UNBRIDLED GREED

Money is the Motive – Fraud is the Means

A Novel

Barry Johnson

Rocochi Ridge Publishing
Ashland

This Rocochi Ridge Publishing edition is published by arrangement with BookMasters, Inc., Ashland, OH

Published in the United States by Rocochi Ridge Publishing
1500 Split Rock Drive #121
Ivins, Utah 84738
www.RocochiRidgePublishing.com

Printed in the United States of America

First Trade Edition: September 2012

10 9 8 7 6 5 4 3 2 1

LIBRARY OF CONGRESS CATALOGING-IN-PUBLICATION DATA
Johnson, Barry
Unbridled Greed/Barry Johnson

ISBN 978-0-9860246-0-3
eBook ISBN 978-0-9860246-1-0

To Joyce

For

Her limitless faith and patience,

Her constant encouragement and inspiration,

Her valuable perspectives and sensitivities, and

Her tireless review and critiques of endless drafts.

Prologue

Las Vegas, NV
October 15th
10:40 AM

Southwest Flight 1916 from Chicago's Midway airport landed on time, shortly after ten-thirty Saturday morning. Fausto Guzman was without a carry on and wanted off the morning's first non-stop to Las Vegas as fast as possible. He was exhausted and annoyed. Why are they moving so damn slow? he wondered. They all seem half dead! Then he recognized he probably looked as worn-out as the rest the passengers, who had all missed sleep to be at the airport for the six AM departure. But he had no sympathy for them; he was tired for other reasons.

Guzman hadn't slept at all since he'd left Las Vegas for Chicago twenty-six hours before. He'd spent eleven of those hours traveling, leaving him only fifteen hours on the ground to practice his craft. Guzman was pleased with his efforts and the twenty-five grand he was paid. He smiled in spite of his aggravation with the crowd, as he recalled how the alleged accident he created had gone virtually as planned.

The proof of his skills was validated earlier as he waited in the boarding area for his flight from Chicago. He'd heard the newscaster report, "Early Saturday morning, Morton Grove Police discovered an overturned, partially submerged Volvo in a shallow branch of the Chicago River. The driver and owner of the car was Republican Congressman Reuben Horowitz, who was found dead in the front seat. The preliminary police ruling is accidental death, but an investigation continues into the circumstances surrounding the accident."

Just after three the previous afternoon, Guzman had arrived in Chicago on Southwest's Flight 711. By four-thirty he'd stolen a silver Cadillac Escalade from a parking lot near Midway and swapped license plates for a set poached from a car on an adjacent street. Then he made his way to the Stevenson Expressway and drove downtown.

His next task had been to make contact with a courier carrying details of his assignment from his employer, along with the agreed upon fee for his services. He'd previously been informed the messenger was someone he'd recognize, a former felon associate from his earlier days in and around Chicago, where Guzman was still known by his real name, Ernesto Morales.

The McDonald's restaurant at 600 North Clark Street occupied an entire square block bordered by La Salle and Clark on the west and east and by Ontario and Ohio on the north and south. Both the drive-thru as well as the parking lot could be accessed by vehicles heading west on Ontario or East on Ohio, so countless cars and people were always around the busy restaurant. It was an ideal location for occupants of two vehicles to hold a brief meeting or exchange items and never be noticed.

At the appointed time, Guzman entered the driveway from Ontario and veered right into the main part of the lot. Almost immediately he saw a familiar man leaning against the trunk of a car. He stopped the Escalade with the open driver side window less than a foot from where the courier stood and greeted him, "Dimas, I see you're still dressing like a gangster, but it's good to see you."

The man nodded, then showed Guzman a large, heavy manila envelope, "Good to see you again, too, Ernesto, and I see you're still eating demasiado. Everything you need is here in the envelope. There's a disposable cell phone, a map, and an untraceable gun. You should get rid of everything as soon as you're done."

Dimas then pulled a map from the envelope and pointed to an X, telling Guzman, "You should park here on Foster near Lockwood at this place we marked on the map. The Congressman drives a blue Volvo station wagon. I'll call you when I see him leave his date's house. Wait for his car to pass. He'll be traveling down Lockwood headed for home. There's a picture of him and his car in the envelope."

Dimas looked around, then continued, "He should be alone. The woman's house is their little love nest, so she should stay there. But if for some reason she's in the car, you're not to leave any witnesses. His pattern is to go home between eleven-thirty and midnight, but you must be parked and ready no later than ten-thirty, just in case he runs low on Viagra and heads home early."

The courier stuffed the map back into the packet and handed it to Guzman. "More details and the phone number for my cell are also in the package, along with the twenty-five thousand agreed upon. Now, I think we should both get the hell out of here. If we stay too long, someone checking the surveillance videos might notice us. Good luck. Be ready for my call around eleven-thirty."

Guzman placed the hefty manila envelope on the passenger seat, then drove south out of the parking lot, exited onto Ohio Street. He turned left onto Clark and left again onto busy Ontario. He crossed five lanes of traffic in the space of one block so he could make a right turn onto La Salle. Heavy rush hour traffic heading north already crowded the road.

Guzman had nearly six hours to kill before he took up his position on the blue Volvo's route, and in the meantime, he needed a private place to study the details and photos in the package. He considered some bars he once patronized in Old Town as he continued north on LaSalle toward North Avenue and Wells. Two of his old haunts he passed were closed down, one turned into a florist's shop, and the other just empty, but the third was still in business.

He parked the stolen car legally in a self-park lot and walked across the street to the tavern. The place was getting crowded already, but he managed to find a small, empty table in an isolated but noisy corner of the bar. He ordered a beer and a hamburger, then carefully reviewed the package's contents and his instructions.

Four beers and two and a half hours later he returned to the parking lot for the Escalade, relieved to see the SUV where he left it. He could steal another vehicle easily enough, but he hated last-minute glitches. He had mapped out his route before leaving the bar and, preferring interstates to more meandering routes, he took North Avenue to the Kennedy, connected to the Edens, then headed north.

After a few miles he left the expressway and headed east onto Golf Road. Seconds later he reached the Old Orchard Shopping Center, where he parked the Escalade, then found a restroom. It was now after eight-thirty and long since dark, the sun having set right after seven that evening. When he returned to the SUV he took a few minutes to get his bearings before heading for the girlfriend's house.

The envelope contained two home addresses, one for the Congressman and the other for his girlfriend. He first made a slow pass by the woman's house and noticed the blue Volvo already parked in the driveway. Then he headed for the location on Foster, where he was to be parked and waiting for the man. He looked at his watch. It was nearly nine thirty-five. So he headed for the target's residence, to trace the likely route the Congressman would take from his girlfriend's to his own home, where his wife and family waited. Guzman concluded the man's only logical path between the Lockwood Avenue love nest and the his residence on Park Lane would be to use Golf Road, traveling west to Overlook Drive, where he would make a right turn.

After three round trips back and forth on Golf Road between Lockwood and Overlook, Guzman confidently chose what he believed to be the ideal location for his ambush, about a mile west of Harms Road. His only concern was how busy the road might be in two or three hours. But the stretch of asphalt was already dark and deserted, so he casually decided he would deal with whatever situation he was faced with at the time of the choreographed accident.

At midnight, Guzman was still waiting to hear that the blue Volvo was on the move. He considered calling the messenger's cell to ask if there was a problem. Maybe I have time to drive the two blocks to the woman's home and see if the Volvo is still there, he thought, but immediately dismissed both options. He decided the later the Congressman headed home, the better off he'd be because there would be less chance of any cars being on the road.

After another tedious half hour of waiting, the four beers once again had Guzman's bladder insisting on relief. He looked for a sheltered spot and saw that a large hedge along the side of a house across the street offered the best nearby privacy. Ten more minutes passed; he couldn't wait any longer and rushed to the shrubbery. Guzman had placed the cell phone he was given on the center console of the Escalade, and in his haste he forgot to grab it as he ran for relief. Three minutes later, his comfort restored, he returned to the SUV, but his relief vanished when he read 'Missed Call' on the screen of the cell phone, and then he saw headlights approaching on Lockwood from less than a block away.

"Shit," he said out loud, trying to decide if he should start the car then or dial the messenger first. He collected his wits just barely in time to verify the passing car was definitely a blue Volvo station wagon with what appeared to be only one occupant. He knew from past experience mistakes happen when he lost his cool, so he willed himself into a calm state. By the time he got the Escalade running, not a simple task in a stolen vehicle with theft protection features, the Volvo was two blocks away, already turning left onto Golf Road. If he goes where I think he's going, I'm fine. I can catch up, he thought, then anxiously pressed 'Call Back' on the phone.

"Where the hell are you? Why didn't you answer? If you screw this up, we're both in trouble," he heard the anxious and angry courier shout.

"I'm on him. Shut up and get off my ass. I'll call you when I'm finished." Guzman raced to Golf Road and was already heading west at a high speed in pursuit of the Volvo by the time he pressed 'End' and tossed the phone onto the passenger seat. As he passed under the Edens Expressway, he noticed only one set of taillights on the road ahead for as far as he could see and assumed it must be the Volvo.

A check of his rearview mirror bolstered his confidence. "Not a car in sight in back of me, and only one in front. That's got to be the Congressman," he said out loud. The Harms Road intersection lights were already in sight, and Guzman knew he needed to quickly overtake the car ahead to verify it was the Volvo. He wanted to be in the ideal position to force the car off the road at his chosen location. When the car entered the well-lit intersection, the Escalade was only ten yards behind. Guzman pounded a fist of relief on the dashboard as he saw the Volvo station wagon clearly illuminated by the traffic signals.

Guzman had numbered the power poles on the north side of the road using them as markers for two key locations he had earlier determined were critical to his plan. The count started with the first pole after the intersection. He planned to force the Volvo off the road just before the fourteenth pole, which marked the east end of a small bridge over a river. If both cars were going fast enough, the Volvo should crash through the low concrete bridge barrier and plunge into the water below.

He decided the poles could also be used to time other aspects of his assault on the station wagon. His strategy was to closely tailgate the Volvo, flashing his bright lights several times to either intimidate or aggravate the Congressman, causing him to move his car into the right hand lane by the time he reached pole number seven. The large and heavy Escalade needed to pull even with the Volvo by pole number ten, and exactly at pole number thirteen he planned to turn hard, directly into the left front fender of the smaller vehicle.

Everything was working perfectly, Guzman thought, as he scanned the road ahead and checked his rear view mirror one last time. "Not a car in sight in either direction. It's only me and the Congressman out here on Golf Road tonight," he said out loud as he neared the end of the pole count. "Twelve, thirteen, go!" he shouted, then slammed his foot on the accelerator and crashed into the Volvo at over fifty miles an hour.

The violent impact from the SUV destroyed the left front side of the smaller car and spun the vehicle ninety degrees from the direction it was traveling. In under a second, its right front wheel and fender impacted the curb and concrete barrier. Almost immediately, the entire front end of the Volvo crashed directly into and over the solid wall and through the two metal bars along the top of the barrier. A four-foot section of the top bar snapped loose and sliced through the windshield and air bag, then shot out the driver's side window, narrowly missing the Congressman's head.

The car's speed combined with the initial angle of impact had launched the Volvo into an upward trajectory, defeating most of the stopping power of the protective wall. Guzman saw the car's slide over the wall end abruptly when the rear wheels got entangled with the twisted remains of the steel bars. The Volvo wagon was now precariously perched atop the wall, with its nose dangling down toward the water below.

Inside the station wagon, Congressman Markowitz was unconscious and bleeding profusely from multiple lacerations to his head, face, and neck caused by shards of lethal flying glass and metal. The Volvo's air bag system had prevented his ejection through the windshield and any direct impact of his chest and face with the steering wheel. Because he wasn't wearing his seat belt, the last conscious sensation his mind recorded was the pain caused by the explosive expansion of the air bag as it smashed into his face and snapped his chin up and his head abruptly backward against the head restraint.

Almost at the same instant, the trajectory of the javelin-like piece of fractured barrier bar destroyed the integrity of the safety glass and collapsed the air bag, leaving the Congressman totally unprotected from flying debris, which soon showered his face, neck, and chest. Exposed carotid arteries made easy targets for thousands of glass daggers that bombarded the vital conduits on both sides of his neck and spilled enormous amounts of blood in seconds. The unchecked hemorrhaging quickly overtook the initial unconsciousness caused by the impact of the crash and triggered a steady and rapid descent into brain death. Within minutes massive blood loss from the deep neck lacerations produced irreversible anoxia in the Congressman's brain.

Proof of the violence of the crash was more evident on the smaller car, but the SUV was also damaged. Guzman was able to halt the Escalade before it vaulted over the cement barrier, but the right front fender and wheel had rammed solidly into the wall. The front air bag deployed, and the shoulder and seat belts automatically tightened, so Guzman had escaped without injury.

After he deflated the airbag and freed himself from the Escalade, Guzman hurried to the smashed station wagon. He discovered the rear part of the car's frame was precariously teetering on what remained of the crushed section of the concrete barrier. The still rotating rear wheels and the cargo space behind the rear seat were the only parts of the car not yet across the wall. The Congressman wasn't moving; numerous air bags had deployed on the driver's side of the car, but were now limp.

Guzman shined the flashlight he discovered in the SUV on the Congressman, and even from his angle, to the rear and side of the driver, it was clear there was already heavy blood loss, far more than he expected. He saw multiple gashes on the man's head and face, and blood was literally gushing in pulsing spurts from a wound on the right side of his neck just under his jaw line. The left side of his face rested against the steering wheel, now draped by an empty airbag covered with blood. Quickly he glanced back at the road in both directions. He still saw no lights and heard no cars. Because the Congressman was still breathing and blood was still flowing, Guzman reasoned there was still a chance his victim might survive in spite of his obviously serious injuries.

After a few seconds he decided that so far the scene still looked like an accident, but if he used a gun to finish the job, it would eliminate any chance of an accidental death ruling, so he put his revolver back into his pocket.

No loose ends, he thought, and reached his right arm into the car from the back seat window and grabbed the victim by the hair. Next he judiciously extended his left hand and arm through the shattered glass of the driver's window and firmly grasped the Congressman's head between his two massive hands, then violently twisted it unnaturally to the right, breaking his neck. He observed the grizzly scene for nearly a minute afterward, then said quietly to himself, "No more blood squirting anywhere now."

The killer then went to the rear of the Volvo and attempted to push it off the wall into the river below. Even though most of the car angled downward at ninety degrees and the weight of the engine even seemed to drag it toward the water, Guzman quickly discovered he couldn't muscle it over the wall. He decided only one option remained, then rushed back to the Escalade.

The motor was still running, so he jumped in, jammed the transmission into reverse, then lined up the front of the SUV directly in back of the Volvo and inched forward as though planning to push the damaged station wagon. The front of the Escalade made contact with the rear of the stranded Volvo, but he realized the SUV now entirely blocked the two westbound lanes of Golf Road and he needed to hurry. With the SUV in position against the Volvo's exposed and elevated rear end, he determined that what he intended to do should work.

He checked the road in both directions one more time and saw no cars or lights. Then he backed the Escalade up across all four lanes to the opposite side of the road, tightened his seat belt, and put the automatic transmission into its lowest gear. He jammed the accelerator to the floor, crossed all four lanes in a flash, and hit the Volvo squarely at nearly thirty-five miles an hour. The end result was another crash between the two cars, but this time the Volvo was no longer on the highway or atop the safety barrier. It was upside-down in the water below.

Less speed would have been better, he decided, once he recovered from his second collision of the night. To his satisfaction, the Volvo was now upside-down in the river, but the Escalade's front end and right front quadrant were both battered as well. He backed the SUV away from the damaged barrier to the other side of the road and pointed it east toward the Edens. Then he steered the car onto the shoulder somewhere near pole number eleven and got out to survey the damage more closely.

The right front light assembly was destroyed, so now the car had only one headlight. The front tire on that side still looked all right, except that part of the bumper was rubbing against it, so he yanked on the broken plastic until the troublesome piece broke free. He re-entered the battered Escalade and began to have serious doubts he would make it to Midway Airport without breaking down or getting stopped by a state trooper. He decided to head back toward Skokie, because he remembered a hospital near Golf Road just east of the shopping center. There are always cars parked in hospital lots at all hours of the day and night, he thought.

Guzman soon located the hospital near the junction of Golf and Gross Point Roads, then circled back to a shopping center two blocks away. He parked the Escalade with the front end nosed against some bushes, concealing most of the damage, then wiped down the SUV and removed all the contents of the envelope that might connect him to the car. After leaving the shopping center, he walked the two blocks back to the hospital. As he approached the somewhat secluded employee parking lot, he searched for the security cameras he knew would be scanning the lot to protect employees and their property at all hours of the day and night.

Satisfied that several cars appeared to be out of range of the hospital's surveillance system, he set his sights on an old Oldsmobile he knew would be easy to steal. Five minutes later he was heading back toward the Edens. He planned to take the expressway until he could exit and work his way to Cicero Avenue near the Kennedy junction. He would then take Cicero all the way back to the airport.

At two in the morning, Guzman dialed the messenger's cell and heard him pick up, "Hola."

"Dimas, the assignment is completed. I'm headed home now."

The messenger said nothing and hung up.

Guzman began to relax and, when he realized he hadn't eaten in over eight hours, he decided he was hungry. He spotted Ruby's All-Night Diner south of Fullerton and decided to stop, take a break, and grab some food. As he reached for the handle on the restaurant's glass door, the bright lights from inside exposed spatters of blood on his hands and forearms. He glanced toward the counter and saw that neither of the two customers nor the cook had taken any notice of him. So he located the door to the restrooms and casually strolled in that direction to wash away the tangible proof of the evening's activities.

Five minutes later the killer was inspecting Ruby's menu. He found himself struggling with a choice between spaghetti and a French Dip sandwich. Oddly that decision seemed to be the most troubling problem on his mind. Eventually he decided on the spaghetti with apple pie for dessert.

Around three-thirty in the morning he saw the signs signaling his approach to the Stevenson Expressway and knew that immediately after passing Pershing Road he'd cross a river, where he'd earlier planned to discard both the gun and cell phone. With the bridge approaching and no other cars on his side of the road, he slowed the car to a crawl, opened the passenger window, then first tossed the gun, followed by the cell phone. He heard neither object splash into the river, and that didn't concern him because he knew the water was deep and far below the bridge.

Twenty minutes later he found a rare parking place in a neighborhood off Fifty Ninth Street where he decided to leave the Oldsmobile. For the second time that night he carefully wiped down anything he might have touched inside and outside the car, and when he finished, gathered the remaining contents of the envelope and walked away from the stolen car. He intentionally left the doors unlocked, hoping someone would steal it again before morning to further muddle up any possible evidence he might have left behind. At that moment a troubling impression crossed his mind. Did I leave something in the car? he wondered. Unsure, he went back and checked again, and found nothing. So he ignored the nagging sense that he'd overlooked anything.

After he killed more time at a Dunkin' Donuts and consumed enough caffeine to keep him awake for the next two days, he walked a circuitous course to the Midway Airport Terminal. Along the way, he systematically discarded shredded photos, maps, and detailed directions into four separate trash cans and arrived at the terminal as planned at exactly five in the morning.

Once he cleared security and made his way to his gate, Guzman secretly congratulated himself while he looked at the only thing he kept from the large manila envelope he was given twelve hours ago. Twenty-five thousand dollars in cash; not bad for a few hours' work, he thought. But he was still slightly troubled by something he couldn't quite put his meaty finger on.

By five AM, Chad Gates and Keri Sandler, two teenagers from Glenview, were starting their third round of questioning by State Police and Morton Grove detectives. Chad and Keri had dialed 911 after seeing something strange happening about five hundred yards, or eight power poles, from where they were parked just off Golf Road. Apparently passionately preoccupied at the time of the first crash, the teens had initially taken notice of transpiring events only when they saw the lights of an SUV back up from the north side of the road and park directly across the two westbound lanes.

They were curious and feared someone might be injured, so they got out of their car and ran up the shoulder on the opposite side of the road. As they approached, still about two hundred yards from the car, they saw from the headlights of the SUV that there was another smaller car perched on top of a concrete barrier. A man had gotten out of the SUV and was looking at the front of his car and the back of the car on top of the barrier. What they saw next terrified them and caused them to slow their approach, retreat from the shoulder of the road, and hide in the trees at a spot police later determined was near power pole fifteen.

The driver, they later explained, jumped back into his SUV, backed it up across all four lanes and sped forward at full speed, crashing into the back of the smaller car and launching it into the river below. Afterward the man remained in the SUV for a minute or two, which allowed them to move closer. They initially reasoned he may have been injured, but when they got to within about fifty yards of his car, it began backing up again, causing them to retreat to the safety of the trees.

The SUV, which they could then clearly see was a silver Cadillac Escalade, then pulled forward about thirty yards and the driver got out. Fearing he might have seen them, they remained in the trees until they noticed he was only inspecting the damage to his car. As he stood and surveyed the front of the Escalade, Chad and Keri both got a clear view of his intimidating face and physique.

Then, while he was preoccupied with tearing off a piece of the plastic front bumper, Chad and Keri crouched low and inched their way toward the SUV until they were close enough to read the license plate. They keyed the numbers into Keri's cell phone along with notations of the man's description, which they doubted they would ever forget. When the driver moved from the front of the Escalade toward them, they quickly ducked down behind the thick leafless bushes, again fearing he might have seen or heard them. But then he immediately climbed back into the crumpled Cadillac and headed east on Golf Road.

As soon as the SUV was out of sight, the two teens ran back to the place on the other side of the road where they had seen the smaller car slammed into and pushed off the cement barrier. As they looked down, they could see the overturned car's large taillights still glowing red under the water. It was then they dialed 911 and reported the strange details of all they had witnessed.

At about the time Flight 1916 crossed over the Iowa line and into Nebraska on its way to McCarran Field in Las Vegas, a mall security car at the Skokie shopping center stopped behind a Cadillac Escalade. The security guard decided to get out and take a closer look at one of the few vehicles in the lot a full two hours before any of the stores opened. He hadn't seen this car before, so it was unlikely it belonged to an employee, and there appeared to be some damage to the right front side of the SUV. Minutes later he notified the Skokie Police of the damaged and possibly abandoned car.

Later that morning the Morton Grove Police had alerted surrounding authorities they were looking for a damaged Cadillac Escalade. A Skokie patrolman was then finally dispatched to check out the car at the shopping center. Sixty minutes after the policeman first saw the SUV, a full blown crime scene was in place and a forensic lab team was dusting the outside of the car for prints.

When one of the technicians opened the rear door, she immediately saw a black cylinder on the floor just barely protruding from under the front passenger's seat. By three that afternoon, a blood sample and two sets of fingerprints had been successfully lifted off the metal flashlight. One set belonged to Roy Jefferson, the man who had reported the car stolen the day before. The owner of the second set of prints had not yet been identified. DNA analysis was also started, investigators assuming they could establish a direct match from the blood sample on the flashlight and one taken from the body of the late Congressman Reuben Horowitz.

Certain the killer had overlooked the flashlight, Detective Barnes from the Morton Grove police was able to convince those involved in the investigation that the discovery of the flashlight should be kept confidential along with the existence of the eyewitnesses. A pact was made and honored, and news of the teenage witnesses, the flashlight, and fingerprints were never leaked to the media.

Chapter 1

Evanston, IL
September 28th
10:30 AM

For the second time in less than a month, Bryan Hampton and Ted Kucharski sat slumped down in their "undercover" dark, blue Crown Victoria. They were across the street from Dr. Hugh Patterson's office on Maple Street in downtown Evanston. The unimposing brown brick building where the dermatologist practiced looked more like a retail storefront than a medical office, but the large windows and single floor design of the structure provided the ideal environment for their surveillance.

This particular Wednesday was one of those rare fall days near the Lake Michigan shore when the sun was shining, the humidity was low, the temperature was an ideal seventy-two degrees, and the leaves were just beginning to turn. But Dr. Patterson was running late, forcing the two agents to remain confined in their car for over an hour. Ideal weather conditions or not, they were relieved to know their long wait was about to payoff.

The two investigators were watching and listening to a surprisingly clear live audio and visual feed from the miniaturized surveillance gear worn by Nina Moretti, an undercover FBI agent posing as a patient named Alice Rizzo. She'd just finished explaining to the middle-aged dermatologist how desperately she needed cosmetic surgery "or at least Botox" because "being single at my age, there's no way I can stand up to all the competition out there with all these wrinkles." The truth was Nina had been carefully selected for this assignment and brought to Chicago from her current posting in Detroit because, at thirty-eight, she was wrinkle-free and probably the best-looking Justice Department employee in the entire Midwest.

Dr. Patterson struggled to appear attentive while fighting his growing impatience with his new patient, Alice Rizzo's, monologue. He'd heard this same spiel, or some variation of it, from so many of the self-absorbed patients who visited his office that he could barely force himself to listen any longer. Finally, he thought, when Nina got to the point and said, "I really can't afford the treatment I need and my insurance doesn't pay for cosmetic services, but I've heard from a friend that you still find ways to help your patients get their work done."

Skillfully, he began his pitch, but understanding his billing tactics were marginal at best, he first posed what he believed was a shrewd and qualifying question, "Well, Alice, I'm quite sure I can help you with your insurance problem, and just so I can thank your friend next time I see her, who referred you? I ask because you didn't indicate you had been referred by anyone here on your patient registration forms."

Agent Moretti was prepared with a name. "Ginny Flowers," she cautiously offered, then added, "I didn't want to get her into any trouble."

Patterson felt both relieved and pleased because the name was vaguely familiar, so he responded quickly saying, "Nonsense, Alice, why would you get Ginny in any trouble by telling me she referred you? I've built my practice primarily on recommendations from satisfied and pleased patients like Ginny."

When Hampton and Kucharski heard Nina give Ginny Flowers' name, they both held their breath for a second hoping Dr. Patterson still had no idea Ginny Flowers had called her insurance company to ask about the very conversation he was about to repeat with Agent Nina Moretti. Kucharski looked at Hampton, then offhandedly shared an observation, "This guy still doesn't know Ginny Flowers never came back for any treatments. I guess she was an anomaly in Patterson's equation of greed. Apparently he didn't believe anyone would take exception to the idea that insurance companies will legitimately pay for services clearly excluded in their policies."

Hampton reminded him of an important detail. "Don't forget it took Ginny Flowers two days of thinking about what the doctor promised her before she decided to make the call. To her credit, she did figure out if she benefitted from his guarantee to get payment for non-covered services, she'd become a party to what seemed to her like insurance fraud."

"Yeah, and by the time I talked to her, it was clear she wanted no part of that," Kucharski added. "So I agree she mostly placed the call to protect herself, and to make sure Sidereal HealthCare knew she wasn't going back to Dr. Patterson, for any further care.

"You know Bryan, I guess patients don't realize it, and I don't know how you handle these calls at the Justice Department, but when any large insurance carrier gets a complaint or call hinting at some impropriety or billing irregularity, that call is immediately referred to the Special Investigative Unit. Once the caller is in contact with an SIU agent like me, we do a comprehensive interview designed to establish the caller's credibility and the legitimacy of their complaint. I don't know why but most fraudulent healthcare providers seem to be unaware of the fact that nearly half of the medical fraud cases we investigate are triggered by phone calls or written complaints from disgruntled and suspicious patients, spouses, or employees."

Kucharski then continued with a story Hampton already had some knowledge of, but it was better than hearing Patterson's oft repeated standard sales pitch, so he listened without much complaint. "You'll recall I ended up with Ginny Flowers because she told the customer service representative she had a question about Dr. Hugh Patterson in Evanston, IL, and as soon as Patterson's name was entered into the software, the agent saw I was already investigating several open cases against him. After five minutes of talking with Flowers, I knew we could add another complaint to the growing list of cases against Dr. Patterson."

As Kucharski had guessed, they could tell Dr. Patterson didn't remember anything about Ginny Flowers except her name. Based on his behavior, he also had no idea Nina Moretti, whose name he thought was Alice Rizzo, had never met Ginny, and he also seemed to be completely oblivious to either woman's role in earning him the attention he was getting from the United States Department of Justice that day.

It seemed to both Hampton and Kucharski that Patterson didn't really care about anything but the sales pitch he was preparing to deliver to Nina. As they waited for the doctor to begin Hampton commented, "This guy is a textbook crook. There are red flags all over the place with him. All the patients I've interviewed tell me he's naturally charismatic and handsome, and because he's had an established practice for years they believe he's trustworthy."

Kucharski interrupted Hampton, "He did look legit for a long time, Bryan, but over the last three years it seems like he's had a midlife crisis or something, and he's transformed his previously routine dermatology practice into what his website advertises as a *Full Service Cosmetic Dermatology and Skin Care Service* that *provides comprehensive skin care and surgery to our many happy patients.*"

Hampton responded, "Ted, once you called our attention to his website, which clearly highlights multiple popular cosmetic services such as Botox, Restylane, and Juvederm, as well as *Laser and Cosmetic Rejuvenation Surgery*, it became clear to us he's trying to attract an entirely new type of patient. He wants to focus on more profitable cosmetic services and less on treating acne and warts. That's fine and legal, but his tactics to get insurers to pay for services excluded in their contracts is not okay, it's fraud."

"The overriding factor here is money Bryan. Since his evolution into the world of cosmetic skin care, his practice has boomed, his payments from Sidereal Health have tripled, and from what we can tell, his honesty and sincerity have evaporated. Based on what I've heard during our surveillance, his charisma, although apparently unnoticed by patients, has been replaced by a series of memorized sales pitches."

Dr. Patterson at last began his well-practiced response to the "insurance dilemma" Nina had presented him. "You know, Alice, the insurance companies, and even Medicare, are at war with patients like you and hardworking physicians like me. You pay them premiums believing they'll cover the medical care you need and they generally don't live up to their side of the agreement. The truth is, they take your premium dollars and try hard to pay as little as possible for the care you deserve."

Patterson paused for effect, then continued, "And it's all so they can get rich and reward corporate executives, while you and other patients are deprived of needed services. And when they do pay us, they always pay less than we doctors deserve. But I take care of my patients, Alice, and we'll get everything I believe you deserve from your insurance company. I have some well-trained people working for me, and I've taught them how to bill the insurance companies so our patients are well taken care of. We have a motto here in our office, 'You have our assurance that all bills will be paid by your insurance.' I hope by now we've eliminated any doubts you might have had about your insurance paying."

Listening outside in the blue Ford, Hampton and Kucharski looked at each other and could hardly believe Dr. Patterson was being so cooperative in building their case against him. They had actually recorded him taking responsibility for how his office staff bills and submits, what under federal law, are classified as False Claims.

"Bryan, this dipshit was officially grandstanding for Nina because she's so hot. Next thing he'll recommend is a full body scan followed by a full body exam," Kucharski noted sarcastically.

Hampton laughed at another of Kucharski's cynical comments. He found it hard to believe they'd become such great friends in only a few weeks. Earlier that month, the two investigators had been unaware that both of their organizations were conducting separate investigations of the dermatologist. Then, during an interview with a former employee of Dr. Patterson's, Hampton was told, "You're asking me the same questions a guy named Ted Kucharski from Sidereal HealthCare asked me last week. Maybe you guys ought to team up." And that's exactly what they had done after Hampton sought out and met with Kucharski.

During their first get-together, Hampton discovered Kucharski was a lead investigator in Sidereal HealthCare's SIU, where he had worked for over six years. He soon learned Kucharski had little patience or respect for physicians who cheated insurance companies and took advantage of their patients.

Hampton found out Kucharski had been a Madison, WI police officer for fifteen years, but was shot while trying to resolve a domestic dispute. The shooting left him with a physical limitation that disqualified him for duty as a patrolman, and when he recovered, he was assigned to do investigative work, which ended up being a desk job.

After a year of paper pushing in Madison, he applied for and accepted an offer in Appleton to work for Sidereal HealthCare as a medical fraud investigator. In six years he had progressed to become a mid-level manager over a team of ten investigators, responsible for investigating the most egregious Sidereal medical fraud cases in the Midwest.

After Hampton finished laughing, he responded to Kucharski's comments, "Yeah, you can just tell he's a real caring and compassionate servant of mankind. If she was a real patient, she'd eventually get a couple of Botox injections and he'd submit a claim for ten other things that he never did. And since his patients are never asked to pay anything, everyone's happy."

"Everybody but my company, Medicare, and every other insurer who've paid this bum over two million dollars in the last two years for work he probably never did," Kucharski responded disgustedly. "And if he did do anything for them, the cosmetic stuff isn't covered anyway, at least not by my company, and for damn sure not by Medicare."

They quickly stopped their dialogue as they saw Dr. Patterson reaching for a photo album showing pictures of all the incredible work he claimed to have done over the years. Then he launched into the technical elements of his sales pitch during which he discussed every aspect of her facial anatomy and described each procedure he recommended for Nina.

Nina had been instructed to question one or two of the procedures Patterson suggested. She already knew none were medically necessary because two prominent Chicago cosmetic surgeons had previously evaluated her, and both had recommended she return in five or ten years "when you might actually need us."

As scripted, Nina decided to challenge his recommendation for a Blepharoplasty, a surgical modification of both the upper and lower eyelids, which Patterson recommended for the "slight bags under both eyes."

"Do you really think I need my eyelids worked on?" she asked.

"Oh, just the lowers. We can do the uppers next year," he conceded.

The treatment plan discussion, which eventually included nine different procedures Dr. Patterson was recommending, finally concluded. Nina, unlike most patients he'd previously treated, understood that Patterson was simply a dermatologist and not a Board Certified Cosmetic Surgeon, and that he wasn't qualified to undertake many of the cosmetic procedures he routinely recommended and performed.

Ten minutes later after meeting with Sandy Barnes, the insurance specialist, Nina Moretti, alias Alice Rizzo, a thirty-eight-year-old beauty, was about to exit Patterson's office holding her copy of a $14,000 treatment plan soon to be submitted to her insurance company.

"Alice, I'll call you in a week or two to schedule appointments for your treatments," the receptionist at the front desk told her. "We have to get authorization from your insurance company before the doctor can do your work. But don't worry, Alice, we'll push it through all the hurdles. It's our problem, not yours."

Hampton and Kucharski watched as Agent Moretti left the office and got into her car for the short drive to a McDonald's just a few blocks away. They'd previously agreed to meet there, grab some lunch, and debrief prior to the DOJ agents heading back south to their offices on Roosevelt Road just west of the loop in downtown Chicago. Ted Kucharski had to go in the opposite direction, a long drive north to Appleton where he lived and worked.

****

When they arrived at the McDonald's where they had agreed to meet Agent Moretti, they realized she was already there. Oddly, they saw her standing in the parking lot near her car surrounded by three large white males of "undetermined national origin," Kucharski quipped to Hampton. They parked as close to the group as possible, then hastily exited the Crown Vic. As they approached the group, they heard one of the men urging Nina to show them the gun she claimed to carry and prove she was an FBI agent.

Kucharski reached them before Hampton, and at six seven and 278 pounds, he was bigger, but older than any of the three men who surrounded Nina. As a former Madison police officer, he had frequently dealt with confrontations between intoxicated students, football fans, and excited political zealots, but he had no idea what was happening here at mid-day in a McDonald's parking lot in normally safe Evanston. However, instinctively he saw that Nina looked threatened and nervous. "Gentlemen," he shouted, "can you tell me what business you have here with my friend Agent Moretti?"

The apparent leader of the group turned and yelled at him, "Back off, tubby. This bitch took our parking place, and FBI agent or not, she needs to move her car or I'm going to move it for her."

"Did you just call me tubby and her bitch?" Kucharski bellowed as he approached the man, who appeared to be reaching toward Nina. "Because if you did, I hope you already had lunch because in two minutes you won't have any teeth to eat with!"

"Are you knuckleheads kidding us?" hollered Hampton who had since joined the squabble. "Do you know it's a felony to threaten a federal officer?"

"Mind your own business!" yelled one of the other men as he tried to shove Hampton out of the way.

After more than two hours of sitting in their car, both agents needed some physical exercise, and when knucklehead #1 took a swing at Kucharski and missed, Kucharski leveled him. At the same time, Hampton grabbed the man who tried to shove him and five seconds later he was on the ground and in handcuffs. In defense of gender toughness, Nina drew her gun and prevented knucklehead #3 from joining in or fleeing and quickly cuffed him as well.

"Well, that was fun, boys," Nina quipped a minute later. "Parking must be at a real premium here in Illinois. Even in Detroit we don't literally have to secure our parking places at gunpoint."

"What are we going to do with these idiots now that we have fifty people watching us?" Kucharski asked no one in particular as he struggled to tuck his shirt back into his pants while he secured his attacker face-down on the ground with his left leg.

"We'll call the Evanston police and have them picked up and just tell them to hold them for a few hours and hope they learned a lesson," Hampton decided.

"What lesson is it they're supposed to have learned?" Nina asked. "Not to be so possessive about a parking place? Not to threaten and confront a woman and call her names? Not to ask to see my gun?"

"All those and two more things; don't get between Ted and lunch, and especially don't call him tubby!" Hampton answered.

While they waited for the police, Nina noticed a student on the opposite side of the parking lot, who was wearing a Northwestern University sweat shirt and seemed to be intensely watching the agents and the men they had subdued. She thought she had seen him using his camera phone while all the commotion was taking place, but couldn't be sure. Now she couldn't see his phone; he was just watching.

Shortly after the police arrived she noticed his camera phone was definitely out recording the activities of the police. When Nina started walking toward him, he stuck the Droid X2 smartphone into his pocket and took off before she could get halfway across the lot. Nina asked a girl who had been standing near him if she knew him. "I think his name is Tony, but I'm not sure," she told her.

"Do you know where he lives?"

"I think he stays in one of the dorms. He's in journalism and he's on the staff of the paper, the *Daily Northwestern*. I've seen his picture with his articles. That's the only reason I know who he is."

After they wasted nearly an hour dealing with the Evanston officers who were already well acquainted with two of the three assailants, Kucharski, Hampton, and Nina settled on another restaurant for lunch, since the crowd that had gathered at McDonald's would likely interrupt the quiet lunch discussion they hoped to have.

Chapter 2

Evanston, IL
September 28th
1:00 PM

Fifteen minutes later, Hampton, Kucharski and Nina reconvened at the nearby Wendy's on Touhy, where there was plenty of space in the parking lot. The smell of cooking beef and fries triggered Kucharski's appetite, and he ordered big, two double Baconator combos, while Nina opted for an apple pecan chicken salad and Hampton found middle ground and chose a chicken filet combo. So they could talk without being overheard, Bryan grabbed a table near the front of the building in a corner with windows on two sides and only one adjacent booth that was currently empty.

While they waited for the number on their receipt to be called, they discussed the recent encounter in the McDonald's lot, still puzzled by how suddenly the unprovoked violence had erupted. Their food was ready sooner than expected and, being unable to reason through any logical motivation other than testosterone-induced stupidity, they decided to get on with the business they should have been discussing for the past hour.

"How do you guys think it went? Did we get what we needed? From my perspective he said far more than we had hoped for," Nina offered.

"Absolutely. I believe we now have the evidence we needed, and since this is the second time we've been able to record the good doctor promising patients he can get their insurance companies to pay for procedures that aren't covered, we're in reasonably good shape. When we add those recordings to the statements we obtained from his other patients, I'm confident we have the evidence we need to get a search warrant and make an arrest," Hampton responded without much reservation.

"And don't forget, Bryan, my company has five cases of our own, including the false claims he submitted and the paid checks he cashed for stuff he never did for those patients," Ted added, his mouth already stuffed with the first bite of two Baconators.

"Okay, you two, then how about filling me in on the exact case we're building. You brought me here for a few days to impersonate a patient hoping to get a free facelift, but other than the fact that I don't need any cosmetic surgery and he says I do, I'm a little embarrassed to admit that I don't totally understand the case we're building against him. Specifically, what are we accusing Patterson of beyond promising his patients that he can get their insurance company to pay for services they don't actually cover?" Nina asked cautiously.

"Don't worry too much about not understanding everything, Nina," Kucharski responded. "Medical fraud's complicated, hard to find, and changes all the time. After six years of investigating it, I'm still surprised at all the different ways people screw with the system. We have over two hundred investigators in our SIU, and we could use twice that many because we process claims for twenty million people. For years we've been chasing guys like Patterson trying to recover money that's already been paid, instead of preventing bogus payments in the first place. But now we're finally getting systems in place to actually detect questionable claims before they're paid."

"You know, Nina, between Medicare and Medicaid, over half of the nearly three trillion dollars we spend annually on health care services is funded by taxpayers. Healthcare fraud, waste, and abuse costs the country over three hundred billion dollars every year," Bryan pointed out.

"That's like a thousand dollars a year for every person in the country, and nearly three thousand dollars for every family," Nina observed.

"Using round numbers you're right," Bryan told her. "In recent years the problem has spread. Before, we just focused on providers of health care services, but over the past twenty years the list of perpetrators has expanded. These days there are more doctors, bigger hospitals, and far more ancillary health care providers like home health agencies committing fraud. And as you know from the work you've been doing, currently our biggest challenge is that common crooks and organized crime rings have discovered health care fraud is a lucrative opportunity."

"You mentioned organized crime rings, Bryan, and I'm surprised at how ingenious and belligerent their schemes are becoming," Nina responded. "We just closed down a Russian crime ring in Michigan last week that had purchased a radiology clinic from the widow of a deceased doctor. For over six months they used the former owner's old patient records along with his license and other credentials, including his National Provider Identity number, or NPI, to submit false claims for all types of radiology services.

"At this point, what we know is that they would send in a claim for a traditional x-ray, like a chest x-ray, then if Medicare or a private insurance company paid the claim, they would send in a barrage of bogus claims for expensive services like CAT scans, PET scans, MRI's, and even EEG's or brain scans. Interestingly, the dead doctor's practice they purchased never even owned the equipment to perform most of those services, and the deceased radiologist had never billed for anything other than standard x-rays. It appears they managed to operate for six months without being challenged because many of the claims were for Medicare patients, and apparently no one was watching," Nina explained.

"We were alerted to this operation by a private insurer. After receiving EEG claims for ten different patients, the company started requesting the electroencephalograph results, which are complex tracings something like you'd see from a lie detector. Turns out EEG's are like fingerprints, and no two are alike.

"Apparently, the Russians had gotten hold of two legitimate tracings and when the insurer requested results for some of the patients, the Russians kept sending in the same two tracings. An astute medical consultant who reviewed the EEG's for the company noticed the problem after he saw the same one the third time around. Problem is, by the time we were brought in and started looking into the case, the crooks had closed down the scheme and disappeared. They had been alerted by a letter from the insurer asking if they had sent in the same EEG tracing by mistake, but we were too late, and as far as we can tell, in six months they billed for and were paid over eight million dollars."

Bryan was shaking his head, then responded, "I hadn't heard the details of that scheme, but part of the reason organized crime is targeting health care is that it's safer than, say, drug running or prostitution. Criminals have found health care fraud to be more abuser-friendly, and if they're caught, the punishment is far less severe than they'd receive, if convicted of other felonies.

"Of course, we can't forget the individual entrepreneurs like the guy *60 Minutes* did the piece on a couple of years ago. Tony, I think they used as his alias, managed to operate a network of Durable Medical Equipment stores. He stole millions from Medicare and never even opened a single storefront with any supplies in it. He just used stolen patient identities, got business licenses under false names, and operated for months before anyone even noticed. And then he was only stopped because he got greedy and careless.

"But Patterson's case is an example of what for me is even more concerning," Bryan mused as he finished another bite of his sandwich. "Another reason health care fraud is growing is that more and more legitimate health care providers are willing to operate in gray billing areas, which many are able to justify because of the low fees they receive from Medicare and especially from Medicaid. Doctors constantly complain the payments they receive from Medicaid don't even cover their expenses. This growing category also includes large hospital chains, home health agencies, and pharmacies, or essentially every provider category.

"But let's get back to Dr. Patterson's specific case. We've proven at this point that he's submitting claims and being paid for services he doesn't provide to his patients. By definition, those are False Claims, and the False Claims Act prohibits individuals from defrauding the government by filing false claims. As to the specific allegations, we'll assert Patterson is performing simple procedures and falsely billing for more complex services as well as padding every claim he submits with procedures he never provides his patients."

"Two questions then, before you go on," Nina asked. "First, how do you know what he actually did, compared to what he billed on the claim he submitted, and second, how do you establish the amount of money he's stolen from the false claims?"

"Good questions, and I'll answer them both," Ted volunteered. "Nina, medical coding is the language providers use to tell insurance companies what they did for their patients. Forget hospitals for now and focus on codes physicians use, because that's complicated enough. Two coding systems are in play on every claim. Procedures or services are represented by CPT Codes. To communicate the reason the procedures are done, one or more diagnosis codes can be attached to each CPT code.

"Some providers will actually falsify their medical records and charts to support the codes they bill, but most don't. So the answer to your first question is we can compare the codes billed on the medical claims to services documented in the medical records and determine if they match or not. If the doctor's willing to falsify medical records to support the fraud, then we end up interviewing patients and the office staff. Are you with me?" Ted asked.

"Yes, Ted, and I wasn't aware of the medical record analysis," Nina answered.

"Okay," Ted continued. "So let me tell you how fraudsters would handle a case like yours. Since you need nothing done, every service billed would be fraudulent, making yours an exceptional case. So we need to assume you do need some surgery. Let's say you want the size or appearance of your nose improved. Essentially you're asking for a nose job or a reconstruction of your nose.

"Instead of billing the code for a Rhinoplasty, which is normally a cosmetic service and is generally not a benefit covered by most insurance plans, a fraudulent doctor will bill a code identifying the procedure as the repair of a deviated septum, and maybe an extra code or two for a nasal turbinate reduction or some other nasal procedure associated with difficulty in breathing or snoring.

"To justify the services, diagnosis codes are also submitted to indicate that you're suffering from some functional problem that requires a repair to facilitate breathing or one that says you're suffering from sleep apnea or some other condition that would be covered by your insurance.

"If a cosmetic or plastic surgeon submits a claim like this, it'll be carefully scrutinized by the insurance company because everybody already knows this particular scheme. However, if an otolaryngologist or a provider of some specialty other than plastic surgery bills the service, it'll be less suspect, and that's the reason some fraudulent physicians often even submit claims using different specialties."

"Another thing Patterson chronically does is habitually up-code and consequently over-charge for every office visit. Office visits can be $50 to $400, depending on what a patient complains of and how long it takes the doctor to decide what needs to be done. Patterson always charges the more expensive visits that take more time, so if he actually spent the time the codes he bills on his claims indicate, he'd be working more than sixteen hours a day most days, which we know he never does," Bryan added.

Ted forced a swallow and nearly shouted, "But that's not all that Patterson does. He also up-codes the surgical services. If he removes one small mole, he'll usually bill a code that says he removed four large moles. He cheats on every claim he sends in, billing codes that overstate the services he actually provided, then on top of that he generally throws in a few extra codes for totally unrelated procedures, simply to get paid more.

"And he also uses diagnosis codes that indicate he's treating patients for diseases they don't even have, because that justifies services that might otherwise not be paid. The collateral damage is that, if you're the patient with a wart, he may have indicated you have skin cancer, and a false diagnosis is now attached to your medical record, and you know nothing about it."

Nina understood and drew a parallel. "That's like taking a car under warranty to the dealership to have a faulty door lock repaired and, without your knowledge, the dealer charges the factory to repair of your shocks, brakes, fuel pump, and electric seats, even though none of that work was ever done. In the auto industry, that's clearly fraud, but somehow in health care the industry seemingly has trouble calling what Patterson is doing fraud until ten patients complain or the cost is in the hundreds of thousands."

"That's a great analogy, Nina," Hampton answered, "and in Patterson's case we think we know the amount he's been overpaid by Medicare and by Ted's company, but he probably bills ten other insurance companies we haven't even looked at yet. So right now the two million dollar figure we're using for the past two years is likely low.

"Medical fraud's become a fertile field for all classes of criminals as well as dishonest providers, and there's no sign the industry or our own government really wants to aggressively commit the resources needed to cure the problem," Hampton concluded.

"Well, my friends, nice little chat, but you two are depressing me and I need to hit the road because it's a long drive to Appleton. And Bryan, you still need to drop me off at my car back by Patterson's office. So what are the next steps here, Bryan? What do you need from me?" Kucharski asked.

"Yeah, Ted, Nina and I also need to get back to the office and log this surveillance and do our paperwork. I'm going to set up a meeting with Al Tacovic, the U.S. Attorney, and if possible I'd like you to be there," Hampton answered.

"I'm good with that, but call me a pessimist, because I always worry about the kind of support we're going to get for a prosecution," Kucharski commented as he got up to leave, trying in vain to brush two catsup stains off his well-worn white shirt. "It was a real pleasure working with you today, Nina, and make sure you never let Patterson near that pretty face."

"Don't worry about that, Ted, he'll never touch me. But you two have me worried about all my doctor visits now. How do you really know what you need and what's being done? I've always assumed my doctors are honest and competent, but now I'm going to be suspicious of everything," Nina responded with concern.

"You know, Nina, in our business, we're always focused on the bad guys, and what we need to keep in mind is more than ninety percent of the physicians are honest and never get involved in the stuff we're talking about. All of us need to be as careful and wise in purchasing and consuming health care services as we are when we're buying anything else," Hampton reassured her.

The three agents were soon on their way; each feeling this had been one of their good days fighting crime, and hopefully one that would result in putting Patterson where he belonged. But all the way back to Appleton something was worrying Ted, something he saw or heard that day. "What was it?" he kept asking himself.

Chapter 3

Chicago, IL
September 30th
9:30 AM

The U.S. Attorney's Office for the Northern Illinois District was located on Dearborn in the heart of the Chicago Loop. Anyone who had been there would likely remember *The Flamingo*, a huge red metal sculpture in the Federal Plaza, as the most familiar landmark in the area. The trouble was that few, if any, would call it by that name. Since 1974, when Alexander Calder's sculpture was erected, most people had always called it "that big red metal thing," unable to associate it with a flamingo or any other bird or animal.

Hampton and Kucharski were scheduled to meet with U.S. Attorney Albert Tacovic at nine forty-five and had arrived early so they could review the case and the documents they planned to present to him. For the past thirty-six hours Hampton had worked diligently with others in his office to prepare a succinct but well-documented initial outline of the case against Dr. Patterson. The objective of the morning's meeting was to get Tacovic to agree he would prosecute the case once all of the evidence had been gathered. Today's session would provide Tacovic with an initial overview of the case and a summary of the evidence gathered to date, but most significantly it would allow Bryan the opportunity to stress how much money this doctor had stolen in two years from the government and private insurers.

What Bryan and Ted both knew from experience was that no prosecutor, and especially a U.S. Attorney, wanted to bother with a medical fraud case unless the loss was significant or a patient had died or been seriously injured. The sad fact was health care fraudsters who steal less than a million dollars rarely get any attention from the overworked legal system.

After waiting half an hour past their appointment time, Bryan approached the receptionist, who after ignoring him for several minutes, grudgingly acknowledged him, "Can I help you?"

"I hope so. Can you tell me how much longer we can expect to wait?" he asked with a touch of cynicism in his voice.

Her answer was well-rehearsed and delivered with sarcasm, "Mr. Tacovic is a busy man, but I'm sure he'll be with you as soon as possible."

Just as Bryan was about to let her know that he was also busy, Tom Bilbray, one of the paralegals, arrived to escort them to the meeting. Bilbray, up to that point in their investigation, had acted as a liaison between the investigators and the prosecutor's office, so Bryan was pleased to see he was participating in the gathering.

Bilbray escorted them to a surprisingly plain corner office with an unexceptional view of the city. Tacovic stood, then walked from behind his uncluttered desk to expedite the introductions. He appeared younger than Hampton expected, not particularly handsome or imposing, slightly overweight and short. And before he uttered a word Bryan sensed he was going to be all business or all BS, or maybe both at the same time. Always a challenge to tell which, with professional politicians, Bryan thought.

As they shook hands, Bryan noticed the U.S. Attorney's Armani suit, diamond cuff links, and especially his Bulgari Ergon watch, which, if not a knockoff, would go for about fifteen thousand dollars. He started to wonder what Tacovic's night job might be.

Hampton caught Kucharski's eye and touched his watch and gave a subtle nod toward Tacovic, trying to get him to notice the watch he was sporting. But Kucharski apparently had no interest in expensive jewelry because he simply looked at his own watch and mouthed, "It's ten forty-two." Hampton just nodded.

Once they were all seated, Al Tacovic's first words were, "As you gentlemen obviously know, I'm running behind today, and the time I scheduled for this meeting has already passed. So let's get right to business. Mr. Bilbray has briefed me on the progress of the case over the last couple of months, but frankly I don't recall the details so, Agent Hampton, please give me the forty thousand foot overview."

"That's precisely what we had planned today, Mr. Tacovic," Hampton responded.

"Call me Al and I'll call you Bryan, if you don't mind."

"That's great with me and I'm sure Mr. Kucharski will be happy if we both call him Ted," Hampton suggested, somewhat pleased by the implied team approach in Tacovic's suggestion to be less formal.

Hampton immediately began a comprehensive yet efficient discussion of the case against Dr. Patterson. He described the specific allegations, the evidence collected to date, and emphasized the suspected theft was in excess of two million dollars. He then explained the incriminating video and audio recordings, describing how Dr. Patterson is shown explaining to two different undercover agents posing as patients, how he can get their non-covered cosmetic services paid for by their insurance companies. Hampton then invited Kucharski to describe the cases his SIU has investigated and developed.

Once Kucharski finished Hampton turned and faced the U.S. Attorney. "We're here today asking for your commitment to support prosecution of Dr. Patterson once we finish gathering additional evidence. And more specifically, we need your immediate approval to seek warrants to search Patterson's office and home, and to arrest Patterson."

Hampton knew Tacovic was ambitious, politically motivated and part of the Chicago Democratic machine. His Congressional campaign against a Republican incumbent was already underway, notwithstanding his ongoing duties and obligations as the U.S. Attorney. With the primary less than six months away, Hampton expected Tacovic to be slow and deliberate in considering their request for warrants, knowing he would need to weigh the political risks and benefits.

Before he accepted his current position in Chicago, knowing Al Tacovic would be his boss and in large part would control the progress of his cases, Hampton had investigated the man's background and credentials. In his opinion the law degree Tacovic received from Northwestern University was the only accomplishment he'd actually earned. Following a lackluster stint at one of Chicago's largest law firms, Tacovic had received a federal appointment to his current position. That had been two years ago when Tacovic was only 35 years of age.

Hampton's conclusion was the appointment was clearly undeserved and obviously the result of his family's political connections. His father Edmund,

Big Ed, Tacovic, a man with only a high school education, had managed to hold office as a Chicago Alderman representing the 44th Ward for thirty-six years.

After several minutes of silence had passed, Hampton began to grow concerned over the longer than expected delay, and he sensed reluctance on Tacovic's part to grant their requests. Kucharski and Hampton both noticed that Tacovic incessantly tugged at the cuff of his left sleeve, and it seemed as if the tugs-per-minute were increasing as they watched him conduct an erratic review of the documents they had given him only minutes before. They knew their misgivings were warranted because the logical next steps they had requested should have been an easy decision for an impartial U.S. Attorney.

So after what seemed like ten minutes of dead air, but was actually only four, or about twenty tugs on his left sleeve, the U.S. Attorney finally responded. "Gentlemen, you've presented a good case here, but I'd like to think about it over the weekend. It's Friday, so nothing's going to happen today anyway. I want to see how this case stacks up against the other work we have going on in this office, and I'd also like to have more time to review the materials you've brought me today. Let's set a time on Monday afternoon for a conference call, and I'll let you know how I want to proceed."

Then turning to Bilbray, he said, "Tom, please arrange a call with Agent Hampton on Monday. Bryan, you can relay the outcome of our call to Mr. Kucharski after we talk, so it won't be necessary for him to participate. I want to thank you both for your time and the good work you've done so far. Now, I need to get to my next meeting, so Tom can show you both out."

And with that comment, they were dismissed and led out of the sparsely appointed corner office and away from its less than enthusiastic occupant, who most likely subconsciously tugged at his left sleeve to keep others from seeing the Bulgari watch Hampton had concluded was likely not a knockoff.

Since the elevator was crowded with government workers headed downstairs to various coffee shops and fast food outlets, Hampton and Kucharski said nothing until they were out on the sidewalk headed for their cars. "What the hell just happened there?" Kucharski asked.

"Not sure I know either," Hampton answered. "Seemed like he was considering some privileged or new information he needed to add to the simple equation we presented to him and was struggling with the math."

"You want to know what I think he was adding to a simple calculation, which then made it complicated?" Kucharski asked.

"Lay it on me, Ted. Tell me what your paranoia meter is reading."

"Word on Tacovic is he's a major political animal. That, I'm sure, is not news to you, but what might be is the fact he has his sights set on one of the Illinois Senate seats, meaning he has to make sure he doesn't step on any toes in the next four years. So he'll check with all his political hacks over the weekend and find out if our crooked dermatologist might be somebody's relative," Kucharski asserted emphatically.

"Take it easy, tiger! Don't be such a cynic. Not everyone is a crook just because this is Chicago," Hampton responded with limited conviction. "Let's give the guy a little more credit than that. After all, we're asking him to support us on a major case here, and it's not unreasonable for a someone in his position to want to understand all the facts before jumping in with both feet and authorizing us to raid someone's home and office."

Kucharski was becoming agitated and almost shouted at Hampton, "How old are you, ten? Are you still such a newbie here that you don't understand how things work in this town, and the rest of Illinois for that matter? If you keep living in La La Land, you'll never get anything done.

"Maybe you need to take a trip north with me. Apparently the two hundred miles between here and Appleton allow me a much better grasp on reality than you seem to have. Something stinks here, and I'll bet big money when you call me on Monday to fill me in on your conference call with your new friend Tacovic, neither of us will be high-fiving each other because this dog is definitely not gonna hunt."

"Ted, I'm pretty sure the two hundred mile commute is just turning you into a pessimist. I think we're fine and that we'll both be happy with his decision. This is going to be a big win for us, wait and see. I'll call you as soon as I'm done talking to him Monday afternoon, so think constructive thoughts and don't be so negative."

As they parted ways, Hampton's thoughts soon brought him to a realization that, more than he wanted to admit, he, too, shared Kucharski's concern about Tacovic's response and possible motives. As he arrived at the garage where his car was parked, he decided there was nothing that could be done about it then, and resigned himself to thinking positive thoughts until Monday's call, hopeful that his continued optimism might offset potential political roadblocks that could negate all the hard work they had already done on the case.

Nineteen miles to the north in Dr. Patterson's Evanston office, another busy day was finally ending, and Debbie Barnes, his insurance clerk, went to his private office to ask a question. "Dr. Patterson, I've been looking at this video since last Friday when it was first posted on YouTube. Have you seen it?"

"I generally don't have time to look at trash posted on YouTube Debbie, so you can be certain the answer is no."

"Well, there's a woman in it who looks so familiar. I keep thinking she's a patient, and I thought you might be able to place her. Could you look at it and tell me if you know who she is? It's driving me crazy. The video is funny, you might even enjoy it."

Debbie cued up the video and handed the phone to Dr. Patterson. The first thing he saw as the caption, *Federal Agents Assaulting Students in Evanston McDonald's, Your Tax Dollars at Work.* He watched a brief scuffle between five men and one woman, which ended abruptly when the two men in suits and the neatly attired woman somehow swiftly overpowered the three sloppily-dressed aggressors.

As the video ended, the camera zoomed in on the faces of each of the assailants, then panned up for the same shot on the three people still standing. The last close-up focused on the face of the only woman in the group, the patient Debbie couldn't place.

Dr. Hugh Patterson knew instantly who she was and two seconds later was stricken with anxiety and fear. What a horrible start to the weekend, he curiously thought, not yet fully grasping the implications of his discovery.

Chapter 4

Chicago, IL
September 30th
5:30 PM

Edmund Tacovic was completing his light Aldermanic duties for the week when he noticed a message to call his youngest son Al. "Finally a bright spot in my day," he whispered, just loud enough to hear his own thought. In recent years Ed had become preoccupied with the notion that Al would someday become President, and that obsession had on many occasions caused him to knowingly stretch even his own hazy boundaries of political propriety.

Now in his seventy-eighth year, this son of Polish immigrants with no education beyond the eighth grade found that more and more often he could rationalize and justify nearly any behavior, if he believed it would advance Al's political fortunes. "You'll become what I never could be," he would tell Al whenever rancor was required to deal with their adversaries.

Al Tacovic, the U.S. attorney, was on his cell creeping along the Lake Shore Drive just north of Oak Street Beach in Friday night rush hour traffic when he saw his father was calling. He quickly disengaged from his current conversation and clicked over to Ed. "Dad, glad you could get back to me, four hours later."

"Don't give me a hard time. You're lucky I called back at all on a Friday night," Ed replied just as sarcastically. "What's up?"

"Well, I'm not sure I want to discuss this by phone, so I'm wondering if you have a few minutes tonight for me to stop by the house and talk in person."
"How about right now?" his father asked. "Where are you anyway? Sounds like you're driving."
"I am, and if you're at home, I can swing by and be there in no more than fifteen minutes. I'm just about to Fullerton on the Outer Drive."
"Then come now, because I'm just leaving the office and I'll be at the house in ten minutes. If you beat me there, spend some time with your mother. We hardly ever see you anymore," Ed chided.

As Al crept along, he thought about his father's rise in Chicago politics. In 1966 Ed officially left his job as a Chicago Transit Authority bus driver, although he remained on the CTA payroll, and began a full-time position as an "advisor" to the Mayor. Daley had several advisors living off the city coffers, and the general public didn't know what they did, nor did they wisely bother to ask. Al had been told about the rumors years ago that Ed was an "enforcer" of some kind for the Democratic machine, but he'd always believed it was unlikely that role really existed. Nonetheless, opponents almost continuously voiced allegations of corruption against the Democrats, but neither Daley nor "Big Ed" were ever personally charged.

Over the years Al witnessed first-hand that loyalty to the Party and to Daley had paid off for his father. He'd heard how his father had the full support of the machine when he first ran for Alderman of the 44th Ward in 1975 and won by a landslide. During his tenth run, the previous fall, Ed announced to his constituency this campaign would be his last for the Aldermanic seat.

Al realized if his father managed to complete this current term, Ed's time on the Chicago City Council would span forty years; not the longest on record, but certainly one of the lengthiest tenures in that body without being indicted or jailed for some impropriety. But more critical to Al than any record for longevity was the realization that, once Ed retired, his ability to pull many of the strings that had facilitated Al's career so far, would no longer exist.

He exited onto Fullerton and thought of all the lessons he learned from his dad, the master politician. All of Ed's associates spoke of his incredible instincts, and while many in his vocation were caught in nets of corruption, he avoided those snares by being shrewd and cautious in all his undertakings, legal or otherwise.

Al was only sixteen at the time, but could still remember Ed's return to the center of power, when the late Mayor Daley's son, Richard M. Daley, became Mayor of Chicago in 1989. And under the second Daley's administration Ed enjoyed the added benefits of being an elected alderman with a more than respectable salary, as well as all the additional financial opportunities his position presented to a politician who worked tirelessly to serve those who needed special favors.

Al realized he would beat his father to their house because he knew the office was at least twenty walking minutes from the home he grew up in, where his parents still lived. He also knew Ed never drove anywhere unless it was a trip out of town. According to plan, Al arrived ahead of his father and had a nice visit with his mother, who as usual tried to force-feed him with all the things he loved, but knew would add pounds to an already large frame. But he couldn't resist and, when Big Ed did arrive, they both indulged in some lethal homemade pastries, but then soon got down to business. Elena Tacovic excused herself soon after, but not before urging Al to come back more often.

"Dad, do you know a doctor by the name of Hugh Patterson?"

"Of course I do and, so do you, if you think about it for a minute. He's married to your sister Janeska's friend Alicia. Remember her? She practically lived at our house while they were in high school, but you were young then, I guess only about eight or so," Ed explained. "And by the way, the last I heard his office was in Evanston, and I'm sure it's in your district."

"You're right about the office location, but I don't remember him or his wife. I wasn't much interested in Janeska's friends then. But I do remember you and mom telling her she should find herself a doctor to marry like her friend Alicia did a few years back. That was probably about the time she was getting married to the guy, and something about the name stuck with me. Is Janeska still friends with Alicia?" Al asked.

"What's this all about? You need a doctor or something?"

"I could maybe use a doctor, this one especially, but not for any medical reason," Al answered. "Let me tell you about the visit I had today from one of the medical fraud investigators working for the department, and the case he dropped on my desk."

Al then explained the case against Hugh Patterson and asked Ed, "So, what's the opportunity here?"

"There's several opportunities I can see, so let's talk about two in particular. But first let me remind you about the way I measure opportunities," Ed responded. "I like to take advantage of opportunities and situations that deliver long-term, recurring dividends.

"Now, opportunity number one is you prosecute Dr. Patterson for medical fraud, and from what we know at this point, the case appears solid. And if by chance it went to trial, a long shot normally in a medical fraud case, and you get a conviction, the payoff for you is some good press for a few days at best. And, of course, you also get a gold star on your record as a prosecutor for whatever that's worth.

"Then again, opportunity number two is Dr. Patterson somehow avoids this mess, keeps his license and stays out of jail, and as a result owes you a sizeable debt of gratitude for your help and compassion. So the question we must ask is how much that gratitude is worth to the doctor and to you, the up and coming congressman and soon to be senator?"

Ed paused, then continued, "As with any opportunity, there are risks in pursuing either one. With opportunity number one, you could lose the case and look incompetent. And with opportunity number two, there's a chance that it might backfire; that is, if Patterson becomes righteous and reports any proposal made to him. But since we already have an inside connection through his wife, we can almost eliminate that risk by indirectly testing his willingness to cooperate."

"So Dad, we're definitely both on the same page, but how do we quickly make something happen here, because I've promised the investigators I'd give them a decision on Monday as to whether or not I'll support their case and the warrants they're after."

A few minutes passed with Ed staring at the wall and slowly tapping his finger on the kitchen table. Raising his head with what Al saw was a shrewd gleam in his eyes, he leaned in closer to Al and almost whispered, "Let's both think this through carefully, but I'll venture a guess you're going to like my idea!"

For the next hour father and son, both trusted servants of the people, planned the scheme down to the smallest detail. Ed's primary rule was that both father and son would avoid as many direct conversations with Patterson as possible.

Ed's idea was to have Al's sister Janeska call her friend Alicia Patterson and tell her she overheard her brother, the U.S. Attorney, discussing a potential fraud case against a Dr. Patterson. In querying her brother, Janeska discovered that the case in fact did involve Alicia's husband. Irrespective of how Alicia responded, Janeska must say to her, "Maybe something could be worked out for a friend of the family, and if your husband wants to talk with my brother, then let me help set up a call between them."

When Janeska did receive a return call confirming Dr. Patterson's interest in a meeting, and father and son were certain she would, she was to instruct her friend on the explicit ground rules governing any conversations with Al. The exact arrangements were that the call was to be placed by Dr. Patterson from his home phone to Janeska's cell phone, the number she was currently calling from, and the same number would be used for any conversations between them in the future.

By eight-thirty that night, all the Tacovic family participants were clear on the game plan, and they quickly put it into motion. Janeska set her cell to 'Speaker,' so Al could listen, then dialed Alicia Patterson, who surprisingly picked up on the second ring and answered with a tentative, "Hello?" because she hadn't recognized the number.

"Alicia, this is Janeska, is that you?"

"Jan Tacovic?" Alicia, shocked for several reasons, nearly shouted, "I can't believe it. Hugh and I were just talking about calling you, but it's been so long I didn't even have a phone number. We were just debating about calling your mom to get your number. Based on the number I see on caller ID, you're still in Chicago, right?"

"Oh absolutely; never left, and I'm still Jan Tacovic, since I never found the right guy like you did. But why were you trying to contact me? I hope there's nothing wrong."

Alicia paused a little too long searching for the right words, but after hesitating continued, "Well, Jan, there is something wrong, and Hugh and I were hoping maybe your dad or brother might be able to give us some advice."

"What kind of problem, Alicia?" Janeska asked.

"Listen, Jan, Hugh is right here and I think it would be best if he explained it to you rather than me."

"That's fine with me, if that's how the two of you want to handle it," Janeska answered encouragingly.

Janeska could tell when Dr. Hugh Patterson took the phone from his wife he was hesitant, so for a few seconds he didn't speak, but eventually he began the conversation. "Jan, we hardly know each other, and so this is difficult for me, and I hope you'll not judge me until you hear the whole story."

Al and Janeska looked at each other, sensing an unexpected twist was about to be introduced into their scripted plan, one that could streamline the potentially awkward approach they had carefully devised. So Janeska wisely responded by saying something she believed would alleviate the awkwardness Patterson was feeling, "Hugh, I come from a family of politicians, and we've been taught from our childhood the first commandment of politics is, *Judge not that ye be not judged*, so don't worry about me or anyone in my family criticizing you. But you should also know my father and brother are big believers not only in repentance, but also, and maybe more important, in atonement."

Hugh paused and finally said, "That's good to know and I'll keep it in mind. I'd like to tell you what's happened and see if you can arrange for me to get some help from your brother or father."

"Go on, Dr. Patterson, I'm listening."

Patterson began by relating the story of what he at first believed was a routine visit from a new patient earlier in the week. "She was interested in some cosmetic procedures, so I examined her and explained what she needed done. Because she was concerned about her insurance benefits, we discussed how my staff is able to get most insurance companies to pay for the services we provide, even when patients are told those services aren't covered. This is all a routine process for new patients as well as existing patients in our office.

"As it turned out, later that same day, Sandy Barnes, our insurance clerk, who spends too much of her time at work on the Internet; saw a video posted on YouTube. The video link was entitled *Federal Agents Assaulting Students in Evanston McDonald's*. As she viewed it, she saw that one of the agents was a woman who looked familiar, but she couldn't place her.

"This all happened on Wednesday, then late today, since she still hadn't been able to figure out why this FBI Agent looked familiar, she showed me the video. I instantly recognized the agent as our new patient, Alice Rizzo, whom I had seen the very same day the video was posted. So we pulled her patient file and checked her occupation, which she had listed as administrative assistant.

"The phone number she gave us rolls over into voicemail right after the first ring. When we checked her address on Google Maps, we see it's a high rise on Sheridan, but she failed to list an apartment number. My staff always checks everyone's insurance coverage before we even bring them into the exam rooms, and they had verified Alice Rizzo's benefits and confirmed her policy was in force.

"The employer she listed was a small business, which has a website and a phone number. That number also rolls instantly to voicemail, and there's no street address. The website only lists Skokie, IL as the company's headquarters. But it was late this afternoon by the time we called, so the employer could still

be legitimate. But I'm concerned the FBI may be investigating me for some
reason, and I don't exactly know what to do, and I'm scared and worried."

Janeska interrupted at that point and asked, "Dr. Patterson, since you do seem
uneasy, I must ask the obvious question here, because we're all friends. How is
it you can get insurance companies to pay for things that aren't covered? Are
you just smarter than other doctors? Do you have friends at the insurance
companies, or what?"

"I don't do anything different than any other medical provider does. We all
have to look out for our patients, so we do what's needed to get them the
benefits they deserve," he replied, much too defensively.

"Just so I'm clear here and know what to tell my brother, are you saying
you've done nothing wrong, but you want to know if there's something you
should do about a possible investigation? Or are you concerned that you actually
have been, let's say, pushing the envelope a little, and if someone looks too
closely, you could be in trouble?" Janeska asked, reading from a quickly
scribbled note Al had passed her.

This time there was even a longer pause before Patterson responded. "I think
I could have a problem."

"A problem or lots of problems?" Janeska asked without any prompting from
her brother. "And can you be specific about what you promised Alice Rizzo,
which is obviously not even her real name."

"Okay, now I think you're asking me more than I'm comfortable telling you.
Maybe I need to talk to my attorney at this point."

"Talking to your attorney is always a good idea, Hugh. But once you go
there, anything dad or my brother can do for you is no longer a possibility.
Maybe you and Alicia need to talk this over, then get back to me," Janeska
cautioned him.

Another pause on Patterson's end, while Janeska and Al listened to a partially
muffled conversation in the background, but then both Tacovics clearly heard
Alicia say, "Tell her the truth, damn it. I'm not going to see you go to jail and
live with the shame of this if we can avoid it by asking a friend for help!"

"Jan, did you hear Alicia?" Patterson asked.

"Of course I did, and I agree with her. Let's get to the point here."

No pause this time; Patterson was resigned to confessing his transgressions.
"Okay, the answer to your question is lots of problems. We know what
procedures insurers will and will not pay for, so irrespective of what procedures
we perform, we bill the services we know will get paid.

"And as to the second question, you asked what I said to the agent. I pretty much used the same speech I use twenty times a day. I told her not to worry; we know how to get whatever you need done paid for. But to make matters worse, this particular woman's face is almost flawless, and beyond some tiny lines around her eyes when she smiles, she doesn't actually need any work done. But in reviewing the treatment plan we gave her, there were nine procedures we recommended, totaling about fourteen thousand dollars."

On the Tacovic end of the line Al signaled Janeska her part was complete, then whispered in her ear, "Have him call this number in one hour to talk to me."

Janeska knew the script from there and, with a thoughtful tone in her voice, proceeded to give Patterson the instructions the Tacovics had agreed on earlier. "Thanks for being candid, Dr. Patterson. Now I think we can get down to business. I'll try to reach my brother and arrange for him to take a call from you at this number in one hour. You need to call back in exactly sixty minutes, unless I call you before then and tell you differently. Do you understand so far?

"You should expect Al to answer the phone. I'll update him on our conversation, but you'll need to give him an abbreviated version of the whole story without trying to sugar coat it. He's a busy man and doesn't have time for anything but the facts. I suggest you spend the next hour outlining everything he should know, not just about the FBI agent's visit, but anything else that goes on in your business affairs that may be illegal, whether you think everyone else is doing it or not. Make a numbered list of whatever the FBI might have evidence of, and be prepared to quickly go over the list with Al."

Then Janeska delivered the most ingeniously phrased part of her message, "I'm fairly sure he can help you, but you can expect it won't come without some significant consideration from you. So don't act surprised when that topic is raised. In fact, you'd be wise to suggest at some point that you're eager to support his election campaign for Congress."

Precisely one hour later Janeska's cell phone rang once, and Al Tacovic immediately answered, asking, "Dr. Patterson, is that you?"

Patterson, surprised by the swift pick-up as well as by Tacovic's directness, responded with, "Yes, is this Mr. Tacovic?"

"It is indeed, Hugh. May I call you Hugh? And you can call me Al or Mr. Tacovic whatever you prefer." Without waiting for an answer, the U.S. Attorney purposefully rushed on with another question. "Hugh, I'm going to record this conversation, and I want to ask your permission to do so, while at the same time asking you to confirm that you're not recording it. I want to make it quite clear that I'm forbidding you to record this or any other call we might have in the future. Are we clear on those points, Hugh?"

After a too long pause, Patterson answered, "Yes, you can call me Hugh. No, I'm not recording the call, and I guess if you insist on recording it there's not much I can do about it."

"Hugh, we need to get some ground rules straight. I need you to respond to my questions with specific answers. Saying I guess, and there's not much I can do about it, are not the kind of answers that will facilitate our discussions. I need an affirmative response to my question. Do I have your permission to record our call tonight?"

Patterson reluctantly answered, "Yes, you have my permission."

"Good. Now, I understand you have a problem, and I'd like you to walk me through the situation you find yourself in, so I can see if there's anything I can do to help you. Keep in mind this needs to be an unembellished and factual description of the problem, holding nothing back that might pertain to the case the FBI is apparently building against you."

Twenty-five minutes later Hugh's narrative was complete, and to his credit Patterson had related generally the same facts and issues about the case Tacovic had heard from Bryan Hampton earlier that same day. In spite of his earlier excuses and claims of innocence to Janeska, he had been remarkably insightful and detailed about possible wrongdoings that might be included in any case against him.

After asking him a few questions to determine if he was aware that another undercover agent, also posing as a patient, had visited his office a week or two before, it became clear to Tacovic Patterson was completely oblivious to the recording of that visit as well. So Tacovic suggested the doctor have his staff review all other new patient visits in the last three weeks, which could have been set-ups as well. If they discovered any new patients who appeared questionable, Tacovic advised Patterson to withdraw any pending insurance claims for those patients.

Tacovic then paused for what he believed to be the appropriate amount of time to thoroughly consider how best to help Hugh with his dilemma. But before he gave the doctor hope he thought it would be advantageous to soften him up with some 'left jabs and hard body blows,' a method Ed Tacovic and his cronies employed on many occasions. For Al, the tactic was only a metaphor; however he'd learned from experience verbal punches were often even more effective than the physical ones.

So Tacovic first summarized every law and statute Patterson had violated, then moved to potential penalties. "You know, Hugh, you're in a boat-load of trouble here. This is a grave situation for you and your family. You can be charged on multiple counts of filing false claims. If you're found guilty, you'll not only lose your license, you'll be looking at a long prison term, possibly twenty years or more.

"And that will just be the beginning. All your property and assets will be seized to pay the associated penalties and to make restitution to Medicare and the other insurers. This is bad, Hugh, very bad and very serious."

Tacovic knew Dr. Patterson would agree to almost anything he proposed after hearing his dire summary of possible consequences. "Hugh, I'm going to discontinue recording anymore of our talk, is that okay with you? But before I do, I need to remind you again that you don't have my permission to record the rest of our conversation. Do you agree?"

Patterson uneasily agreed, then, as instructed earlier by Janeska, tried to be proactive, "Mr. Tacovic, I'm appreciative of any help you can possibly give me. Furthermore, I want to show my appreciation and demonstrate my respect for your public service by making a substantial contribution to your Congressional campaign in the 9th District, where my family lives."

Although out of sequence with the original plan, Al decided now was a good time to get specific, so he spelled out the terms as though Patterson had proffered them himself. "Hugh I appreciate your offer and your expression of gratitude. Your proposal to make an initial two hundred thousand dollar contribution to my campaign fund is much appreciated. We're running low on funds right now and your suggestion to wire the money to my account by Monday afternoon is extremely generous and timely." Tacovic then told the doctor to carefully write down the wiring instructions he was about to give him.

Tacovic then outlined the bail-out plan they had cooked-up for Patterson just hours before. Once he was satisfied Patterson understood the legal processes that needed to take place, the ground rules of the arrangement, and the exact sequence and timing of each event, he emphasized their current conversation would be the last time they would speak directly.

"You're never to call me directly. If anything unexpected comes up, you can contact Janeska, who'll relay any information I need to know about.

"This is my liaison Tom Bilbray's phone number. You're to instruct your attorney to call him on Monday afternoon." Tacovic had already asked Patterson for the name of his malpractice attorney and written down the name Dynah Edelmann. "I want to stress to you that your attorney, Ms. Edelmann, needs to understand very little about what's actually happening between the two of us. It would be imprudent on your part to disclose any details about this case or our arrangements to her or anyone else.

"Remember, Hugh, Ms. Edelmann's only role is to act on your behalf as an officer of the court to deliver a decision from a higher court that protects you from the warrant the agents will present when they enter your office. They'll believe they have the right to conduct a search, and they'll have a legitimate warrant, but Ms. Edelmann will present them with a subsequent decision that overrides the authority granted in their warrant. Don't forget, how we arranged for all this to transpire is none of her business!"

As Tacovic said goodbye to Patterson and clicked 'End' on Janeska's phone, he noted the call had lasted a total of 52 minutes. "Not bad," he said to his sister. "Less than an hour, and by Monday we'll have another two hundred thousand dollars in the war chest, with the promise of more to come." Then he thanked Janeska for all her help and reminded her to let him know immediately if either of the Pattersons contacted her.

Strangely, as he left the house where he was raised and drove home to his family, he seemed to be without any remorse or sense of wrongdoing over how he was conducting the affairs of the U.S. Attorney's office. Just before he turned-up the volume on his car's CD, he even smiled at his thought, Chicago politics; ya gotta love it!

Chapter 5

Chicago, IL
October 3rd
9:30 AM

"Clear skies, plenty of sunshine, with a high of sixty-five degrees is the Chicagoland forecast for today," Hampton heard the WBBM radio announcer repeat for the sixth time. But in spite of the sunny weather, for some reason other than the extra-long commute, he felt an oppressive gloom enveloping him as he inched along the road on his way to work. The Eisenhower Expressway traffic always aggravated Hampton, but today the combination of his concern over the voicemail he heard before he left his apartment and a growing frustration over delays caused by an accident somewhere ahead had compounded his irritation and was feeding his growing anxiety.

Hoping for additional insight he might have missed the first three times he'd heard the message, Hampton decided to listen to the voicemail Tacovic's paralegal left him one more time. He grabbed the cell off the seat and pulled up the voicemail. "Agent Hampton, this is Tom Bilbray calling on behalf of U.S. Attorney Al Tacovic. He's asked me to schedule a call with you today, Monday the third of October, at three in the afternoon. Mr. Tacovic told me to remind you that Mr. Kucharski is not invited to participate in the call. He's also requested that you be alone when you place the call, and stressed that you're not to use a speakerphone. And, of course, he's also specified that you're not to record the call nor share any specific details that will be discussed with Mr. Kucharski."

After Bilbray paused for emphasis, he went on, "At precisely three this afternoon please call the number I'll provide you, then wait for us to join the call. You'll also need the security code that I'll give you as well." After providing both the number and code, Bilbray added, "Thanks for your cooperation. Mr. Tacovic looks forward to speaking with you later today," then he abruptly hung up.

Finally out of the car and behind his desk, Hampton paused, absentmindedly surveyed his surroundings, and thought, I'm fifty-four years old, and I'm sitting behind a metal desk from the seventies, when steel was king. I have an office without a view that's ten times crappier than one I had in Utah a week after I graduated from law school. And I'm spending my morning wrestling with my instincts trying to convince myself there's no logical reason to feel uneasy about a conference call four hours from now, with someone who's supposed to be on my team.

After a few more minutes of fruitless reflection, he concluded that his observations with respect to his accommodations were his own fault, the consequence of his choice to become a civil servant. And in regard to his nagging intuition, he decided there was no obvious answer, hoping his concerns were only imagined. Still uneasy, he opted to follow an impulse and talk through the issues with Kucharski, an action he determined wasn't a disregard for the instructions Bilbray had given, because the call with Tacovic had not yet taken place.

Using his office phone, he dialed the main number for Sidereal HealthCare's SIU in Appleton. On this particular day he wanted to avoid any record of a direct call from his office to Ted's cell. When the operator answered, he asked to be transferred to Agent Kucharski, hoping he was in the office.

"Kucharski," Ted answered, sounding like he'd partially swallowed the last large bite of breakfast.

"Ted, it's Bryan. Do you have a minute?"

"For you, my friend, I have a minute and a half," Ted responded.

"I got a call from Tacovic's boy Bilbray, and I want you to hear it. This is all confidential, of course," Hampton explained.

"Do you mean against regulations or confidential?" Kucharski chided.

"Listen and draw your own conclusions. Are you ready?"

"Okay, dude, let me hear it, because I can already tell I'm not gonna like it."

"After you hear what he said, I want to go over the call point by point and have you give me feedback on what your gut tells you is going on."

Kucharski had Hampton run the voicemail for him, then insisted on hearing it a second time. "Weird is my first impression, but not really unexpected," Kucharski concluded.

"All right, so let's dissect this message into a series of individual points, and as we go through them, we'll make some observations and try to draw some conclusions; not just about the content, but also about the tone and delivery, and see if we can read between the lines. I don't want to get blindsided this afternoon when I'm on the call," Hampton explained.

"First, Tom called me Agent Hampton, then used his own full name, and when he referred to Tacovic, he used his official title. Like I wouldn't know who he was if he just said, this is Tom from Mr. Tacovic's office. He hasn't used this level of formality with me since the first time we talked over two months ago. Second, he stated time and date for the call, which is only normal, so nothing noteworthy there. His third point was to remind me you were not to be on the call, which is just reiterating the instructions Al gave us last Friday, so I guess nothing unusual in that either.

"But now we get to the fourth point, which really concerns me, because instructing me to be alone and not to use a speaker phone is bizarre and explicit. The first part of the fifth point is probably the most curious, his warning me not to record the call. I understand his motive to restrict specific information going to you, but I wonder why they believe it would occur to me to record the call?"

Hampton continued, "There's nothing unusual about the sixth point; his giving me a number and security code for the call is only logical. But what I wonder, is why do any of this by phone? Normal protocol would be to send me an Outlook appointment by email that would include all the information he left on the voicemail. And, point number seven, telling me to call precisely at three, then wait for them to join the call, raised questions about two of the words in that sentence, 'wait' and 'us.' So, Ted, what do you think? What's going on?"

"My first thought is what I said to you Friday, just before you told me to take it easy. The fix is in, my friend. Dr. Patterson is connected in some way to Tacovic. The big tipoff to me has nothing to do with me not being on the phone, or you not telling me anything detailed about the call. But there are three things about the voicemail that make the hair on my back, neck, and legs stand at attention; first, as you already noted, he told you no speakerphone because others could be listening on your end without them knowing, which they definitely don't want happening. Second, they didn't send the instructions or numbers in an email because they don't want any discoverable digital evidence. Third, telling you to call in and wait for 'us' allows them to have someone listening for any uninvited guests who may try and join the call.

"But more important, it leaves you without any idea of who else might be listening on their end, to act as a future witness should one be needed. This gives them the leverage they need to refute anything you might later say about the call. My prediction is we're screwed, and you'll hear some heavy duty BS this afternoon as to why they're not going to give us the warrants."

Hampton paused momentarily while he processed the logic thread and information Ted had just summarized, then said, "Ted, I guess we've both reached basically the same conclusions, but why wouldn't the voicemail from Bilbray be evidence or proof? It seems to me we could still use it as evidence, if we needed it at some point in the future?"

"Evidence of what?" Kucharski asked. "If Tacovic ends up in a tough spot because you out him, then he just claims Tommy Boy said all those strange things totally on his own, because he sure never told his paralegal to say any of it."

After they shared some additional opinions about the voicemail and discussed next steps, Hampton told Kucharski he would contact him after the three o'clock conference call with Tacovic. Their call concluded, Hampton looked at his watch and saw he still had four hours before he talked with Tacovic and decided he would try and distract himself from more negative thinking by working on another case that needed his attention.

Shortly before two that afternoon, Al Tacovic called Vincent Morales, his campaign's 'financial advisor,' "Vince, its Al. Have you verified the arrival of the funds?"

"I just checked about fifteen minutes ago and the wire was received a little after one our time, for the specified amount. All is well," Vince reassured Tacovic.

Having received the confirmation, Tacovic needed to execute the next several steps in his plan, so at five minutes after two he called Tom Bilbray and summoned him to his office. Bilbray arrived almost immediately and closed the door as he entered. Al instructed him to sit and be ready to take notes. "Tom, I think you already know this, but I want to reiterate that I believe you and I have a great future together. Your discretion and respect for the confidential matters I've assigned you in the past has earned my confidence and trust."

Bilbray felt himself redden at this praise from the man he decided several assignments ago was his ticket to success. In recent months he'd already eagerly handled several of Tacovic's questionable projects, which he wisely had never discussed with anyone and probably never would.

As he prepared to record directions from Tacovic, he naively thought, look at me; only three years since the night I decided what I wanted to do with my life, and I'm in a private meeting with my boss, the U.S. attorney, and he's about to ask me to do something for him he can't assign to anyone else in the department but me, not even to any of the hot-shot lawyers who work here.

Bilbray constantly struggled with his self-confidence and tried hard not to think about himself as a once thin, frail young man, born and raised in a farming family near Momence, IL, about an hour south of Chicago. All through his miserable high school years he believed there had to be something more in life than staying on a farm raising corn and soy beans. A revelation of that brighter future had come to him late one night while he was trolling around on the Internet. He stumbled across an ad for a twenty-four month, online course to become a paralegal. At the time, he didn't totally understand what a paralegal did, but the thought of associating with attorneys, working in an office, getting out of Momence and off the farm had thrilled him.

"There's an important and delicate matter I need you to assist me with in the next few hours, Tom, and I want to know if I can depend on you to once again manage an issue with absolute confidentiality?" Tacovic asked him and Tom quickly nodded his willingness.

Tacovic continued, "Tom, write down the name Dynah Edelmann. She's an attorney who represents a doctor named Hugh Patterson, and this morning she was advised by her client to contact you, on your cell, between four and five this afternoon. When she calls and identifies herself, you're to tell her you represent the U.S. Attorney's Office and she must carefully listen to and follow the instructions you'll give her.

"Begin by telling her that a final draft of an important legal document will be delivered to her office tomorrow at noon. The document will reference a specific court and judge. It's an appeal directed to that court to prevent grave legal actions against her client Dr. Patterson. She's to transfer the document to her letterhead, sign it, then have it delivered personally by someone from her office to the referenced court early Wednesday morning.

"Continue by telling her on that same afternoon a courier will deliver the court order she requested from the judge to her office. Those documents will temporarily stay the enforcement of other warrants for her client's arrest and for searches of his office and home."

Tacovic paused to be certain Bilbray was keeping pace with his instructions, then continued. "Make sure you stress to her that Federal officers are planning to exercise their search warrant on Thursday morning between eleven and noon. So she must be at Dr. Patterson's Evanston office no later than eleven that morning. She's to bring the court documents she received the previous day with her.

"Impress upon her that she must remain at Patterson's office until she's prevented the federal agents from performing their search or arresting her client. Emphasize the court documents she possesses supersede the warrants the agents will try to serve. Tell her Agent Bryan Hampton, a veteran attorney in the Justice Department, will be the agent in charge that day. He'll immediately understand he's lost the legal high ground once he examines her documents."

Tacovic continued his instructions after swallowing a gulp of coffee, "Remind her that she'll be acting as an officer of the court, and will be protecting the interests of her client. Then make it clear once the agents have gone, her responsibilities in this matter are at an end, and she need not be concerned about any further efforts to seize her client's property or to arrest him.

"Then ask her if there's anything unclear about the instructions you've given her. You're only to answer questions about the specifics of your directives, should she be unclear about any of them. Do not, under any circumstances, address any peripheral matters or questions she might pose pertaining to the who, what, or why's of this matter. Finally, tell her if she needs to speak with you again to call you at the same number.

"One more thing, Tom; in the morning I'll give you a sealed envelope containing the document you told her to expect by noon tomorrow. Don't open it, but make sure you deliver it between eleven forty-five and noon. When you arrive at her office, simply give the document to the receptionist, explaining it's important that Ms. Edelmann see it immediately, then walk out without saying anything else. Now that's a lot of information. Did you get everything and do you have any questions?"

"I have it all down, Mr. Tacovic. I'll take care of it and tell you how it went after I speak with her. Can I ask why the attorney is calling my cell phone and not the office number?"

"Because I don't want anyone but you to handle this important matter, and also because Ms. Edelmann may need to contact you after regular office hours due to the critical nature of this matter," Tacovic explained, knowing by now the obedient paralegal would likely not even speculate about other possible motives.

"Just make sure you come and tell me in person how the call went. No emails on this."

After Bilbray left his office, Tacovic next placed a call to a long-time friend of the family and close political confidant of his father. After only two rings, the man answered his cell with a gruff "Hello?"

"Judge Markowski, it's Al Tacovic."

"Little Al, my adopted godson. It's not my birthday, so you must need a favor."

Tacovic realized the judge knew as soon as he picked up the phone some favor was needed. Tacovic depended on this long-time relationship and called upon it often. Judge Andrzej, Andrew, Markowski had been a close friend of Ed Tacovic and his family for over thirty years. He was also the son of Polish immigrants, but wasn't a resident of the Forty-Fourth ward. The Judge and Big Ed first met during a city council meeting in the early part of 1981, while Ed was serving his second term as an alderman.

At the time Markowski was an up and coming attorney, who on that particular day was appearing before the Council arguing a zoning matter for a wealthy client. Their chance encounter during the meeting developed into a long and solid relationship, and with Ed's influence and help, Markowski climbed the Party ranks until his loyalty finally earned him a seat on the bench.

Al was only seven when Andrzej Markowski first came to their home for dinner, an evening Al would never forget because he'd never heard language in his home like Mr. Markowski freely used at the dinner table. The Markowskis had no children and, when Al was twelve years old, Markowski's wife had died. After that loss, this giant, loud and boisterous man spent a great deal of his spare time with the Tacovics, so much that he eventually asserted Al was his godson, and no one ever challenged the claim.

The bond between Markowski the judge, now seventy-two years old, and Ed the seventy-eight-year-old Alderman, was partly their common heritage, partly their political ties, partly their love of power, but mostly their unconstrained greed. Al, the godson, depended on and funded that greed whenever the opportunity arose, and the Judge never let him down.

"Judge, you know me too well, so I'm not even going to try to make something up. I do need a favor, and there's a short fuse on this one. Bryan Hampton, an agent over at the DOJ, has a suspect in a medical fraud case and he's requesting warrants to arrest him and to authorize searches of his home and office. Their suspect is Dr. Hugh Patterson, who happens to be an important constituent of mine, and I need to prevent all of this from taking place.

"I'd like you to issue an order to dismiss their warrants and to stop their intrusions and his arrest. Dr. Patterson has an attorney, and we'll need to make it look like she requested the stays on behalf of her client. I'll prepare the documents for her here and have her sign and deliver them to your court early Wednesday morning. The warrants the DOJ agents are seeking haven't yet been issued, but it must appear like I'm supporting our agents in this investigation. So I'll authorize them to pursue their warrants later today, meaning they'll likely be issued tomorrow sometime.

"However, I won't allow the agents to proceed with their planned arrest or their searches until Thursday. So, it'll look like there was a leak of some kind from the court that granted the warrants and somehow Patterson was alerted to his pending arrest. The assumption will be the doctor immediately contacted his attorney for help, and she then petitioned your court to stop the whole process.

"With the information in the petition I prepared for her to sign and submit to your court, it will appear you made a reasonable decision to simply slow down a relatively drastic action against a pillar of the medical community. So there's no reason anyone should suspect anything or point any fingers in your direction."

"You know, Al, nothing is ever simple with you, but everything is always impeccably planned," Markowski commented. "What's the name of Patterson's attorney, so I can watch for the paperwork?"

"Dynah Edelmann is her name, but you've probably never heard of her. Based on our research, she's primarily a medical malpractice specialist, who incidentally has done quite well for herself. She's already represented Patterson in two or three malpractice suits."

"As a matter of fact, I've heard good things about her, and anyone who's opposed her speaks highly of her competence and veracity," Markowski responded, then asked, "Does she know what's going on with this particular situation?"

"Only that her client might be in trouble and he needs her help to prevent his arrest and searches of his office and home. I have this thing at arm's length with one of our paralegals doing limited communication with her as well as all the leg-work and handling of documents. If anything is ever linked back to this office, it'll look like a junior paralegal went off the reservation, because it'll be his word against a U.S. attorney's."

"I've got one more relevant question, Al. What happens on Thursday afternoon when those agents come screaming into your office after being thwarted in their plans to make an arrest? They'll likely have accumulated mountains of evidence, and they've probably been working on this case for months. You don't expect them to just walk away from it, do you?"

"You're right about that, Judge! They won't want to leave this alone, and they do have substantial evidence that's taken months to gather. However, when they do confront me, I'll maintain that I got the decision from your court at the same time they did, and after reviewing the court's position, I could see there were some problems with their case and their warrants. I'll clearly tell them I have no interest in taking Patterson to court, explaining my office has too many, more important cases right now to waste time on this one.

"I'll suggest it would be far more efficient to bring Patterson in with his attorney, present the evidence we have, and negotiate appropriate penalties along with a significant financial settlement. This course of action, I'll explain, will avoid the costs and time commitment of a court case that could potentially backfire.

"Then I'll point out Patterson's attorney is already making allegations of entrapment related to two visits by FBI agents posing as patients to Patterson's office. The assertion, I'll tell them, is the agents induced the physician into committing an illegal act by pleading for badly needed medical treatment, which their own insurance companies told them they wouldn't pay for. From a legal perspective, what the agents did, in my opinion, was definitely not entrapment. But my rationale with them will be, 'Who knows how a jury might view it.'

"The part I won't tell them is the ultimate disposition of the case will be a reasonable monetary penalty with no jail time for Patterson, and I also plan to work with the state licensing boys to just give him probation. After all, we need him to continue working. Think of the money he'll generate, so he can support the politician of his choice."

"Okay, Al. I've heard enough. It sounds like you have it all figured out, so just make sure I have time to write my opinion on the case and get the paperwork turned around on time. I assume you agree this case is a fifteen on our value scale of one to a hundred," Markowski suggested in closing.

Tacovic paused briefly, somewhat caught off guard, having first thought this was a five thousand dollar favor not a fifteen thousand dollar one. But he was in no position to bargain, the judge held all the cards at that point. And why should I care anyway? Tacovic thought. With my hundred percent mark-up on all expenses, it's Patterson's thirty thousand, not mine. The Judge's greed just means more money for me, a hard working U.S. attorney. So he told Markowski, "You're definitely right about it being a fifteen, Judge. See you in church."

After a quick bathroom break and a cup of coffee, Al Tacovic confidently returned to his office just as Tom Bilbray was arriving for their three o'clock conference call with Hampton. Bilbray asked if he was too early, but Tacovic told him his timing was perfect, then with the deceitful smile of a corrupt politician, invited him into the office and waved him to one of the chairs in front of his desk. "You're clear on what we're doing here, right?" he asked Bilbray.

"Yes, sir, I believe I am. You'll tell Agent Hampton you're approving his request for the warrants, but he's to delay serving them until Thursday morning between eleven and noon. The timing is because you want coverage on the Thursday night TV newscasts as well as press coverage in the Friday morning papers, so our agencies will get maximum publicity, and the doctors inclined to commit fraud will be put on notice."

Al responded in a way designed to further reel Tom into thinking he was one of the engineers and masterminds of the plan rather than a potential victim and scapegoat by saying, "Yes, Tom, but only you and I know the real reason we want them to wait until Thursday. We also know there won't be any press coverage, because Hampton's raid and planned arrest of Patterson will be non-events.

"Now, it's time for us to get on the call. You listen and let me do all the talking. We're going to make this quick and to the point. The fewer questions I need to answer, the less likely we are to get into any details that might complicate things." And with that, they joined the conference call with a suspicious and conflicted Agent Hampton as the only other participant.

At four that afternoon an elated Bryan Hampton sat in his office, still trying to figure out how he and Kucharski could have been so wrong in their assessment of how Tacovic would respond. Nearly an hour had passed since he hung up from the five minute call, and he still felt mostly positive about the outcome, but remained mildly concerned about waiting until Thursday morning to serve the warrants, a condition Tacovic insisted on.

However, he understood the political advantages of capitalizing on news coverage, so he wrote off his concerns as nothing more than minor annoyances. Minutes before, Hampton had initiated the formal process to request the warrants, then delegated the rest of the work to one of his assistants. So now, he decided, it was time to share the good news with Kucharski.

He placed the call directly to Kucharski's cell phone to avoid any delay in reaching him with the news. Because his message was positive, he wasn't anticipating any covert or negative remarks from either of them, so he decided there should be no problem with a direct call from his office to Kucharski's cell.

After eleven rings, Kucharski asked, "Hampton, is that you again? What's up with calling my cell from your office phone no less?"

"Are you sitting down or standing?" Hampton asked.

"Don't you also want to know what I'm wearing right now?" Kucharski responded sarcastically.

"Okay, if you're going to act like that, I'm just going to hang up and not give you the news."

"I don't need anymore bad news today, so why would that threat change anything for me?" Kucharski asked.

"All right, I'm going to just tell you because you're hopeless. What are you doing next Thursday morning?"

"Well, at nine I'm having my nails done and at ten--"

"Ted, we got the warrants and we serve them this coming Thursday morning between eleven and noon."

After several seconds Kucharski finally responded, "I gotta tell you Bryan, I'm blown away. I never expected you to bring me good news on this case. My antenna was way off on this one, because I was sure Tacovic was gonna mess with us and let this guy off for some reason known only to him and his bank account." Pausing again, only a moment this time, Kucharski asked, "But why Thursday and not tomorrow afternoon or Wednesday?"

"Tacovic wants press and TV coverage and knows the headlines in the Friday morning papers will maximize the publicity from the arrest, and he also knows if we do it by noon it'll be on TV an hour later and will make both the early and late Thursday evening newscasts. So he's requiring us to do it on Thursday in a specific timeframe," Hampton explained.

"I guess that makes sense if you're a politician, but getting Patterson behind bars one day sooner would be my first priority. But then for some strange reason I always look heavy in pictures, so I don't care much about press coverage anyway. Speaking of which, have you seen us on YouTube?"

"What are you talking about?" Hampton asked.

"Oh, sorry to burst your happiness bubble, but you need to check out the video on YouTube of our little altercation in the McDonald's parking lot last week. I'll text you the link, because I know you struggle with technology. Anyway, I need to go, one of my kids is in a play tonight and I'm already late.

I'll call you tomorrow and see what you thought of our performance on the video." Then Kucharski hung up and immediately texted Hampton the link.

After watching the video the second time, Hampton felt waves of apprehension encroaching on their beachhead of surprise, the one element of their case they believed would assure a positive outcome. When he noticed the video had already attracted over a million hits in five days, anxiety completely overwhelmed any sense of confidence he'd felt only minutes before.

Simple math, he thought. Two and a half more days before we raid his office, the current rate is about two hundred thousand more views a day, meaning at least another half million people will see Nina by eleven in the morning on Thursday. What's the probability somebody in Patterson's office hasn't already seen the video and recognized her? And if they haven't seen it yet, what's the chance someone there won't be one of the next five hundred thousand people to view it and recognize Nina, who they think is Alice Rizzo?

Chapter 6

Chicago, IL
October 3rd
7:30 PM

"Finally, you're home! Where've you been?" Dynah Edelmann anxiously asked her husband Gabe. "Did you get the message I left right before five, over two and a half hours ago?"

"Honey, I had a long case, an emergency surgery, and as soon as the patient was out of recovery, I changed and dashed out of the hospital."

Dynah realized Gabe's responsibilities as an anesthesiologist were constantly in conflict with normal everyday living and strict schedules. She knew he was tired and exhausted when he simply turned to her and said, "What's up? You seem to be overreacting. You know when I don't return calls it's because I'm tied up with a patient or in the middle of a case. Is something wrong? The kids look fine."

"I'm sorry, Gabe. I guess it's possible the combination of my hormones going crazy with this pregnancy and the strange conversation I had with a guy named Tom Bilbray from the U.S. Attorney's Office this afternoon, that I'm overreacting, but I really don't know. I want you to listen to the recording I made of the conversation and tell me what you think."

"You recorded the conversation?" Gabe asked.

"I did and let me explain why. To me, it was an odd situation to have a client call and tell me he wanted me to contact a particular person in the U.S.

Attorney's Office at a specific time, then follow the instructions I was given. When I tried to get more information from my client, he simply told me the directions he'd given were all I needed to know for now and to please just do as I was asked.

"Then he wanted to know if I would agree to those terms, so I told him I would make the call and decide, then get back to him. Because I had no idea what to expect, I decided I was going to record it. Since I did it without telling Mr. Bilbray, it would never be admissible as evidence, if we ever had a reason to need it. I don't even know why I just said that," Dynah added as an afterthought.

"Whoa, counselor, please tell me we're not in trouble with the federal government," Gabe asked anxiously.

"No, no, it's not anything about us. But it could become a problem for my legal career at some point if my suspicions are valid. I'm becoming more and more concerned because the longer I weigh the implications of what I'm being asked to do, the more I feel like I'm getting drawn into some shady deal I don't understand. The first red flag is the person who asked me to call this Bilbray guy and to follow his instructions is my least favorite client."

"Not Patterson! Are you telling me that sleaze ball has something to do with this? Now he's graduated from just practicing bad medicine to having problems with the Feds, and he's trying to involve you in it? Now I'd like to hear the call, because I doubt it's any worse than what I'm starting to imagine."

After listening, then re-listening to the recording, they both decided to put some space between the questions raised by the message and the decisions they needed to make by morning to answer them. As working parents, Gabe and Dynah had made an unalterable commitment to play with, read to, or otherwise interact with their girls every night before bedtime. So they agreed to return to the recording later, when the girls were asleep and Gabe had eaten his dinner. They hoped by then they could consider the call in a more calm and less hectic atmosphere.

By nine-twenty the house was quiet and a degree of tranquility had replaced the turmoil of less than two hours ago. They hesitated to revisit the recorded call, but knew they must, and after hearing the message a third time, Gabe asked Dynah to explain the legal issues that concerned her.

"I'd prefer to summarize the problems rather than dissecting the call issue by issue," she told him. I think that approach gets us to solutions faster."

"Have at it. After all, this is your area of expertise, not mine."

"So let me summarize what I'm being asked to do, so I'm sure we're both considering the same issues. Tomorrow morning sometime before noon, they've told me a legal document will be delivered to my office. I'm supposed to sign it, then early the next morning forward it to a specific judge. Simply put, I'm being instructed to sign a legal document I didn't draft and represent to a judge that it's my work.

"I can review what they send me, and if it's well-drafted and presents a sound argument, which I assume it will, then there's no legal problem with representing it as my work. Large firms have paralegals and associates draft documents all the time and the partners take the credit. So, let's assume I receive a solid, well-prepared document to submit to the court, and I feel fine about the integrity of the legal arguments it contains, so I sign it."

Dynah paused, then continued, "The next step in this process, according to Bilbray, is in the afternoon of the same day, Wednesday, the judge I sent my appeal to will return a favorable court order granting the requests contained in the petition I submitted that very morning."

Gabe interrupted his wife at that point and volunteered, "Well, I'm no attorney, but I can tell you what I would conclude from that scenario. Whoever's running this show already knows the judge is going to decide to rule favorably on the petition you send him. That seems like a problem, or is that just the way things work?"

"Yes and no," Dynah answered. "For some things like granting warrants or restraining orders, most attorneys know how certain judges will usually rule, and that's particularly true for senior prosecutors and U.S. attorneys. The questionable aspect in all this is the timing. I submit my petition early on Wednesday and I have the requested court order back the same afternoon? Unless this is a simple case and the documents are brief, that kind of turnaround time is unusually short.

"My guess is the judge and the U.S. attorney have already discussed this and the judge has agreed to grant the requests, and it's possible he could already have the same legal draft they're sending me tomorrow. If both those assumptions are true, then the judge and Tacovic both know I'm a passive and willing player in this process," she explained.

"But that's a two-way street, Dynah. Using the same logic, you understand what's going on between them as well."

"But I'm just one of thousands of attorneys in this city, while they're influential, powerful, and well-positioned politicians. In any dispute with them, I'd be squashed. My assumption is they view me as a puppet and plan to pull my strings for a while, so I can fill a required role in their little production. My participation prevents this from looking like the U.S. attorney was stopping federal investigators from executing a warrant he likely authorized.

"The judge and Tacovic know the end of the play, and I'm only there in a scene or two, and as a consequence I have no idea what the story's all about, and that's precisely how they want it. That perspective is reinforced by the last thing he told me before he asked if I had any questions, but I'll come back to that in a minute.

"So once I have the court documents, which apparently supersede and revoke some warrants the federal agents will try to act on, I'm to show up at Dr. Patterson's Evanston office no later than eleven o'clock on Thursday morning. When they arrive, I'm to present my documents to the agent in charge and thereby prevent the DOJ team from searching Patterson's office and arresting him. None of that should be problematic because Tom Bilbray assured me Hampton, the senior agent, is an attorney who'll respect the court orders I present him with. My final task is to remain on the doctor's premises until I'm positive Hampton and his team are gone and aren't coming back.

"You have any questions up to this point?" Dynah asked. Gabe merely shook his head no and signaled her to continue. "So, as I started to say a minute ago, the last instruction I was given by Bilbray is after I'm sure the agents have departed and aren't coming back, I'm to leave the office and assume my responsibilities in this matter are at an end. He then assured me there would be no further warrants on this matter targeting Patterson."

"Okay, Dynah, so to me that part sounds like a problem, too. How do they know that no other warrants will be issued? Do they know the case is over at this point, and if so, how? It seems like they can predict with too much confidence exactly what's going to happen at every step along the way. How can they possibly know there will be no more warrants?" Gabe asked.

"The answer to those questions is primarily what bothers me about this whole process and any involvement I would have in it. I think you've reached the same obvious conclusion that I have. A deal has been made between Tacovic's office and a judge to prevent the scheduled arrest of a physician who's being investigated by the FBI. But I don't know if this action simply delays his inevitable arrest or if it implies a permanent suspension or dismissal of the case against him. And if it's the latter, then the implications of being complicit in any aspect of what's legally a conspiracy would be far more serious."

Gabe interrupted his wife with more questions. "Why do you think the FBI is planning to arrest him? Just how serious is the trouble he's in, Dynah? And what's your guess as to the crimes he's being accused of?"

"Those are important and valid questions. I think I've narrowed it down to only one likely possibility. Because it's a federal investigation, and after having represented Patterson three times, I know something about the type of crime he's likely to commit. So because it's federal, you think drugs, fraud, or taxes. I eliminate trafficking in drugs or illicit use of drugs because in my experience with him there've never been any indications he personally uses drugs or is in any way connected with that element of society.

"I also logically believe we can eliminate taxes, because I doubt there would be this kind of interest in a simple tax case. And besides, I've seen his last two years of tax returns. They were subpoenaed by the plaintiff as evidence in his last malpractice case, and I know for a fact he pays ridiculously high taxes. I also know he had a taxable income last year of more than five million dollars.

"So, knowing all that, I've concluded this must be a health care fraud case. And also, because I've seen some of the claims he's filed in the malpractice cases I've handled for him, I think that's the most reasonable deduction. So, I believe the FBI is investigating and planning to charge him with Medicare fraud."

Dr. Gabe Edelmann had just heard two words, 'Medicare fraud' that even for honest medical practitioners almost instantly caused a cessation of rational thinking. Gabe understood there's nearly unanimous agreement within the medical community that Medicare and Medicaid fees were grossly inadequate. From his own experience he knew Medicaid often paid less than twenty-five percent of his customary fees. This persistent and growing deficiency had created a constant undercurrent of frustration about the two government programs, which for some physicians are responsible for over half their income.

Even more frustrating to Gabe and other doctors was the general public's failure to understand the simple economic reality that when fees paid by government programs don't cover physicians' costs, it makes it impossible for them to operate their practices profitably, and there are no subsidies for medical practices running in the red. Additionally, in recent years, private insurers had more and more often based their payments on a multiple of the Medicare fees.

Dynah had asked Gabe about the multiple concept once before and he'd explained it by citing an example, "If the fee Medicare sets for a certain procedure is fifty dollars, a commercial insurer may set their fee for that service at one hundred and twenty percent of the Medicare fee or sixty dollars.

"Physicians can no longer realistically set their own fees if they treat Medicare patients or belong to provider networks managed by major health insurers. The resulting frustration of shrinking margins, longer hours and lower profitability has inspired a strategy in the industry to increase reimbursement by emphasizing optimized coding and billing strategies."

Gabe returned his thoughts to Patterson's case and asked his wife a question. "Dynah, do you remember when you had me look at several of Patterson's insurance claims involved with one of his malpractice cases? Do you recall I told you coding and reimbursement seminars frequently tout how the inaccurate use of billing codes can result in lost revenues? The reality is, changing a single digit on a code can result in a dramatic increase or decrease in reimbursement, so everyone stresses the importance of accurate coding.

"The problem is, as with many concepts, the meaning of 'accurate coding' can be precisely defined and carefully adhered to, or it can be distorted and abused to serve any rationalized need. Courses are taught, seminars offered, and medical billing services have been created, all with the promise of 'optimizing reimbursement' for health care providers.

"For busy providers focused on caring for their patients, medical coding is a discipline left to their staffs or a vendor who manages their billing. When payments are less than expected providers become frustrated with the system. The result is they become almost subconsciously sympathetic to the plight of any fellow practitioner who appears to be targeted for simply trying to be paid equitably."

Gabe continued, "Honest doctors, and the vast majority of them are, often don't realize some of their cohorts are patently dishonest and should be censured rather than supported. Alarmingly, there's a growing segment of otherwise honest providers who have been persuaded by professed 'coding experts,' to employ questionable billing strategies, which they represent as legitimate and permissible practices.

"These programs are successful because as health care providers, we believe there should be a way to get paid properly, if we just understood how to code and submit our claims correctly. Sadly, many, if not most, of the strategies taught in many seminars are at best are in gray zones and at worst are blatantly fraudulent."

Dynah knew Gabe had no day-to-day involvement in the selection of the codes used to bill for his services, but he was keenly aware of the low fees he received in comparison to the complexity and risk of the care he provided every day. Consequently, in spite of what he had just explained, his natural inclination was to rally in defense of any member of his profession, whenever there was any hint an insurer or government payor was making accusations against a fellow health care provider related to payments for their services. She had expected the lecture he'd just given and she knew it wasn't the last time she'd hear it.

As a result of his biased thinking, Gabe began shaking his head and in a cynical tone said to his wife, "You know, Dynah, I'm now going to make a hundred and eighty degree adjustment in my thinking here. If this entire conversation and case is about a Medicare fraud investigation, then I strongly urge you to do everything you possibly can to help Dr. Patterson. To me, it's unthinkable the Feds are planning to conduct a mid-day raid of a doctor's office due to billing issues with Medicare, particularly while he's in the middle of treating patients and with the waiting room full of people. That seems intentionally damaging to his reputation and a harsh and inappropriate way to handle the situation.

"Besides, I hear surgeons at the hospital constantly talking about how little Medicare and Medicaid pay them for complicated and difficult cases. And we both know how meager their fees are for my services, and I'm literally responsible for my patients' lives all day, every day. This kind of ongoing harassment of the medical profession is inexcusable! Why wouldn't you want to stop them from barging into his office? If the judge and the U.S. attorney are working to slow down the process and save Dr. Patterson embarrassment, particularly when we don't even know if he's guilty, then what's wrong with that?"

"You make a reasonable argument, but don't you think there's anything suspicious about his income? You don't make anything even close to that," Dynah responded.

"That's true, but what's also true is normally, you wouldn't know anything about his income and wouldn't be factoring it into your decision process. Don't forget this guy's been in practice for over twenty years, and cosmetic dermatology services in recent times are in amazingly high demand. All the new and pricey filler materials and Botox procedures are making cosmetic services possible for a whole new segment of the population who would previously never have been candidates for traditional plastic surgery," Gabe argued convincingly.

"All right, so let's assume his situation doesn't justify a raid on his office, and the intent of the process they want me involved in is purely to slow down the FBI and encourage a more timely arrest. Then why are they asking me to petition the court?" she asked.

"They haven't asked you to do anything, Dynah. Patterson asked you to get involved on his behalf because you're his attorney. They're just instructing you how to accomplish what must be done quickly because of the scheduled FBI arrest. You're the closest thing he has to a defense attorney, and there's no doubt in my mind Patterson has connections in the U.S. Attorney's Office, and they're simply helping him avoid an embarrassing situation.

"I think, as his attorney, the person who's previously defended him, you've been selected by default as a convenient component of a legal process someone else has designed and is executing. I repeat, if I were you, I'd help Dr. Patterson as a matter of principle in resisting what is over-aggressive law enforcement."

"I understand that must be your position as a physician defending your profession. I'm an attorney, and I must consider all aspects of the law. I guess I'll sleep on it and decide in the morning what I want to do. I'll have more information about the specific allegations against Patterson once I get the documents they'll deliver to me tomorrow by noon."

"We need to get our minds off this for a while, get comfortable and decompress. Let's watch an hour of *King of Queens* reruns and call it a night," Gabe suggested.

By five the following afternoon, Dynah had reviewed, transferred to her letterhead, and signed the impeccably drafted petition. After writing 'His Honor Judge Andrzej Markowski' in the center of the envelope, she carefully printed the Judge's office address below it. Dynah then provided her assistant with explicit instructions regarding the urgency of completing the delivery early the following morning, making sure she knew the exact location where the documents were to be taken. Dynah then sealed the large envelope and made sure the return address clearly identified her as the sender.

Her last task was to stamp the envelope 'Confidential' in several places. As she did so, another pang of doubt caused her to continue grasping the package a little too long while her assistant tried to pull it away from her. "Sorry," Dynah offered weakly, "just trying to make sure I didn't miss anything."

Chapter 7

Evanston, IL
October 6th
10:30 AM

The fourth consecutive sunny and already warm fall day had forced them to lower their windows to lessen the pungent odor of interior disinfectant, common only to cars in government fleets and New York taxis. The influx of fresh air forced a greasy, cinnamon scent mixed with the aroma of coffee to rise from the bag that once held Kucharski's breakfast, causing Hampton to subconsciously consider a trip to a Starbucks down the street. He decided to resist the urge because in less than twenty minutes they would take action. Eight days ago the blue Ford had been parked not far from its current location, but this day was different, because today was the day they planned to make an arrest and finally reap the rewards of months of relentless and sometimes boring investigative work.

A little after eight o'clock that morning Hampton had met Kucharski at Union Station in downtown Chicago. Kucharski had driven from Appleton to Milwaukee on Wednesday for an all-day meeting, and to avoid extra hours on the road he decided to stay overnight there and take the Hiawatha Line commuter train to Chicago early that Thursday morning. Departing on the six-fifteen train, he was scheduled to arrive in Chicago at seven fifty-seven, allowing plenty of time to connect with Hampton and the other two agents slated to serve the warrants at Patterson's office. His train was ten minutes late, but heavy traffic delayed Bryan as well, so when Kucharski finally exited the station, Hampton had arrived only minutes before; nonetheless, he began complaining of a much longer wait the second his friend got into the now too familiar Crown Vic.

"You're wasting government funds when you keep me waiting." Hampton chided Kucharski, who already looked tired and disheveled, presumably from too little sleep and the two-hour train ride.

"Yeah, at your salary I'm sure my tardiness has caused a serious jump in the sixteen trillion dollar U.S. debt. Speaking of which, when do we eat?" Kucharski asked.

Hampton had anticipated Kucharski's gnawing appetite, and he smilingly handed him a hefty McDonald's bag, saying, "Here you go, big guy. Two sausage, egg, and cheese McGriddles, a large coffee, an extra-large orange juice, and some cinnamon melts for dessert. We might have a long wait before your next meal, and I don't want you getting tired and useless and claiming you're hypoglycemic."

Kucharski responded sarcastically, saying, "Thank you Bryan, you're a gentleman if not a gourmet, and I want you to know I won't let you down. I plan on eating and drinking everything in this bag except the paper products. All so I'll be strong and can protect you from the evil Dr. Patterson," and without another word, Kucharski opened the bag and began his assault on breakfast.

They had been waiting for over thirty minutes, the result of Hampton's decision to observe foot traffic going into and coming out of Dr. Patterson's office for at least an hour before their scheduled mini-raid. The other two agents had arrived just minutes before in a black Mercury, model and year unknown, and had parked at the end of the block giving them a clear view of the rear door to the office, just in case someone inside attempted an unexpected exit into the alley. Two cars were necessary as the plan was for Patterson to be transported to the lockup by the other two agents, while Hampton and Kucharski, after finishing their work at the dermatologist's office, went to Patterson's home to assist the agents in their search efforts there.

"Starting to look like it's a slow day for the doctor," Kucharski observed.

"I was thinking the same thing myself," Hampton agreed glancing at his watch. "But we know he's in there because the lights are on, and his car is in the lot along with another one belonging to an employee. But where are the patients?"

"Seems strange to me. It's ten-forty, and no one has gone in or come out all the time we've been here," Kucharski commented, with obvious growing concern.

Four minutes later, their optimism was rekindled when a black Mercedes 450GL pulled into the lot and parked near the employee's car. Before long, a thirties-something woman opened the driver's door and, with slight awkwardness, emerged from the SUV. As she turned to open the rear door, withdrawing what appeared to be a large purse, she revealed both a striking face and a sexy mid-pregnancy profile. Adjusting her dress, she began walking toward the office door, then paused, reached into her purse, extended an arm back toward the Mercedes, and locked the doors with her remote. Once inside, the agents lost sight of her.

"Finally, a patient! I feel a little better now," offered Kucharski. "But she must be going in for stretch mark prevention because she's even better looking than Nina, so she doesn't really need him."

"More relevant to our concerns about his lack of business today, her car fits the profile of many patients who come here for the cosmetic procedures he advertises. As we both know it makes no difference if she needs anything or not, she'll be told she does. So I'm hoping her arrival just signals a late start to one of his normal busy days," Bryan responded.

Inside the office, out of their sight and earshot, Dynah Edelmann was sheepishly greeted by Sandy Barnes, Dr. Patterson's trusted insurance specialist, and the only employee he had allowed to work that Thursday. Five other staff members had been given the day off having been told the doctor was attending a seminar. During two of Dr. Patterson's malpractice cases Sandy had been assigned to act as Dynah's resource for providing copies of claims and charts and other materials used to defend the cases.

After telling Dr. Patterson Dynah was in the reception room, Sandy returned to her post at the front desk and anxiously asked the attorney, "What exactly is going to happen when they come in, and what am I supposed to do when they get here? Hugh told me an hour ago on the phone you had explained to him exactly what'll take place from the minute they come through that door, and he assured me nothing will happen to me because you'll take care of everything."

She's calling him Hugh! Now I know why she's the one he picked to be here today, Dynah thought, then recovered and reassuringly responded to Sandy, "I think there are four of them as far as I could tell when I circled the block before pulling into the lot. Probably two of them will come in the front door, and the other two will stay outside making sure Dr. Patterson doesn't make an unexpected dash out the back door. The two who come inside will present their IDs or badges to you. I want you to inspect their credentials, and hopefully one of their last names will be Hampton."

Pointing to one of the waiting room seats, Dynah continued, "I'll sit in that chair, and when they ask to see Dr. Patterson, you're to point to me and say, 'Dr. Patterson is busy now, Agent Hampton, but I'd like to introduce you to his attorney, Dynah Edelmann.' At that point you're done and are not to say another word other than goodbye when they leave. Do you clearly understand what I want you to do?"

After confirming Sandy could deliver her line perfectly, Dynah told her they probably still had a ten or fifteen minute wait, and suggested she try and relax. After a quick trip to the ladies room and a hurried hello to her client, Dynah sat in the chair she had pointed to earlier, a position that gave her a clear vision of the front door as well as a profile view of anyone standing at the reception window speaking with Sandy.

Dynah wasn't nearly as confident as she tried to appear. She had never confronted a federal agent attempting to serve a warrant and only hoped everything took place as she anticipated, because she wasn't sure what she'd do if Agent Hampton chose to ignore her and the clear directives of the court order in her possession. She hoped the agents would be so astonished at her presence and so completely stunned and discouraged by the court documents she presented them they would peacefully retreat, realizing any further actions on their part would be unlawful. In her heart she knew such a scenario might be a major miscalculation on her part, but hoping for the best never hurt.

At exactly eleven, Hampton called agent Sanchez, who headed up the team of four agents assigned to search Patterson's home, and confirmed they were in position. He reiterated his earlier instructions reminding them to wait until he called back in approximately ten minutes before they knocked on the front door to serve their warrant. After Sanchez acknowledged his instructions, Hampton disconnected and immediately called the two agents observing the rear of the office, explaining, "Bill, in two minutes we'll walk through the front door and ask for Dr. Patterson, so in one minute I want you to move your car as close to the back door as possible, then both of you should get out of the car and make sure you stop anyone trying to leave, but don't enter the office until I call you back and authorize it."

Bill Jones acknowledged the orders. Bryan hung up and told Kucharski, "It's time to dance. Make sure you have your credentials and your game face on. I have my ID, the warrants and a gun, which I'm positive we won't need because I think this guy is going to collapse the minute he sees us."

Thirty seconds later they crossed the street, opened the front door, and for the first time observed the inside of the office they had previously only seen on video. Surprised by the silence as well as the extravagance of the decorating and furnishings in the reception room, they noticed the attractive pregnant woman was its sole occupant. Behind the large open glass panels separating the reception desk from the seating area, they recognized one of Dr. Patterson's employees, Sandy Barnes, who had appeared on both of their video recordings explaining insurance guidelines to their agents posing as patients.

Sandy stood and asked, "Can I help you gentlemen?"

Almost as Dynah scripted, the younger, better looking and more athletic man produced an identification case, then flipped it open to clearly identify him as a DOJ Agent, and introduced himself by saying, "I'm Agent Bryan Hampton from the United States Department of Justice, and this is Agent Ted Kucharski. We're here to see Dr. Patterson. Please inform him we need to meet with him immediately, either here or, if he prefers, in his private office."

Recognizing how easy Hampton had made it for her by introducing himself by name, Sandy realized all she had left to do was to recite her single line and her part would be finished. With forced coolness she looked Hampton in the face and gesturing toward Dynah, she gulped briefly, then said, "Dr. Patterson is extremely busy right now, but let me introduce his attorney Ms. Dynah Edelmann." Exhaling a deep, but quiet breath of relief, her part over and her delivery flawless, she backed slowly away from the window and stood motionless, waiting to see if the rest of the morning turned out the way Dynah had predicted.

Dynah Edelmann stepped forward, offered her hand, and began, "Agent Hampton, I'm pleased to meet you. As Sandy has already explained, I'm Dynah Edelmann, and I represent Dr. Patterson. Here's my card. May I please see your credentials?"

After looking at his DOJ ID, she turned to Kucharski and said, "I'm not sure I caught your name Agent. May I see your credentials as well, just for the record?" She then offered him her card and extended her right hand, actions which permitted her to appear both assertive and courteous.

Kucharski looked inquisitively at Hampton, shaking his head as he reached for the wallet containing the ID, which identified him as an agent of Sidereal HealthCare's Special Investigative Unit. While Kucharski showed his ID to Dynah, Hampton explained his role in the investigation saying, "Agent Kucharski is part of a joint task force investigating your client. We realized several weeks ago his company was also in the process of developing cases initiated by patient complaints against your client. The federal cases we're investigating involve allegations of false claims submitted to Medicare."

Dynah handed Ted his ID, then asked both agents, "May I inquire why you're requesting to see Dr. Patterson today?"

Hampton then explained, "We have warrants to search both this office and his home and to arrest him on suspicion of medical fraud, specifically filing of false claims to Medicare and Medicaid."

Dynah's mouth was suddenly dry. She found it strange and even surprising her presence in the office to intercept and confront the agents had seemingly not caused them more concern, noting Hampton, at least outwardly, appeared not to suspect she might have any legal cards to play that would trump the warrants he planned to serve. Fighting off growing apprehension, she decided to press forward, so she asked to examine the documents he smugly, at least in her mind, appeared so anxious to present. After accepting the warrants from Hampton, she scanned the documents for several minutes while both agents watched.

Several minutes passed, and Dynah glimpsed Hampton checking his watch. She was aware it was six or seven minutes after eleven and realized Hampton probably needed to update the agents outside on the events occurring inside Patterson's office. He probably expects me to spend another five minutes or so reviewing the warrants, Dynah thought, then noticed Hampton was about to excuse himself, probably to make a quick call to his fellow agents.

Dynah decided to surprise Hampton and passed the warrants back to him before he could say anything. She concluded it was the ideal time to drop the bomb she had received from the court of the Honorable Andrzej Markowski late yesterday. Fighting hard to steady her shaking hands, she reached into her oversized purse and withdrew the written decision from the higher court, an order which prevented any actions Hampton's team planned for the day, both here at Patterson's office as well as his home.

She passed her documents to Hampton, mustered what remained of her dwindling courage, and with steely outward confidence and forced bravado announced, "You'll find the court orders I'm presenting you revoke the warrants in your possession and require you to immediately and permanently cease any further actions against my client until you're able to convince Judge Markowski, who issued them, you have sufficient evidence to move forward with any legal procedures against Dr. Patterson."

Both men had sensed something was wrong as soon as Brenda introduced Dynah Edelmann. Just how wrong wasn't apparent until they heard Dynah pronounce the words "revoke the warrants" and "cease any further actions." Stunned, Hampton took the documents Dynah offered and began his review, not believing for one second his examination would change the consequences of the documents' directives, so well summarized by Patterson's attorney. Notwithstanding his acquiescence to the current reality, he pretended to continue inspecting the court order, hoping to delay long enough for his frustration and anger to subside, allowing him to retreat gracefully and professionally from this legal highjacking.

Hampton knew Kucharski also entertained no doubts about the effect of the court order, summarized by Dynah Edelmann. And he also knew Kucharski had absolutely no interest in a refined or polite exit, or in withholding expressions of contempt for the situation. So while Hampton struggled to restrain his emotions, he knew Kucharski likely had no plans to curb his sentiments. He watched as Kucharski faced Dynah and asked, "How can you possibly feel good about what you're doing here? I don't understand how attorneys like you can sleep at night when you're protecting criminals like Patterson."

Hampton, regardless of his own inner struggles, realized Kucharski was so angry he was inappropriately confronting an officer of the court, and any further comments or actions on his part could cause them both problems. Extending his arm across Kucharski's chest to prevent him from further invading Dynah's personal space, he made eye contact with her and said, "Ms. Edelmann, I'm sure you can realize this decision is a stunning and disheartening setback for our investigation as well as our plans to gather additional evidence against your client.

"We're both frustrated, and I believe you can appreciate the anger we're feeling right now because we obtained our warrants following appropriate procedures. We couldn't be more surprised, not only that you've secured this particular court order, but that we had no knowledge of it. Can you tell me when you petitioned the court on behalf of your client, and how you became aware of our warrants?"

Hampton knew she wouldn't answer his second question, but hoped he might gain some insight into how she found out about their warrants and when they were going to serve them by knowing the day and time she petitioned the court. He knew Dynah as a fellow attorney would understand how disappointed and frustrated the agents felt seeing their efforts thwarted at this point in their investigation.

Hampton had seen by her expression Dynah was enormously relieved he'd been able to manage his own emotions and restrain his large companion. He understood the ethics of their profession prohibited her from revealing the source of her information, but was hopeful his apology had earned him some consideration from her. Maybe she would at least tell him when she filed her petition.

"I submitted my request to the court early yesterday and received the judge's response late yesterday afternoon. I'm sure you don't really expect me to tell you how I was aware of your warrants, so I hope you'll be content with learning half of what you wanted to know. And now, Agent Hampton, I respectfully request you comply with the order of the court and withdraw from these premises.

"I also want to clearly point out any search of Dr. Patterson's home is also prohibited. So please contact your team there immediately to prevent any invasion or search of his home. And one more thing, please tell the agents outside to stand down as well." With that, she gestured toward the door, indicating it was time for them to leave.

When they were back on the street, Hampton placed the two calls Dynah suggested and he already knew had to be made. In both cases, the agents were surprised and puzzled by his instructions to immediately stand down and return to their respective posts. But it wasn't the first time any of them had been disappointed by the actions of a court.

"Shit, did we ever get sucker punched in there? What the hell is going on in the Department of Justice, Hampton?" were the first words out of Kucharski's mouth as Hampton started the car and began to exit the parking lot. "You requested our warrants on Tuesday, and she petitioned another court to revoke them on Wednesday morning and got papers that afternoon? The only way that's possible is if there's a leak somewhere in the court system or in your own office."

"Accurate logic, Kucharski, but let's carefully think through this together, because there are two other important details not yet included in your equation. The first element is the one day delay Tacovic imposed on our little raid, which you've not mentioned. And why were we supposedly waiting for twenty-four hours?" Hampton asked rhetorically.

"Because Tacovic wanted to get some free publicity from the press coverage of our operation," Kucharski answered. "And where were the reporters and cameras that were supposed to record and create the publicity? Are they just late or were they never going to be here in the first place?"

"Exactly! That bastard Tacovic set this whole thing up and sold us out," Hampton realized. "I should call some of the reporters and newscasters I know to create my own publicity and expose him for the crook he is. I can't believe he would screw with us like that."

"That's what it looks like to us now, Hampton, and it's one possible scenario, but we have no proof. Stop and think about this. Tacovic also needed a judge to agree to issue the orders revoking our warrants, warrants the U.S. attorney himself authorized. Additionally, Dynah Edelmann would also need to be part of their little plot. Is all that possible? I realize this is Chicago, but there could be another explanation. You can't go off halfcocked against Tacovic or you're gonna be looking for work."

"I don't know, but looking at this purely from an objective perspective, without the delay Tacovic imposed on serving the warrants, this never could have happened. So he's got to be the architect of this whole charade, but what's his motive?" Hampton asked.

"How about heading for Union Station, so I can try and catch an early train? And while you're driving I'll share some advice and a suggestion," Kucharski continued. "Ever heard the name Davee Da Silva? I think you may know this guy, but if not I'll be glad to make an introduction."

"I've heard of him, but have never met him. He's an investigator at the Medical Fraud Crime Bureau here in Chicago is about all I know," Hampton answered.

"You're right. For the last three years he's been with the MFCB and just recently was put in charge of their new medical fraud prevention task force. I'll introduce the two of you, by phone at least, so you can start talking to each other tomorrow, if not today. Let me tell you a little more about Da Silva and why you need to know him. He's a former Chicago police investigator, over twenty-five years on the job. He knows everyone who's anyone in Chicago politics, meaning if he wants to, he can probably find out exactly what happened here today and why.

"Trick with getting Da Silva to help you is he first needs to trust you or he won't do anything for you. His contacts are the source of his information, and he never discloses them, and if he thinks you will, he won't tell you anything. I can vouch for you, but it'll take a face-to-face meeting between the two of you before he'll lift a finger or tell you anything. But when and if he decides he wants to get answers for you, you'll have them fast."

With light traffic and good driving, Hampton was able arrive at Union Station in time for Kucharski to catch the one o'clock train to Milwaukee. They had travelled from Evanston to downtown Chicago by way of Sheridan Road, Lake Shore Drive, Michigan Avenue, and finally a turn on Adams to get to the station. The stunningly warm and sunny fall day, coupled with intermittent views of Lake Michigan throughout one of the most beautiful and scenic urban routes anywhere in America, had eased the anger and hostility they felt after leaving Patterson's office.

When Kucharski finally exited the blue Ford to catch his train, Hampton realized they had spent more time during the drive discussing the Bears, the Packers, vacations they would never take, and who was better looking, Dynah or Nina, than they had recounting the disappointing events of the day or how much they disliked Al Tacovic and Chicago politics.

Standing on the sidewalk, Kucharski leaned in through the car's open window and promised Hampton, "I'll get hold of Da Silva sometime today or tonight when I can catch him. After I talk to him, I'll call and let you know what he said. You should plan on meeting him tomorrow. I'll set a time and place good for him, and you'll need to get yourself there. Okay?"

Hampton nodded his agreement, thanked Kucharski for his advice and help, then drove away. Uncharacteristically depressed more than angry, he steered the blue Ford onto Jackson and headed east with no particular destination in mind, even though it was the middle of a workday.

Chapter 8

**Chicago, IL
October 7th
11:40 AM**

Hampton took a cab from his office to the restaurant on Superior Street just
east of Michigan Avenue where Kucharski had arranged for him to meet Davee
Da Silva at eleven forty-five for lunch. Kucharski explained the restaurant and
time had been specified by Da Silva because he was attending a meeting at a
nearby business that morning.

Gino's East, one of the great Chicago deep dish pizza restaurants, had a
national cult following perpetuated over the years by a never-ending stream of
struggling students who found refuge there during their rigorous graduate
training at Northwestern University's Medical, Dental, Law, and Business
Schools located a block to the east. The uninitiated sometimes claimed the
incessant sidewalk waits just to get in the door, weren't justified by the quality
of the pizza. But no holder of an advanced degree from Northwestern ever
ventured such a blasphemous opinion.

Hampton was five minutes early and wondered if he should wait because
Kucharski had told him to ignore any line outside, go directly to the person
taking names, and ask for Da Silva by name. He decided to stay outside for a
few minutes in case his host had not yet arrived. Minutes later, Hampton felt a
large hand on his shoulder. Turning, he saw a solid, swarthy, early fifties, figure

attached to the paw by a long arm. "Bryan Hampton, if I'm not mistaken?" a deep voice asked.

"Yes, sir, that's correct," Bryan answered in a too reflex and military-like manner, instilled by his FBI training when encountering a superior. "But how did you know?"

"I saw you and Ted duking it out with those punks on YouTube." They shook hands, then Da Silva suggested, "Let's get inside before the place gets really crowded."

After they were seated in a relatively secluded part of the already noisy restaurant, both men ordered soft drinks and Hampton began looking at the menu. "My guess is you've never eaten here before," Da Silva observed, and not waiting for Hampton to confirm his suspicion, continued, "This is the best deep dish pizza in Chicago, and if you've never had it, then I'm going to order for both of us, because I'm buying. Is there anything you don't like on your pizza? I can't do onions anymore, so I skip the Supreme and go with large Meaty Legend and add mushrooms. There's plenty for both of us if we just order a large. Is that okay with you?"

"If that's the best option then I'm all for it, and I don't do onions or garlic anymore myself, so I'm glad you don't want the Supreme."

Hampton noticed the waitress showed up almost immediately, called Da Silva by his first name, and asked if he wanted his usual or if he was going with a large since he had a guest. Da Silva agreed to the large, then asked Marge, who wasn't wearing a nametag, "How's your son Jim doing in football this year Marge? He's a senior now, right?"

She responded with a huge smile, "Thanks for asking, Davee. He's having a red letter season on defense. His old man and I are hoping for a scholarship offer from at least one of the universities in Illinois or Michigan."

As soon as Marge left the table, Hampton thanked Da Silva for seeing him so quickly and explained he hadn't expected to get to meet with the MFCB agent until Monday at the earliest.

Da Silva then interrupted Hampton, "I know you and I are both busy people, and we have limited time today. Kucharski filled me in on the case you two are working on and told me all about the hit your investigation took yesterday. To save time, I want you to know without asking anyone anything, from what Kucharski told me about Tacovic and Judge Markowski's involvement, there's about a ninety-nine point nine percent probability Chicago politics are in play.

"As a rule of thumb, in this town the unexpected only happens when cash changes hands, and in a deal like yours, probably several hands got greased. So the important questions are, what do you want from me and why? And what do you intend to do with the information I give you, if I get and give you the facts?

"I know Kucharski told you I was an investigator in the Chicago PD for many years, and over time I've been able to earn the trust of the people I worked with as well as others who trust the people who trust me. Because I'm honest and keep my word, I've gained what some people might call inside connections, but I more accurately describe them as long-time friends and associates. These people care about justice and are willing to give me information as long as it doesn't come back and expose them as the source. So, DOJ Agent Hampton, talk to me before the pizza comes and I get distracted."

Bryan realized this was the litmus test moment Kucharski had warned him about. In the next few minutes he would either earn Da Silva's trust or all he would get out of the man was a slice or two of the Meaty Legend. So he carefully considered his answers to each of the questions Da Silva had asked, then began, "Since a year after I graduated from law school when I started with the FBI, I've spent over half of those twenty-eight years investigating crimes involving drug diversion cases, the sale of illicit drugs, and more recently medical fraud in most of its varieties, meaning medical provider fraud, organized medical crime rings, and just plain vanilla criminals using stolen patient ID's and provider ID's to bill insurers and Medicare.

"I asked to be transferred from my previous posting in Florida because I was frustrated by the pervasiveness of medical fraud in Dade County, as well as the failure of the prosecutors and courts to pursue legal actions and appropriately penalize the criminals we investigated. I thought that another state, another set of courts and prosecutors, and maybe a different gang of criminals might change what was becoming for me in Florida a hopeless and bleak situation.

"I was tired of busting my butt day in and day out to build cases against obvious criminals, and not being able to get a prosecutor to take the case because it was less than a million dollar theft from Medicare or a commercial insurer; or the case was less than a slam dunk; or the doctor was crucial to the insurer's ability to offer services in a particular section of the state, meaning we couldn't touch that physician; or the clinic belonged to someone with connections to a politician, in which case they'd give us no reason at all and the case would just disappear.

"No insult intended to you as a long-time Chicago police officer, but Chicago was definitely not on my top five list of choices for a new beginning. But I also must admit until yesterday I had been optimistic, committed, and enthused about working with the people in our Justice Department office here, because they're all hardworking and dedicated."

Continuing after pausing a second or two in case Da Silva had questions, Hampton went on, "I'm sure Kucharski told you how well our case against this dermatologist Dr. Patterson was going. We'd met with Tacovic a week ago today to request warrants and he'd agreed this past Monday to authorize them. We secured the warrants on Tuesday, but agreed with Tacovic's condition not to serve them until yesterday morning at eleven, and that's when everything fell apart."

Da Silva interrupted, "So I already know the details about what happened next at the doctor's office. I need you to take me back to the phone conversation you had with Tacovic on Monday when he wouldn't allow Ted to listen in. Tell me as near as you can remember exactly what was said, how long the call lasted, and who else was on the phone."

"First, the only ones who said anything were Tacovic and me, but I think his paralegal Tom Bilbray was with Tacovic and heard everything."

"What makes you think Bilbray was with Tacovic?"

"I heard some background noise, and it was Bilbray who left the instructions for the call on my voicemail. Also, we've worked with him for several months on the case, so I'm making a logical assumption."

Da Silva then asked him, "Did you think it was peculiar Tacovic required you to wait nearly thirty-six hours after obtaining the warrant to serve it?"

"Well, in retrospect it should have seemed highly suspicious in light of all that's happened, but at the time his explanation was the timing would allow the press to cover the event, and it seemed reasonable."

Da Silva was quiet for a moment, then asked Hampton, "Anything else you or Kucharski might have left out?"

Hampton searched his memory, then reviewed with Da Silva the crucial highlights of what occurred the morning before, making sure Kucharski had reported all the essential details, then told Da Silva, "I guess there's not much more to tell you than what you've already heard."

"Okay, Bryan, we have the facts up to now, but what are you planning to do next? Have you contacted Tacovic yet?"

"I tried to reach him this morning and was told he was off site at a meeting and not expected to return to the office until Monday. I told his assistant my business couldn't wait until Monday and she suggested I speak with Tom Bilbray. An offer I declined since I knew I was going to talk with you at noon. I did have his assistant schedule an appointment for me with Tacovic on Monday morning at ten-thirty, which was the earliest time she said he had available."

"So what are you planning to do in that meeting, Bryan? Have you worked it out in your mind? Are you going to report what happened and ask for his advice, or are you going in with guns blazing, accusing him of wrong doing?

"I ask because I now believe I understand you're passionate about and committed to your job. But I also realize you suspect Tacovic either temporarily highjacked or maybe permanently killed your case. And if you meet with him in that state of mind without a definite strategy, whatever he says, and I absolutely guarantee he'll deny any responsibility, is going to piss you off, and if you're not careful and tactical, you're likely to get yourself into a serious and possible career-ending confrontation."

Da Silva stopped and looked directly at Hampton for a few seconds then went on. "So I ask again, what will you do with any information I give you? Because if there's any chance in the process of confronting him, using facts I provide you, you somehow lose your cool and accidently or out of anger divulge where you got the information, then we're done here.

"The way the world works in Chicago is what you learn from one experience must be factored into the probable outcome of your next experience, so you don't make the same mistake twice and get bad results over and over."

"Look, Da Silva, I'm at a crossroads in my career here. I love the work when everyone plays fair. I've dedicated my life to this job. My wife divorced me years ago and my two married daughters have pretty much written me out of their lives because I was never home. I was always too busy with my work. So there's no way I can promise you I'm going to stay calm and not start telling the SOB what I think of him, if you confirm he sold us out. And if that means my career at Justice is over, then so be it.

"What I can promise you is I'll never involve you or get so specific with facts you provide me that any source you used would ever be jeopardized. Right now, where I am once again with my career is I can't work in a corrupt system, and if Tacovic is responsible for what happened yesterday and in some way profited from it, then I'll either transfer out or leave the DOJ altogether.

"What I need to know from you, Davee, is exactly how yesterday's events were arranged and executed, and who's responsible for them, because if someone planned the whole thing and was bribed to let Patterson off the hook, and if that person is Tacovic, then I won't spend another minute working in this district."

Both men were silent for a short time and, as they paused to see who would speak next, Marge delivered the deep dish Meaty Legend. Then Da Silva broke the awkward silence, simply saying, "Time to eat, my friend."

Bryan waited for Da Silva to grab the first wedge, then reached for a slice for himself, and immediately dropped it onto his plate, "Seems a little too hot right now!"

"Are you talking about the pizza or your predicament?" Da Silva asked jokingly, but with a serious look on his face, then fell silent while he dabbed at some cheese sticking to his chin.

Not knowing what the man would say or do next, Hampton chewed carefully, marveling at how Da Silva could eat the hot pizza so rapidly. But more important he wondered if he was capable of considering Bryan's problem at the same time he was gobbling down his lunch. After he finished his fourth slice, Hampton's unspoken questions were answered.

"Bryan, I've decided to take a chance on you, thirty percent because Ted vouched for you and sixty percent because I feel like you're a decent guy. You'll note that only totals ninety percent, meaning there's a ten percent chance I'm wrong, but it's a chance I'm willing to take. So let me tell you what I know, then I'll see what else I can find out before Monday morning at ten, so you'll know as much as possible before you meet with Tacovic."

At that point Davee Da Silva described the relationship between the Tacovic family and Judge Markowski. He explained the judge was so close to Tacovic that for years he had falsely claimed Al as his godson, noting there was a long Chicago political history between Ed Tacovic and Markowski going back thirty years. Given that background and his knowledge of past deals involving the two older men, Da Silva told Bryan a deal to get the judge to rescind warrants previously issued was possible and highly probable.

Then he asked Bryan, "Do you know Tacovic's running for Congress next year and he's already raising money? His old man, Big Ed, believes Al is presidential material, and he's started collecting on a long career of political favors to position his son for a senatorial run four years from now. Ed and Al both know a senate seat is the obvious launching pad for anyone planning to be president. Just look what it did for Obama, in all other respects an unqualified amateur."

Da Silva continued laying it out for Hampton. "Dr. Patterson's office is in the same Congressional district where Al plans his congressional run next year. If I were a betting man, my money would be on a scenario wherein Patterson somehow paid off Tacovic and the judge to save his ass. All of which culminated in yesterday's disastrous outcome for your case."

Amazingly, in less than eighteen hours after first talking to Kucharski, Da Silva had been able to reason through most of the conspiracy. His experience and knowledge of the participants allowed him to almost perfectly analyze what had likely taken place, except he couldn't yet account for the crucial timeline or the connection between Patterson and Tacovic. These were critical missing pieces of the puzzle he would need to discover over the weekend. That information must come from a trusted associate with the innermost inside information possible.

Chapter 9

Chicago, IL
October 10th
10:15 AM

A dark, ominous day greeted Chicago commuters traveling to their jobs in the city Monday morning. The storm was the first of a series scheduled to march through the region during the coming week, a succession of fronts guaranteed to prematurely relieve trees of their brilliant fall colors. Increasingly uneasy about the probable aftermath of his upcoming confrontation with Tacovic, Hampton once again found himself riding the elevator to Tacovic's dismal office.

He had a plan; a strategy to achieve what he decided was the most he could reasonably hope for under the circumstances. But he was uncertain how Tacovic would react once he detailed the accusations and assertions of extortion Da Silva had now confirmed. Would Tacovic abandon any façade of decency and reveal his true character, summoning a different kind of darkness into his office, or would he be constrained by Hampton's revelations and remain neutral? The only unknown was how incensed Tacovic might become and whether or not Hampton would remain in control of his passionate dislike of the man and his conduct, if Tacovic reacted too aggressively.

Less than an hour ago Da Silva had called Bryan's cell and described in great detail the facts he'd discovered and confirmed over the weekend. He began by revealing a previously unknown connection between Tacovic and Patterson uncovered by one of his friends at the police department, who at Da Silva's request had searched phone records for Patterson's office and home. Da Silva explained he'd instructed his source to focus on calls made from those two locations between the previous Friday and last Wednesday.

"My friend discovered a fifty-two minute call made at ten on Friday night from Patterson's home to a cell phone that, with some difficulty, he was able to discover was registered to Janeska Tacovic. This solved the big unknown for me," Da Silva explained to Bryan. He went on to speculate after Bryan met with Tacovic Friday morning, Tacovic had done some snooping around to find out who Patterson was and how much he was worth.

"In all likelihood, he discussed the situation with his father Ed, and between them they came up with a plan to extort money from Patterson in exchange for killing the investigation. There's no doubt in my mind Ed was the mastermind in this scheme, because of the involvement of his daughter, Al's sister," Da Silva explained.

Then he continued, "My source looked for other calls between the two numbers and found only one. It originated from that cell phone and went to Patterson's home number at eight thirty the same night. So, my theory is father and son cooked up the idea to offer Patterson a deal. To protect themselves, they used Janeska's phone, so no record would exist of a call to any of their personal, office, or cell lines. Whether or not Janeska was involved, we don't know, but my guess is she reached out to Patterson's wife to test interest in a deal. If you question the last guess, let me tell you why I believe it's accurate."

"I did wonder how you could make that leap, but I have to tell you how amazed I am at what you've already discovered, especially since all this was done over the weekend," Bryan commented.

Accepting the praise without comment, Da Silva continued, "One of my sources who does background checks for me specializes in family connections. Short story is, when feasible, he gets a marriage date, then checks newspaper archives to see who was in the individual's wedding party or attended their reception, because in this state and city those events often yield some unique insights. Turns out Patterson's marriage was covered extensively in the *Sun Times* Society Section, including a captioned picture of the wedding party. Guess who was the Maid of Honor?"

"You're not going to tell me it was Tacovic's sister Janeska."

"Yes I am. The article clearly lists the Maid of Honor as Janeska Tacovic. So we have a clear connection between the two families, making a sleazy deal like this easy to arrange. So I'm confident the agreement was made Friday night on the ten o'clock phone call. Another of my sources discovered Patterson sent a two hundred thousand dollar wire transfer to an offshore bank account the following Monday, so that must have been the agreed upon payoff."

Da Silva next explained, "Tacovic was forced to support the warrants you requested to avoid any suspicion or appearance of incompetence for not backing such a solid case. So a court order voiding those warrants was required. That order needed to be the response to a petition from an attorney representing Patterson, and the request as well as the related decision of the court all had to be processed within a tight window of time, impossible to achieve without the one day delay Tacovic imposed on the serving of your warrants."

Da Silva went on to explain a friend in the Judge's office supplied the crucial details confirming the arrangement between Markowski and Tacovic. "Another interesting fact I learned from my source is the petition to stay the warrants submitted to the court on Wednesday morning by Patterson's attorney, Ms. Edelmann, was exactly the same document as a draft Tacovic sent to Markowski marked CONFIDENTIAL the day before.

"Apparently the Judge wanted more time to prepare his response, and Tacovic agreed to send it over. This could imply Edelmann was a bribed participant in the scheme, or possibly she just agreed to submit the document prepared by Tacovic's office on behalf of her client without being aware of any serious impropriety."

Da Silva paused, then added, "I checked her out with my attorney buddies as well as a couple of the judges who presided over some of her cases. She gets good marks all around for competence and honesty, so I'm not sure what we can assume regarding her culpability in this mess.

"We also discovered Tacovic didn't deal directly with Patterson's attorney, according to another friend in Tacovic's office. Instead, he used a paralegal named Tom Bilbray as the intermediary. My source told me Tacovic manipulates and maintains Bilbray as a fall guy in case anything goes haywire with any of his shady agreements."

Da Silva then concluded his report, highlighting crucial details and warning Bryan to be cautious and pragmatic in how he used the information. "Bryan, I gotta tell you, I feel this is a no-win situation for you. We have inside information which can't be proven in court because my sources won't testify; they have too much to lose. What we do know is we have first person confirmation clearly indicating a U.S. attorney, a paralegal in his office, a Federal judge and possibly a Chicago alderman conspired to prevent the arrest of a physician suspected of committing medical fraud totaling over two million dollars.

"We're also certain we could eventually prove the two hundred thousand dollars the physician wired from his account to an offshore bank last Monday went to an account linked to the U.S. attorney. We know the conspiracy likely involved a sister of the U.S. attorney and possibly the physician's attorney, but our best guess is the doctor's attorney wasn't part of any pay off and was likely just an unwitting and not too savvy participant in the overall extortion plot."

Da Silva paused, apparently to gulp down some coffee, then continued, "Those are the facts, and if we wanted to sacrifice three of four of my sources, we could trace the money to Tacovic's account and get Patterson's attorney to tell us how her specific involvement was arranged. We could prosecute at least Tacovic, Bilbray, and possibly Markowski, and there's a fifty-fifty chance we'd get a conviction.

"But a much more likely outcome is the Chicago political machine would somehow stop the whole process before it even got started. Your problem, Bryan, is you can't confront Tacovic with most of the details we uncovered without burning my sources. And while this case is a big deal for you, no one's going to risk their neck or career for an iffy deal like this one. All you can safely do is go in there and give a fly over view of what we know happened, then listen to him deny it.

"What's going to really infuriate you is my source in Tacovic's office told me eventually, probably in a week or two, Tacovic will announce internally he's decided against prosecuting the case because Patterson's attorney is claiming entrapment. Consequently, he'll disclose a negotiated settlement and fine to settle the case. Patterson will be forced to pay back the money plus interest he overcharged Medicare and Medicaid, along with the mandatory fines imposed by the government. Patterson will be put on probation for six months, and afterward there won't be any sanctions on his medical license. I was also told Tacovic won't include any of the Sidereal HealthCare cases as part of his negotiation, a fact I haven't yet shared with my friend Kucharski, but will as soon as we're finished with this call."

Da Silva concluded with a warning and a question, "Please don't burn any of my bridges here and make me regret I trusted you. Before you meet with Tacovic you must have an answer to one all-important question for Bryan Hampton, and that question is 'What am I going to do after he denies everything I confront him with?' The only way you can be successful in this situation, on this particular day, Bryan, is to understand you have only two viable alternatives, and you defined them on Friday. You've either got to transfer to another district or you need to leave the Justice Department altogether.

"If you get too crazy with Tacovic and start threatening to expose him, he wins and a transfer within Justice won't be and option, because he'll destroy you. So now you're down to one alternative, which makes you one more attorney looking for a job in an over-saturated market.

"My sage advice for you is to remember the quotation from Kipling's *A Father's Advice to His Son*, 'If you can keep your head when all about you are losing theirs and blaming it on you, If you can trust yourself when all men doubt you, but make allowance for their doubting too;'

"So remember that challenge and apply it when you're face to face with Tacovic, and you'll prevail, but if you lose your cool, you're screwed. And Bryan, should you decide not to leave the DOJ and opt for a transfer, I have an idea you might be interested in, but I won't tell you anymore about it until you've decided what you're going to do.

"Good luck, Bryan, and don't forget, bad guys eventually lose, but today isn't that day for Tacovic. However, his time will ultimately come, and several Illinois politicians are sitting in jail cells right now as proof of that eventuality."

"Agent Hampton, Mr. Tacovic is ready to see you now," Bryan heard Tom Bilbray say from across the room while he held open the security door leading to the maze of cubicles and offices just beyond.

"Sure, Tom, sorry; I guess I was lost in thought there for a moment and didn't see you open the door."

Bilbray responded with a "No problem," then led Bryan to Tacovic's office.

Tacovic, as expected, was on the phone. Always trying to reinforce the image of the preoccupied and busy executive, Bryan thought. Then he allowed a slight smile to escape when a second theory crossed his mind; he's probably just ordering his morning coffee.

Tacovic made no effort to stand or even extend a hand of greeting across his desk. He simply nodded acknowledgement Hampton had arrived, then gestured for Bryan to sit down while he continued listening to what Bryan perceived as an extremely one-sided conversation. Almost as an afterthought, Tacovic conveyed with a dismissive wave of his right arm the signal to Bilbray he was to leave the room and shut the door.

Bilbray complied so quickly Bryan wondered if they were on the Starship Enterprise and Tacovic had just beamed Bilbray out of the room. The phone remained glued tightly against Tacovic's ear, and after two more minutes of silence, Bryan assumed he must be listening to a weather report or just dead air. Finally, Tacovic uttered three words, "Fine then, goodbye," and hung up.

Bryan decided to immediately go on offense against Tacovic and asked, "Was that Mrs. Tacovic? I had a lot of those conversations with my wife just before she divorced me. Mostly I listened, and near the end of our marriage, I got to the point where 'fine' was my answer to everything, because it meant the next word was going to be 'goodbye,' then the conversation would be over."

"Do you always eavesdrop on other people's conversations, Agent Hampton?"

"Not always, but I usually can't help listening when someone has me sit around watching them hold a phone for five minutes. Maybe it's just the investigative gene I've been blessed with. It makes me naturally snoopy."

"Why are you here today, Agent Hampton? My supposition is you want to discuss your botched raid on Dr. Patterson's office last week, and if so, then get on with it. I want an explanation for a situation that could have turned out badly for this office had you been allowed to raid his home and office and move forward with his arrest, which you had convinced me was justified. In light of the accusations of entrapment against your investigative team raised by Dr. Patterson's attorney, we're fortunate Judge Markowski had the wisdom to vacate the warrants you had me request, thereby preventing a public relations nightmare."

After listening to Tacovic's distorted version of last Thursday's sabotage orchestrated by the arrogant and corrupt politician himself, Bryan took a mental deep breath and marshaled more self-restraint than he believed was possible. Maintaining a calm expression and tone while suppressing internal rage, he resolved to state his case in no uncertain terms as quickly as possible and exit Tacovic's office before he heard the man utter one more lie. He now appreciated the significance of Da Silva's warning and advice to have a planned response to the fabrications Tacovic would so skillfully articulate.

If you can keep your head, Bryan thought. Then, in a calculated move, he jumped from his chair, bent completely over Tacovic's desk, got nose to nose with his adversary abandoning any consideration for Al's personal space, and began his prepared, but ostensibly spontaneous listing of assertions against the US attorney.

"Listen to me, you crooked bastard. I know exactly what you did last week. I know Patterson paid you off because you solicited a bribe to keep him from being charged and exposed. I also know your friend Markowitz, your father, and even your sister are involved in your extortion and flagrant abuse of your office and the judicial system. I also know your flunky little paralegal Bilbray handles all your dirty work.

"You're so corrupt you don't even look surprised I know all about your scam, because you simply don't give a shit about right or wrong, do you? I can't touch you now; you have all the connections and I have nothing but truth on my side, and in this city, truth counts for zilch. I won't work another day here with you and your cronies, so here's what you're going to do for me. I'm going to request a transfer to somewhere as far from you as I can get, and you're going to do everything you can to see I get assigned where I tell you and my superiors I want to go."

Hampton could see Tacovic was already beginning to regain his composure, realizing in spite of everything Hampton already knew, he was powerless to take any action against him. Tacovic lost the neutral expression he'd maintained during Hampton's verbal barrage and started to smile.

"You better wipe that smile off your face right now because, if you don't, my evil side will take over, and I'll forego any future career with the Justice Department and start beating the shit out of you. My last warning to you is if you don't facilitate my transfer and keep your mouth shut about our little conversation here this morning, I'll come after you, legally, physically, and any other way I can possibly think of. And if you force my hand, you'll never make it to Congress or any other elected position, because I'll expose you, your corrupt old man, and your godfather the judge, and you'll all spend your days in Marion with the rest of your political friends."

With that, Bryan straightened at the waist, still looking directly into Al's eyes, and promised, "Expect my call in a few days to let you know where I want to be transferred." Then he turned toward the door and walked out of Tacovic's office.

Stunned, Al remained where he was, still behind his desk, but without the imposing figure of Bryan Hampton two inches from his face, threatening to ruin his political future. How can he know about Bilbray's role and my sister's involvement? He wondered. Unable to answer any of the troubling questions running through his mind after forty-five minutes of careful and secluded deliberation, he decided the best course of action would be to do as Hampton demanded.

So unless Hampton violated his end of the pact, Tacovic would tell no one what had taken place, especially not his father or the judge, because both of them would likely overreact and things might get complicated. No, he thought,

I'll keep this to myself, but I'll tell Patterson we've encountered an unexpected complication, and I'll need another hundred thousand to fix the problem. As Big Ed always says, every problem is looking for a solution, and politicians get paid for solving problems.

Hampton, out of the federal building and back on the street, decided his session with Tacovic had accomplished his objectives. He suspected he had sufficiently frightened and alarmed Tacovic so he'd support Bryan's transfer out of Chicago. He also believed he'd created serious concerns for Tacovic about how he'd discovered such intimate details of the extortion scheme. Hopefully those concerns would cause Tacovic to be less bold in future abuses of his position.

Still, Bryan had no real illusions Tacovic and his cronies would discontinue their shakedowns, because there was an election next fall and his coffers required a constant flow of funds. And even when there isn't an impending election in Chicago, it's never too early to prepare for the next one.

As he walked across the plaza, his eyes were drawn to a scene farther up the block where the sun had broken through the cloud cover and rays of brilliant light bathed a narrow section of the street and sidewalk, illuminating for a moment the cars and pedestrians passing through it. Bryan interpreted this scene as a metaphorical reminder of his experience over the last half hour. He was emerging from the moral darkness surrounding Tacovic and was moving toward a brighter future.

His reasoning was further confirmed by the warmth he felt as he passed through the small sunny area of the sidewalk on his way to an early and tranquil, but regrettably solitary, lunch.

Chapter 10

Chicago, IL
October 18th
12:30 PM

A driving overnight rain had dwindled into a gentle but still dousing shower as the midday sun struggled to defeat the cloud cover. Waiting for his guests to arrive, Hampton stood sheltered under the brown steel awning that stretched from the revolving door across the sidewalk and ended at the curb of One Hundred East Chestnut. The restaurant was just west of Michigan Avenue, adjacent to the Tremont Hotel in the heart of the Gold Coast.

Almost everyone who dined at Mike Ditka's became an evangelist for a variety of reasons; the food was exceptional; the atmosphere was varied, ranging from a main floor tavern feel to an upstairs dining area with private rooms; the walls were tastefully adorned with sports memorabilia and art; and on many days customers might even catch a glimpse of celebrities who regularly patronized the eatery. Frequent visitors and fortunate first timers often even got to meet The Coach himself. Ditka regularly roamed among the tables, unlit cigar in hand, greeting patrons.

The private upstairs dining rooms at Ditka's were secluded and, depending on the group and the event, could even be tranquil. It was the ideal venue required for the discussions Hampton and his three associates, Kucharski, Da Silva, Dr. Josif Stolic, a friend of Da Silva's, would undertake that day. Hampton had purposefully chosen Ditka's for what he expected to be a memorable and maybe even celebratory meal, one he anticipated would further confirm the direction he had started to believe his life and career should follow for the next several years.

Three days after Hampton's confrontation with Tacovic, he called Da Silva and asked him to describe the idea he'd mentioned a few days earlier. Da Silva responded with a question, "How did your meeting go the other day?" After Hampton had related in some detail the tone and substance of his discussion with Tacovic, Da Silva inquired further, "Tell me how you're feeling right now, and what you think you should do."

Hampton explained he thought he would stay with the Justice Department unless Tacovic unexpectedly tried to undermine him with his superiors or refuse to support his reassignment. "In that event I'll go after Tacovic and do everything in my power to expose him and the rest of his corrupt cronies and relatives."

Da Silva paused, then suggested, "Bryan, why don't you call me back in two days and let's talk again. Until you're beyond the anger and your appetite for revenge, where you seem to be stuck right now, I don't think you can appreciate or accurately weigh the opportunity I want to discuss with you. Let's talk in a couple of days," he declared, then hung up.

For the next forty-eight hours Hampton grappled not only with the Tacovic issue, but also with the growing frustration he was feeling about how Da Silva was handling him. He felt like he was somehow being manipulated. After a restless Friday night, he'd gotten out of bed, thrown on his sweats and running shoes, and jogged six miles to a Starbucks, far from his neighborhood and apartment. He'd hoped for clarity and insight and thought the run and new surroundings would help provide some of both.

When he'd cooled down, he ordered the Bold Pick of the Day, Grande size, grabbed the October 15th morning paper and settled in. Once he finished a quick inspection of the sports section, he spotted the girl at the counter signaling his coffee was ready. After he retrieved the already overfull cup, he added two packs of Splenda, some skim milk, stirred carefully, and replaced the lid, all without spilling any of the hot brew on himself or the counter.

After working his way back to his table, he noticed the headlines on the front page for the first time, "Congressman Horowitz Found Dead in One Car Rollover." The article lacked detail, but the essence of the story was, early that very morning, police had discovered Horowitz dead in his car in what appeared to be a one-car accident near the Harms Woods Forest Preserve. His car had apparently been traveling west at high speed on Golf Road and veered off the north side of the highway, crashing through a bridge barrier and coming to rest upside-down in the densely forested North Branch of the Chicago River, just east of the Glenview Country Club.

The cause of death was unknown, but there was evidence of serious head trauma, according to police at the scene. No one actually saw the accident, but a 911 caller notified police they had seen a car speeding away from what they eventually identified as the rear taillights of an overturned car off the side of Golf Road. The article ended by noting police hadn't ruled out foul play.

Hampton was familiar with the Republican and his politics, and was almost certain Horowitz's death hadn't been an accident. The Congressman had been an outspoken critic of a number of powerful and prominent Illinois politicians and business people since his election as the representative from the 9th District less than one year ago. No sooner had Hampton thought the words *Ninth District* than he recalled Da Silva had told him Al Tacovic planned to run for Congress in the 9th District, and now the Republican incumbent was conveniently out of the way.

At that moment he came to the harsh realization that fighting the Tacovics and their associates at the current time, on their turf was an unwinnable and extremely risky battle. He'd played all his cards, told the man more than he should have, and revealed himself as a serious and unpredictable adversary, even having gone so far as to threaten to expose Tacovic irrespective of what the consequences might be for himself.

By the time he drained the Starbucks cup, Hampton had made a decision. At the beginning of his brisk walk back toward his apartment, he forced himself to articulate out loud what he had decided to call his *Starbucks Decree*. He was convinced hearing the decision in his own voice would solidify his resolve and preclude any rethinking or backtracking in the future.

So, speaking only to himself, he quietly but resolutely pledged, "Right now, I'll forget about Al Tacovic, Hugh Patterson, Judge Markowski, and Tom Bilbray. I'll leave Chicago and live to fight those crooked bastards another day. If they can murder a Congressman, they can get rid of me without a second thought. I'll stay in the Justice Department and continue investigating medical fraud cases if I can find an honest U.S. attorney I can trust and work with. I won't risk getting killed just because Al Tacovic believes I could cause him trouble. But for the rest of my career, I'll covertly never stop looking for opportunities to expose all of them, and eventually I'll do just that."

He had recited his pledge five more times during the trek back to his apartment and by then was convinced his decisions were sound, his strategy focused, his tactics restrained and, for the most part, his reasoning process was rational and unemotional.

The passage of time, a bit of middle-aged introspection, and a realistic understanding of how dangerous Tacovic could really be had inexplicably blended over coffee and a newspaper to provide Hampton with clear decisions and some valuable insight into a path forward. He had realized then the delays Da Silva had imposed before suggesting a solution for him were necessary to give him time to prepare himself intellectually and emotionally to appreciate any opportunity his new friend might suggest.

As soon as he arrived at his apartment, he called Da Silva and told him he was ready to talk about the future and wanted to hear about the opportunity he had in mind. Da Silva had then asked the same questions as before, but this time Hampton was ready and had recited his *Starbucks Decree* for the seventh time that morning, but this time Da Silva had heard it, too.

"Excellent, Bryan, that's the message I've been hoping to hear, but even more important I think you've now made a much needed attitude adjustment so you can appreciate what I want to propose. So let me tell you about what I believe would be the ideal situation for you, the Justice Department, and my organization.

"For the last two years the MFCB has been working closely with Dr. Josif Stolic, who for many years was a practicing orthopedic surgeon, but for the past twelve years has been the CEO of BeatMedFraud.com, a firm he started that works with health insurers to detect and prevent fraud in health care claims. Ted's SIU had used BeatMedFraud.com services for two years before my company started working with Dr. Stolic just a little over a year ago. The MFCB project is an industry-wide commercial insurance initiative to pool all medical claims from all Property and Casualty and Health Care insurance carriers into one massive database.

"BeatMedFraud.com can then apply their sophisticated analytics and systems to that data to identify abnormal and suspect billing patterns linked to certain providers or groups of providers. This is a unique approach using cutting edge technology. It's the first time all the medical bills from these two industries have been gathered into one large data repository. This database will enable BeatMedFraud.com clinicians, analysts, and investigators to examine the overall billing practices of any provider submitting bills for medical care covered by health care insurance, auto insurance, Workers Compensation insurance, and general liability insurance policies."

Da Silva paused to make sure Hampton was following, then went on, "This project is evolving into a unique and vital tool for the health care and P&C industries, and several months ago the MFCB began organizing special teams to investigate potentially fraudulent medical providers identified by Stolic's company. I was chosen to be the national head of those teams, and I've been gradually hiring senior investigators to act as regional supervisors."

Bryan interrupted Da Silva, asking, "So you want me to work at the MFCB? I thought you wanted me to stay with the Justice Department."

"No I don't want you to work at the MFCB. Let me finish. As I was saying, we've been organizing regional teams and, even now, I continue to search for and hire leaders for those teams. About five months ago I received a job inquiry from an FBI Agent named Gayle Baker, who's been working medical fraud cases out of the DC office for the last several years.

"I won't go into details, but let me just say the combination of her mother's illness and a failed personal relationship had prompted her to look for a career change. I eventually hired her and assigned her as the supervisor of the Southwestern Region, based out of Las Vegas. She's a committed and effective by-the-book investigator, and so far, we love the work she's done for us.

"Now here's where it gets interesting, and where you might fit in. Two months ago, the former governor of Nevada, an attorney named Paul Dixon, accepted an appointment to be the new U.S. attorney for the District of Nevada, headquartered in Las Vegas."

"Wait a minute! Paul Dixon, the guy who was a County Commissioner there for years and years and graduated from the University of Utah and Stanford Law? Because if that's the Paul Dixon you're talking about, I knew him when we were both at Utah majoring in Political Science."

"I don't know where he did his undergraduate work, but he did graduate from Stanford Law School, and he was a well-respected Clark County Commissioner for twenty-one years. So you probably do you know Dixon."

"Sounds like the same guy to me. I finally agree with you, Da Silva; this is starting to sound interesting."

Da Silva then went on, "Well, if you do know him, that's another huge plus in this equation. So here's the punch line; Dixon is looking to close out his career in public service by making a difference in an area he's passionate about. He announced in a recent interview the main reason he accepted the appointment was because he intends to focus most of his efforts on prosecuting medical fraud and medical identity theft. His plan is to encourage cooperation between public agencies and private businesses to detect, pursue, prosecute, and punish medical fraudsters.

"Ultimately he believes it's possible to prevent most of the medical fraud now wasting billions of dollars every year. Gayle Baker had an opportunity to meet with him briefly, and she's convinced he's sincere and extremely motivated for some personal and otherwise interesting reasons. His exposure to the fraud problem began when one of his married daughters was an unknowing victim of medical identity theft, which later caused a denial of coverage.

"Apparently, their family went without any medical insurance for several months from the time her husband lost his job until he found work again. When they sought coverage on his new employer's plan, the insurer denied their request and accused them of falsifying their application by omitting vital information in their medical history, specifically for failing to report she'd been treated for cancer. They discovered over one hundred thousand dollars in false claims for tests, office visits, and chemotherapy she never received had been paid for by her husband's previous insurer.

"Dixon's daughter tried to explain to both insurance companies there was some type of error because she'd never been treated for any type of malignancy. When she was unable to straighten things out after weeks of letters, emails, and discussions with both her past insurer and the new company that rejected their applications, she turned to her father for help. So Dixon, being a wise executive, contacted an old friend, Dr. Josif Stolic for advice. Stolic is a physician and also happens to be one of the nation's leading experts in preventing health care fraud."

Pausing for emphasis and any questions, Da Silva then continued when Hampton remained silent. "Dr. Stolic was able to get the defrauded insurer to send electronic copies of the last five years of claims for Dixon's daughter. His staff then used that data to identify the suspect claims and, through a complex process, they were able to trace them to an organized fraud ring. Once informed of the cause and source of the problem, the insurer was more than willing to clear-up Dixon's daughter's records, particularly when BeatMedFraud.com offered them an additional analysis of all their claims.

"The subsequent report from that evaluation by Dr. Stolic's team disclosed the same ring was still actively submitting additional false claims to the insurer using different stolen patient and provider identifications.

"Those experiences alerted Dixon to the magnitude and pervasive nature of medical fraud and he decided he would try and do something to remedy it.

Understanding the difficulties his daughter encountered while trying to correct her medical records on her own, then recognizing the specialized skills and knowledge it required from Dr. Stolic and his team to ultimately find the source of the fraud, he pledged to do more to protect average citizens and to pursue the criminals who perpetrate health care fraud. Any questions before I go on?"

Bryan simply said, "I'm still not clear on where I fit into this whole story, other than I knew Dixon thirty years ago."

"I'm getting to that if you really need it spelled out. What we have brewing here is the Perfect Storm, the A Team, the Dream Team or, whatever other name you want to use to describe the opportunity and people who are gathered in a single place, with a single purpose, at this opportune time," Da Silva said excitedly.

"Using Dixon's pledge and initiative as our core, or you might want to call it our political foundation and safety net; it's possible for us to operate an all-star process; one that has all the components and staff required to detect, investigate, arrest, and prosecute any person or organization engaging in fraud, waste, or abuse against our health care system.

"If you transferred to the Nevada District of the DOJ and were working out of Las Vegas, we would have two seasoned and expert investigators, one from the MFCB and one from the DOJ. We already have the data and software assets of Dr. Stolic's company, and we have a U.S. attorney we know to be honest and committed to this cause, and whose trusted friend knows more about health care fraud than anyone else in the country. Bryan, I think you should ask to be transferred to Las Vegas as soon as possible because that's where you belong and where you'll be able to make a difference."

After Da Silva had finally explained the opportunity in Las Vegas to Hampton, the two men talked for another hour. Most of Hampton's questions were answered during their long conversation, but he felt it was crucial he have an opportunity to personally meet Dr. Stolic and Gayle. He also wanted to renew his acquaintance with Dixon to be certain the man he once knew hadn't been corrupted by his long tenure in politics. So Hampton had agreed to Da Silva's suggestion he meet with Dr. Stolic as soon as possible, and Da Silva had agreed to arrange two meetings, one with Dixon and one with Gayle Baker, before Hampton made a final decision.

Three days later Hampton stood outside the restaurant, semi-protected from the drizzle, and waited for the three people he was meeting to arrive. Moments later an overcrowded silver Hyundai Elantra angled into the open space at the end of the metal awning. Da Silva was driving, Kucharski was crammed into the back, and an imposing, bearded, Slavic giant was hunched over in the other front seat, apparently searching for something on the floor. Hampton realized the man must have been looking for the door handle after Da Silva reached over him and the door popped open, freeing the captive from the passenger's seat.

Kucharski was the first to see Hampton and reached out to shake his hand after avoiding the cross traffic of pedestrians marching east on the sidewalk. Never one to waste words, he omitted any greeting and immediately launched a volley of complaints, "I'm never going to ride in that damn sardine can Da Silva calls a car again."

Soon both Da Silva and the large stranger had also extricated themselves from the car and, after navigating the sidewalk, they approached Kucharski and Hampton, and Da Silva did the honors, "Bryan Hampton, I'd like you to meet Dr. Stolic." After the two men shared a brief greeting, the group moved through the revolving door into the restaurant. Hampton then led the group upstairs to their reserved dining room, which he'd previously examined to confirm its privacy and seclusion.

The usual formalities and niceties a civilian might expect to be customary conduct in any business gathering or meal were ignored most of the time when two or more law enforcement officers assembled, especially for meals. The trio of agents wasted no time getting down to business, notwithstanding the fact that the fourth person in the group was a physician turned fraud expert and was a total stranger to Hampton. As soon as everyone had scanned their menus and placed their drink and food orders, Hampton turned to Dr. Stolic and asked, "Is it okay for me to call you Josif or do you prefer Dr. Stolic?"

"No one I work with calls me Dr. Stolic, Agent Hampton. Since I left my medical practice, I only hear my title used when I'm being introduced as a guest expert on a TV show, or as a speaker at a seminar or conference. The individuals hosting those events like the additional credibility inferred by my medical certificates and title. Call me Josif. Here's my card in case you need to know how to spell either of my names," he answered, handing Hampton his business card.

"Great and all the rest of us just use our first names as well, and you don't need to add my agent title either. So I know both of my friends here have worked with you and your organization, but please tell me about yourself and also about your company so I can catch up with the rest of the group."

Hampton and the others then listened as Dr. Stolic spent the next twenty minutes highlighting his background and the history of his company, which he'd formed with two partners eleven years earlier. "We started with no clients and no software and grew our business to where we now have over three hundred employees. We provide fraud and abuse prevention services to over eighty different organizations paying health care claims. We have contracts with countless health care insurance companies, numerous Medicaid managed care companies, and several property and casualty carriers. And we also do extensive work with many state and federal government agencies."

After touching briefly on the MFCB master payor database initiative which Da Silva had previously explained to Hampton, Dr. Stolic also covered his own professional experience. "I had a large orthopedic surgery practice for over twelve years, but I became fascinated with medical informatics, so I worked part-time as a consultant, but then decided to give up my practice and become a full-time employee for a successful start-up company, which was soon acquired by a large corporation. I wasn't ready to work in a big conglomerate, so I left that company and, with two partners, started the business I now oversee."

He then shared with Hampton the basic business model of his service company, explaining how their systems and clinicians reviewed millions of claims insurers processed for payment every day. "Our automated systems look at millions of claims and find the suspect ones, which are potentially fraudulent or in some way questionable. For complex claims or large cases flagged by our software, our clinicians review all of them, and either validate or reject what the systems have detected as possible problems. Then we specify an action on the claim or the provider to our customers, and they decide how to implement our recommendations from that point on."

Stolic then stressed how his organization coordinated their analytic and investigative services with SIU's like the one where Kucharski worked, as well as with organizations like the MFCB. When Stolic finished, he asked Hampton to reciprocate with similar explanations of his background and current duties. And he also asked him to explain him why he wanted to meet him today and why he wanted to leave Chicago.

Hampton spent only fifteen minutes describing his training and work history with the DOJ. He factually and dispassionately recounted the events of the past few weeks without using Tacovic's name, but may as well have, because he mentioned the man's position and title several times.

Saving for last his answer to Stolic's inquiry concerning why he wanted to meet him personally, he concluded by saying, "I firmly believe no job is worth the eight to ten hours a day you spend doing it unless you can trust, respect, and even enjoy those who work with and for you. You can't ever understand who someone is, what caliber of man or woman they are, until you can judge their character. And you can only truly judge someone's character when you see how they consistently react and behave in times of stress and in moments of choice, when one's ethics and integrity are either sustained or surrendered.

"As an investigator if you're going to be effective, you need to develop the ability to recognize integrity or lack of it in the people you interview during an investigation. In my job, you need to be sure the associates you work with and the supervisors you work for have integrity. So over the years I've tried to nurture the ability to recognize this attribute as a kind of sixth sense.

"I've found few people can hide their true character and personality if you sit and talk with them one-on-one for thirty minutes to an hour. When I'm the one doing the interview, I have some twisted questions I like to use, depending on how the conversation evolves, but I'm usually not wrong unless the person is extremely clever, which means they've become skilled at hiding who they really are."

"Interesting," Stolic commented when Bryan finished. "You and I share a common philosophy, and both of us claim a similar ability, what I call a gift; the gift of discernment. So tell me, Bryan, what have you learned so far about me today?"

"That's like one of my twisted interview questions. Let's see, I've determined you're a no BS guy, you say things straight up without any apparent holding back on facts. I think the givens are you're a bright and hard working person, and it seems like you're fully engaged with your business, your employees, and your customers. You're without a doubt a hands-on type of leader, which I believe is the only effective type of leadership. You're not a braggart, and you say 'we' a lot rather than 'I,' indicating you share credit for success with those you work with rather than having everything be about you.

"These two guys tell me you know more about medical fraud than anyone in the country, and I have a lot of respect for them, so I take them at their word. I sense your self-confidence, yet you remain humble, and I bet you're the same person irrespective of the company you happen to be with. You speak about gifts and discernment and intuition rather than how talented and clever you are, which tells me you're likely a religious or spiritual person as well. I've heard nothing about your family as yet, and if this was a job interview I couldn't ask these questions, but how about a little personal and family information, if you don't mind?"

Stolic smiled and answered with little deliberation. "In answer to your question, let me first share a couple of questions I always ask prospective employees in one form or another using language like the following; tell me about the most important decision you've ever made in your life. And tell me how you would describe yourself, who you are in a nutshell, and what accomplishment you're most proud of up to this point in your life."

After pausing and looking at Hampton for a few seconds, Stolic continued, "For me, the answers to those questions are interrelated and don't require a lot of thought. The most important decision any of us ever makes is choosing a companion, so in my case it means the most important choice I've ever made is asking my wife to marry me. As to my most important accomplishments, I would say being married to my best friend for thirty-five years, along with being the father to five married children, who so far have given us three beautiful grandchildren.

"And as far as describing myself, I'd say I'm a husband, a father, a physician, and an entrepreneur responsible for taking care of my family and for guaranteeing over three hundred employees a healthy and growing environment in which to work, so they, too, can care for their families."

After Stolic finished, Hampton remained silent for several seconds, then looked deliberately and directly at the physician and spoke, "Well, Josif, I have no more questions. You've answered all I planned to ask and some I hadn't thought of. I'm comfortable with your answers and have no reservations about working with you. I thank you for your candor and willingness to meet with us today. Is there anything further you'd like to ask me?"

"I'd like you to answer my two questions, those I just responded to, if you don't object."

"Wow, I guess I should have expected that," Bryan replied. "First I have to tell you I'm divorced with two married daughters, one living in Virginia and the other one in Southern California. My ex-wife is remarried and lives in Gaithersburg, MD. We've been apart for five years. The hardest decision I ever made in my life was to agree to my wife's request for a divorce. Admitting we needed to separate and go our different directions was difficult, but it was the best thing for our family, because I was ruining her life and forcing our daughters to pick sides. So we parted as amicably as possible, and we can still talk civilly to one another, although less and less frequently now since she remarried two years ago.

"If you ask me who I am, I'd say I'm a DOJ Agent, and it's sad I think of my vocation as who I am, especially since I've been seriously considering leaving my job. With respect to accomplishments and what I'm proud of, I would say my two daughters and my two grandkids, and earning my law degree.

"I'm an Army brat. I lived all over the country growing up and I continued that nomadic lifestyle as a result of my career at the Justice Department with all the required transfers, which I like to think were major contributors to our failed marriage. I'm sure that's a far cry from answers you would have liked to hear from me, but it's the truth and it's all I have to tell."

Stolic then responded, "Well, it is what it is, but if you end up coming to Las Vegas to be part of our team, you'll definitely appreciate Da Silva's lead investigator, Gayle Baker. She's about your age, unmarried, bright, great looking, and she's also an attorney and a former FBI agent. That's a lot of things in common for the two of you, so maybe she'll end up being the real reason you need to leave Chicago and move to Las Vegas."

Lunch and conversations continued for another hour until two-thirty, when everyone decided they needed to stretch their legs and go their separate ways, back to offices, homes, and hotels. Before parting ways, Hampton and Da Silva agreed on plans for their upcoming trip to Las Vegas. The trip would hopefully afford Bryan and Dixon the time to begin restoring a thirty-year-old friendship and would also allow him the opportunity to meet Gayle Baker for the first time.

Da Silva agreed to set up the meetings and insisted on accompanying Bryan on the trip. They decided a two-night stay in Las Vegas would allow adequate time for their planned appointments as well as for any unanticipated meetings. They targeted their trip for the following week, and Da Silva agreed to call Bryan once the meeting days and times were set, so he could make his travel arrangements.

Hampton lingered behind the others to pay the check and to thank the server for her attentiveness and respect for their privacy over the past two hours. He left a generous thirty-five percent tip, then headed downstairs to leave the restaurant.

Emerging from the revolving door, he glimpsed the valet closing one of the Elantra's doors while Da Silva prepared to ease the car into traffic. Kucharski needed a second try to force the rear door closed, and in the process saw Hampton standing under the metal canopy. He shook his head, pointing at his door, but then smiled and gave Hampton the double thumbs-up signal. *I hope so, my friend,* Hampton thought, then walked east toward Michigan Avenue.

Chapter 11

Las Vegas, NV
October 27th
1:00 PM

The main office of the U.S. Attorney for the District of Nevada was located on Las Vegas Boulevard in the old downtown section of Las Vegas. Several federal buildings were clustered in a four square block area only two blocks from the entrance to the Fremont Street Experience, a section of older casinos and hotels trying to compete with the more celebrated and better frequented Strip resorts.

Even though southern Nevada had been hit harder by the bad economy than almost anywhere else in the country, the seven mile drive from the airport had still taken Hampton and Da Silva over forty-five minutes because of busy streets and congested freeways. After an arduous process of establishing their identity and clearing the metal detectors, they rode the elevator to the fifth floor and finally arrived at Suite 5000. As soon as they walked through the door, they were greeted by a stunning Hispanic woman who looked to be in her mid-thirties.

Approaching the men, she offered her hand and greeted them, "Agent Hampton and Mr. Da Silva, welcome to Las Vegas. I'm Charlie Cruz, Mr. Dixon's assistant. He's running fifteen minutes late, and he's asked me to make sure you're both comfortable and have everything you need while you wait."

Everyone shook hands and the two men introduced themselves, then Charlie asked, "May I offer either of you coffee, a soft drink, or water before I show you to his office?"

Bryan stared at the woman for an uncomfortable few seconds without responding. He had actually never spoken to Dixon's assistant before, although they had traded emails in the process of confirming some of the details about today's meeting. He was surprised to learn Charlie was a woman and was stunned by her beauty. He found himself clearly off balance and struggling to regain some degree of composure and poise. Da Silva looked amused by his friend's awkwardness and answered Charlie, "I'd love a cup of black coffee and Agent Hampton could use a cold shower."

She smiled, having apparently understood what Da Silva had meant by the shower comment. Thankfully she encouraged no further remarks from either of them at that point, almost certainly because she'd noticed Bryan's reddening face. Just before she left them waiting in Dixon's office, she simply said, "One coffee and one ice cold glass of water coming up."

As soon as Charlie closed the door, Da Silva turned to Hampton. "I thought you were supposed to be this smooth and experienced man of the world. What's wrong with you? You're red as a baboon's butt, and you never said anything but hello to the woman. I'm a little worried about introducing you to Gayle after that performance. I've been telling her what a gracious and seasoned guy you are, and now you choke the first time a good looking woman says hello to you."

"I thought Charlie was a man! I was trying to remember if I wrote anything inappropriate in the emails we exchanged. The double whammy of worrying about that and dealing with how good looking she is ended up being too much for my jet-lagged brain to process. I was just about to recover with a clever comment when you interrupted me, and I definitely could've done without the damn shower remark."

"Yeah, I'm sure you had something dazzling to say that would have completely changed her first impression of you had I not interrupted the great rhythm you had going for you."

After a few more exchanges Da Silva let Hampton off the hook, and by the time Charlie returned with their beverages his red face had mostly faded to a normal color. Once she had set down their drinks, Hampton asked her to tell them a little about Dixon; how long she'd worked for him; what she admired about him; how he treated people who work on his team; and anything else she cared to discuss about the man. He ended his questions by telling her, "You probably know we were acquaintances when we were in undergraduate school, and I've only talked to him once since then. What I want to know is if he's changed much, or if he's still the same person I knew and respected then."

After a thoughtful pause Charlie responded, "Agent Hampton, you've asked a lot of questions that could put me in an awkward position if Mr. Dixon wasn't the type of man he is. If that were the case I'd simply decline to answer.

"First of all, I've only worked for him for about four months. He inherited most of the staff, including me, from the former U.S. attorney. When Mr. Dixon was appointed to replace our former boss, on his first day in the office he assembled the entire staff and introduced himself and told us about his family, his values, his style of management, and what he wanted to accomplish during his time in office. But he went beyond the group meeting and took the time to meet with all ninety of us individually.

"Because I'd been the personal assistant to his predecessor, I was particularly concerned about my own future. But he explained he felt my experience was invaluable, and he'd like to see how we both felt about working together after a few weeks. He promised he'd find me another job in the department if I was unhappy. What we've all learned is that he expects us to be accountable for our individual job responsibilities, to be creative in approaching our work, to be self-motivated, and to work hard and care about results."

Hampton interrupted with a question, "How did that go over with people?"

"So far, after four months, fifteen people have voluntarily left their jobs because they preferred an environment with less accountability. But the rest of us enjoy the new energy he's brought to the workplace."

"How's morale after losing fifteen people?" Hampton asked.

"Well. I guess I can answer that question by telling you we've come up with a name for ourselves, because we don't want to be thought of as just another slow-moving government agency; you know, like the DMV or Medicare. We call ourselves 'The DOJ Special Forces Team.' It's a reflection of the sense of pride we have in our work and our belief that we can make a difference."

Charlie paused to look at her watch then continued, "Mr. Dixon should be here in about five minutes, but I want to make sure I answer your other questions. You know he served as a Clark County Commissioner for over twenty years. That means he was re-elected five times to a powerful position in the southern Nevada area. He was asked to run for the Senate and for governor several times, but declined because he didn't want to disrupt the lives of his family.

"Just a couple of years ago, after his children were grown, he agreed to run in a special election for governor after his predecessor was forced to resign. He garnered eighty-eight percent of the votes and, had he wanted to continue as governor and seek re-election, he could've easily won, but he wasn't interested. He wanted to make a difference in a focused role he was passionate about, preventing white collar crime, especially medical fraud and identity theft.

"Unlike most politicians, in every position he's held he's shown he's focused on the mission and not on his own popularity or career. He works hard, he's fair, and he's respected by the staff and by his peers. He's a quiet and humble man, not what you would expect given his accomplishments.

"I don't know what his IQ is, but he's brilliant, and he remembers everything you tell him. Another thing I admire about him is he never takes credit for someone else's ideas or work. He's definitely someone you should want to be associated with if he offers you the chance."

As Charlie concluded her remarks, and at almost exactly the time she had originally assured them he would arrive, Paul Dixon entered his office and greeted Hampton and Da Silva. "Bryan, it's great to see you again, and you must be Davee Da Silva from the MFCB," he said while shaking their hands. "I see Charlie has taken good care of you, and I apologize for being late, but sometimes you just can't end a meeting at the time it's supposed to be over if the business isn't done."

"Can I get you anything to drink before I go back to work?" Charlie asked Dixon.

"No, I'm fine for now, thanks."

As Charlie left the office, Dixon turned back to the men and invited them to bring their drinks and gather at a small conference table where he suggested they could sit and talk more comfortably. Once they were all situated, he began, "I've carved out the remainder of the day for our meetings. I'd like to suggest the following agenda, but I'm willing to amend it based on any suggestions either of you would like to offer. I think we have several objectives today. First and foremost, Bryan and I need to catch up, and I believe we can do that throughout the course of the day, but I also feel we need some one-on-one time together if neither of you object.

"Second, Davee, I'd like to understand your personal objectives here, as well as those of your organization. Third, I'd like to share with both of you my goals and explain what I'd like to accomplish during the years I remain in this position. And then, of course, Bryan, I want you to tell us what you see as your role and the opportunities you envision for us working together. Does that all sound reasonable?"

Both men nodded their agreement, so Dixon continued. "So, let's approach our time together in this way; first, I'd like to give an overview of what I believe to be my limited understanding of the issues surrounding medical fraud, followed by a discussion of some of the goals I believe my office should set in fighting the problem.

"Next, I'd like Davee to explain his organization's current focus in combating medical fraud and specifically what he believes the unique opportunity could be here in Nevada. Then, Bryan, if you could tell us how you view the overall landscape of health care fraud and what your experiences have been over the years battling it. Also, please then explain what you see as the real advantage of joining forces in what would be a combined effort between government and private industry to do something unique.

"Once the three of us get through those discussions, I want Bryan to spend an hour or two with me talking about issues which might be confidential government business, so if we could ask you, Davee, to let us have some privacy at that point, it would be appreciated."

"Mr. Dixon, by the time we get to that point I'd be more than happy to excuse myself and take a nice long walk, so the two of you can take all the time you need. I just want to thank you for allowing us an entire afternoon of your time."

With that, the three men began their discussions. Dixon started by explaining his own family's personal experience with medical identity theft and the resulting false claims filed in his daughter's name. Dixon went on to detail how he'd asked his life-long friend Dr. Stolic, the fraud expert, to help with the case. Although Bryan gleaned far more details from Dixon's account, the bottom line was the same; it took one of the country's leading experts on health care fraud to resolve an issue faced annually by millions of other Americans who don't share Dixon's access to expert professional help.

Dixon continued, "I thoroughly investigated the laws and statutes applicable to health care fraud and what governments and private insurers were doing to combat the problem, and after all my analysis and research and from everything Dr. Stolic taught me, I'm convinced there's much more we could be doing to detect and prevent health care fraud at its inception, and to aggressively prosecute perpetrators of the fraud."

Dixon then went on to state in detail the goals he had set for his office. "I can best summarize my goals by telling you we envision a joint effort between federal and state governments, and private organizations, to share information and relentlessly prosecute anyone proven to be involved in committing or contributing to fraud against entities paying for health care services."

After pausing thoughtfully, he went on, "Our plan is unique in the sense that I don't believe in setting thresholds or buffers for cases to rise to a level where my office will prosecute them. If fraudsters know they'll be left alone as long as they don't steal over fifty or a hundred thousand dollars a year, or if no one is injured or dies as a result of their schemes, a buffer is created inviting otherwise honest providers to test the waters of creative billing. This initial testing of the system, when left unchecked, is what I believe becomes an open invitation to abusive, then outright fraudulent billing schemes.

"A second unique aspect of our plan is we won't limit our focus to fraud against health care insures, but we'll also concentrate our efforts on the growing abuses in billing for medical services in workers compensation and auto accident claims handled by property and casualty carriers."

Dixon's subsequent narrative lasted a little over an hour and, after a few questions and answers were handled, he turned to Da Silva and asked him to take over for the next part of the discussions.

Da Silva spent fifty minutes explaining the revolutionary new All Carrier All Provider Medical Claims Data Base, or the ACMDB as he called it for short, and how it would be used to detect and prevent fraud in medical billing. "This new initiative to combat fraud against health care insurers and property and casualty carriers will enable our investigators to compile every medical claim submitted to every commercial insurer into one massive database.

"By aggregating over two years of previously paid claims in one place, it's possible to examine the billing patterns of every provider submitting any bill for any medical service to any insurer. Using those millions of claims, medical analysts and statistical experts can determine average or normal patterns of billing for treating a particular condition or injury."

To be certain Dixon understood the significance of his last statement, Da Silva gave an example, "If a person fractures his knee cap, years of claims for treating fractured knee caps have already been compiled into a separate data cube. Our analysts and clinical experts are able to ascertain from actual claims submitted, a normal series of services commonly provided to treat fractured knee caps. Services on any new bill can be compared to normal care already established from previous claims."

Da Silva then went on to explain how the information was applied to identify fraud. "So, by using the millions of claims in the database, it's possible to determine a normal course of treatment for every injury or disease, then examine how each provider's individual billing practices compare to those averages or norms. By identifying providers who submit claims significantly deviating from statistically normal treatment patterns, it's possible to focus our evaluations and investigations on those doctors who routinely submit bills appearing to be atypical or unusual. This works both ways, in that we can identify treatments that are either excessive or inadequate."

Continuing, Da Silva emphasized, "This is the first time such a massive multi-insurer database has been created for health care claims and, as a result, the MFCB has organized special medical fraud investigation teams to more efficiently and effectively use this database in fighting rising health care costs as well as the fastest growing cost component of workers compensation and auto insurance."

Next Da Silva explained how the MFCB teams were staffed and organized by regions and specifically mentioned Gayle Baker. "The Southwest Region is headquartered in Las Vegas and headed by Gayle Baker, a former FBI medical fraud investigator, who I'm sure you recall meeting recently, Paul. Gayle was excited and enthused at the prospect of working with your team after just the brief time she spent with you."

Da Silva then made his pitch, "I believe we have an opportunity to do something unique in Nevada by assembling what I think of as the A Team or Dream Team. I talked about this idea with Bryan when I urged him to look into coming to Nevada. The combined efforts of teams led by Dixon, Hampton, and Baker could produce innovations in health care fraud prevention that can make a difference in solving this massive national problem."

Da Silva's obviously complimentary reference to Dixon and Hampton as potential members of the Dream Team felt patronizing to Hampton, but Da Silva was selling an idea, so Hampton let it pass without comment. Dixon had a few questions covering the last hour's discussion, then he suggested they all take a bio-break, refresh their drinks, and reconvene in fifteen minutes.

It was three-fifty when Hampton began the first part of the discussion Dixon had asked him to address, and it would be nearly seven-thirty before they finished their one-on-one conversation, after Da Silva was excused. For the first hour Bryan reviewed his career assignments at the DOJ, with most of the emphasis on the years he spent investigating drug cases and his more recent focus on health care fraud in general. He touched on specific locations where he'd been assigned and mentioned specific cases both successfully and unsuccessfully pursued by the teams he worked with.

Next he reviewed the various reasons why he believed joint efforts with Dixon and the MFCB could be a unique and valuable opportunity. Most of the motives he mentioned had already been discussed by Da Silva, but eventually he touched on something Dixon had stressed as part of his goals, "Paul, your position on not setting minimum dollar loss thresholds for prosecution will be difficult to administer, but I believe it's a crucial part of a successful program.

"Many private insurers and most prosecutors ignore cases where the loss is below some set dollar amount that's usually ridiculously high. Commonly, SIUs won't open and investigate a case if the loss is less than fifty thousand dollars, and getting a prosecutor to take a case where the fraud totals less than a million dollars is often impossible. We spend a lot of time investigating cases where we can definitely prove substantial fraud losses, but when we can't meet the high loss standards set by local prosecutors, nothing happens and months of our work ends up wasted.

"Then there's the political side of the whole matter, and by political I mean both government politics and corporate politics. Health insurers and Medicare have a real challenge in trying to deal with the fraud problem. On one hand they can't allow the fraud to continue unabated, but on the other hand, exposing the magnitude of the fraud can make them look incompetent for allowing it to happen in the first place. And in many cases the fraud schemes have gone on for months if not years before they're discovered."

Hampton was emotionally engaged, and he pressed on, "Another dilemma is private insurers have contracts requiring them to have a provider network with a certain number of physicians and specialists in a particular geographic region to render care to their insured population. If a provider is removed from their network for abusive or fraudulent billing, and the insurer's network falls below their required number of contracted physicians for the area, they can incur stiff financial penalties from state insurance regulators.

"We need to figure out how to stop anyone and everyone who commits the fraud without making Medicare or private insurers look negligent. And the other part of the success equation is we need to deal with smaller loss cases, meaning we'll need to prosecute a much higher volume of cases that aren't nearly as newsworthy. But those are the abusive predecessors of medical claims fraud that will grow when left unchecked. So those are my experiences and my frustrations. Now do either of you have any questions or comments?"

After some discussion and questions, Dixon suggested he and Bryan should segue into an internal discussion to cover current and past confidential DOJ cases, as well as other private matters. Da Silva happily excused himself and suggested Bryan call his cell when he and Dixon finished their discussion.

Dixon stood and, while shaking Da Silva's hand, said, "Thanks for understanding, Davee. Why don't you give Bryan and me about two hours? If you're a gambling man, the Fremont Street casinos are a short walk to the north of our offices; you can't miss them. There are also plenty of good and inexpensive places to eat there. As residents of Clark County, we'd appreciate it if you could do all you can in the next couple of hours to bolster the local economy."

After Da Silva left, Dixon wasted no time. "What's going on Bryan? I'm obviously missing something here. What happened in Chicago that has you planning to leave and move to Vegas? Although I have no problem with it, I'm also trying to figure out why you're hooking up with the MFCB. You seem on edge or agitated, and it also feels like you're holding back. Let's get candid and talk openly and actually show some trust in one another. I've got no agenda here other than what I've already outlined, and I need to know if that's true in your case."

"You know, Paul, we were once friends, but not close friends, and that was over thirty years ago, and time and circumstances change people. But as far as I can tell you're still the honest, straightforward, and brilliant guy you were then, and your career and accomplishments indicate the people of Nevada trust and respect you. I noticed driving in from the airport they even named part of the Beltway after you. Now that's some kind of tribute for a politician who's still alive.

"However, tilting the trust scale in your direction even more than your name on a freeway or your record of public service is the sincere and glowing, yet objective, endorsement Ms. Cruz gave you. She cited many of the positive personal qualities and values I recognized in you back in college, and because she sees them thirty years later, that tells me success and power haven't compromised your integrity.

"It's crucial for me to work with people who are honest, dependable, committed, and fair. I'm sick of the politics that cause people to make wrong decisions for the sake of their careers. I'm not so naïve I believe we can operate in a vacuum, but I need to know when you tell me something and I leave your office that you won't change your mind five seconds later and not tell me why."

Bryan then explained in detail the circumstances surrounding the investigation and carefully constructed case they built against Dr. Patterson. He shared how Tacovic, along with a federal judge, solicited a bribe from the physician and betrayed Bryan's team. He then told how he confronted Tacovic and described the circumstances surrounding the death of Congressman Horowitz, and what he believed really happened.

He told Dixon after the murder of the Congressman, he decided he needed to either leave the Justice Department or transfer out of Chicago or he could become Tacovic's next target. Then he explained his association with Da Silva. "I didn't even know Davee Da Silva until a couple of weeks ago when an SIU investigator I was working with hooked us up. Da Silva sourced some revealing inside information about how our investigation got politically sabotaged, then he gave me some good advice.

"He suggested I look into this opportunity with you, and he introduced me to your friend Dr. Stolic and, between the two of them, they convinced me Las Vegas could offer the situation I've been looking for. I'm here today because I wanted to meet you and Gayle Baker and find out for myself if this is the opportunity they promised it would be."

"Bryan, I can't accept responsibility for your happiness or for your career. But I'll tell you we share a common goal, and I believe we can work together, and you can be sure I'll never betray you or lie to you. There's a lot of work to be done in Nevada, and we need good experienced leaders to accomplish what I envision. I've heard Tacovic was a product of Chicago politics, but I had no idea his character was compromised to the extent he would solicit a bribe or be party to a murder. Do you really believe he's involved in the death of Congressman Horowitz?"

"I have no proof, but there's certainly motive and, inside law enforcement circles, the word is evidence exists linking the murder to a specific suspect. But to prevent alerting the assailant and any associates, they're not releasing any information about what evidence they have or who the suspect might be. But even if they find the killer, most of the time that person doesn't know who hired him or ordered the hit."

The two men talked for another hour and thirty minutes, becoming increasingly more at ease with one another. They shared personal details of their lives and careers since college and were soon reminiscing about professors, friends, and even their individual law school experiences. Bryan was surprised at how comfortable he was discussing a wide range of topics with his friend from many years ago. Interestingly, their wide-ranging conversations revealed they shared similar views on everything from politics to movies. Bryan even commented to Dixon he was surprised at how easy it had been for them to rekindle their friendship.

"It's interesting, isn't it, Bryan? Plato is credited with saying 'Friends have all things in common,' and while we probably can't tell if that's one hundred percent true for the two of us, clearly we share important basic values.

"You know, it's getting late, and if Da Silva did go gambling, he's probably either rich or broke by now. I hope you see this as a great opportunity and will agree to come here, so the two of us can do something unique and meaningful. I believe we can work together and would be a strong team. Give me the word and I'll do everything I can to facilitate your transfer to the Nevada District, and the sooner, the better, from my point of view."

Dixon then looked at Hampton seriously and continued, "There is one relevant matter I want to share with you before you leave, so you can factor it into your decision. But you can't discuss this with Da Silva or Gayle or anyone else at the MFCB at this time. The information I'm sharing must be held in the strictest confidence until we decide if we want to include them or not.

"What I'm going to describe relates to the first case you'd be assigned to investigate. This case is one where we could potentially work closely with the MFCB team. We believe a local attorney, Bennett Watson, heads up a crime ring, that among other offenses, stages auto accidents, then defrauds auto insurers with injury claims involving hundreds of thousands in false medical expenses, as well as millions in settlements for bogus long-term injuries.

"The schemes cover everything from phony towing and storage fees for the damaged cars to personal injury settlements for fake physical impairments. We've decided to begin our investigation where we believe we have the best opportunity to uncover the scheme. We plan to focus our initial investigation efforts on the Accident and Injury Health Restoration Clinics, which are all run by a chiropractor named Ari Mirzoyan.

"In every auto accident case where Watson or one of his associates is the attorney, all medical care is rendered in one of Mirzoyan's clinics. Every one of these cases has exorbitant medical expenses that maximize whatever insurance benefits are available, and every accident victim ends up with a disability that yields a huge financial settlement and legal fees.

"This could be a case where the MFCB data and their trained medical fraud investigators could complement our team and efforts, and prove the value of their database and the advantages of joint public and private shared investigations. It would also be a great case for you to begin making inroads into the quagmire of healthcare fraud in Nevada."

"Paul, I appreciate your time and the opportunity to get to know you again. This has been an encouraging and enlightening afternoon for me, and that case excites me just thinking about the impact it could make and the signal it would send about your goals and your commitment. I'd love to be part of it. What I can promise you is unless something totally unexpected happens when I meet with Gayle Baker tomorrow, I'm ready to pack my bags and be here by next week."

With that, the two shook hands and Hampton agreed he would call Dixon tomorrow after his meetings with Gayle Baker and Da Silva to plan their next steps. After surrendering his security badge, Hampton called Da Silva to let him know his meeting was over, and Da Silva told him he'd pick him up in front of the DOJ building's entrance in a few minutes. Later, as they drove away, Da Silva asked, "So how did it go?"

"It couldn't have been better actually. It was amazing how we were eventually able to pick up where we left off thirty years ago."

"Did you get Charlie's cell phone number before you left?"

"I never even saw her again. She was gone home by the time I left, and I wouldn't have asked her for it anyway."

"Well then, you should thank me for having the balls to get it for you." Da Silva handed Hampton a small piece of paper. "Here you go, and she said she'd be happy to help you with any relocation needs, should you decide to move here. By the way, have you made that decision yet?"

"I'm close, but I want to meet Gayle first so I'm sure she's someone I can work with. Is this really Charlie's cell number?"

"What do you think? Oh, by the way, we're meeting Gayle for breakfast tomorrow morning at nine at the Verandah Restaurant at the Four Seasons. She has a friend who's some kind of pit boss or something, and he's going to comp our meal and make sure we have a nice quiet place to talk while we eat. That way we'll be close to the airport and our hotel, and we don't have to deal with the freeway traffic going into town again. So where would you like to eat tonight?"

Chapter 12

Las Vegas, NV
October 28th
9:00 AM

Gayle Baker left her car with the Four Seasons parking attendant and immediately rushed to the Verandah Restaurant to make sure her friend had made the arrangements he promised to take care of. After waiting for over half an hour at a table, which as promised was in a private but also picturesque location overlooking the terrace, she realized her unnecessarily early arrival was typical obsessive behavior on her part.

Gayle had spent the last fifteen minutes of her wait thinking about her recent decision to give up a career with the FBI and move to Las Vegas to head-up the Southwestern Region Medical Fraud Investigation Unit of the MFCB. She still wondered if she had made the right decision.

Hampton and Da Silva had left a little late for their breakfast meeting knowing Las Vegas was over-crowded with out-of-town visitors that Friday. In addition to the large Halloween parties scheduled by several strip hotels, there were three other major events taking place over the weekend, a soccer tournament, a rodeo, and drag races. Regardless of the crowds, they had managed to arrive fifteen minutes early, but by the time they got inside the hotel, unbeknown to them, Gayle had already made her way to the Verandah.

"So tell me all I need to know about Gayle Baker," Hampton prodded Da Silva as they sat waiting for her in the lobby.

"Okay, Bryan, but I shouldn't be telling you all this stuff because I'm her employer and some of this is personal. You can't ever let on I told you, but I think you need to know enough about her to help you make your decision about a career change. She's in her middle forties, reasonably attractive, and I might add she has a nice athletic body. She's never been married as far as I know. When she graduated from law school she went directly to work for the FBI, and she's been there since. She told me until the last few months, her life had been severely unbalanced, confessing she was almost totally focused on her career."

"So what prompted her decision to leave the FBI?" Hampton asked.

"Gayle had a few on and off relationships over the years, the most recent one with Dave Barnes, a fellow FBI agent. She told me they dated frequently for the first year, steadily for the second year, and were even discussing possible marriage dates, but then Gayle's mother was severely injured in a car accident. When she was discharged from the rehabilitation facility, she was unable to live alone and needed some temporary help.

"As an only child, Gayle welcomed her widowed mother into her home to provide whatever care she required. Temporary turned out to be nearly eighteen months. Dave Barnes lasted eight of those months. Compassion, it seems, wasn't his strong suit. Nearly a year ago now, her almost fully recuperated mother was able to return to her own home here in Las Vegas.

"Gayle told me the combination of that separation and the earlier breakdown of her relationship with Barnes convinced her she needed to make some major adjustments in her life. She decided to start by changing her career, then her place of residence. Eight months later she left Washington, her job with the FBI, and moved to Las Vegas to be near her mother.

"Apparently she believed securing the position with the MFCB was divine intervention because the role was a perfect fit for her skill set, and it allowed her to relocate where she wanted to live. So far, after just a few months, she says she's more than satisfied with her job, pleased to be near her mother, but admittedly lonely. I think that's where you can help Bryan."

"You can forget that part of this gig, Da Silva. I'm not looking for a relationship or romance. I just want a job where I can focus on my work and not get bogged down in political crap," Hampton emphatically countered. "Look, it's past time for her to be here. Maybe we should check and see if she's already in the restaurant waiting for us."

"You're probably right, Bryan. Let's head back there. Fair warning, my friend. When you see her, you'll change your tune on the 'I'm not looking for a relationship' idea."

Then they both left the lobby and headed out by the pool where the Verandah was located. As they neared the restaurant Da Silva immediately saw Gayle sitting alone at a table set for three.

"Gayle!" Da Silva almost shouted, standing two feet from where she sat staring at the palm trees lining the Verandah's outside seating area.

Appearing startled, but recovering quickly, Gayle looked up and saw Da Silva and Hampton. She stood and greeted her boss, who then introduced Bryan, "I'm happy to finally meet you, Agent Hampton. My boss here has been telling me all about you for the past several days and, based on the high expectations he created, I was watching the sky over the pool, half expecting you to fly in wearing a red cape and light blue tights."

For a second too long Hampton looked at her, then at Da Silva, his plan to be clever and witty that day by not repeating yesterday's pathetic performance with Charlie Cruz already stymied. Da Silva looked at him and shrugged, then turned to Gayle and said, "Bryan's a little slow on the uptake when he first meets a woman, so please excuse him for not understanding you were making a small joke, which if I may add, was a great comeback considering you seemed to be off in La La Land when we first walked up to the table."

Hampton, thankful to Da Silva for taking a little heat off him by putting Gayle on the defense, took a shot at both of them by saying, "I'm starting to think inborn sarcasm is a job requirement for anyone who works at the MFCB. Maybe I need to sign up for a course at the Don Rickles School of Personal Communication so I can fit in."

"Okay, let's all sit down now and be nice to each other and order some breakfast," Da Silva suggested.

Over the next half hour, Gayle highlighted her career with the FBI, summarized her personal goals for her new position with the MFCB, and touched evasively on her private life. However, regarding personal matters, she made one definitive string of declarations. "I live alone, I'm not married, I'm not involved with anyone, and I'm not gay."

For his part, Bryan highlighted his education and his career, omitting any references to Tacovic, the Patterson case, and any thoughts he had about Congressman Horowitz's accident. Da Silva, out of respect for Bryan, hadn't mentioned any of these issues to Baker, believing Hampton would discuss them with her when and if he decided they were relevant.

The breakfast meeting with Gayle had gone so well Hampton decided, when he got the opportunity, he would suggest he and Da Silva take a late afternoon flight back to Chicago rather than spending another night in the overcrowded city. During a quick bathroom break the two men made the decision to do just that and to wrap up as soon as possible.

Once their discussions resumed, they continued for another hour, but then noticed the staff of the Verandah had begun the change-over from the breakfast buffet to the lunch items. Four or five other tables were also still occupied, but it was nearly eleven-thirty, and they all sensed it was time to wrap-up their meeting.

Bryan took the initiative by saying, "Gayle, I've enjoyed meeting you, and I feel our time together this morning was well-spent. You're an accomplished and talented investigator and an enjoyable person to talk with. I'm impressed by your background and your thoughts about how the DOJ and MFCB might combine forces. My hope is our work together will be a model for other joint efforts between government and private sector organizations to combat health care fraud.

"I hope you share similar thoughts and feelings about me personally, and the perspectives and goals I've shared as we've talked this morning. If you do, I'm going to get back to Chicago as soon as possible and begin the process of relocating to Las Vegas. Paul Dixon has already extended an invitation for me to do so, and meeting you and gaining the confidence we can work effectively together has sealed the deal for me."

"Bryan, I couldn't agree more. I, too, have enjoyed our meeting this morning, and I believe there's a lot of common ground both in our goals and in the things we think can be developed as we work together to improve the tactics and objectives of fighting and preventing healthcare fraud. I'm looking forward to partnering with you. My immediate hope is you'll be able to get Mr. Dixon to commit to at least a trial joint investigation between our two organizations. I'm a little concerned because in my meeting with him, he was reluctant to promise anything, but seemed open to the idea."

Gayle seemed to change her focus, then went on, "I do have one final comment. I need to add a note of caution, based on some things I think you were implying as we talked. As a disciplined investigator, I'm a stickler for following proper protocols and not taking shortcuts. Should I have the opportunity to work with you, I hope you'll respect that perspective and support the disciplined approaches I believe are critical to success. If you have no problem with that, I think we could be a great team."

Da Silva quickly interjected himself into the conversation before Hampton could comment. "I know Bryan is totally supportive of that approach to working cases, so there's no problem there at all, Gayle. And now, Bryan, you and I need to get to our hotel, check out, and make some new plane reservations, if you really want to get back to Chicago tonight."

With that comment still hanging in the air, Da Silva stood and offered to help Gayle with her chair. It was a not-too-subtle signal to Hampton the meeting was over and it was time to quit while they were ahead. The two men said their goodbyes to Gayle, who stayed to verify their breakfast was complimentary as her friend had promised.

In the rental car on the way back to their hotel, Da Silva carried on a seemingly endless monologue on how well he thought the meeting had gone. He finally paused or ran out of anything else to say, allowing Bryan to interrupt. "Why didn't you allow me to address Gayle's last comments about being strict on process and protocol? You know damn well that's a problem for how I like to work a case, and now you've deliberately misled her into believing I agree with her methodical hamstrung approach. She has a right to know my style is controlled spontaneity. More often than not, it's a follow-your-gut technique. I believe in disciplined investigative techniques, but I also believe when the situation calls for creativity you either adapt or the bad guys get away."

"Yeah, Bryan, but let's not be too honest with Gayle quite yet. From what I hear, nine times out of ten your successes are the result of you following your gut and instincts more than working a case by the book. My position is we had a good meeting today and there's no reason to mess it up with an unresolvable discussion over how best to investigate and develop a case. Let's let her get to know you first before we go there.

"The two of you can deal with the details of working together once you actually have a suspect to investigate. You hold all the cards anyway, Bryan. If you decide you don't like working with her, then you tell Dixon it's not working out, and the MFCB is no longer partnering with the DOJ. She's smart enough to realize that would be bad for our organization and for her career. Besides, with your sophistication, charm and polished approach to women, she should be putty in your hands, making it simple for you to get her to see things your way."

After they checked out of their hotel, and while Da Silva drove them to the airport, Bryan called Paul Dixon's office and reached Charlie Cruz. She greeted him pleasantly and asked how his day had gone. "We had a great meeting with

Gayle Baker, and we've decided our work is done here for now, and we're heading home tonight. I was calling to see if there was any chance I could speak to your boss."

She teasingly responded, "Absolutely. You know Mr. Dixon has installed a special red phone in his office to accommodate any calls from you. And no matter who he's talking to or how busy he is, I'm instructed to put you through to him immediately."

Then she laughed and told Hampton to hold while she made sure Dixon was available. Less than a minute later, he heard Dixon come on the line. "Bryan, it's great to hear from you before the weekend. What's up? Are we a go?"

"We absolutely are a go, Paul. That's the purpose of my call. The meeting with Gayle went well and I'm calling to ask you to pull every string possible to accelerate my transfer. I want to get back here as soon as possible to join your team. I'd appreciate it if you'd send Tacovic a formal request to have me immediately transferred to your district, and please stress the immediate part."

"That's excellent news, Bryan. We'll get that email off before I leave the office today. I'm going to copy both the AG and the Director on my message, which I suggest you do as well once you submit your formal request. That way we'll make sure everyone is in the loop, and no one can discreetly undermine our efforts to facilitate your transfer."

"That's good advice, and I'll definitely follow it. Thanks for your support, and I can't stress enough how much I'm looking forward to getting back here as soon as possible to begin our work together."

By four-thirty Hampton and Da Silva were sitting in the United Airlines boarding area for Flight 866, which was scheduled to leave Las Vegas at six-twenty, arriving in Chicago just before midnight. Hampton used the available time to call Tacovic's office and leave him a voice mail. The message was brief and straightforward. He told Tacovic he was formally requesting an immediate transfer to Las Vegas to work for Paul Dixon, the U.S. Attorney in the District of Nevada.

He advised Tacovic he should expect an email from Dixon supporting the transfer, as well as one from Hampton himself documenting his formal request. He stressed both he and Dixon would copy their emails to the U.S. Attorney General, as well as the Director of the FBI.

After hanging up from that call, he used his iPhone to send Tacovic the promised email, including copies to all the referenced parties. He managed to complete all his correspondence long before the Chicago-bound flight was called for boarding.

At eight o'clock Pacific time, Flight 866 was nearing Laramie, WY. Da Silva and Bryan were nursing the four extra bags of pretzels they managed to coerce the flight attendant into giving them when Da Silva asked, "How did we manage to forget to buy food, Bryan? What's the matter with us? We sat in the airport for over an hour and a half, five feet from a deli, and we never made a move to get dinner."

Back in Las Vegas at that very moment Bennett Watson huddled in a dark corner of a bar near Flamingo and Decatur, waiting for his associate to arrive for a quick meeting. Uncharacteristically, the man wasn't early, but not yet late. Watson, always careful not to be seen with any of his unsavory colleagues, was anxious for the hasty get-together to be over with as soon as possible.

From where Watson sat, he had an unobstructed view of the tavern's front door, and he watched attentively assuming his guest would arrive any minute. Unexpectedly, he sensed someone peering down at him and was slightly alarmed he hadn't detected their approach. Then he heard an ominous but familiar voice, "Mr. Watson, may I join you?"

Watson was both relieved to see his associate had arrived, but at the same time, he was, as always, ill-at-ease in the man's presence. Knowing it was important for him to project authority and not appear intimidated, he pretended to be pleased to see Guzman. "Fausto, how nice you could come, and right on time, as always. Please have a seat while I order you a drink."

Chapter 13

Chicago, IL
November 3rd
4:00 PM

Through some quirk in the federal bureaucratic process, after only three business days, Hampton's official transfer from the Illinois District to the Nevada District had been approved and the authorizing documents forwarded by email to both U.S. attorneys and Hampton. But Hampton was away from his desk when the message arrived in his inbox. Regrettably, he first heard the good news from the last person he ever wanted to deliver it. After being summoned to see Tacovic, he once again found himself waiting in the man's drab office, just minutes after Tom Bilbray advised him Tacovic had requested the urgent meeting.

Sooner than he expected, the office door opened. Al Tacovic hurried toward Hampton, smiling and extending his right hand as though he was greeting a voter or a close friend and said, "Let me be the first to congratulate you. I just received official word the transfer I worked so hard to get you has been approved. Your official start date in Nevada is November twenty-first. You have a full two weeks to make your relocation arrangements. Tomorrow will be the last day you need to come into the office here, so you'll have plenty of time to prepare for your move.

"I want you to know I appreciate the outstanding work you've done during your time in Chicago. I know we've had some minor disagreements, but that's because we're both strong-willed and dedicated to the cause of justice. I want to wish you the best of luck in working with Paul Dixon. I hear that, like me, he's a committed and dedicated public servant with a long record of success."

Bryan stared at the man as he delivered his duplicitous congratulatory remarks. He was stunned by his own response to Tacovic's tactics, realizing he was actually standing there and shaking hands with the hypocrite whom he knew was corrupt and whom he believed was in some way linked to the murder of a Congressman.

Dozens of gut-driven emotional reactions countered by the restraints of rational thinking born of experience bombarded his psyche as he thought, I want to choke him or at least kick his ass, or maybe smash his face in, but what's the smart thing to do here? Do I play along and just get the hell out of here, or is that dishonest? Should I tell him what I think of him, and what I suspect he's involved in? Maybe I should do an Arnold and tell him he won this round, but I'll be back? What's the wise and winning play for my career, my future, my integrity, and how do I ensure justice will eventually be served?

Seconds after Tacovic concluded his insincere commentary, Hampton simply said, "Thanks for your help. I'm looking forward to working with Mr. Dixon. I believe he's an honest man." With that said, Hampton turned away from Tacovic and left the man's office for what he hoped to be the last time.

As soon as Hampton was in the hall recalling the bizarre encounter and how he'd been able to overcome his initial outrage and exercise prudent restraint in his response to Tacovic, he found he was incapable of arriving at any plausible explanation for his judicious behavior. But he was thankful for whatever force tempered his emotions and gave him the power to avoid a contentious exit that would have accomplished nothing, and perhaps could have threatened his future career or even his life.

The following morning, Bryan met with fellow agents to summarize and transfer all his active cases. By three in the afternoon he'd cleared his office of personal effects and visited a few of his co-workers to express his personal thanks and say goodbye. His last unofficial act after leaving the office was to call Ted Kucharski in Appleton. He tapped Kucharski's cell number on his iPhone contact list, and his friend answered on the third ring. "Bryan, so are you coming to Appleton this weekend to say your farewells? You know my kid is performing in a school play for the next two nights, and you don't want to miss that, do you?"

"That's a tempting invitation, but I need to pack and get ready to drive west as soon as I can, so I'm going to take a rain check on the play and the weekend in Wisconsin for now. As I noted in my text last night, I got official authorization for my transfer to Las Vegas yesterday, and I'm just leaving the office now for the last time. So my stint in the Midwest is rapidly coming to an end.

"I'm scheduled to report for work on the twenty-first. I'm planning to ship my personal stuff, what little there is of it, and take some time driving my sixty-three Corvette out west. I think I can only plan on doing four hundred miles or so a day. So I'll be at least four days on the road, barring any unforeseen problems, which could be more than a few driving a nearly fifty-year-old Chevy."

"Good luck with your plan, because that drive is an agonizingly long and monotonous trip. Basically, it's Illinois and Iowa corn for eight hours, then Nebraska corn for eight more hours, then you have eight hours of Colorado mountains, and finally Utah and Nevada desert for another five or six hours. About ten years ago, I made that drive with some friends, and calling it thirty hours of pure boredom is the most positive thing I can say about it.

"But, anyway, I'm glad you called because I wanted to share some good news with you. A few days ago, we got a call from another female patient complaining about our friend Dr. Patterson. We interviewed her yesterday, and she's eager to go after Patterson because not only did he bill Sidereal HealthCare for treatments she never received, but his office apparently screwed up and they sent her a bill as well for over ten grand.

"But here's the best part. She's married to some big shot attorney in Waukegan. He called Patterson's office about the bill, and the doctor's billing clerk apparently threatened to take the wife to court if she doesn't pay whatever Sidereal decides is not covered. So now we have an ally, an angry attorney who wants to go after Patterson, and therefore, this becomes a case my superiors can't ignore.

"So, Agent Hampton, my going away present to you is the encouraging news we're reopening all of our past cases against Patterson, along with this new one. And for starters, we're going to oust him from our network, after which we'll prosecute him for fraud. Our friend the Waukegan barrister guarantees he'll find us a prosecutor who has jurisdiction and who'll take the case. He claims he has lots of friends in the legal community who owe him favors and has no reservations at all in calling in a few to make this happen. Bryan, we're going to be all over Patterson, and we'll get him in spite of his connections."

"That's awesome news, Ted, and I hope you're successful. Keep me posted on the progress of your investigation and hopefully the prosecution. I'd love to see your case somehow circle back and tie Tacovic and his friend Judge Markowski to the bribe Tacovic solicited from Patterson. Maybe there'll be an opportunity to get Patterson to testify against Tacovic in exchange for a lesser sentence. If you ever get to that point with your case, I'd love to help in any way I can."

Then Hampton wrapped up the call. "Well, my friend, I guess we both have our work cut out for us. I'm anxious to get to Las Vegas and start work. Dixon seems like someone I'll enjoy working with, and I think our team is going to make a difference. I'll make sure you get all my new contact information, but in the meantime, just phone or text me because my cell number's staying the same. I want to sincerely thank you for introducing me to your friend Da Silva, because none of this would ever have happened if not for you. If there's ever anything I can do for you, just call, and if it's legal, it's a done deal."

"I'll stay in touch, Bryan, you can definitely bet on that, and I'm glad Da Silva's idea has worked out so well. He thinks a lot of you and he desperately wants the MFCB to have a chance to work with your DOJ team."

After Bryan ended the call, he checked his watch and saw it was just after four, which meant in Las Vegas it was only a little past three, so Charlie Cruz should still be at work. He punched Dixon's office number and, as he hoped, Charlie answered. "Charlie, it's Bryan Hampton. Do you have a minute?"

"Agent Hampton, it's nice to hear from you and yes, I have as many minutes as you need. What can I help you with?"

"Well, as you must know by now, I'll be starting on the twenty-first, which is just two weeks from this coming Monday. My plan is to be packed up and out of Chicago by the middle of next week. Then I'm allowing four days of driving to get there, which means I'm hoping to arrive in Vegas sometime Saturday or Sunday. I was wondering if you could give me some suggestions on the areas of Las Vegas where I should start looking for an apartment or a house to rent."

"As a matter of fact, Mr. Dixon already asked me to give you whatever assistance you require, and I've already started gathering some information that should help you. I'm planning to compile some apartment listings, and if you're interested in renting a house, I can look into those options as well. Since you're not firm on a Saturday or Sunday arrival, I'd like to suggest you plan on coming into town on Sunday sometime in the early afternoon. Most of the weekend tourists leave by midday, so you'll find the city is far less crowded on Sunday than Saturday."

Charlie paused then continued, "If that's a plan you're okay with, I want to offer to spend Sunday afternoon showing you around the various parts of town where I think you might be interested in living. And if we have time we can even drive by and look at some of the apartments and houses I think would be workable choices. Then, starting on Monday, you could actually go back to any specific properties that looked promising to you."

"Charlie, that's a generous offer. I think it sounds like a great plan for me, but I don't want to take you away from your family on the weekend."

"Actually, that won't be a problem because I have a friend Jenni who has two children, and we actually help each other out on the weekends by watching each other's kids for half a day. So one weekend she takes my kids from one to seven on Sunday and the next weekend I take hers. It'll work out perfectly because I have her two girls this Sunday."

"Well then, you're on, if you promise to let me buy you dinner that Sunday. I guarantee I'll have you back to your children by seven. Incidentally, what part of town do you live in? Is it close to the office?"

"First of all, you don't want to live close to the office, because I assume you prefer to live somewhere nice, which is not downtown. A high rise condo near the strip, which is fairly close, would be an option, but with that exception, commuting thirty minutes or more each way is something you'll need to plan on every morning and afternoon if you want to find a good neighborhood.

"I live south, but mostly west of downtown where the office is, and it's usually a forty minute drive at the time I have to travel. The place I live is called Summerlin South. The schools there are great, and that's a priority for me, but not an issue for you. So you could find a nice apartment closer to the office than where I live. Give me some guidance on number of bedrooms as well as your price range. I also want to know if you need something furnished or if you have your own furniture. I'm wondering why you would want a house; aren't you a family of one right now?"

Bryan eventually answered those questions as well as several more and, after twenty minutes on the phone, they had made fairly detailed plans together for a week from Sunday. Once they hung up and he had a few minutes to reflect on the call, he realized he had divulged far more about his personal life and affairs to Charlie than he could remember sharing with anyone for years. He decided it was okay under the circumstances, but soon he needed to get her to reciprocate.

He actually knew only a few sparse details about her personal life that he'd picked up from some of Dixon's comments. He knew she was the widow of a Navy Seal and had two boys ages nine and seven. He knew where she worked and how long she'd been there, and that she was the trusted assistant to a man he already respected. And, from their conversation, he'd learned her address and that she wanted to have dinner at the Claim Jumper Restaurant near her home.

But he also knew one more fascinating thing. He would be spending an afternoon with Charlie in nine days, and he was more excited about that than anything that had happened to him in nearly a year.

Chapter 14

Las Vegas, NV
November 21st
8:00 AM

Bryan's first week in the Las Vegas Justice Department office was a short one. It was Thanksgiving week, and although the only official Government holiday was Thursday, nearly everyone used a personal day on Black Friday. Like millions of other Americans, DOJ employees either spent the day with their family or joined the mobs in search of Christmas bargains.

Charlie warned Hampton against planning to work on Friday because office tradition dictated only a small voluntary crew be present to manage the affairs of the DOJ, and he wasn't scheduled to be part of that skeletal staff. Since their Sunday afternoon excursion a week ago, Bryan and Charlie had spent some part of every day together and they were both enjoying their developing friendship.

After he'd considered three different areas of town and driven by six different apartment complexes and two houses that Charlie had identified as good prospects, Hampton eventually selected an apartment less than two miles from where Charlie and her children lived. He settled on a two bedroom, two bath, unfurnished, ground floor unit that was ideal except there was no garage for his Corvette.

Charlie was with him when he discussed possible solutions to his garage problem with the manager of the complex, and she made a suggestion that surprised them both. "Why don't you store your car at my house, at least for a while, or even permanently, if it works out for you? I have a three-car garage and only one car. I could move the kids' bikes and other junk around and there'd be one dedicated bay for your cherished Corvette."

Hampton looked dubious, but Charlie forged ahead with her suggestion, "As the Senior Agent, the first day you show up for work, they'll assign you a standard government issue Crown Victoria that you use like your own car. So you won't even need to drive the Corvette often anyway."

"That's a tempting offer, Charlie, but I'd never do it without paying you a rental fee for the favor. In Illinois, it was costing me a hundred and fifty a month for a garage to store it, so I could pay you that much. But why don't you think about it for a day and let me know if you really think that's a good idea."

"One hundred a month and we'll try it for three months, then either of us can kill the deal if it's not working without giving a reason, and we'll still be friends. Deal?" she had asked, then offered a hand to shake on her proposal and the arrangement was official.

An unfurnished apartment meant beds, tables, couches, and various accessories had to be purchased. Charlie offered to help Bryan shop for the things he needed, and during the week they had gone on several buying expeditions. Late one afternoon she called to tell Hampton, "I'm bringing my two boys, Aaron and Becham, along tonight to help us look for your living room couch. Is that okay?"

Three stores and two hours after their search began, all four of them had finally agreed on a dark brown sectional, and Bryan suggested they go have dinner. "You boys get to pick the restaurant," he told them. After some intense debate they were able to settle on tacos at their favorite Mexican restaurant a few minutes from their home.

By week's end, Bryan knew considerably more about Charlie and understood a few of the many challenges facing a young widow raising two young boys and working full-time. His admiration and respect for her as a competent, dedicated, and loving parent of her two children had only added to his initial attraction to her beauty and poise. He recognized she was an extraordinary and amazing woman, but he also realized she was closer to the age of his oldest daughter than she was to his own fifty-four years, and that troubled him whenever he considered how long he should prudently leave his Corvette parked at her home.

By nine on his first day of work, Bryan hadn't quite settled into his office, but he was at least able to send and receive emails and handle phone calls and voicemails. He spent the following half hour preparing for a meeting Dixon scheduled for nine-thirty with the other attorneys in the Las Vegas office. During the meeting, Dixon had asked him to introduce himself and tell a little about his background and goals.

Normally, that type of presentation wasn't a concern for him, but Hampton knew there were already rumors in the office about the motives for his recent transfer from Chicago. He'd decided he would tell the truth, but withhold details about Tacovic. "The simple explanation," he told them, "is I requested the move because I wanted to work with a leader like Paul Dixon who's committed to the same goals and standards I believed in. Tacovic wasn't passionate about prosecuting medical fraud, and he had too many ties to Illinois politics to be completely objective in his decisions."

Later he wondered if even that explanation might have been too condemning and would somehow get back to Tacovic and cause him problems, but he'd decided to address the issues surrounding his transfer in enough detail so he would never need to deal with the subject again.

Later than morning, Bryan met with Dixon in his office. "Bryan, you did a nice job today with the staff. I'm sure you realize one or more of them will know an associate who works in the Chicago office, and they're sure to report what you said about Tacovic having too many political ties to be objective. In fact, I'm guessing a few emails have already been exchanged, and, of course, every sender will have paraphrased your remarks with their own slanted and likely inflammatory version of what you actually said. I don't really care, but we'll likely hear more about this at some point, and my bet is soon."

"I'm sorry if I overstepped my bounds, but I felt I needed to give a fact-based reason for coming here, with enough detail so people would stop asking about it. I've already heard two false rumors floating around the office, so I felt I needed to be specific and definitive, and be done with discussing it. I guess I should have run it past you first."

"Would you have followed my advice if I'd told you not to say what you felt you needed to?" Dixon asked, not smiling.

Bryan paused for a second to consider the question, then answered, "No, probably not, but then I also would've wondered if coming here was the right decision."

"Right answer, Bryan! On matters of personal conscience, none of us has the right to muzzle another person. The people I trust and prefer to work with are those who voice their opinions and can rationally reason with others who have opposing views. The only thing I ask of my staff is, once we agree on a course of action, we're united and committed in pursuit of it. And as the person ultimately responsible for this district, I reserve the right to make final decisions, and I'm intolerant of those who, for whatever reason, independently decide to deviate from an agreed upon path. That leads to confusion and inefficiencies and often failure, and I can't accept any of those outcomes. Are we clear?"

"Very clear, Paul. I appreciate your candor and agree with your approach. I've never been one to come at things sideways, nor do I believe in backdoor assaults, so we should be in great shape here."

"Good, now I want to bring you up to speed on that case I discussed with you last time we met, but first I want to ask how you feel about working with Gayle and the MFCB. I realize that may not be an entirely fair question with the sparse amount of information we've given you so far, but I'd like to know how you're leaning at this point."

"Paul, I say we've got nothing to lose and a lot to gain by giving them a shot. Since this case involves medical treatment for auto and workers compensation cases, and they have all that medical bill data, why wouldn't we want to test the value of their information and the competency of their staff? Gayle appears to be an experienced and skilled investigator, and what better opportunity will we ever have to see what can be gained by working with them? And besides, a fraud-fighting partnership between the public and private sectors is one of the core goals you've already announced to the staff, the politicians, and the public. If it works out, you hit a home run."

"We hit a home run, Bryan. This isn't about me; it's about our team and the MFCB team, and you're the captain of the combined squad. I'm just the Manager, and if Da Silva participates, he'll be a coach. I also plan on using my friend Josif Stolic as pinch hitter anytime he's needed. So we actually will be, what Da Silva likes to call the Dream Team, and we'll use our assembled talent to shut down Bennett Watson, Ari Mirzoyan, and anyone else associated with their crime ring.

"This case will be our line in the Nevada sand, our message to criminals as well as the vulnerable public that our team is serious and more than capable of finding medical fraudsters, prosecuting them, then taking away their white lab coats and exchanging them for orange jump suits, with numbers."

Hampton had worked with political appointees his entire career. He'd endured uninspiring pep talks and insincere stump speeches many times, and he knew Dixon's response hadn't been planned nor prepared. Dixon had extemporaneously and passionately restated his intentions to meet the commitment he made to root out medical fraud and jail those guilty of it. In doing so, he'd demonstrated palpable passion and sincerity, and Hampton couldn't help but feel a sense of profound gratitude he had escaped the frustration and despair of Tacovic's influence and found an ethical and honest leader who wanted to aggressively enforce the law without exception. He smiled involuntarily, causing Paul to ask, "What are you grinning about?"

"I'm just happy to be here, Paul. I'm thrilled you're just an older version of the quiet, solid, and honest guy I knew thirty years ago. Now fill me in on everything I need to know on this case so I can get to work."

Dixon then called Charlie. "Please let Abe Slater know we're ready for him."

For the next hour Dixon, with Slater's help, outlined in detail what had been learned so far in their investigation of the suspected crime ring and the schemes they believed were organized and overseen by Bennett Watson. Abe Slater was the current lead investigator of the team working the case. It soon became clear to Hampton that Dixon had already advised Abe that Hampton was going to be in charge of the investigation moving forward, and that he would report directly to him from then on.

Earlier Abe had suggested to Dixon that Eli Wilson be assigned to the case, because both Abe and Eli had been working the investigation together for the past two months. Dixon tentatively agreed to the proposal, but told Abe he wanted Hampton to meet Eli as soon as possible, so he could make a final decision about including Eli as part of his team.

As the meeting progressed, Abe outlined a plan they had been considering. "We're thinking about sending four agents posing as patients into the Accident and Injury Health Restoration Clinics. Three would impersonate victims of car accidents. The fourth agent would claim he was injured at work, but he'd eventually confess to the treating doctor that he'd really been hurt playing in a family football game. He'll explain to the chiropractor that he needs his injury to be documented as job-related because his back is so painful he can't work, and without the salary benefits from workers compensation, he'll be unable to pay his bills."

Hampton intentionally maintained a neutral expression which Abe was evidently unable to interpret, so he gave up, and continued cautiously with more details. "The plan was to have each of the agents go to one of the four offices the clinic operates. They'll all claim lower back injuries because it's often impossible to initially diagnose the authenticity of back injuries unless there are fractures, ruptured discs, or nerve damage verified by various tests. Otherwise, the symptoms are generally back pain, sciatica, and limited range of motion, and the agents will be well versed in how to describe the actual symptoms they'd be experiencing if they really had sustained a serious back injury."

"I like the concept, Abe," Hampton offered. "But will we prove what needs to be established? Seems like we'll have patients with fake injuries, but our agents will be claiming legitimate symptoms, and in that case, wouldn't we expect the clinicians to run the indicated diagnostic tests and follow appropriate treatment protocols?"

"Yes, but once all the tests are run and there's no indication of any reason for the pain our agents are claiming, the question becomes, what will the doctors do then? Will they stop aggressive treatment and manage the patient conservatively, or will they keep running expensive tests and continue bringing the patients into the office for physical therapy, acupuncture treatments, and chiropractic manipulations that do nothing but run up their bills?" Abe responded.

At that point, Dixon interrupted the conversation, saying, "I can see the two of you have a lot to discuss and you're off to a good start. As fascinating as this discussion is, I have a far less interesting meeting I need to oversee. Why don't the two of you reconvene in Bryan's office and continue your discussions there. Abe, invite Eli into the balance of your talks today so Bryan can meet him right away and get a chance to see how he fits in.

"Bryan, I think you and I should get on a conference call with Da Silva and Baker, preferably this afternoon if Charlie can arrange it. We'll invite them to work with us on this case. We won't go into any detail yet, and we'll definitely not give them any names until we have all the necessary non-disclosures and confidentiality documents signed. All of that will likely take a week with the Thanksgiving holiday coming up, but we can't do anything officially with them until all the paperwork is completed.

"The MFCB will likely also have some documents we need to review and complete. I'm going to ask you to work with Charlie to make sure all the paperwork and required clearances get taken care of on both ends. We'll let them know on the call you and Charlie are responsible for all the logistics.

"Also, Bryan, ask Charlie to make it a priority to set up the call today, wherever there's space on my calendar. Abe, thanks for joining us and good luck to both of you, I'm anxious to move forward on this investigation before Watson and Mirzoyan know what hit them."

Outside Dixon's office, Hampton asked Charlie to arrange the call with Da Silva and Gayle. With both men still meeting near her desk, she couldn't help overhearing Hampton talking to Abe. "Abe, I'd like you and Eli to join me in my office in half an hour. Bring all your files and any other documentation either of you have assembled so far. We'll discuss in detail everything you and Eli believe is pertinent. I think it's crucial we first focus on facts, not theories. After we deal with the facts we can also talk about impressions, ideas, and suspicions either of you might have for advancing the investigation.

"I think we should all plan on spending the remainder of the day together so you can get me up to speed on the case as fast as possible."

Abe Slater, an agent in his middle forties, was usually friendly and open to Charlie and the rest of the staff, but as she watched him listening to Hampton, she noticed a subtle change in the man's demeanor and body language.

After Abe walked away, Charlie looked up at Hampton. "Too much too fast, Chicago man. Everybody here already knows you're a star. Telling two guys who've been on a case for months to drop everything they're doing and report to your office in half an hour is bad enough. But asking, actually ordering, them to tell you their ideas, suspicions, and impressions when they don't even know if you can be trusted or if you're some kind of back-stabbing, glory seeker isn't a great way to enlist their help. If I were you, I'd spend the first hour letting them ask you questions, right after you apologize for being such a butthead."

Hampton was caught off guard and was speechless for a few seconds. "Okay, Charlie, I guess I got a little too excited and forgot this was my first day on the job. Your points are well taken and probably valid, so I'll do my best to follow your suggestions."

"Probably valid? Try some humility, too. Less efficiency and more dialogue will go a long way in letting people see the side of you I catch glimpses of now and then. You're basically a nice guy, but most of the time you're wound up too tight. You suffer from what we psychologists call tightassistis, or TA for short, a condition men who live alone without the supervision of a wife often suffer from. Now, I need to set up a conference call if you'll excuse me." And with that, Charlie turned and started punching numbers on her phone.

Thirty minutes later Hampton closed the door to his office after he greeted Abe and introduced himself to Eli Wilson. After they were all seated, Hampton began the meeting with an apology and a suggestion that they spend some time getting to know one another before attacking the case. Abe and Eli actually used more than an hour discussing their professional training, work experience, families, and aspirations with Hampton. They questioned him about his family and probed for more details about his exodus from Chicago.

Hampton was as open as ever about his family, which meant he gave minimal details. In reference to Chicago, he simply explained, "I've said all I'm going to say about leaving Chicago, but anyone interested should know my departure was my own decision. I'd appreciate the two of you not asking me about it ever again." When their conversations reached the two-hour mark, they decided to break for lunch, then reconvene after the conference call Charlie had managed to schedule for one o'clock.

The phone discussion with Da Silva and Baker lasted less than fifteen minutes, and Dixon did most of the talking. He started by shrewdly telling the MFCB investigators that Hampton had recommended his team work on a trial basis with the MFCB to jointly pursue a case currently under investigation by the DOJ staff. After he paused briefly to let that news sink in, Dixon continued, "I've decided to go along with Bryan's suggestion, with the understanding that Agent Hampton must have complete authority and control over the combined task force and final say on any actions undertaken by the team."

After the group exchanged a series of verbal high-fives about Dixon's decision, tactical issues related to the required paperwork and other procedures that had to be followed were discussed in some detail. The call ended a few minutes later, but not before both sides voiced a series of enthusiastic declarations of optimism about their anticipated future successes.

"Well, Paul, that was masterful. You got them to believe I had influence over a decision you'd already made, but only if we control every aspect of the investigation. You gave them what you knew they desperately wanted and got the terms you knew we needed. At the same time you sent them a signal that you're reluctantly moving forward, guaranteeing they won't challenge the leadership conditions you stipulated. Now that I've seen you in action, I understand another of the reasons you were re-elected five times; you're an architect of consensus."

"Could there be a better credential for a professional politician, Bryan?"

"There should be a few more adjectives added, but from what I've seen of you so far, they're already part of your résumé." Hampton then smiled, thanked Dixon for the call, and explained he needed to get back to his discussions with Abe and Eli.

As he passed Charlie's desk on his way back to his office, she stopped him. "Hey, I ran into Abe in the kitchen a couple of minutes ago. Apparently your boat managed to find some smoother water late this morning, so congratulations on being teachable."

At precisely half past one Abe and Eli were back in Bryan's office, and their discussions resumed. Bryan began, "I think we should focus our conversations for the rest of the day on the operation and staffing of the four locations where the Accident and Injury Health Restoration Clinics do business."

Abe interrupted Hampton with a question, "Because the name of the clinic is so long, can we just use the code named *RACHI* that we've already created to save time?"

After a pause and a strange look from Hampton, Eli wrote the code name on a note and handed it to him. Hampton finally realized the name was created by reordering the first letters of the clinic's ridiculously long name. His mind involuntarily began trying to reconfigure the letters into a real word, when Abe explained, "Eli and I like the code name because you can pronounce *RACHI* as RAUNCHY, and that's definitely a fitting name for both the clinics' operation and its staff."

"That's awesome! I like it." Hampton said with a relaxed smile that had set the tone for the rest of the day's discussions.

Throughout the afternoon, the detailed briefing revealed several critical factors about the clinics' operations that, for Hampton, exposed a disciplined and carefully structured system of fraud. He learned there were actually five offices with business licenses where the clinics operated. Four were treatment centers, and the fifth was a business office where only four people worked, one being the owner Dr. Ari Mirzoyan.

Abe explained the basics of the *RACHI* operation. "The treatment centers are spread throughout the Las Vegas Valley, but the business office is located in a posh high-rise building on Corporate Drive just west of Paradise Road a few blocks off the Strip. We estimate there are approximately forty-two employees throughout Mirzoyan's operations, including the doctor himself.

"His current wife, who after two months of surveillance has never been seen entering or leaving any of the five locations, is a paid consultant to Mirzoyan's clinics. According to IRS records, the consulting firm she allegedly operates has only one customer, the *RACHI* clinics. It pays her firm two hundred thousand dollars a year, most of which is offset by annual expenses of over one hundred and ninety thousand dollars."

Eli then offered some background information on the doctor himself. "Dr. Mirzoyan, who owns the *RACHI* clinics, refers to himself as a 'holistic practitioner of chiropractic medicine' who 'specializes in restoring the health of victims of auto accidents and job related injuries.' Our investigation over the past several weeks has revealed Mirzoyan is of Armenian descent and was loosely associated with the Armenian fraud network based in Southern California that was exposed less than a year ago. Mirzoyan somehow avoided being one of the many participants who were arrested and had their assets seized.

"He's fifty-five years old, divorced four times, and in spite of all the divorce settlements, quite wealthy. But it appears there's never enough money to satisfy his wants. He's practiced in six different states, leaving five of them because of sanctions or potential sanctions against his license. But with every near conviction he's perfecting the art of fraud, or so he believes.

"Mirzoyan's lived and practiced in Vegas for the past five years and has built an empire of sorts. As Abe said, his four treatment offices and one business office currently employ forty-two people. Every treatment location has one or more physical therapists, one acupuncturist, one personal trainer, one licensed chiropractor, one x-ray technician without credentials, operating unsupervised and illegally under a single licensed radiology technician for all four locations, and one or two front office receptionists, depending on the volume of patient traffic in that location.

"Three of the offices have MRI systems and a fourth office has a CAT scanner. He's created an operation that can, and literally does, generate millions of dollars in charges every month, as long as there are patients to feed the machine. And we believe his association with Bennett Watson guarantees there will never be a shortage of warm bodies passing through the doors of the *RACHI* operations."

Eli paused to see if Hampton wanted to comment, then went on, "From interviews with two former employees, we've learned Dr. Mirzoyan runs a disciplined and incentive-based operation, and every employee understands their role and the owner's expectations for their productivity. The clinics are run much like a large legal practice in that each employee knows their productivity determines their salary and continued tenure with the clinics."

Hampton interrupted Eli asking, "So you're telling me every clinic employee is incentivized to support the fraud we suspect, and they believe their jobs depend on their complicity in the scheme?"

"Even though there may be eight or more ancillary personnel in each office, all services rendered by any employee are billed under the name and National Provider Identifier number, of the one chiropractor in that office. What at first mystifies most new staff members is the endless stream of injured patients who find their way into the practice. These newly hired employees initially believe the ads featuring Dr. Mirzoyan, which run constantly on TV, are responsible for the flow of people. However, it eventually becomes clear to those actually involved in patient care that many of the injuries are suspect, and most of the services being provided to patients are unnecessary, redundant, or ineffective.

"But the high wages seem to corrupt those who stay, and employee turnover is low. The two former employees our agents have located and interviewed so far claim few of the clinics' employees say much except the money is great and the working environment is fast paced. Under those circumstances, the already compromised staff generally can rationalize that if it's okay with the doctors, who am I to question them?"

Abe then jumped in to stress an important fact. "About a year ago, however, that reasoning was re-examined by two former staff members who left their jobs. These are the people Eli and I later interviewed, and they told us last fall one of the chiropractors mysteriously left the practice to 'pursue new opportunities in another state,' but since then no one's been able to locate the doctor or his family, or even forward his mail."

By four-thirty, all three men agreed they were exhausted and should quit for the day. But just before they adjourned, Eli asked Hampton a troubling question, "Can you please explain to me how in the hell a doctor like Mirzoyan can lose his license in one state and get a license to practice in another state over and over again, without someone checking into his past?"

"Eli, that's the question we're asked by nearly every victimized patient; how can something like this happen? How can someone lose his license in one state, then open up somewhere else with valid medical credentials? There are many reasons it can happen, because there're so many holes in our licensing and tracking systems for health care professionals.

"We've all heard of cases where someone has been working as a doctor for years, then someone dies or is injured due to the provider's negligence, and it's discovered the provider never had a license in the first place.

"Those are the more unusual cases, but Dr. Mirzoyan's migrations are unfortunately the more common problem, and it happens for two main reasons. First of all, the court system is responsible for judging providers accused of violations, but licenses to practice medicine, dentistry, nursing, physician assistants, and so on are granted by entities other than the courts. Generally they have names like the Department of Professional Licensing.

"These entities, the courts and licensing bodies, don't always communicate with one another, so actions by a court in Ohio may never be known by a licensing board in New Mexico. It's also true that a restriction or sanction placed on a doctor's license by an entity in New Mexico may not be picked up by the licensing body in Ohio.

"You guys already know something about the National Practitioner Data Bank or NPDB, which is maintained by the Department of Health and Human Services. The Data Bank is intended to be a supplemental source of information used by credentialing and licensing entities to evaluate health care professionals' credentials. The NPDB cannot be accessed by the public and is generally regarded as flawed, due to outdated and incomplete data."

Hampton continued, "Another challenge is that each state and Medicare maintain their own separate sanctions databases, and in some cases they're updated regularly, and in other cases the updates occur months after the reportable events take place. Then to further muddy the waters, providers can be sanctioned, but the sanction won't be recorded in the database."

"Bryan, what about the problems we see with biased peer review, where doctors charged with judging their fellow practitioners fail to act and no sanctions are ever imposed on negligent providers in the first place? We've seen this happen especially in small towns where doctors sit in judgment of providers they attending church with, or socialize with." Abe asked.

"While provider peer review is good in many respects, we know it's potentially problematic in those very situations. When licensing boards, peer review committees, and hospital credentialing bodies are composed of providers who see each other on a daily basis, it's not surprising justice is not always served." Hampton agreed, then finished by saying, "One final reason providers can move around in spite of prior crimes or licensing problems is they may have originally obtained licenses in multiple states, and over the years they kept their licenses current in several of those states. Then, if they get in trouble in one state they migrate to a state where they already have an active license and lie about any past sins."

By the time Bryan finished his licensing discussion it was nearly five, but before stopping, he made a recommendation. "You guys, we have basically a day and a half before the Thanksgiving holiday, so I'd like to suggest we spend tomorrow focusing on whatever information you have on Dr. Mirzoyan's billing office procedures and personnel. And I want us to review everything you've already learned about the four other chiropractors who work at *RACHI*, and especially the one who was hired a year ago to replace the doctor who seems to have dropped off the face of the earth.

"I think we need to carefully look at anything we have on that disappearing doctor as well, if you've actually had time to check up on his whereabouts. If not, we need to assign someone to run him down wherever he's gone, then we need to interview him and find out why he left.

"Thanks a lot for today, guys, I'm amazed by all the information you two have already turned up and by everything I've learned from both of you here today. Are we good for now?"

Both men nodded yes, which Hampton hoped was their confirmation things were feeling much better to them and, with that, Abe and Eli headed back to their offices.

After they had gone, Bryan closed his door and relished a moment of quiet satisfaction over the day's events, fully aware that had it not been for Charlie's advice the day could have had an entirely different outcome. He went to his phone and dialed Charlie's extension, but it immediately rolled to voicemail, which he assumed meant she was already gone for the day. Then he realized they had no shopping excursion scheduled for that night and was surprisingly a little shaken by the void he felt.

Chapter 15

Las Vegas, NV
November 22nd
2:50 PM

The day's discussions had gone by so quickly that none of the three investigators could believe it was already approaching three o'clock. They had worked through lunch to maintain the momentum they had going throughout morning, and as they left his office, Hampton suggested, "Abe and Eli, you guys should head home right now. As far as I'm concerned we've already done more than a full day's work." Unexpected time off was a great perk, even when it was only an hour or two. So both men were pleased not only to get home earlier, but also to have discovered another important quality about their new boss through his simple but thoughtful gesture.

Earlier, Charlie had delivered each of the three agents a burger and fries when she returned from her own lunch break. During the few minutes the men needed to eat their food and drink their Diet Cokes, Abe and Eli had discussed their upcoming Thanksgiving Day plans, while Hampton mostly listened. When Abe asked Hampton what his schedule was for Thanksgiving Day, he weakly explained, "I have nothing planned. I need to finish setting up my apartment. I have boxes still waiting to be unloaded and tables screaming to be assembled, so I'm planning to work, then dine out."

Hampton realized immediately they knew that was BS, when after his response, an awkward silence settled over the group. So Bryan quickly added,

"There's a good chance my daughter and her family might be coming in from LA, if her husband is able to get Friday off work."

Once the men left, Hampton sat in front of his PC, called up a new Word document, then opened his notebook to the first entry he made during that day's meeting. He began his work by typing a header that read *Accident and Injury Health Restoration Clinics Investigation*, then a sub-header entitled *Billing Office Procedures and Personnel.*

Bryan always preferred to first record his notes and ideas informally using a word processing application, so he wasn't tied to the ridged structure demanded by the agency's case tracking software. Eventually, he would transfer all the relevant and accurate data to that system and enter it in the required format. But Hampton's own analytical process called for him to first document a mix of case facts, peppered with free form thoughts and speculation.

Throughout the investigation his approach was to record all his spontaneous impressions about what some fact or series of facts might or might not actually mean. He preferred not to expose most of his early or initial ideas to anyone until he had sufficiently mulled them over and discarded any he decided were irrational. He had learned by experience a hard but important reality; tangible written ideas on a screen or printed on paper were far less forgiving than squishy, less disciplined thoughts rattling around in his head.

An important fact he recorded from that day's meeting revealed only two individuals ultimately prepared and submitted every insurance claim from all four of the treatment centers. He also learned Mirzoyan had equipped his operations with the latest practice management system, and it interfaced with one of the most costly and advanced electronic medical records system on the market.

All four offices were linked by a Virtual Private Network to the billing office. According to the ex-employees who were interviewed, every patient's bill and medical record entries originated from each of treatment clinics. These initial entries were closely scrutinized, and, if necessary, modified by the two employees in the billing office, each of whom had a different and vital role in the process.

One of those individuals, Lance Beasley, reviewed the electronic medical records to verify every possible injury and medical condition had been accurately and optimally recorded, and assigned a diagnosis code, and that all plausible treatments and tests had been documented in the medical record, regardless of whether or not they were actually performed.

Once that process was completed, the second billing expert, Amanda Booth, compared the draft bill produced in the clinic to the newly enhanced version of the medical record. Amanda's responsibility was to make certain every documented service in the patient's medical record had the procedure code with the highest charge possible recorded in the final version of the bill that would be sent to the insurer.

The former employees both emphasized that a performance record was maintained by the billing office personnel listing all errors of omission in both the draft medical record and the initial version of the bill. Scores were determined by tracking the amount of lost revenue that would have resulted if those mistakes had not been detected and corrected in the billing office.

Neither of the two women interviewed was able to describe the scoring formula, but they both knew staff members and doctors received a combined performance score every month. If anyone's score was below a certain value, everyone in that particular clinic suffered a reduction in their following month's wages. It was a generally held belief habitually low scores would result in the dismissal of the billing and coding person as well as some unknown but severe penalty to the doctor; although neither of the former employees had ever witnessed either of those outcomes.

The practical reality was, after experiencing their first pay cut, every worker at the clinic was focused on any and all reasons for their reduced income. The resulting operation became self-policing, with every employee checking and double checking their own work as well as the tasks of their fellow workers.

Patients were commonly queried about any pain or disease they might have, which could require care from the clinic's staff. Both former employees told of a diligent, but imprudent billing clerk at one of the clinics who had actually placed a small sign on the staff side of the reception desk, visible only to the employees. It read: *If You're Not Sure, Bill It Anyway.*

After summarizing and documenting the facts, Bryan recorded his immediate observations and initial conclusions. "The *RACHI* operation has been designed to optimize revenue with every employee accountable and financially vested in accomplishing and facilitating that goal. Failure on the part of clinic workers to maximize tests, treatments and charges for any real or possible injuries or pre-existing conditions results in a reduction in pay for every employee at that particular facility. As a result, employees police themselves and their fellow workers to make certain no error ever occurs that could reduce billable charges for any patient. This creates a medical process focused far too little on patient wellness and far too much on generating maximum revenues.

"It seems fair to assume that nearly every employee with any reasonable tenure is likely complicit in most crimes and fraud committed. Two employees at a remote billing office have enormous responsibility and control over billable charges and insurance submissions, and more critically on the contents of every patient's medical record, which may routinely be falsified to justify overcharging and unnecessary treatments."

Hampton then proceeded to produce a long list of nine crucial questions his team needed to answer. He also created a list of eleven next steps his investigative team needed to allocate and prioritize. The majority of the questions required the gathering of specific and detailed information about Amanda and Lance, the two key employees in the billing process. His list of 'Next Investigative Steps' mostly addressed how the tasks associated with collecting that information would be divided up between the members of his team.

By the time Bryan finished recording his observations, questions, and next steps, it was after four-thirty and near the time most people started preparing to leave for the day. After hearing a gentle tap on his door, without looking up he said, "Come on in."

But when he heard Charlie's voice asking, "Are you busy?" he quickly turned toward the door and got up from his chair to greet her. "Charlie, I'm glad you came by, because I'm just finishing up."

"I thought I'd drop in and see how your day was going. I saw Eli and Abe take off nearly two hours ago, and I was afraid you might be gone as well."

"No, I'm obviously still here, but I let them take off because we worked through lunch and got a lot done today, and we have a big day tomorrow. So I thought it would be nice for them to quit a little early."

"Well, I'm glad you're not gone and I was able to catch you before you left. I won't be in on Wednesday because both of my boys have parts in their class Holiday Plays, and Paul told me to take the day off, so I could see them without the stress of driving into work and back out to their schools twice in the same day."

"That's nice, but what's a Holiday Play?" Bryan asked.

"Oh, that's the politically correct substitute term for the Christmas programs we all took part in when we were their age. I guess around here they first quit calling them Christmas Programs, and changed them to Holiday Celebrations, but because they were still held right before the Christmas break, the ACLU complained they were still primarily commemorations of Christmas. So now we have Holiday Celebrations and Holiday Plays held right before the Thanksgiving vacation.

"Christmas events, when and if they're held in our schools, have become Winter Festivals, and our kids sing Frosty the Snowman rather than Christmas Carols. I'm sure some do-gooder will soon protest Thanksgiving celebrations claiming we're insensitive to the plight of turkeys. My husband was always baffled by the fact that in this great country, the silent majority constantly gets pushed around and loses their rights to the vocal minority of anti-religionists."

"Wow, Charlie, I can see that's a topic you're obviously passionate about. I agree with you and share your husband's inability to understand why most Americans sit by watching our rights be eroded by loud but small minorities. But I'm also baffled by most people's lack of concern about medical fraud."

"Well, anyway, Bryan, I didn't come in here to preach to you. I really wanted to ask you to have Thanksgiving dinner at my house with the boys and my parents. I had planned to ask you last week, so you wouldn't think this was a last-minute invitation, but I missed seeing you on Friday before I left, and you never called the entire weekend, so this is the soonest I've had a chance to talk to you."

"Charlie, that's a really thoughtful and welcome offer, but I don't feel right about crashing your family's holiday meal. I'll be fine. My Thanksgiving plan is to get some work done around the apartment, then have a quiet meal out."

"Bryan, you're not crashing our family dinner. I want you there, and my parents are anxious to meet you. The boys want you there as well. The last thing they told me when they left the house for school this morning was to be sure and invite you over for Thanksgiving."

"Well, if you're positive it's not a problem, then I'd love to come."

"Be there by two. We eat at three or so. The dress is casual and, since I'm supplying the food, we'll expect you to bring the wine. I'll see you tomorrow if we need to cover any other details." And, with that, Charlie said goodnight and left his office.

Bryan's mood changed immediately. He now had something to look forward to over what could have been four days of football games on TV and long days alone in his apartment. But now he'd enjoy at least one of those days with Charlie and her family, and maybe he'd invite them to a movie and dinner on Saturday if they're not busy.

While Bryan was considering his weekend plans, across town in Dr. Mirzoyan's Henderson Clinic, Dr. Gerald Washburn, or Dr. G as the clinic employees called the popular and well-liked chiropractor, was nearing the end of a long and heated conversation with his boss. "Look Dr. Mirzoyan, I'm telling you for the second and last time, I'll no longer treat patients who have nothing wrong with them, and neither will anyone else working under my supervision. I told you this two months ago and you promised to look into the billing procedures, and you've never done anything about my complaints since.

"From now on, the only medical treatments my staff will be providing and billing are the services I believe will actually benefit the patients. The same goes for all the tests, physical therapy, and x-rays you demand we bill, whether we perform the services or not. In this office we're no longer going to be running unnecessary and redundant diagnostic tests or billing for services we don't provide. What you're ordering us to do is fraud, and if you don't know that, I certainly do, and I'm not going to be part of it any longer!"

Dr. Mirzoyan's face was blood red and his fists were clenched when he finally lost his temper and began shouting at Washburn. "Those decisions are not up to you or to any other clinic employee. This is my business and my practice, and I make the policy decisions, not you! If you keep making these demands, you'll be permanently dismissed, just as your predecessor was."

Washburn wouldn't back down. "What did that mean? Is that what happened to Dr. Smith? Did you permanently dismiss him, because no one's heard from him since he disappeared twelve months ago, apparently right before you hired me. I can't believe it took me this long to see what was going on right under my nose.

"Don't ever threaten me again, Dr. Mirzoyan, I know way too much about your shady operations, and I won't hesitate exposing you to the police. I insist on running this practice in an ethical and honest way, and if you don't support that, then we're done."

Mirzoyan realized things were getting out of control and the office staff could undoubtedly hear their argument and everything Washburn was saying. He had to defuse the situation quickly and get out of the office. "We're both too excited to rationally discuss this now Gerald. Let's schedule a meeting after the holiday weekend and come to a workable compromise."

Before Washburn could reply, he hurriedly left the office through the private rear entrance to avoid encountering any of the eavesdropping employees. Mirzoyan realized then he had made a big error hiring Washburn, in spite of the young doctor's ideal test scores and the careful interview he himself had conducted.

This particular bad result was extremely frustrating because after the problem with Dr. Smith, Mirzoyan had commissioned a psychologist friend to develop a test along with a list of interview questions designed to measure what the psychologist termed a 'corruptibility score.' Based on Washburn's test results and responses in the interview, he should have been highly corruptible and therefore a prime candidate for a position with Accident and Injury Health Restoration Clinics.

As he approached his Jaguar XKR convertible he was still fuming with anger and realized he needed to contact Bennett Watson to disclose this serious and unfortunate development. He feared he might have revealed too much by using the words 'permanently dismissed' when he referred to the missing Dr. Smith.

Chapter 16

Las Vegas, NV
November 29th
10:00 AM

The second workday after the long Thanksgiving weekend began with encouraging news for Hampton's investigative team. Gayle's documentation process was complete, and the Justice Department had received notification she was cleared to participate in the investigation. Hampton concluded the speedy approval by Lockheed Martin, the government contractor in charge of the process, might have been due to the urgent status Dixon placed on it, but more likely Gayle, a former FBI agent with existing background checks and security clearances, was an easy candidate to process and certify.

His reasoning was corroborated by the fact the other four MFCB employee names submitted at the same time showed a status of 'In Process' when he checked their applications on the contractor's website.

Nonetheless, he realized bringing in Gayle immediately would allow his side of the investigation to proceed without the delay he feared they might encounter waiting for paperwork. So Hampton placed a call to Gayle's cell and left her a message asking her to call him as soon as possible. Next he phoned Da Silva. "Davee, it's Bryan, I've got some good news I wanted to share. We've received all the clearances and paperwork today allowing Gayle to begin work with us immediately."

"Hey, Bryan, that is great news. Can I call you back later and you can fill me in on the details? I picked up your call in the middle of a staff meeting in case it was something urgent."

"No problem, we can even talk tomorrow if today's bad. I just wanted you to hear the news from me because I've got a call in to Gayle and thought you should know before I spoke with her."

The last few days had been a welcome relief from the hectic pace Hampton had been keeping for several weeks. He'd spent most of the Wednesday before Thanksgiving organizing his office and left work around three in the afternoon to do some grocery shopping. As he looked back on the holiday weekend, Thanksgiving Day had been one of the best days he could remember for many years. Charlie's parents proved to be warm and enjoyable co-hosts for the day, and while Charlie and her mother prepared the meal, her father had shared enlightening information about his daughter and the difficulties she dealt with after her husband was killed in Afghanistan, information Bryan might never have learned directly from her.

He gained even more respect for Charlie as her parents also shared insightful stories about her high school and college accomplishments during dinner conversations and later in the day as they talked and watched football on TV. The more time he spent with her family, the more he saw how they influenced, supported, and strengthened one another.

As the day wound down, Bryan decided to head back to his apartment around nine, and Charlie walked him to the door. "Thanks for spending the holiday with my family, Bryan. We all enjoyed having you here, and I hope you weren't overwhelmed with all the talk and commotion."

"I had a great day, Charlie, and I loved meeting your parents and spending the day with the boys. The food was amazing, but I ate too much. I'll need to run three times my normal distance in the morning. Good night, and thanks again."

"Call me tomorrow sometime if you want to, Bryan, and let's see if we can get together."

Oddly, when he turned to leave, an overwhelming realization of loneliness began to creep over him as he realized the temporary gratification of great food and terrific company was being overrun by the emotional emptiness that had become his life. With each step he took away from her door he felt more isolated and alone. His only comfort had come from Charlie's parting suggestion to call her sometime the next day.

As it turned out Friday ended up being a day of mixed activities for Hampton. He spent the early morning hours detailing plans for the following week's investigative efforts, then later weaved his way through the apartment complex to the Durango Fitness Center. After a rigorous workout, he returned home, checked his email and voicemail, and found no messages so he decided to shower, then call Charlie. The solitary privacy and steamy confines of a shower had long been the one place where Bryan was able to think clearly and reason through any problem or decision pressing on him.

Friday's shower, however, proved to be more of a discovery and assessment session than anything else. The reality that neither of his daughters emailed or called him on Thanksgiving, a holiday their family had always celebrated and enjoyed together, triggered some long overdue soul-searching he usually tried to avoid. Yesterday's experience with Charlie's family reminded him of the missing dimension in his life that at one time provided the balance and clarity he now realized was so essential to genuine happiness. The shower turned cold before he could plan a complete strategy, but he managed to reason through a few initial steps he would take to begin rebuilding the relationships he hoped to reestablish with his children.

By four that afternoon, Bryan had spoken with both of his daughters. Each conversation began awkwardly, but eventually their dialog moved a little closer to the familiar ease they once shared when their father-daughter chats were frequent and open. Recalling the two conversations, Bryan was grateful both girls, now adults with their own families, actually preferred to look forward to better days, rather than dwelling on any of his past parental failures and shortcomings.

His call to Charlie, however, had been a disappointment in one respect, but positive in another. "Bryan, I'm beat from shopping all day and, if you don't mind, I'd rather we did something tomorrow and skip tonight."

Because Bryan had hoped for a Saturday outing as well, he already had a partial plan for the day and quickly suggested it. "That's fine, Charlie. I'll bet after all the work you did on Thanksgiving, then shopping today, you're probably exhausted. How about we take the boys to an early movie tomorrow, then the four of us go to dinner? We can let them pick the movie and you can choose the restaurant."

Charlie loved his idea and told Bryan, "The boys have been bugging me to see the new Muppet movie if that's something you wouldn't mind watching. I already know there's a five-ten showing at the same theatre we went to last week."

Bryan had no clue about the Muppet movie, but faked it, probably unsuccessfully. "Sure, Charlie, works for me, if that's what they want to see. I'll go online and get the tickets tonight. How about a restaurant? Maybe we should get reservations because it'll be around seven when we're out of the movie, and that's a busy time."

"I'll make the reservations, Bryan. I know exactly where I want to go and it'll be my surprise for you."

The persistent sound of the office phone returned Bryan's attention to the reality of Tuesday morning and the Watson case. Before he pressed the speaker button, he revisited Saturday night's activities with a final thought. The movie was almost tolerable, the dinner was excellent, and the company was amazing, then he pressed the button and answered, "Bryan Hampton!"

"Bryan, this is Gayle Baker returning your call. What can I do for you?"

"Gayle, thanks for getting back to me so soon. I wanted to let you know all your paperwork has been processed, and you've been cleared to participate in our investigation. I talked briefly to Da Silva a little while ago, so he knows the good news as well. I was wondering if there was any chance you could meet with us today so we can get started."

"To say I'm amazed by that news would be an understatement. Someone must have done something to speed things up because I wasn't expecting to hear anything until next week. Da Silva has already emailed me, obviously after you called him, and he's directed me to clear my calendar and do everything I can to assist your team with the investigation. Unfortunately, I know little to nothing about your case, so it's hard to assess how much help I can be and exactly what MFCB resources will be needed. But I have my orders, so if you're still set on this afternoon, I'll arrange to be there."

"That's good news. If you can arrive by one, first I'll bring you up to date on the background and basics of the case and how we've initially divided up the investigative tasks. Then I thought we could meet with the other two agents on our team, so you can get to know them. During those discussions, I'd like you to explain the data you have, how it's organized, and how you think we can use that information and any other MFCB resources or staff to advance our investigation. Then, if we still have time today, the two of us need to get specific about the next steps you think we should take to leverage your database and analytic capabilities."

"That's an aggressive schedule for a single afternoon, Agent Hampton. I think you're minimizing the complexities involved here. First, as you've already noted, you and your team will need to understand our data, how it's interpreted, and finally the different ways in which it can be analyzed and used to identify abusive and fraudulent providers and claims. Covering all that in an hour or two is overly ambitious, but we can try. I'll be there by one and we can start, but I'm not optimistic about meeting your schedule."

"Agent Baker, let's get something clear at the outset. We value your participation in this trial project, but at the same time I think Mr. Dixon was quite clear the DOJ is responsible for the decisions and outcomes, as well as the pace of the work. I've been assigned to lead the investigation, and for the duration of our work together I'll expect you to interpret my requests and suggestions as your directives. If you're unclear on any of that, or if you feel you'll be unable to take directions from me or my team so we can achieve the goals we set, then we might have a problem. We'll expect you at one."

Gayle was silent for several seconds and decided at that point any rebuttal to Hampton's assertion of his leadership authority was a no-win situation for her, so she simply responded by saying, "See you at one." But at that moment she was actually thinking, this guy is a capricious jerk and I'm not sure I can even deal with him. Hopefully he's just having a bad day.

When Gayle arrived for their afternoon meetings, the receptionist led her to a large conference room where Bryan sat with two other men and Charlie, whom she recognized as Paul Dixon's assistant she'd met during her previous visit. Gayle was immediately thrown off balance because she was expecting to first meet with Hampton in the private session he described earlier that morning. Her hope was during their time together, she could better assess his unpredictable temperament while trying to assert some of her own ground rules. Her agitation was compounded when she realized she was about to meet the two agents they'd be working with, while still struggling with the distraction of trying to recall the name of Dixon's assistant, a woman with a man's name, she thought, while searching her memory in vain.

Bryan stood to greet her, then proceeded with introductions, "Gayle, welcome to our offices. I want you to meet Agent Abe Slater and Agent Eli Watson, and, of course, you already know Charlie Cruz, paralegal and special assistant to our investigative team on loan from Mr. Dixon."

It was a quick sequence of three names she needed to remember, but she relaxed slightly after Charlie greeted her by flashing a warm smile, then invited her to help herself to a beverage from the nearby credenza before taking a seat at the conference table. Opting for water and, while still standing, she removed four business cards from her briefcase and distributed one to each member of the group. All four reciprocated by returning one of their own. Now she had names and contact information, and her anxiety dropped another notch.

She could tell Bryan wasn't going to waste any time with social pleasantries as he immediately began the session and explained, "After your warning concerning the complexity of the information you need to share with us, I revamped the attendee list, but left the agenda the same as we discussed this morning. As I originally explained, the first order of business will be an overview of the case and the suspects. I'll lead that discussion, with Abe and Eli adding any relevant or important details I fail to mention.

"After that, we can talk about how we propose to pursue the investigation. Then I've asked Abe, Eli, and Charlie to each spend a few minutes highlighting their professional experience and backgrounds with the Agency, after which I'd like to invite you to give an overview of your career. Then we'll break for fifteen minutes and resume with your description and explanation of the MFCB data and any other resources you have that are relevant and could benefit us in this investigation.

"A central focus here is we're looking at a case which should be an ideal fit for your organization's tools and data. This is a medical fraud case, but one in which the suspects are defrauding mostly property and casualty carriers and only some health care insurers. As I understand, the MFCB database includes a large amount of property and casualty medical bill data, so this should be your sweet spot and provide both our organizations with the optimal opportunity to understand its benefits. Incidentally, throughout our discussions, let's cover questions as they arise rather than leaving them for the end of each presentation."

At the Four Season's breakfast meeting, Gayle had decided Hampton was an awkward but affable individual who wasn't good at compromise. After her phone call with him a few hours ago, and after listening to his presentation so far, if pressed, she would describe him as an uptight, inflexible, and insecure jerk.

With his preamble over, Bryan spent nearly an hour describing the activities of the alleged fraud scheme and identifying the principal participants and structure of the organization behind it. He also shared estimates of the monetary losses involved, based on the assumed three-year duration of the well-organized operation. Abe and Eli volunteered facts and details when Bryan either failed to mention them or misstated a name or other minor fact.

By prior arrangement, when Bryan signaled Charlie, she documented information new to him or statements by the other participants he believed were critical details. Once the case had been summarized, Bryan presented an abridged version of proposed tactics for obtaining more specific details about the clinic operations; for establishing clear links between Watson's referral machine and Dr. Mirzoyan's clinics; and for identifying one or more employees with a good understanding of the operation who could be pressured into serving up their employer and fellow workers to avoid jail time themselves.

Abe was then asked to explain the tentative plan to send healthy undercover agents posing as injured victims into each of the four clinics. Their objective would be to gather first-hand information specific to the diagnostic procedures and other services the agents actually received, then compare those facts to the bills the clinics submitted to insurers for those same visits.

Gayle had remained quiet for the entire hour. She hadn't asked any questions nor made any comments because her mind was racing far ahead of Bryan's descriptions and explanations about the case and how they proposed to better understand and prove it. Gayle was trying to decide how best to play her hand, because she already knew a great deal more about Mirzoyan's operations than Hampton's team had even come close to discovering to that point.

Several months ago, MFCB investigators identified the suspect billing patterns Hampton was discussing, and they had already verified links between the clinics and Watson's law firm, along with other far reaching and enlightening details about this case. She needed some time to think through exactly what she'd already been told and what additional information the team might have unearthed since she was last updated on the case. She decided she needed to consult with Da Silva on how best to disclose any information the MFCB had already learned before she said anything to the DOJ team. She heard Hampton speak her name summoning her away from her thoughts and back into the meeting. "I'm sorry, Agent Hampton, what did you ask?"

"I was wondering if you had any questions before each of you discuss your backgrounds, experience, and credentials?"

"No, I'm following everything I've heard, so we can move on." Not a lie, she thought, because she had qualified her answer by claiming to understand only what she heard, which wasn't much for the last half hour.

With her attention again on Hampton, she heard him ask Abe to lead off the career highlight reel presentations he requested each of them to share, reminding them Eli and Charlie would follow. "Since we're already running long, after

Charlie finishes her part, we'll take a quick break, then Gayle will pick up after we return," Hampton told them.

Sadly, Gayle heard little of what was said during the next hour. Instead, her attention, aided by her laptop, which was currently connected to the MFCB VPN, was focused on reexamining a case in her company's files. She was reviewing the current summary and timeline of the MFCB's investigations, discoveries, facts, and assumptions concerning the very case Bryan had just introduced. She began with the chronologic story line; how the case was initially exposed and developed even before she joined the MFCB; what was subsequently learned and discovered; then ended with a careful review of the summary document created by the MFCB investigators. In one of the first meetings Gayle attended after joining the MFCB the document had been presented to their leadership during a confidential briefing on the case.

She distinctly recalled the analytic team warning the leaders that the billing anomalies detected in some Las Vegas chiropractic clinics were some of the highest scoring patterns of fraudulent billing discovered in the entire MFCB database. Beginning with the first scoring analysis received from BeatMedFraud.com, and every week since, four chiropractors in Las Vegas had been on the top ten most suspect providers list.

However, it took MFCB analysts over six months to determine all four clinics were owned by one person, Dr. Mirzoyan. Ownership of medical facilities wasn't information required for submitting a claim nor was that information tracked by any claims processing system. Claims were traditionally submitted, processed, and analyzed using the identity of the treating provider, irrespective of who owned the clinic where the work was done. Associating the four clinics with a single proprietor was done on the Internet by Lisa Taylor, an MFCB investigator, using the Google search engine.

Lisa was chasing down more information on one of the suspected chiropractors when she noted the doctor's affiliation with the Accident and Injury Health Restoration Clinic. Two days later she was performing a similar search on another suspected chiropractor from Las Vegas and discovered that he, too, was affiliated with a clinic by the same name, but with a different address. Further web browsing identified a total of four clinic locations with that same name in the Las Vegas area.

Lisa's next step was to place a routine phone call to each of the four clinics and request an appointment. Her script was generally the same on each call. "I'd like to make an appointment to see Dr. Abenaz," a name she made up following an exhaustive search of licensed providers in Clark County, which revealed no one by that name practiced anywhere near Las Vegas. "Oh, you don't have a doctor by that name? Can you tell me the names of the doctors who do work in your office? Maybe I just misunderstood my friend." At that point Taylor discovered each clinic gave two names, the first one being the actual working doctor in that location, while the second name was always Dr. Ari Mirzoyan.

A credible and strong link to Watson wasn't so easily established. Making that connection required a more confidential and comprehensive accident claims data repository exclusively maintained and hosted by only one organization in the entire country, All Risk Analytics. FelonFinder, the flagship solution offered by All Risk Analytics, was a comprehensive system for improving claims processing accuracy and detecting fraudulent claims. The system provided users with access to all recorded accident claims information and allowed them to data mine by conducting queries and research on all reported claims. The database was all-inclusive and was comprised of over ten years of property and casualty claims history.

All Risk Analytics clients received reports on any of their claims with unusual patterns or any other questionable information. Each client could then investigate these dubious and suspect accident claims. Also, the Internet interface enabled users to perform searches that could focus on a single data element or a specified string of data elements as long as the information was present in the millions of claims residing in the unique database.

One of the data segments or grouping of data elements included in FelonSearch contained the name, address, and telephone number of the claimant's attorney. The MFCB was a client of All Risk Analytics, and Jon Metcalf was the analyst who used FelonSearch every day. For several weeks Jon had been conducting regional investigations of auto accident cases with high medical costs, and once he began reviewing cases in Clark County, NV he uncovered a link between ninety percent of the cases he was studying and two established attorneys. The data showed both attorneys shared the same phone number and address, and eventually he established they were both employees of Bennett Watson's law firm.

Either dumb luck or wise management strategy accounted for the next major breakthrough on the case two weeks later. Monthly case presentation and review sessions allowed analysts and investigators to discuss their cases and brainstorm new ideas with their peers about how to advance stalled investigations. When Jon Metcalf presented his discovery regarding the Las Vegas cases and divulged the connection between ninety percent of them and Watson's law firm, Lisa

Taylor had looked up from her iPad browser and asked, "Jon, can you repeat the attorney's name please?"

After hearing Metcalf repeat Watson's name, Lisa thought, who says you can't multi-task? But to the group, she said nothing more. However, immediately after the meeting she approached Metcalf with an idea. By the end of the following week, after multiple queries of the FelonSearch database and further interrogations of the MFCB medical bill database, Jon and Lisa had established a definitive link. They could now show that over the past three years, over eighty-five percent of injured claimants treated at Dr. Ari Mirzoyan's four clinics were represented by an attorney employed by the Watson law firm or by Bennett Watson himself. In the report they prepared and sent to their superiors they had summarized their findings and deductions and provided a series of bulleted findings and facts.

Gayle scanned the first paragraph of the summary and reviewed Jon and Lisa's list of findings; "Based upon our analysis of comprehensive data, which includes three years of aggregated paid medical bills from all four Accident and Injury Health Restoration Clinics in Las Vegas, sourced from the MFCB database, and the associated claims information sourced from the All Risk Analytics FelonSearch database, the following facts have been validated and are indicative of fraudulent activity:"

Gayle noted over twenty different items on the report that she decided could be conceptualized and summarized more easily in paragraph form. She constructed it in her mind, believing it might fall to her to communicative those findings to this group.

The data showed excessively high numbers of suspect medical bills were being submitted by Mirzoyan's clinics. Even a higher percentage of claims scored as likely fraudulent were being handled by Watson's law firm.

The clinic's high fraud scores could be easily summarized; the clinics billed too many services and tests; charged too much for what they did; treated the patients longer than any other provider; and violated every possible billing rule and guideline in the book.

As for the high fraud scores nearly all of Watson's claims earned, the most highly suspect issues revolved around his shady clientele and the frequency of their auto accidents and workplace injuries. Watson's cases also had highly suspicious vendor relationships and associations.

Gayle decided the report's final paragraph said it all. The bottom line was the statistical interrelationships between Watson's law firm and Mirzoyan's clinics were off the charts, and clearly this was a fraud scheme that had been in operation for over three years. The recommendations encouraged investigators to look for other participants and extensions of currently identified problems, because without a doubt they existed.

About midway through Charlie's description of her training and background with the DOJ, Gayle shut down her connection, closed her laptop, and reengaged with the group. For the time being she had completed her hurried review of the MFCB team's assembled facts and theories. The question she needed an answer to was when she should reveal what the MFCB team already knew and in how much detail. The answers to those questions, she realized, needed to come from Da Silva.

Charlie finished her presentation by commenting, "I want each of you to know how much I admire and respect our new boss Paul Dixon and how fair and caring he's been to all of us. I look forward to working with all of you and helping you in this investigation in any way I can."

Hampton then thanked her and the two agents for their informative and efficient reports, and announced a twenty-minute break, reminding Gayle she had the floor when they returned.

As the group prepared to leave the room, Gayle asked Charlie, "Is there a private space I could use to make an important call?"

Charlie immediately and graciously accommodated her request, taking her to a small conference room where Gayle used her cell phone and amazingly reached Da Silva on the second ring. After quickly recounting the specifics of the case Hampton had just outlined, the two MFCB agents spent the next fifteen minutes planning how best to leverage the advantage of the head start the MFCB already had on the investigation. Since Dixon declared the ground rules, Gayle and Da Silva had felt their organization and their unique data have undeservedly been relegated to a runner-up, back seat role to the DOJ team.

"We have a strategic opportunity to gain a more equal role in the leadership of this investigation, Gayle, and we're going to use it," Da Silva declared. "Let's not let the cat out of the bag today until we've thought this through more, but I have an idea. I want you to use the rest of the day lecturing about the data and the analytics in general, then suggest the group reconvene in our offices in the morning for a demonstration. I'll fly there tonight. We'll have a show-and-tell with them tomorrow, using the actual information we've compiled on

Hampton's case. We'll blow them away. Then I'll use the credibility our analysis has earned us as leverage to negotiate a more equal role in our partnership as we move forward."

"I was sure you'd see this exactly the way I did. I'm glad I was able to reach you so I would know how you wanted me to manage this opportunity," Gayle answered. "The twenty-minute break is nearly over and I need to get back to our meeting. Any other instructions?"

"Not for now, but we've got a long night of work to put this together by morning. Call your team as soon as possible and get them to update and re-skin the presentation they gave internally on this case. Tell them we'll need to see it before the meeting with Hampton's group in the morning, and find out how soon they'll be ready for a dry run. Then talk to me or leave me a voicemail so I'll know when to meet with all of you. One more thing, Gayle; I want you to do everything you can to get Paul Dixon in the meeting at our offices tomorrow. I want him to see our presentation, not just hear about it."

Bryan was the last member of the group to return to the meeting, and as soon as he was seated, he invited Gayle to proceed. She had hurriedly prepared a Power Point presentation including several handouts that very morning describing the medical bill database in great detail. She proceeded slowly over the next two hours, detailing every aspect of the unique MFCB resource.

She explained, "This venture required an initial two million dollar investment and over three years of intensive effort to bring it to its current state of development. The first fifteen months were devoted to just securing permission and cooperation from the insurers to provide digital records of their medical claims. After authorizations were granted, the data needed to be collected and normalized, then aggregated and stored in a manageable data warehouse.

"The data warehouse must be frequently updated by regularly scheduled imports of new claims. And finally the data must undergo constant analysis using the latest and most advanced software tools and technologies available, all designed and created to identify suspect medical claims, and the abusive and fraudulent medical providers who submit them."

Gayle then explained, "The funding, data hosting, and analytic competences required for this project were beyond the scope and capabilities of the MFCB, and as a result, a partnership was established with Dr. Josif Stolic's company, BeatMedFraud.com, a vendor of health care fraud prevention and detection services. I understand you've already been briefed about Dr. Stolic and his company, so I won't bother explaining anymore about what they do."

Gayle then proceeded to discuss in painful and excruciating detail each piece of information required for the analysis of a medical claim. She explained the meaning and use of each field of data sent by the insurers to the MFCB database. As Da Silva directed, she paced her presentation so that it occupied the remainder of the workday.

At four fifty-five, she dropped her first bomb. "Agent Hampton, now that you all have a thorough understanding of the contents of our database, how we created it, and how we keep it updated, I'd like to propose we reconvene at the MFCB offices tomorrow morning to continue our discussions. I suggest this because we can actually show your team our reports and other analytics, including the latest link analysis tools I think all of you will better appreciate and understand, if you can view them dynamically in operation on our systems."

"Perhaps we can hold that meeting in another few days, Gayle, but I'd prefer to first spend a session or two outlining how we might be able to apply the database and the software you use to advance the investigation of our case we outlined today. I'd prefer to focus on a real case rather than spending time viewing hypothetical applications of your technology and data."

"Bryan, Mr. Da Silva is taking a red-eye flight to Las Vegas tonight. He'll be in our offices by nine-thirty in the morning and has asked me to invite all of you, and Mr. Dixon if possible, to be there at ten. We'll demonstrate our capabilities precisely in the way you just specified. I think you'll see it will be unnecessary to spend any sessions outlining ways to use our data and tools to advance the Watson case, because it's already been done.

"I want to thank you all for an informative and productive day. Now if you'll excuse me, I need to go back to my office to make preparations for our session in the morning. Charlie, if you could confirm Mr. Dixon's availability for tomorrow's meeting even as late as nine AM, it would be helpful and much appreciated. Thank you all again, and I'll plan to see you tomorrow. I know you're going to be surprised and possibly amazed by what we're going to show you." And with that, Gayle left the room and, soon afterwards, the building.

Several seconds after the door closed, four perplexed DOJ employees sat looking at each other wondering what had just happened, and what was going to happen the next day. Charlie was the first to speak. "Boys, to quote my kids' favorite Ghost Busters phrase, somehow I think we're going to get slimed."

Chapter 17

Las Vegas, NV
November 30th
10:00 AM

Dixon, Hampton, Abe, Eli, and Charlie arrived at the offices of the MFCB at exactly ten. They were promptly escorted to a conference area set up like a classroom, dominated by a giant video projection screen at the front of the room. Da Silva and Gayle, along with two analysts introduced as Jon Metcalf and Lisa Taylor, were already standing by the door waiting to greet them. Three other staffers were also present, but ignored. Two were IT types, futzing with the projector and laptop, and the third was a woman arranging bagels, cream cheese, and pots of coffee. Soon the three unnamed workers silently slipped away, their work done, at least until the first AV mishap or empty coffee pot raised its ugly head.

Da Silva acted as the host, thanked Dixon excessively for finding the time in his busy schedule to participate in the morning's meetings, then welcomed the remainder of the group with overdone enthusiasm.

Hampton's antenna was immediately in the alert mode warning him of an ambush he felt was coming, but couldn't quite yet grasp. He wanted to try and maintain control of the meeting, so he decided to go on offense. "Davee, we want to welcome you back to Las Vegas and hope you're not too exhausted from your overnight flight. We're all anxious to know why you decided to make this unplanned trip on such short notice."

"I'm glad you asked, Bryan, because I want to be crystal clear about why I felt it was important for me to get here as soon as possible. When Gayle heard you introduce the basics of the investigation we'll be working on together, she realized it was critical for us to get with you immediately and share what we currently know and suspect as a result of the work our staff had already put into this case."

After hearing Da Silva's opening comments Abe and Eli glanced quickly at Hampton with surprised and puzzled expressions. Hampton looked at Dixon, both men already appeared troubled by what they had just heard. No one ventured a question at that point, but clearly many remained unspoken.

Da Silva had noticed the silent exchanges between members of Hampton's team. Realizing he had already accomplished one of his goals, he continued, "We've actually been looking at various parts of this scheme for months, but it wasn't until recently that Jon and Lisa, the analysts Gayle asked to join us this morning, made some startling connections. Their findings have allowed us to establish definitive links between a series of facts that, until recently, seemed unconnected.

"Because we now know so much, we felt we had a unique opportunity to demonstrate how, by using of our database and analytics, we can leverage limited information and evidence, along with some reasonable assumptions, and begin to construct a data supported case. We've found, once we can factually validate the key aspects or attributes of a fraud scheme, it's then possible to infer the associated functions required to support that central process. Said another way, once we know what they're doing, we have a good idea who and what they need to keep it going.

"In this particular case we know the basic instrument of the fraud is a false claim and the associated medical bills. We know the bills are being created by all four of Mirzoyan's clinics. We also know an unreasonably high percentage of the clinics' injured patients are represented by attorneys working for Bennett Watson.

"We're just now beginning to understand and identify all the procedures and individuals required to supply the allegedly injured patients to the clinics, and to facilitate the creation of the claims they produced. At this point, we can say it's highly probable there's a link between the activities of the clinics and Watson's law firm." Da Silva paused, noticing Dixon seemed to have a comment or question.

****

Paul Dixon seized the opportunity Da Silva had given him and interjected himself into what was starting to feel too much like a private conversation between Da Silva and Hampton by summarizing the facts Da Silva had just shared with the group. "Mr. Da Silva, are you telling us the MFCB has already identified specific suspicious billing activities of the Accident and Injury Health Restoration Clinics, which we call *RACHI* for short, and that you've already identified and proven a relationship between Bennett Watson and Ari Mirzoyan, the owner of the clinics?"

With too much smugness, Dixon thought, Da Silva answered, "Proven a connection is likely an overstatement, but the automobile insurance data clearly reveals an aberrantly high statistical relationship between patients treated at the Mirzoyan clinics and those who are also clients represented by Watson's firm.

"We've looked at norms for this metric and the average percentage of individual auto accident claimants who share the same doctor and attorney is approximately twenty-one percent. In the case of Mirzoyan and Watson, the percentage is eighty-six percent. Statistically, that's over four times the relationship we would expect based on actual data, and over three standard deviations above what normally occurs.

"To an analyst, when any value is off by three or more standard deviations from the norm, you assume you need to look into the cause of that aberration. It's a red flag and you can't ignore it. Consequently, we've started to more closely examine all claims where Watson lawyers and Mirzoyan doctors are linked to the claimants in any way."

Da Silva asked for question and getting none, continued, "Before we begin to explain how our medical bill data allowed us to make progress on this case, I want to give one more example of how targeting a specific subset of claims has revealed a third organization statistically linked to what we're now convinced is a well-organized fraud ring.

"We started by isolating the data where Mirzoyan and Watson are linked to the claimant, and as I said, that's over eighty-six percent of the auto accident patients the *RACHI* clinics treat, and we discovered one hundred percent of the time Tow4Savings was the towing company that removed the car from the scene of the accident. What we also noted is that their charges are consistently high.

"So we did an analysis of average towing and storage charges in Clark County, really the greater Las Vegas area, and discovered Tow4Savings charges were routinely around two and a half times higher than the average fees charged by other towing companies. The next thing we wanted to find out was who really owned Tow4Savings, because the entity listed in the public records is a dead end, and we haven't been able to link it to either of our prime suspects. We know the DOJ can get to the real ownership roster, and that's why I mentioned this as another area where our mutual strengths can be of real benefit."

Da Silva sensed a change in Hampton's team as he shared the MFCB data and breakthroughs. Skepticism was being overtaken by optimism and excitement. The DOJ team all seemed anxious to hear more. There was no indication Hampton or Dixon were in any way defensive about the progress Da Silva's team had already made on the case or skeptical about the information the MFCB had uncovered. In fact, the way Da Silva read his audience, they seemed as pleased as if they just discovered they were holding a winning lottery ticket. And they should be ecstatic, Da Silva thought, as he looked at his notes, because we picked the winning numbers, bought the ticket, and now we're giving it to them.

Dixon listened as Bryan tried to get the meeting back on course by ending the posturing exercise currently underway and directing a specific question to Da Silva. "Davee, could we get back to the basics of why we're here this morning? We need to get a comprehensive understanding of the data that yielded the facts and the conclusions you just presented. We're anxious to understand how you've learned what you know and how the medical claims database has been the key to your progress. I believe we're all understandably impressed with what you've told us so far, and we're eager to have you demonstrate and explain what Gayle promised we'd see and hear by coming here today."

Dixon added his urging to return to a discussion of the data, stating, "Davee, I agree with Bryan. We're thirty minutes into our meeting, and I have another appointment at one this afternoon that couldn't be rescheduled. If we can get down to detailed explanations and discussions about your data, I'd welcome it. I need to leave by twelve-thirty, and if you're agreeable, I think you and Bryan and I should spend about fifteen minutes together in private before I head out."

Dixon understood what other members of his team would likely soon realize if they hadn't already. Da Silva's primary motivation for flying to town on such short notice, and for staging today's session in the manner he had, was done for a clear purpose. By preceding the formal discussion of their database with a convincing presentation of facts already gleaned from their data, then revealing how those facts identified likely associations with other suspects, the MFCB could legitimately now assert a more co-equal role in leading the joint task force.

In the next ninety minutes, if their data and analysis proved to be as useful as the MFCB team claimed, some organizational accommodation would need to be made. Dixon was fairly certain Da Silva wanted more recognition, as well as additional authority over the management of the investigations they were jointly undertaking. He knew from years of politics that good relationships are based on trust and wins for both partners. And if Da Silva's narrative was supported by sound analysis and detailed data, then the MFCB certainly merits more respect and additional participation in the decision-making process.

Everyone in the room agreed with Dixon's desire to move forward, so Da Silva turned the discussion over to Gayle. The lights were dimmed and the projector display became visible showing a spreadsheet-like document entitled Medical Bill Database Record Layout with a subheading of CONFIDENTIAL AND PROPRIETARY MFCB & BEATMEDICALFRAUD.COM. After explaining the column headings, Baker began by describing each row in the layout and clarifying why each insurer was required to submit that segment of information.

She then told how that information was used by the analysts. "The first data element is called Bill ID, which is the insurance carrier's assigned identification number for that bill. The second data element is called Row Number, which is the number of the row for each line item on a unique bill. The third data element is Claim ID, which is the insurance carrier's assigned identification number for the claim that each bill is associated with. All three of these pieces of information are key to linking bills to claims and line items to a unique bill."

Gayle paused and looked at the DOJ team to stress a fact. "There's an important point of clarification here that's sometimes confusing for investigators or medical personnel not familiar with the property and casualty nomenclature. In health care, a claim, in the most simplistic terms, is a form the provider submits to request payment from an insurance company for services rendered to a patient covered by that company.

"But in P&C language, a claim has a different and broader definition. A P&C claim is the comprehensive demand for compensation for a loss covered by an insurance policy purchased to protect the insured from that loss. For example, if you have auto insurance and you crash your car into a tree, damaging the car as well as causing multiple injuries to yourself, you'll file a claim with your insurance company.

"One of the components to that claim will be the car repairs by the auto body shop, another might be the towing charges to transport the car to the repair shop, and there will also be costs associated with your injuries. There could be ambulance charges, hospital charges, physician charges, surgeon charges, anesthesia charges, physical therapy charges, all of which are lumped into the category of medical costs.

"The charges for those medical services will be submitted the same way a medical provider submits charges for health care services, but this transaction on the P&C side will be called a bill, not a claim. So to be clear a medical bill in the P&C world is a component of the overall claim. So when we speak of bills, we're really referring to what the health care world calls a claim. I hope I've made that clear, but are there any questions so far?"

No one raised their hand or asked any questions, so Gayle continued, "The next data element is the Date of Loss, which is the date of the accident or the injury if it's a worker's compensation claim. The next data element is--."

Gayle's presentation lasted over an hour. By then she had reviewed each of the nearly one hundred data elements or fields of information and answered a host of questions from the agents along the way. Next she explained what she stressed was the most complex and difficult part of creating a large data base comprised of information from multiple sources and told why that process was the key to successfully aggregating and using health care data. She called the process normalization, emphasizing the record layout she had presented was the end product that resulted after experts had interpreted and translated data from over thirty companies into one universal format.

"Also each contributing organization can have different field names, different structures, and unique formats for storing their own information, so it's necessary to map fields from each company's data into the universal format and layout I just presented. We also need to deal with situation where multiple fields from one company, which must be combined into a single field, while in other cases a single field needs to be split into several separate fields.

"I could give you more examples, but I'll conclude by saying Dr. Stolic's staff is incredibly skilled at mapping and translating the data coming in from all the carriers and insurers. It's taken months of effort to ensure the integrity of the database we've created. Knowing the foundation our analytics rely on is irreproachable, gives us great confidence in the anomalies and fraud we detect, report, and investigate."

Once Gayle finished, Da Silva re-introduced Jon Metcalf and Lisa Taylor, explaining they would take the group through a brief tour of what is known about Mirzoyan's clinics and his suspected links to Bennett Watson. Lisa began, "The medical analysts at BeatMedFraud.com have repeatedly identified all four of the chiropractor's working in Mirzoyan's clinics as extreme outliers for their billing tactics. They're not particular either; they exploit nearly every billing abuse we've ever detected anywhere in our data.

"Let me just highlight some of their abuses starting with the practice of up-coding. Ninety percent of the office visits from the Mirzoyan clinics are billed at the highest and most complex level, as contrasted to all the other chiropractors in Nevada who bill the most complex office visit for only five percent of patient appointments." Lisa then went on to recite an entire laundry list of the clinics' identified billing irregularities, emphasizing that every bill for every patient featured gross overcharging, excessive diagnostic testing, and services rendered that had no proven therapeutic value for the medical conditions being treated.

At the conclusion of her discussion of the clinics' billing practices, Lisa summarized, "Every bill from each of the chiropractors from all four clinics in question is identical when viewed from the perspective of a specific injury. If someone has a back injury, no matter which of the four clinics they're treated in, the bill will have the same tests, the same x-rays, the same series of chiropractic services, the same number of visits, the same list of secondary diagnosis codes, and the same charges.

"What I can also tell you is that the medical documentation Dr. Stolic's nurses have reviewed is identical, irrespective of which doctor supposedly wrote it. There's never the slightest variation in the wording or the punctuation; we call it CCC, or cookie-cutter crap. The sad thing is it took us months to realize these four chiropractors were all working in clinics owned by the same individual, whom we all now know is also a chiropractor." Lisa then detailed how she was able to link all the clinics to Ari Mirzoyan by simply using the Internet and a telephone. After fielding a few questions she told them Jon Metcalf would next explain the work he was involved in.

Jon Metcalf began by telling them he'd been involved in an entirely different analysis focused on high-cost auto accident claims when he discovered an interesting connection. "While analyzing the cost analysis by region, I discovered high medical costs were the primary driver of the expensive claims, and this correlation was especially true in Nevada. During a monthly staff meeting I was telling our analysts I could see a connection between ninety percent of the auto claims with high medical costs in southern Nevada, and two attorneys from the same law firm, a firm I discovered was owned by Bennett Watson. After the meeting, Lisa talked to me and suggested the two of us should look more closely at the providers who submitted the medical bills, linked to high cost auto claims."

Jon graciously credited Lisa for approaching him with the idea of linking the attorneys he had identified to medical bills from certain providers, but then his ego got the better of him. "Lisa's theory was insightful, but it could only have been advanced after there was proof that high cost auto claims in Nevada were being driven by the medical bill component, and that those claims were linked to two attorneys employed by Bennett Watson.

"It required considerable effort and expertise with another system and data source to make those key determinations. I'm the primary researcher who uses the FelonSearch application to do those types of studies and research. Once we isolated all the cases from the four clinics into a separate data cube, we were able to link almost all those bills to claims in the FelonSearch database. We determined over eighty-six percent of the claimants treated at Mirzoyan's clinics were represented by attorneys working in Watson's firm. If the FelonSearch claims data had more complete information about the claimant's attorneys, we're certain the percentage would be even higher.

"Another telling fact we also discovered was when Watson's attorneys represented the claimants, over ninety percent of their claims were scored as highly suspect by FelonSearch, meaning they were likely fraudulent." Jon then listed the reasons why the system had scored the claims as suspect, after which he summarized the MFCB conclusions and recommendations for next steps.

It was those conclusions the group would next discuss in detail. But first Bryan restated what he'd just heard then followed-up with questions. "So, Jon, without any reservations are you telling us the data proves there's a long-standing fraud scheme involving five categories of documented fraudulent billing practices and at least ten different identifiable abuses?"

Jon paused to count the specific violations he'd discussed, then said, "That's what I'm telling you our investigative team has determined based upon our review and analysis of the data and the documentation so far."

"Are you also telling us the data you have clearly indicates the number of claimants shared by Mirzoyan's clinics and the attorneys working for Bennett Watson is so disproportionately high that statistically it can't be a coincidence, and that it establishes an unlikely and possibly illegal connection between the two businesses?"

Gayle jumped in before Jon could answer. "What we're saying is we've never seen eighty-six percent of a medical practice's auto claimants represented by a single law firm. We're not saying it proves an illegal relationship exists, only that it's suspect and warrants further investigation."

"What's the normal or average percentage of claimants shared between a medical practice and a single law firm?" Dixon asked.

Gayle looked at Jon hopefully, and Jon smiled. "We wondered that, too. So far, we've only been able to query the data from Nevada and Arizona because those were manageable sized datasets. Across all of Nevada, the average shared percentage is twenty-one percent. For Arizona, with a larger population, the average is eighteen percent. The highest rate we found in either state, other than the case we're discussing, is one in Tempe where one clinic had forty-seven percent of their claimants using a single law firm. But their total number of cases in two years was under twenty, whereas here we're talking about hundreds of cases a year being shared by Mirzoyan and Watson."

Bryan then asked, "And you mentioned other complicit parties and organizations. I'm not focused on the towing company, but I'm interested in your conclusion that many of the clinics' employees are likely parties to this scheme. What leads you to that assumption, and how many of the employees, and what specific roles do you believe are involved? Does the physical therapist know what's going on? How about the person who checks the patients in when they arrive and makes their next appointment? Is that person involved as well?"

Lori answered Bryan's question before anyone else could respond. "Our belief is as follows; the two people in the billing office, all four of the chiropractors, as well as anyone who's actually providing services in the clinics, specifically the physical therapists and their assistants, the x-ray technicians, the acupuncturists, the massage therapists, and the physical trainers are all complicit. They all would have likely had some role in falsifying chart notes, billing documents, and other documentation, verifying services were performed and establishing or confirming a diagnosis necessitating the care provided.

"There may be other members of the support staff with some knowledge of what goes on, but without a direct role in the fraud. In answer to your specific question about the receptionists who control appointments and handle patient traffic in and out of the offices, how could they not know someone billed for a forty-five minute appointment was in and out of the office in ten minutes?"

Dixon then made a strong declaration to the group. "I think we need to narrow our focus and agree on some fundamental objectives about who we're after and who might be peripherally involved. First of all, we want to insure we have a case against the principals driving the fraud schemes. According to what Jon and Lisa have told us, that would be Watson and Mirzoyan, and it's my personal belief, based on what we've seen in our investigation so far, someone other than Mirzoyan is the mastermind pulling the strings. For now let's assume it's Watson.

"So those two individuals are who we want to be sure we charge and convict. We must be certain we have air tight cases against them. Next on my pecking order is anyone who's licensed to provide medical or legal services to the citizens of Nevada, meaning all the involved attorneys in Watson's firm and all the licensed medical providers, especially the chiropractors, in Mirzoyan's clinics. As far as the remainder of the employees in either the law firm or the clinics, we should view them as possible witnesses for the prosecution against the principals in this case.

"I'm excited about the possibility this case could become a state-wide or even a national wake-up call for anyone who believes health care fraud is a safe crime. We need to make it clear that anyone committing or facilitating abuse or fraud in our health care system will be caught, prosecuted, and punished, even those who believe it's okay to cheat just a little.

"For too long Medicare and Medicaid have been easy targets because the bureaucracy associated with our medical programs has been incapable of managing itself, let alone effectively identifying fraudsters. With the implementation of Obamacare, the waste and fraud in our public health programs will literally skyrocket, wasting hundreds of billions of dollars every year."

Dixon paused and looked directly at Metcalf. "Jon, you told us all the bills look the same, and Lisa says all the medical documentation is cookie-cutter. That tells me those documents must be prepared by a limited number of people. You also told us there are only two people working in the centralized business and billing office.

"In my opinion we should aggressively look into the exact role of those two individuals by subjecting them to intense scrutiny and interrogation. If they're uncooperative but clearly complicit, we'll go after them as well. However, if they cooperate and know enough to be effective witnesses in our case, I believe we should offer them reduced penalties or possibly agree not to prosecute them at all. We'll need to convince them it's in their best interests to assist us in our investigation.

"The other objective must be to identify all other individuals or entities in these schemes not directly employed by the law firm or the clinics, like the towing company for example. Patients claiming fake injuries from staged auto accidents need to be recruited, so we need to discover who's responsible for finding these people. Also, we're not even sure we see the whole picture yet. Can there be other facets to this operation we don't yet know about?"

Hampton looked at his watch and saw that Dixon was running out of time. "Paul, it's coming up on eleven forty-five, which means we only have thirty minutes left in this session if you still want to spend time with Davee and me before you leave. I suggest we move on to discussing exactly what next steps this team should take and make some assignments."

"Bryan, I agree, so why don't you and Gayle, or Davee if he prefers, give us some suggestions on how you see us dividing up the duties and moving forward from this point."

For the next twenty minutes Da Silva, Gayle, and Hampton led a collaborative discussion that had the feeling of a veteran football team huddling up to call a series of plays for a last minute drive to win the game. Bryan was clearly the quarterback, but he wisely listened to observations and ideas from his two co-captains as well as the rest of the team. He realized that much of the investigation plan he'd already outlined could still be pursued with some important changes.

Since the MFCB team had already vetted the billing practices and clearly identified specific documented irregularities from their data, it wouldn't be necessary to repeat any of that work. On the other end of the spectrum, the link to Watson's law practice would necessitate additional background investigations. He also decided the plan to send in agents posing as accident victims wouldn't be necessary and could even compromise the integrity of the legal case.

Plans were formulated and assignments made to leverage and optimize the strengths of each member of the team. Everyone seemed to recognize their different skills and assets were complimentary, and if they could work together cooperatively, the investigation would be faster, more efficient, and more likely to result in solid convictions.

By the time Dixon had to leave, they had agreed the DOJ team would call in additional FBI agents to expand the background and financial investigations beyond those already in progress on the four current chiropractors, the clinic doctor who disappeared a year ago, and Mirzoyan. These additional investigators would focus on Watson and the attorneys in his practice, as well as other licensed providers working in the clinics.

The DOJ team would follow-up on any additional individuals or businesses like the towing company that might be identified from further data analysis coming from the MFCB team. The FBI agents would also undertake a comprehensive financial review of personal and business tax returns, investments, and any additional business interests linked to Mirzoyan or Watson.

Jon and Lisa were tagged to head up a team of MFCB analysts to further detail the specific fraudulent billing practices in each of the clinics. For every identified billing irregularity, they would generate statistics to identify the exact degree of variance from normal or average billing practices, documented in the rest of the provider population.

When norms were being discussed, Dixon made a request. "Gayle, I'd like you to enlist Dr. Stolic to help establish and specifically to certify those calculations. As you know, this type of evidence must be presented in clear and unambiguous statements, so a judge, prosecutor, and jury can clearly understand the extent each irregularity deviates from normal activity. We must be able to make clear statements concerning each type of billing fraud.

"To demonstrate what I'm looking for, I'll use the example Lisa mentioned earlier concerning excessive physical therapy services. For this illustration, since I don't know the statistics, I'll use hypothetical numbers, but this is how I think we need to present this information." Paul turned to the white board and began outlining a format while explaining the information he was drawing on the panel.

When he finished, he then turned to Bryan and asked, "There is one area you haven't mentioned or assigned yet Bryan. What about the billing office staff? How are you planning to handle that crucial aspect of this case?"

"I was going to discuss that next, along with asking about the remainder of the employees at the clinic. My suggestion is Gayle and I handle the billing office staff. Abe and Eli have already started looking into the backgrounds and financial affairs of the clinic personnel. Abe, can you give us a brief update on anything you've already learned about the two people in the billing office?"

"So far, Bryan, it looks like Lance Beasley may be the more interesting of the two. From what our sources tell us, he's responsible for all the medical documentation, but does none of the actual billing. He's twenty-eight years old and dropped out of med school, so far for reasons unknown. He's formerly from the southern part of Illinois. Both his parents are physicians, but we don't yet know how he ended up in Vegas or at the clinic. We actually have a couple of agents from the St. Louis office making the thirty mile trip up to Edwardsville,

IL today looking into his background and education. So we expect to know a lot more in a day or two.

"Amanda Booth is the other person working in the business office and she's responsible for all the billing and claim submissions. She's thirty years old, married with a couple of kids, and a husband who apparently never works, according to their neighbors. Their tax returns for the last three years confirm Mr. Booth earned zilch in any of those tax periods. But get this, their taxable income for each of the last two years was over one hundred and twenty thousand dollars.

"A year before that, Amanda grossed forty-two thousand working for Stockman Administrators, a local third party administrator, or TPA, as they're known in the industry. They live in a dump in an old section of town and drive a six-year-old Honda. We're still digging into their finances and her education."

"Thanks, Abe. We need you to be full speed ahead on both of those individuals. I want you and Eli to complete your investigations on them in the next forty-eight hours, if possible. That means a full report on my desk before the end of the day this Friday. Gayle and I will bone up on the information over the weekend, then we'll do a Q&A with the two of you on Monday morning to make sure everything is clear.

"Jon and Lisa, we'll plan to spend Monday afternoon with both of you fine-tuning our understanding of each fraudulent and questionable billing practice you've identified. I'd like five complete patient billing histories showing examples of flagrant and obvious fraud, so we can ask them specific questions about those bills.

"Paul, we'll need a subpoena allowing us to seize and examine all bills and medical records at the clinic. If the judge won't grant that broad of a warrant, then for starters we'll limit our request to the five patient histories I just requested. Then first thing on Tuesday morning, Gayle and I will show up at the billing office to ask Amanda and Lance a few questions. Gayle will interview Amanda, while at the same time, in a separate office, I'll talk to Mr. Beasley. After we grill them for an hour, they'll likely want to talk to their boss, and while they make that call, Gayle and I will give them some privacy, allowing us to compare notes.

"Without a doubt, after they talk to Mirzoyan, they'll refuse to continue talking to us and wait for their attorney to show up. Hopefully, that'll be Mr. Watson himself, but not likely. Whoever shows up will probably tell us to get the hell out of there, unless we have a warrant, which we'll then produce, once again throwing them off balance. While they work to provide the five files we asked for, their lawyer will be calling back to his office for more directions and maybe reinforcements.

"Gayle and I will get both Lance and Amanda into a room and conduct a bill-by-bill review of one of the patient's files. We'll ask them both to tell us specifically what they did to produce those records and each of the bills. We'll keep at it until they realize we highly suspect they're complicit in a fraud scheme. When we see them sweating, getting tongue tied and emotionally drained, we'll call it a day, promising to return soon, but we won't tell them when."

Paul Dixon confirmed his support and enthusiasm for Bryan's plan, then asked, "Bryan, I think we need to be prepared to have agents at every one of the clinics the next morning after you visit the billing office. They should be armed with complete background and financial information on each of the chiropractors running the four facilities. Our agents should enter all four offices at the same time and request an immediate interview with each of the doctors.

"We'll instruct our teams to spend at least one hour doing documented face-to-face interviews with the doctors. They should all use a standardized list of questions, but should also follow-up on any specific personal facts we uncover about each doctor. On Wednesday afternoon we'll regroup at our offices and we'll hear reports on each team's findings. We can assume after the warrants and questions at the billing office, followed the next morning by interviews of the chiropractors, we will have caused significant stress and confusion throughout their operation."

After a pause to think, Dixon continued, "I also plan to secure warrants for wiretaps on each of the clinics' lines, the business office lines, and the home phones of all four chiropractors and Mirzoyan. We'll also try for wiretaps on Watson's office lines, and each of the attorneys' home phones, and, of course, we'll be listening on everyone's cell phones, provided we can secure that information in the time we have available.

"If we can accomplish all those logistics in the next forty-eight hours, we should clearly know who's calling who, and who everyone looks to for instructions and answers. We should also know if any others are involved in this scheme, as we see who they reach out to once they know we're on to them."

Dixon stressed a crucial point. "We want to be careful to limit our questions to the falsification of medical records and insurance bills. No one should mention anything pertaining to the auto accident aspect of this case. We want them to believe we know far less than we actually do. We want to know the individuals who panic first and seem to be the most likely to work with us to avoid their own prosecution. For now, we won't request wiretaps on Beasley or Booth, but we'll see if anyone we're monitoring calls them and what discussions result. Bryan and Davee, I'm out of time. Can we adjourn to another room for a few minutes before I leave?"

The three men excused themselves and Bryan suggested the group take a break, get some lunch, and be back in the conference room in one hour. Da Silva suggested they use Gayle's office for their quick meeting. Once they were settled, Paul began, "Davee, it's clear your team has some important and unique data and analytical assets. I appreciate your flying to Las Vegas to emphasize the value and importance of those resources.

"It's clear to me one of your primary purposes in organizing this meeting and presenting us with this exceptional and comprehensive material was to convey more than just information. You wanted to send a message, and I can tell you Bryan and I have clearly understood the message. We now have a far better understanding of your data and how it can be used to initiate and support medical fraud investigations.

"I was likely too rigid in how I originally structured the leadership and management of our joint effort, and you were shrewd enough to realize you held cards we didn't know were in the deck. You played your cards today, and you had a winning hand. And now I'm anxious for you to tell us exactly what you envisioned would be gained by this successful strategy."

Da Silva looked a little stunned. He found himself totally surprised by Dixon's integrity and his forthright and candid approach to the situation. He'd been in many struggles for power and control over the years, and when confronted by any loss of influence or authority, most leaders would never acknowledge their rival's strengths so honestly. Nor would they have suggested their challenger propose a plan for resolving the matter.

Once those perspectives had flashed through his mind, Da Silva answered, "Paul, we want to be treated as an equal partner. We want our staff and our data respected by your people. We want recognition for our contributions when you make arrests and get convictions. We want some say in the planning and execution of those strategies. And we don't want to be kicked in the balls and forced to take all the blame if our combined team makes a mistake or we spend time chasing a false lead. We simply want a partnership based on respect and trust."

****

Paul responded, "That's fair and reasonable, but you must understand I'm accountable for any actions we take, because in the end, these will be DOJ investigations and prosecutions. So I must retain the right to review and approve any activities involving actions on private citizens. Therefore, I suggest we make Bryan and Gayle co-leaders of all task force planning and execution.

"However, I retain the right to review and approve all external and covert actions, the requesting of warrants, the authorization of arrests, and the interrogation and questioning of anyone who might potentially be indicted. We'll schedule regular bi-weekly conference calls where Bryan and Gayle will update you and me on the progress of all investigations. Our two co-leaders can request more frequent conferences when situations demand. Bryan and Davee, do those arrangements seem agreeable?"

Da Silva answered first, "I'm more than happy working under those terms, and I want to thank you, Paul, for being so amenable to embracing our team and data."

Dixon knew Hampton wouldn't be overjoyed at sharing management of the team with Gayle. But he also knew Hampton would realize his boss had made a decision and defined the rules, and he had no choice but to get on board with the plan as outlined. "Paul, I'll respect your directions and will do everything possible to work effectively with Gayle and the rest of the MFCB team. They've clearly established today that our two organizations together can accomplish things that neither of us alone is capable of achieving. Davee, you have my respect and my word I'll do everything I can to see that Gayle's methods and my instincts and style are complementary and not disruptive. I have one question; who's going to explain the ground rules to Gayle?"

Dixon looked at Da Silva, then at Hampton and said, "Of course, we'll delegate that task to you, Bryan. It'll be your first opportunity to begin harmonizing your two investigation styles. Keep me posted, and get Charlie to set up the Wednesday afternoon meeting and the biweekly conference calls we just discussed. Davee, have a safe flight home and thanks again for coming to see us today." With that, Dixon left the room and headed to his next meeting.

Chapter 18

Henderson, NV
December 2nd
6:00 PM

Fausto Guzman had been shadowing Dr. Gerald Washburn off and on for the past five weeks. His client, Bennett Watson, ordered him to get familiar with the young chiropractor's normal routine and to discreetly get the identities of anyone he might be spending time with on a regular basis. During the first week of November he'd followed Washburn every day, all day long, essentially every minute he wasn't working in Mirzoyan's Henderson clinic or sleeping in his own condo.

Over the first eight days of the surveillance, Guzman had discovered a great deal about Dr. G., as his staff liked to call him. The most self-serving discovery so far, because it made his job easier, was each day's routine was nearly an exact copy of the previous one. Guzman now knew for five days a week Washburn led a boring, routine, and predictable life, but beginning on Friday night and for the remainder of every weekend, anything might happen. Guzman had exposed a side of the chiropractor's life that remained well hidden from his employer, fellow workers, and patients during the work week.

Washburn's surveillance was originally initiated because of a confrontation he had with his boss. After nearly a year of working for Mirzoyan, either the young chiropractor's guilty conscience had finally gotten the best of him, or he wasn't too bright in the first place, and had finally just figured out the clinic's operations weren't entirely kosher. The day before Guzman was told to keep an eye on him, Washburn had actually presented Mirzoyan with a list of the clinic's treatment and billing irregularities and demanded they be rectified immediately. Mirzoyan had tried to reason with his young protégé, explaining there was nothing wrong with the way the clinic was being managed, and that his peers running the other three offices had never voiced any complaints. But Guzman believed Washburn wasn't clever enough to understand he was confronting a professional criminal, and naively persisted in demanding his boss put an immediate end to the list of transgressions.

Guzman knew the conversation wasn't a new one for Mirzoyan, and he also knew there were only two ways it could be resolved. To buy some time, Mirzoyan used the Thanksgiving holiday as an excuse and told Washburn he wanted to study the list of issues for a few days, then review them with his billing staff, and after following those steps he promised they would meet again in a few weeks. Dr. G. had reluctantly agreed to the arrangement, mistakenly believing Mirzoyan was sincere.

Guzman recalled the night he first received this assignment from Watson to keep an eye on Washburn. Guzman's phone had buzzed alerting him that a text message had arrived. When he checked the screen and saw the cryptic message, he knew immediately it was from his employer, *CEJ on Flamingo 8:00 tonight*.

He knew CEJ was the term Watson used for three seedy, out-of-the way taverns he preferred for meetings whenever his business transactions involved exchanging information he wanted to be sure was never recorded or documented in any way. CEJ stood for Controlled Environment Joint, and within seconds he had replied with a simple 'OK,' confirming he would be at the meeting set for eight that night at the bar on Flamingo.

Guzman didn't consider Watson to be his boss, but preferred to think of himself as the problem-solving arm for Watson's diverse and corrupt business interests. Guzman did not appear on any list of employees; instead he was a contractor and the CEO of his own company, a web-based business called wesolveproblems.com. The home page, which was actually the only page on Guzman's website, listed no address, no phone number, and no services. It was essentially a dead end, except for an email address where prospective customers were instructed to forward a description of their problem along with a phone number where they could be reached.

The website promised visitors that "When circumstances allow, we will respond to your email within 24 hours or less." Every request, except those encrypted with a special key word from Watson, was answered after sixteen hours with a response that informed the sender 'Regrettably, due to previous commitments, wesolveproblems.com cannot undertake to assist with the particular problem described in your inquiry.'

Fausto Guzman was actually an immigrant whose real name was Ernesto Morales. Late one night ten years ago he entered the U.S. by swimming the Rio Grande, then fled northward to Illinois, where he joined former associates from Mexico. He'd spent the first few years of his American criminal career in Chicago as a small-time enforcer for several minor drug distribution rings. Eventually he branched out from assaulting addicts who were late with payments to their dealers, and dealers who short-changed their suppliers, to peddling his special talents to a more diverse group of buyers.

A few years later his reputation for brutal efficiency in the expanded marketplace allowed him to become the contractor of choice for two major crime rings as well as other organizations in the greater Chicago area. In particular his services were much in demand by the union and political white-collar criminals. Because these organizations were generally without full-time enforcement personnel, they depended on trusted contractors to carry out violent and illegal acts on their behalf.

All was going well for Morales in Chicago until three years before when, by a stroke of bad luck, a traffic surveillance camera recorded him executing three leaders of an opposing gang during a brutal and messy drug buy, which also resulted in the deaths of a bystander and the wounding of four others. For weeks afterward his likeness was repeatedly plastered on every newspaper and TV news broadcast across the state. Consequently, his former clients seemed unwilling to risk hiring the now notorious killer for fear of being linked to the well-publicized murders.

So Ernesto chose to leave Chicago until things cooled off. However, he didn't go without references, and because a long-standing unspoken connection still existed between some Chicago enterprises and certain illicit Las Vegas interests, he secured an enthusiastic introduction to Bennett Watson. It had been nearly three lucrative years since he'd met the Vegas attorney and agreed to work for him.

When Guzman first got to Las Vegas, Watson had taken care of everything for him, even providing him with a passport, driver's license, and three credit cards, all issued in the name of Fausto Guzman, a name Morales wouldn't have chosen for himself. During his time working for Watson, Guzman had mugged, robbed, threatened, and coerced too many people for him to remember, all in the line of duty. He'd committed arson, ransacked offices and private homes, and had even torched a new BMW 750 while it sat overnight in the owner's driveway.

As a sideline, Guzman had also proven to be resourceful by providing Mirzoyan's clinics with stolen patient identities and insurance information. He had also become the source of an unending number of dishonest people who posed as accident victims for the various schemes run by Watson and Mirzoyan.

Guzman was paid a retainer plus 'extras' for the more physical and violent acts he performed in the line of duty. In the first thirty-five months of working for Watson, his employer had only ordered the assassination of one victim.

As they sat in the bar on Flamingo, Watson explained the most recent incident with Dr. Washburn and told Guzman how he had found out about it. "Before Mirzoyan left the clinic's parking lot, he was on his cell trying to reach me. I wasn't able to call him back until the next morning. Once Mirzoyan explained the situation, I commended him for delaying any immediate confrontations with Washburn and told him before we did anything, we needed to know if Washburn had discussed his complaints with anyone else at the clinic, or at an insurance company, or with anyone in law enforcement.

"He was a nervous wreck, and to calm him down I promised him I'd arrange for you to keep an eye on the young doctor for a few weeks to see who he spent time with. I asked if Washburn dated anyone working at the office, and Mirzoyan had no idea if he did or not. He told me he didn't pay attention to his employees' personal lives. I told him maybe he should start."

As Guzman watched the rear door of the clinic office open and saw the tall slightly built man exit, he thought about an almost identical scene a year earlier. *Here I am again, in the same parking lot keeping an eye on the late doctor's replacement, a man who'll likely suffer the same fate as his predecessor.*

The parking lot at the rear of the clinic was reasonably well-lit to a distance of about twenty feet away from the building. At thirty feet, where his car was parked next to Washburn's, it was so dark the chiropractor likely didn't even see Guzman exiting the car parked next to his until it was too late. *Where did he come from,* was probably the last conscious thought that crossed Washburn's mind just before Guzman delivered a solid blow to the back of his head.

Washburn regained consciousness sometime later, discovering he was blindfolded and sitting upright on the ground with his hands bound in back of him. As soon as he raised his chin off his chest, he was punched hard in the ribs and immediately afterward hit in the face with what felt like a bat or club of some kind, then nothing; only some heavy putrid breathing near his face. "What do you want?" he pleaded. "Why are you doing this?"

"Do I have your attention now?" Guzman asked in a gruff and disguised voice.

"You must have the wrong person. If you want money, you can have what's in my wallet, but it's not much," Washburn offered.

"I have the right person, and you'd better listen, because if I have to come back, I won't be this nice next time. I know all about you, my gay little friend, and this will be your first and last warning. You're nothing but a cog in a big wheel, a wheel called the Accident and Injury Health Restoration Clinics.

"Faulty cogs get replaced when they don't do the job they're supposed to do. If you want to keep breathing, then shut up and quit complaining about anything to do with how our operation is run. Don't ever threaten Dr. Mirzoyan again. Wise up and keep your damn mouth shut and you might live to see thirty. If you talk to anyone or go to the police, you'll be dead before the sun comes up the next day. We know everywhere you go and everyone you hang out with, especially your boyfriend at the billing office. Say anything to him and he dies along with you. Do you understand?"

Washburn was terrified, and a wave of nausea surged over him. The only thing he managed to say was, "Yes, I understand clearly what you're saying. Please don't hit me again. I'll do as you say."

Guzman knew he'd be visiting Washburn again. His intuition told him this dumbass will think he can go to the police or try and disappear or make some other stupid move, then he'd have to come back and actually kill him. But tonight he had orders to simply warn him and give him one more chance to wise up.

Thoughts of needing to catch Washburn off guard all over again aggravated him so much he punched him twice more in the ribs and gave him a long, debilitating blast from his flashlight-sized stun gun. This sent Washburn's body into wild spasms and caused his head to crash into the side of the car, then hit the parking lot pavement so hard it sounded to Guzman like someone dropped a watermelon onto the ground.

When the spasms stopped, Washburn was motionless; exhausted or unconscious, Guzman wasn't sure which, and he didn't care. He removed the zip ties from Washburn's wrists, then propped him up behind the wheel of his car. He left the blindfold in place, started the engine, closed the driver's door, then got into his own car. Guzman parked far enough away so he wouldn't be seen, but close enough to observe Washburn hopefully regain consciousness. As he sat in his car, Guzman carefully aimed a camera at the chiropractor and zoomed in for a tight shot. His plan was to email the video to Washburn the next day with a warning attached, 'Next Time You Won't Wake Up!'

Within twenty minutes, Guzman could see Washburn was almost coherent enough to drive. He watched as his victim slowly maneuvered his Mazda Miata out of the parking lot. Guzman followed at a distance to see exactly where Washburn was headed. When he saw the Miata turn into Washburn's condo complex, he decided the doctor had likely had enough excitement for the night and felt reasonably sure he wouldn't be doing his usual Friday night out with the boys.

But Guzman wasn't inclined to assume anything when working for Watson. He'd previously planted a number of listening devices in Washburn's condo, which he decided to monitor for the next hour or two to be certain he'd guessed right about any plans Washburn might have. Thirty seconds after hearing the front door slam, the next noise Guzman heard sounded like a child sobbing.

After several minutes, the weeping transitioned to barely discernible howling of, "Look at my face" and "What has he done to me?" over and over again. Thirty minutes later all Guzman heard was water running and some persistent sniffling and moaning. It finally ended, then kitchen sounds of an ice dispenser and refrigerator or freezer door opening and closing, then nothing but the TV in the background.

An hour passed and he was about to shut down his surveillance devices and head home for the night, then a cell phone rang inside the condo. He heard six rings and, regrettably, Washburn answered, before it rolled to voicemail.

"Lance, is that you?"

Silence.

"FaceTime? No, I look terrible, and I'm not going to use FaceTime with you or anyone else tonight."

Silence.

"No, I'm not going to make it tonight; I'm not feeling too well. No, don't bother to come over; I'd just be bad company."

Silence.

"Yes, I've been crying because--because--."

Guzman heard nothing for several minutes, but believed Lance was urging Washburn to tell him why he was so upset and why he wasn't at the bar with the boys, where he usually spent the early hours on Friday nights. His assumptions were confirmed when he next heard Washburn sobbingly begin recounting some of the events that transpired earlier that evening. After completing an excessively dramatized and lengthy, but highly embellished, yet incomplete version of the night's events, he heard Washburn explaining why he hadn't yet called the police.

"I can't talk about this to anyone until I figure out who this guy is and why they're after me. I'm scared and for all I know they're watching me right now."

Silence.

"Spend the night at your place? I guess I could, but I don't want you to see me the way I look."

Silence.

"All right then. I guess I would be safer there, and it would help to think through this with someone as brilliant as you are, Lance. I can try and be there in half an hour."

Guzman realized he had a problem and wasn't sure how to deal with it. As soon as Washburn got inside Lance Beasley's apartment, he wouldn't be able to hear their conversations and plans. To that point, he didn't believe Washburn and his friend Lance had ever discussed the fraud taking place every day at the clinics. He suspected Washburn had actually avoided asking Lance because Washburn was smart enough to realize with Lance's responsibilities in the billing office there'd be no way he wouldn't be aware of or even involved in the scheme.

Guzman tried to reach Watson, then Mirzoyan on their cells, but neither answered. A few minutes later he saw the Miata leave the condo complex, but neither voicemail message had produced a return call. He decided to follow Washburn and hope Watson would contact him and tell him what to do next. By the time Washburn parked in front of Lance's apartment building, no orders had come to Guzman, so his only option was to wait for further directions. However, there was something he could do, and he decided to take advantage of Washburn's absence from his condo.

He left his spot outside Lance's apartment and headed back to Washburn's place. Of necessity, a skilled burglar, Guzman entered through the unit's front door as easily as if he possessed a key. Gingerly carrying a small package slightly larger than an egg carton, he walked directly to the chiropractor's bedroom. Lying prone on the floor beside the king-size bed, he flipped a switch on the package, which caused a light to glow red.

Sliding the bundle as far out of sight as possible, he positioned it at the head of the bed near the middle. Quickly he returned to the door he'd entered only minutes before and peered outside to be certain no one was in sight. A few yards away a couple walked to their car, so he quickly closed the front door and waited until he heard their engine start. As they backed out of their parking place, their headlights partially illuminated the room where he waited. He noticed the sleeve of his black shirt covering the arm that just delivered the bomb under Washburn's bed was coated with gray dust. He brushed it off, then smiled thinking, if you were a cleaner person Dr. Washburn, you might find my little gift before it annihilates you.

Earlier on the drive over on his way to stay with Lance, Washburn decided he couldn't risk telling his lover the real reason he was attacked. The two men had been seeing each other for the past few months, but there was still much he didn't know about his friend. Because Lance had never mentioned anything about the illicit business taking place in the billing office, he didn't feel safe discussing everything he knew with him tonight.

Instead, he decided to be vague about the reasons for the attack, while at the same time posing questions that would give Lance opportunities to comment about possible irregularities taking place in the business office.

Once Washburn arrived at the apartment and Lance saw the extent of the beating he'd received, he again insisted they call the police. Two long hours of discussion, ice packs, and hugging ensued, during which Washburn gave Lance multiple opportunities to be candid and revealing about any anomalies or indiscretions he was aware of at the billing office. Lance mentioned none, and Washburn sadly realized his worst fears were likely true.

The beating from earlier in the evening, coupled with the emotional shock of learning his most trusted friend could actually be part of a fraud scheme that now threatened his life, had completely drained any strength or determination that remained in him. So Washburn told Lance he was too tired to talk any longer and explained he preferred to sleep in the spare room tonight because of his painful injuries, then he excused himself and headed off to bed.

Guzman finally got the return call from Watson about two hours after he'd left the bomb in Washburn's condo. After Watson heard an abridged version of the night's events, he confirmed that Guzman had made the right decision to do nothing, but he ordered him to go back and remove the package from the doctor's bedroom as soon as possible.

Guzman argued the device was good insurance and explained it could only be triggered by the remote control he had in his possession. Watson angrily responded, "The device is anything but insurance, and I insist you remove immediately. A bomb is a messy solution and I'd never authorize you to use it, so go get it tonight while Washburn's away."

Guzman agreed to retrieve the package, but uncharacteristically had no intention of doing as Watson demanded.

Chapter 19

Las Vegas, NV
December 3rd
8:00 AM

On Saturdays Hampton often escaped the stuffy confines of the fitness center by jogging outside rather than tolerating another boring hour on the treadmill. An unexpected absence of morning sunlight that normally drenched his living room caused him to peer outside through an east-facing window. What he saw was a blustery and gray Saturday sky. After checking his iPhone, he noted the current temperature was thirty-seven degrees, and the predicted high for the day was forty-eight. Not the kind of day the Las Vegas Chamber of Commerce touted, but probably nicer than Chicago, he thought.

Out of curiosity, he checked Chicago's forecast using the *WeatherBug* app on his iPhone and discovered the temperature at nine AM in the Windy City was thirty-eight, going to a predicted high of forty-nine with calm winds. As it turned out, Las Vegas had winds of thirty miles an hour all day long with intermittent gusts in excess of fifty. He became acutely aware of that reality as soon as he left the confines of the condo complex and suddenly felt the sting of nearly invisible grains of sand that pelted his face and the constraining force of powerful wind gusts that at times nearly halted his progress. He struggled through a fifty-minute battle with the elements, then returned home, pleased to be out of the wind and cold and finally back inside his apartment.

His sleep the previous night had been fitful, punctuated by periods of abrupt awakenings and visions of confrontations with Ari Mirzoyan, and endless struggles for compromise with Gayle Baker that all ended without resolution. He'd studied the background reports for Lance Beasley and Amanda Booth until nearly two AM, when his heavy eyelids ultimately won the battle against four cans of Red Bull.

Once Hampton learned more about their backgrounds and personal lives, along with what he already knew about their duties in the billing office, he started to realize they were both likely complicit in the fraud scheme, but they were also victims of their manipulative and cunning employer. Understanding they were culpable, but also young and inexperienced, he feared one or both might not be wise enough to realize their only possible upside was to admit their role and aid in prosecuting others who were more accountable, especially Dr. Mirzoyan.

After he removed his shoes, socks, and shirt in anticipation of a hot shower to wash the sand and grit from his hair, eyes, and any other part of his body exposed during his run, he heard the front door bell ringing. "Who the hell is at my door at nine on a Saturday morning?" Hampton asked himself out loud. Slipping his sweaty shirt back on, he headed for the door and jerked it open without looking through the peep hole.

Surprised would be understating his shock when he saw Gayle standing there with her briefcase in hand. Before he could open his mouth to speak, a series of questions raced through his mind. What was she doing here? How did she know where I live? Why would she show up here at nine on a weekend morning without calling first? Why is she carrying her briefcase? Why does she look so much better in Levis and a sweater than she looks in her G-Man clothes at the office? Why doesn't she wear her hair like that all the time? How bad do I look right now since I was ready to jump into the shower? When he finally gathered his wits and spoke, all he could deliver was an impolite question, "Gayle, what are you doing here?"

"I'm here to talk about the case. I'm sorry if this is an imposition. I know I should've called first, but I wanted your help in thinking through some things that are bothering me about Lance and Amanda. Are you alone? This is rude of me, I know, and I can come back later or just wait until Monday if I'm interrupting anything."

"The only thing you're interrupting is my shower. How did you know where I live? I don't remember mentioning my address to you or anyone else for that matter."

"Bryan, I've worked for the government for a lot of years. If we can find Muammar Gaddafi, then I sure as hell can find out where you live."

"That's BS and you know it. Who gave you my address?"

"Let's get off that subject and back to why I came here. After you take your much needed shower, could you spare an hour or two this morning working through some facts and laying out a strategy about how we're going to handle our interviews with Lance and Amanda on Tuesday morning? There's no doubt in my mind one of them could be the key to breaking this whole case. I'm especially focused on Lance based on what his background investigation revealed concerning his reasons for abruptly leaving Illinois and how that might be a factor in this case?"

"I'm not even sure which of his reasons for leaving his hometown you're talking about, but I share your views about their potential importance in building our case. But I also feel like both of them have been drawn into this mess by a crooked SOB who could possibly be blackmailing two apparently bright people, forcing them to be accomplices in this kind of scheme."

"I doubt he's blackmailing them or twisting their arms at all. It's about the money, Bryan. It's always about the money. These are crimes of opportunity and they both stepped into a golden one and embraced it. They're doing what anyone would do. I believe it's that simple. But our exchange of opinions just now, this brainstorming we just did, is exactly what I came here hoping we could do. I need opposing and validating opinions for some of my theories, and I'm too stoked to wait till Monday."

"Okay, I'll blow a couple of hours of my day off. I have to admit, I'm wrestling with next steps and motives as well, because I'm not sure it's only about money, at least with Beasley. Why don't you head over to Starbucks on Charleston and get us some breakfast and lots of coffee while I shower and dress. Come back in half an hour and we'll work till noon. Is that a plan you can live with?"

Gayle thanked him, asked how he wanted his coffee and how hungry he was, and agreed to return in thirty minutes. After closing the door he again removed his shirt and headed for the shower, but then heard the front door bell ringing for a second time. With shirt in hand, he returned to the living room and, while opening the door, asked, "Did you forget something?" Stopping mid-sentence, he found himself staring directly into Charlie's inquisitorial eyes.

"I came by to see if you wanted to do something this afternoon with me and the boys, but it looks like you might be too tired after what, a long night's work with Gayle?"

"What are you talking about? She got here about ten minutes ago, unexpected, uninvited, and fundamentally unwelcome. I just got back from a run, and she showed up at the door, wanting to know if I would spend some time with her today working on the case and preparing for our interviews on Tuesday morning. I have no idea how she even found out where I live, let alone being accused of having a sleepover with her. What's the matter with you anyway?"

"Bryan, you need to look at it from my perspective. It's nine in the morning and I came over here to see what your plans were for the day, and just as I'm about to get out of my car I see Gayle walking away from your condo, and when you open the door you're shirtless, your hair is a mess, and you're asking her if she forgot something. Can you blame me for being a little mixed up?"

As Da Silva had repeatedly told Hampton, he wasn't the most sophisticated conversationalist nor the quickest wit when it came to banter with the opposite sex. But he was experienced enough to know the correct answer to Charlie's question wasn't the right answer, if he wanted to avoid days of banishment from the Cruz family circle of trust.

So metaphorically he discarded his Martian thoughts and responded as a true inhabitant of Venus, "Charlie, I can see how it would be logical for you to jump to the wrong conclusion in this odd set of circumstances. I'm sorry this string of coincidences was something either of us had to experience. I hope you know this is all a big misunderstanding, and nothing is going on between Gayle and me. I want you to know she's coming back with some coffee and rolls, and I agreed to work with her until noon reviewing background information on Lance and Amanda.

"I'd love to have you stay and help us go through the analysis, if you have the time and interest. If you have other things going on right now, we can get together a little after twelve, and I'd love to go anywhere you want to go and do anything you're interested in doing. I was planning to call you after I showered, and earlier I thought we might take the Corvette out for a drive, but it's way too windy and I'm afraid the blowing sand will pit the paint."

"Bryan, I'm sorry I flew off the handle. I had no right to question anything you do with your spare time. You know by now I have the temperament of a Latin and we're passionate about everything, especially our relationships. Excuse me, that was a bad choice of words. I didn't mean to say that; it came out wrong, but you know what I meant. I can't stay now because I have twenty errands to run, but come over at twelve-thirty and we'll get lunch and figure out what else to do this afternoon."

"Great, Charlie, but can you do me a favor? Will you stay here until I'm out of the shower and Gayle is back, so there are no more misunderstandings?"

"I guess I can if that's what you want, Bryan."

"I would appreciate it, so please come on in, have a seat and wait until she gets here and I'm dressed."

Bryan gave Charlie a quick kiss on the cheek, then for the third time headed for the shower, silently congratulating himself for avoiding a confrontation, managing a tricky situation, and preventing a rift from developing in his relationship with Charlie. This is good, he thought, and at the same time, I'll send a clear message to Gayle that I'm already involved with Charlie. But then he genuinely wondered if that was really the message he wanted to convey.

Thirty minutes had come and gone, but Gayle decided to remain in her car, giving Charlie the extra time to leave Bryan's apartment before they expected her to return. She decided the five extra minutes were more than enough if Bryan wanted the two women to avoid crossing paths. Approaching the door with both her hands and arms laden with coffee and bags of rolls and muffins, Gayle couldn't press the button to ring the doorbell, so she gently kicked the door twice trying to simulate a normal knock.

She wasn't surprised when Charlie opened the door, or when she saw Bryan fully clothed sitting on the couch. Ball's in my court, she thought, and said, "Hi, Charlie, I saw you getting out of your car when I was leaving, and I thought you might still be here when I got back, so I brought you a skinny latte and your pick of muffins. I hope that was the right choice. I see you as the chic latte type of woman, but if you don't want it, you can have my plain coffee and doctor it any way you want."

For a moment Charlie appeared to be caught off guard, confirming she didn't realize Gayle had seen her when she left Hampton's apartment half an hour ago, but she recovered quickly. "The latte would be great, but I usually go with whole milk and plain sugar, not the artificial stuff, since I don't have a weight problem, and I'm a strong believer in natural foods. Bryan, as we planned earlier, I'll see you at my place around twelve thirty."

Then Charlie grabbed her latte out of the drink carrier Gayle was still holding, walked to the kitchen, picked up the sugar shaker, and dumped a generous helping into her cup. She stirred it deliberately with a little wooden stick, also snatched from the carrier, and finally, after what felt like an eternity to Hampton, turned slowly to leave and said, "Don't work too hard, you two.

Remember, this is a weekend, and Saturday's supposed to be a day of relaxation."

An awkward silence hung over the room once Charlie was gone, which Bryan finally filled by offering a lame, "We had plans this afternoon and Charlie just came over to confirm the time."

"Doesn't she have a phone?" Gayle asked sarcastically.

"Oh, sure she does, but I guess she had the same problem you did this morning and forgot how to use it," Bryan countered, while moving to the kitchen to prevent Gayle from seeing his look of satisfaction over his clever comeback.

Relationship maneuvering at an end, at least for the time being, most of their coffee consumed, and with only one muffin remaining, Hampton and Gayle cleared away the Starbucks remnants. They replaced the food wrappers with the unsettling FBI reports that had thrust them both into a restless night of sleep, then drew them together for this unusual Saturday morning session.

Bryan made a suggestion. "Why don't we each take turns summarizing what jumped out at us about these two? Anything we think might have enticed them to get involved in the first place, their reasons for ongoing involvement, and any Achilles heel either may have that might enable us to persuade them to cooperate with us are the things we should focus on."

"I agree with that approach, Bryan, and I think we need to add one more area of focus, which is looking at any relationships either of them might have inside or outside Mirzoyan's organization. How about if I start? I want to begin by talking about Amanda, because, as we decided, she was my primary focus, and Lance was yours."

"Have at it then," Bryan told her.

Over the next twenty minutes, Gayle summarized what they had learned about Amanda, what her impressions were, and why she was concerned about their ability to get her to cooperate. "Amanda is thirty. She's married to a loser who apparently never works. She sticks with him because they have a thirteen-year-old and two smaller children.

"Amanda and her husband live out toward Henderson, off East Charleston, in a run-down home built over fifty years ago. I doubt the contractors who threw up those four hundred tract homes, which all look the same, ever believed those boxes with flat roofs covered with various sizes of white gravel and stone would ever have families actually living in them nearly sixty years later. Almost every house has bars on the doors and windows, dirt where there's supposed to be grass, and three or four junkers, most without wheels or tires, sitting in the driveway or perched on blocks in dirt where a lawn once existed.

"Apparently she once considered becoming an RN, but the cost of the education and a too early marriage to her high school boyfriend disqualified nursing as an option in her life. Instead of nursing school, she opted to become a medical coder, apparently because she originally thought she could 'Work from home and earn over $500 a day,' as the trade school advertisements promise on TV.

"After completing her coding course, she landed a staff position as a claims processor for one of the larger insurers with a processing operation in Las Vegas. She eventually worked her way up to become an auditor of high dollar claims, and it was that position that became her real training ground and provided a fluky opportunity for eventual employment with Mirzoyan.

"In a crazy set of circumstances, she actually met Dr. Mirzoyan himself when the insurance company she worked for sent her to do an onsite audit for one of his clinics. What's rumored to have happened is strange, but not improbable. When she showed up at the designated site to perform the audit, she was surprised to discover she hadn't been sent to an operating medical clinic, but instead found herself in a beautifully appointed luxurious fifth floor suite that housed a staff of 'billing and documentation specialists' as the receptionist explained to her. As we now know, the entire billing staff is only two people."

Hampton interrupted asking, "Gayle, before you go on, I'm curious to know the source of this information? How do we know what went on at the billing office?"

"Actually, I'll tell you more about that later, Bryan, but we learned all of this from her former department manager at the insurance company.

Gayle asked Hampton if he had any other questions, saw him shake his head, no, then continued. "After being ushered into a large meeting room and finding the materials she previously requested displayed on a conference table big enough to seat thirty or more people, she started to get intimidated. It was unlike any other onsite audit she had ever experienced or heard of. The incident that put her off her game in a big way was realizing the clinic's owner, the smooth and seemingly gracious Dr. Ari Mirzoyan, was standing in the room waiting to greet her.

"He reportedly welcomed her warmly, and offered her coffee, refreshments, and flattery, and assured her she would find nothing wrong with their billing. Three days later, she submitted the results of her audit to her manager. Amanda reported no irregularities, and her written report actually commended the staff for their 'excellent documentation' which supported 'flawless' billing practices. Unwisely, Amanda had mixed too much subjective praise for Mirzoyan and his operation into her summary report, compelling her supervisor to suspect the audit was compromised. The supervisor promptly ordered a new team of two male auditors to repeat the process."

Gayle went on to explain in more detail that when the FBI agent interviewed the supervisor last week, the woman actually still remembered the incident and gave a colorful and memorable account of what happened, which the agent recorded, then transcribed.

Gayle then read the exact words of Amanda's former manager. "I smelled a rat, and the rat was Mirzoyan. We confirmed their operation was highly questionable and likely fraudulent with our second audit, but our timid and indecisive VP of provider relations later convinced the head of the SIU not to do anything about it.

"I had to let Amanda go because the subsequent audit revealed she had overlooked glaring problems, which reflected badly on our whole department. This was a tough decision for me, because Amanda was bright, and I believed she had a promising future with us. But people lost trust in her, and that's a bad situation for an auditor.

"A month later, I actually helped her get a job at a TPA here in town. A friend of mine who managed their claims staff called to ask what I thought of her. I told her Amanda had been let go because of a political situation, but she was a bright girl and they would be wise to hire her. From what I heard she only stayed there for a few months, then I don't know what happened to her."

After reading from the report, Gayle continued her narrative, "The supervisor lost track of her, but apparently Mirzoyan didn't. We believe she applied for a job at the clinic or he actually sought her out and easily convinced her to come and work for him for about three times what she was earning at the TPA. One of the lines of questioning we'll definitely pursue is how she ended up working at the *RACHI* clinic billing office."

Gayle then backtracked to discuss Amanda's upbringing. "Amanda and a younger brother were raised by an abusive, alcoholic father after her mother died when she was nine. She got pregnant when she was sixteen and married her high school boyfriend who's her current, no good husband.

"One more interesting comment from her old supervisor could be a key to why she was initially manipulated by Mirzoyan during the audit and why she went back for more and ended up staying. She described Amanda as a 'prime candidate for Extreme Makeover,' adding without much compassion that, 'She was a plain, frumpy, overweight young woman who actually had the potential of at least looking presentable if she would wash and style her hair and dress decently.'

"So in summary, Bryan, I think fate cued up a perfect opportunity for Mirzoyan to prey on a young woman who'd been abused and exploited by most of the men in her life. He offered a little kindness and attention, a ridiculously high salary, plus who knows what else he did and does for her. She brought expertise in coding, along with years of experience in insurance billing and audits, the perfect pieces he needed to complete his fraudulent puzzle. From his perspective, I imagine the end result seems like a textbook alliance offering him the chance for ongoing exploitation of a needy and vulnerable young woman."

"Gayle, I think you've pretty much nailed the important facts about Amanda's background. Our guys did a great job gathering this information as fast as they did. So how do you assess our chances with her? What do you think her vulnerabilities might be?"

"If you want my honest opinion, I think it's going to be virtually impossible to turn her against Mirzoyan. She'll likely deny any wrong doing, call him the minute we leave the office, and stick by him even if it means she gets charged as well. My only hope is at some point she'll realize she's looking at prison time, and the thought of leaving her younger kids with her worthless husband will wake her up. I just don't think it'll be easy to overcome what I suspect is a high degree of loyalty to Mirzoyan."

"I can't argue with your reasoning, but I hope you're wrong, for her sake and ours, too. I think we're done with Amanda for now, so let me talk about Beasley. Lance is twenty-eight years old. He's the youngest of three children, his siblings being two older sisters. Beasley's parents are both physicians, practicing in Edwardsville, IL, a small town with a population of about twenty-five thousand.

"One of his sisters, also a physician, is a highly respected internist in St. Louis. And the older sister, a super achiever with a PhD in microbiology and an MD, is a full professor on the staff of the Northwestern School of Medicine, in Chicago.

"After a mediocre high school career, Lance did attend Southern Illinois University, got average grades and completed a pre-med program, while earning a BA degree in biology. He was accepted into the SIU Medical School and successfully completed two years of the curriculum with excellent grades, but then mysteriously dropped out. Apparently, from what our investigators learned, he decided he wanted to live a different life than the one mom, dad, and both sisters chose and planned for him as well.

"While in Edwardsville, the agents were able to interview three of his college friends who actually still live there, and in the process of answering questions, the first one hinted that Lance was gay. When they questioned his second friend they worked on the assumption he might be gay and asked a series of lifestyle questions. Friend number two reacted by being amazed their questioning seemed to be trying to circumvent the well-known fact that Lance was openly gay and had been since his third year of college."

"Clearly," his friend ventured, "Lance's lifestyle was the primary reason he left Illinois for parts unknown, because living in a small Midwestern town like Edwardsville with two practicing physicians for parents who didn't accept nor acknowledge his lifestyle was an untenable situation."

After noticing Gayle had a quizzical look, Bryan paused to ask if she had a question, but she answered, "No," so he continued, "Our guys couldn't come up with evidence of why he chose Las Vegas as his destination, but what we might assume is he likely regarded Vegas as the complete opposite of Edwardsville, and therefore a reasonable place to start over. As near as they could determine, his first job in Vegas was as a bartender in a small locals joint on Paradise Road. He began working there a little over three years ago, and stayed for nearly two years.

"Around two months before he quit, he was riding in a car driven by a fellow worker from the tavern, and they got into an accident. We think the accident was legitimate, because the claim has none of the characteristics of the Mirzoyan cases we're looking at. Apparently, he suffered some neck injuries as well as some cuts and bruises on his face and head, and was treated in the ER at the Sunrise Hospital, then released. They recommended follow-up care by the physician of his choice, but he had none.

"We're not sure how he ended up at Mirzoyan's Henderson clinic, but he did. He might have seen a TV ad, or heard Mirzoyan, the huckster, on the radio, or possibly even read one of many bus stop benches advertising the Accident and Injury Health Restoration Clinics. All we know for sure is he apparently decided to look into what the clinics could do for him, and through some twist of fate began working there two months after his accident.

"My theory is that, during his treatment, he somehow got friendly with someone at the clinic, and when they learned of Lance's medical background, they recruited him or at least encouraged him to look into a job somewhere in Mirzoyan's organization."

"Bryan, do you know the chiropractor's name at the Henderson clinic? Is that the office where Dr. Washburn works?"

"I'm not positive, but I think you're right. Isn't it Gerald Washburn? Why do you ask?"

"I'll tell you later, but for now I don't want to taint your trail of logic, so go on."

"That's all the background we need to review, unless you have something to add, but now I want to look at Lance as a possible witness and discuss his vulnerabilities, strengths, and weaknesses. First of all Lance, needless to say, is bright, and absolutely must have known after only a few weeks or months of working for Mirzoyan that something wasn't kosher about the billing operations.

"I think this guy's continued involvement in this mess is largely about two things. The first must be money, because we know he earns over a hundred and fifty thousand a year, and for the amount of training and the skills he has, he's way overpaid. In fact, with bonuses he earns more than either of his sisters, which I'm sure he would love to let mom and dad know.

"The other motivating factor I believe we need to pursue is an existing sexual relationship with someone else working at the clinic or in the billing office. Since both of the other people in the billing office are women, then the logical conclusion would be an employee at the Henderson clinic where he was treated for two months. That connection could even be the person who recruited him.

"If I'm right, then Lance's cooperation, or lack of it, may be closely tied to his friend's culpability in the overall operation. If his lover is one of the professionals at the clinic, he'll realize anything he does to help us will be a betrayal of his friend, which could be problematic for us. If, on the other hand, it's someone lower on the food chain, then we can promise them both immunity, and it might be a slam dunk for our team."

"It won't be a slam dunk no matter what, I can promise you that," Gayle assured him. "So now, I'll tell you what I was mulling over when I asked you about Washburn a few minutes ago. The source of the opinion I'm about to relate to you could be labeled unprofessional and the information could be deemed unreliable, unsubstantiated, and possibly highly biased. But in light of what you just hypothesized, and what I'm assuming as well, it may be relevant.

"Two months ago, one of our local MFCB investigators visited Dr. Washburn's office to review a case we were looking into. When he documented the visit in the case tracking system notes, he made an inappropriate entry, for which he was subsequently reprimanded. Last night after reading about Lance, I recalled the situation with the agent, so I got on the system and read the actual note he recorded along with the sanitized disciplinary action that was released to all personnel. Would you like to guess what the note said? Never mind. I'll tell you. I'll quote it verbatim, as it was written, then deleted."

"Dr. Washburn was cooperative and friendly, but too friendly for my liking. This man is a closet homosexual, and I think no male agent from our organization should ever be sent to that office again."

Bryan was pleased, but hid any reaction from Gayle. The fact her information supported his theory was gratifying, but he didn't want to appear surprised by the accuracy of his hypothesis regarding a crucial factor in the case. He also didn't want to take the chance he might say anything close to what he was thinking, I knew I was right, he's probably involved with one of the medical providers or the personal trainer.

So he looked at Gayle and pressed forward, explaining his revised plan for their interrogations on Tuesday. "In light of the new information we talked about this morning, I think we need to change our strategy for interviews on Tuesday. I'll question Amanda and you handle the interview with Lance. That makes more sense to me, because I think he'll be less threatened by you, and more forthcoming, as long as you avoid being a hard ass and just focus on being kind, understanding, and mothering him into a truthful acknowledgment of his involvement.

"On the other hand, I'll be the kind and considerate male figure Amanda hasn't seen much of in her lifetime and hope we can make at least some progress with her. Do you agree?"

"As a matter of fact I do, but I'm not sure I can mother him because that job description's not part of my resume."

"Well, just do the best you can. You know what I mean anyway, just be nice and leading in your questions. You know, touchy and feely like women are supposed to be."

Gayle shot him a cynical glance, then stood and started gathering her papers and putting them into her briefcase. "It's close to noon and I think we're done here. You need to get ready for your afternoon activities, and I have work to do."

"I agree, we've made good progress, and I do need a few minutes to clean up and get over to Charlie's if I'm going to be on time. Don't work all weekend. We all need a break to keep our minds fresh. Thanks for coming over."

Bryan then led her to the door and opened it. She passed awkwardly by him while buttoning her coat, then walked into the still blustery forty-six degree late morning and was immediately socked by a sudden gust of gritty wind.

Chapter 20

Las Vegas, NV
December 6th
9:30 AM

The billing office hours of the Accident and Injury Health Restoration Clinics were from nine to six, five days a week according to both the answering service and the sign on the wall outside of the suite's entrance. On the first Tuesday of December, Hampton, Gayle, and Eli were parked in the empty lot of a steak house directly across the street from the building housing the fifth floor billing office. They'd already waited half an hour beyond the normal nine AM start of business to be certain all three of the staff members were on the job and engaged in their everyday tasks before they disrupted their routine.

Dixon had recommended Hampton include Eli as part of the mini-assault team, so he could keep an eye on the receptionist and deal with any possible counter-attacks launched by Watson attorneys during the time Hampton and Gayle were conducting their interviews. Hampton had agreed two federal agents on the scene would add credibility, as well as corroborating statements should any problems arise.

Hampton led as the three-agent team entered the plush reception area of the fifth floor suite. Approaching the receptionist, identified by her name plate as Sally Blackburn, Bryan presented his credentials and introduced himself. "Good morning, Ms. Blackburn, I'm Agent Bryan Hampton from the United States Department of Justice. This is Agent Eli Wilson, also from the Department of

Justice, and this is Special Agent Gayle Baker from the MFCB." Both Eli and Gayle then showed their ID's to a stunned and visibly alarmed Sally Blackburn, after which Bryan resumed his matter of fact, yet intimidating introduction.

"We're part of a joint task force investigating health care fraud. We're here to interview Mr. Lance Beasley and Ms. Amanda Booth, and we'd appreciate it if you would please escort us to their offices immediately. Agent Wilson will follow us, then return here with you to the reception area to answer any questions you might have and to be available to assist us should we need to call on him."

Sally seemed frightened beyond her ability to do anything but conform to Hampton's request and quickly opened the door to the inside office, then apprehensively led them down a long, wide hall past a massive conference room, a full kitchen, and a production room full of printers, copying machines, servers, and multiple flat screen monitors. As they approached the part of the office farthest from the reception area, they saw two open doors on opposite sides of the hall, and about twenty feet beyond them, a pair of massive double doors marking the end of the hallway. Even at a distance of twenty-five feet, the tasteful gold lettering on each of those imposing doors was clearly legible. One declared 'Private Office,' while the other simply read 'Dr. Ari Mirzoyan.'

Glancing through the open doors where the group stopped, it appeared to Hampton that Lance and Amanda both had identical, oversized offices. He estimated their spaces were about the size of a large living room, maybe twenty-five feet square, or about three times the size of the average DOJ office. No gold lettering on these doors, but both employees had their names on plaques attached to the walls outside their spaces. Bryan directed Sally toward Lance Beasley's office, telling her, "Please take us to Mr. Beasley first." All four of them then entered Lance's office.

Sally only managed to say, "These Justice Department Agents are here to see you and Amanda." Beasley stood and looked at the group, speechless and noticeably uneasy.

Hampton took charge, instructing Eli to go across the hall and invite Amanda into the proceedings. Once she was in the room and standing next to Lance, Hampton repeated exactly the same message he delivered to Sally in the reception area, but with some further explanations. "Agent Baker will remain here with you, Mr. Beasley, while I step across the hall to chat with Ms. Booth. Agent Wilson will return to the reception area with Ms. Blackburn to help her with any issues she might have. If you all cooperate and answer our questions, we can be out of your hair in no time at all.

"There's one more thing I need to ask before we separate into our groups. There are several patient records we want to review in great detail a little later on. Who should I ask to pull any charts and retrieve any information that might be archived and not part of your current files?"

Amanda answered quickly and with reasonable confidence by challenging the legality of his request. "I don't think we can show you patient information without permission from our attorneys. I'm sure you're aware of HIPAA regulations prohibiting the disclosure of confidential health information."

Hampton responded to her objection by answering, "Ms. Booth, we're respectful of all the laws of this nation. It's the full-time responsibility of the Department of Justice to see that those laws are enforced, and that's precisely why we're here chatting with the two of you today. We want to make sure you and Mr. Beasley aren't violating any laws, specifically the laws prohibiting the filing of false claims.

"We're especially concerned you might be doing something Dr. Mirzoyan the owner of this business isn't aware of and would in all probability not condone. We have the legal right to request and inspect your records, and if you fully understand the HIPAA regulations, you'll recall one of the exceptions to the privacy regulations is your obligation to cooperate, and disclose information to governmental agencies and the courts. Now if there are no more questions, I'd appreciate it if we could move on to our separate interviews so we might all be done by lunch time."

Hampton's session with Amanda went basically as they had anticipated. While he was able to establish a restrained rapport with her, she remained guarded and careful with every answer and explanation concerning her personal life, as well as her duties at the office. She was candid regarding her dismissal following the audit she performed on Mirzoyan's billing practices, but offered a new explanation for her termination.

"The insurance company was determined to find something wrong with Dr. Mirzoyan's claims, and all I could see was the doctors working for him were doing everything they could to provide comprehensive care for their patients. They were making certain their patients got well, no matter how much it cost. I don't believe most insurance companies actually want to pay for good treatment. They just pay doctors as little as possible, and Medicare and Medicaid are even worse."

Hampton did learn Amanda had actually written a letter to Dr. Mirzoyan expressing her interest in a position soon after she started working for the TPA.

Apparently, it took around two months for him to get back to her and invite her in for an interview. She explained to Hampton that part of the interview process involved taking a "weird test," telling him "I must have done well on it, since I got the job."

It seemed clear from the interview that Amanda Booth admired her employer, enjoyed her job, and possibly believed she was involved in a perfectly legitimate operation. Hampton concluded she was either the best actress in Las Vegas, or she had completely forgotten all the rules of appropriate coding and reimbursement that she learned in her training and worked to enforce during her time at both the insurance company and the TPA.

She seemed genuinely ignorant of the fact it was fraudulent to modify documentation submitted by the providers, bill for services they didn't render, and habitually change billing codes to the most complex and costly treatments. As Hampton considered the rationality of that particular line of reasoning, he paused and looked directly at Amanda for one long minute and decided she was definitely a actress, and a talented one at that.

Hampton realized the time he and Gayle had allotted for the initial interviews was nearly up, so he concluded his session with Amanda by telling her, "Ms. Booth, you're an extremely bright and well trained medical billing expert. You've worked for two third party payors, and you once understood right from wrong. Unfortunately, you've fallen into an awful situation here. You're committing fraud multiple times every day, possibly on every bill you handle.

"We're on to this deliberate scheme you're deeply involved in, and our initial belief is you're the one mainly responsible for it. We'll prove our case, and you'll be charged along with anyone else who's had a hand in it, and at this point it looks like you and your friend across the hall will definitely be going to prison for a long time."

Hampton then stared at Amanda for a long moment and handed her a sheet of paper. "Now, here's a list of five patients' names. Please arrange to have all their records available to us immediately. We're going to take a quick break, then you and Mr. Beasley will spend the rest of the day with Agent Baker and me going through ever line item on every bill we already know is fraudulent.

"We'll be asking you both to tell us why we're wrong, requiring you each to justify everything you submitted to the insurance companies on the claims for those cases. You should plan on meeting in the conference room down the hall in fifteen minutes. That will give you time to get the documentation together. I want to start with the bills for Henry James Lattimer, date of birth January 14, 1956, patient ID number 0218624778. See you in a few minutes."

****

Earlier, after everyone but Gayle had left Lance's office, she suggested they sit at a small conference table for their discussion. By then, Lance had partially recovered from the unnerving reality that federal agents had come to question him about a possible fraud scheme. Unpleasant memories of a former life of concealing and suppressing personal interests and choices bolstered his determination, and he silently resolved he wouldn't be intimidated in this or any other situation.

In his first attempt at bravado he told Gayle, "I prefer to stay right where I am here at my desk." Then to allow his courage to gain some momentum, he asked, "Now tell me again, who exactly are you? I'd like to see your ID, and please explain what organization you're from, because I didn't quite catch all those letters the other agent clipped off after your name."

Gayle was troubled by Lance's initial responses and feared Hampton's belief that an understanding mother figure could get Lance to cooperate and open up was about to go down the drain. "My name is Gayle Baker, and I'm with the Medical Fraud Crime Bureau. We're part of a joint task force working with the U. S. Department of Justice to investigate and prevent fraud, and I simply want to ask you a few questions relevant to an investigation we're pursuing that involves the clinics you work for."

After examining her credentials for more time than was necessary, Lance tossed the case onto his desk and said, "Never heard of you or the MFCB. Why should I answer your questions?"

"If you prefer to talk with Agent Hampton, I can arrange to have him meet with you after he finishes with Ms. Booth."

"I prefer not to talk with either of you, and I have no intention of answering any questions. Now, why don't you leave my office and sit in the reception room while you wait for your friend to finish with Amanda?"

In her years with the FBI, Gayle had encountered this type of temporary false courage from suspects on several occasions. Generally, guilty people either breakdown under initial questioning and tell everything they know, or they pretend to cooperate and tell a series of lies mixed with truth. In the latter case, unless they're incredibly skilled liars, they trip themselves up with conflicting or differing versions of what they claim is truth, and most of them eventually capitulate and confess after intensive questioning.

When an accused person like Lance decides to be belligerent and antagonistic, there's only one way to deal with them; scare the hell out of them, which is exactly what Gayle decided to do. "Listen to me, smart ass. You're in no position to be a tough guy because we can bury you and your friend across the hall with the evidence we already have. We're here to decide if it's just the two of you stealing millions from the insurance companies, or if someone else has put you up to it, which is far more likely based on how dim-witted you're acting right now."

Lance maintained his aggressive attitude, saying, "If you had the evidence you claim, you should be here to arrest us, so why are you here just asking questions? You're fishing for information, and you have no evidence of anything. You know nothing about me, and you know less about this perfectly legitimate business. By the way, where are your warrants to inspect our patient files?"

Gayle decided to quit asking questions and try to rattle Lance with facts they already knew about him personally and his duties in the billing office. Then she planned to weave those facts into a modified but plausible story of how the fraud was being committed, indicating clearly how Lance and Amanda were the central figures in the scheme. Her hope was Lance would conclude their case against him was strong, and he would want to cooperate, hoping for leniency. "If you really think we know nothing about you and what you do here for the six figure income you get, maybe you should shut up and listen while I enlighten you about some of what we already do know."

By the time Gayle finished relating detailed facts the FBI investigators had discovered about Lance's personal, family, and educational background, she could see his facade of confidence was beginning to weaken. Once she explained in detail his role in the clinic's billing office, the chinks in his posturing had grown into discernible cracks. With only ten minutes remaining of their previously agreed upon interview period, Baker shared a version of the DOJ's working theory of the fraud scheme operation, in reality a heavily slanted and embellished account that placed Lance and Amanda at the center of the scheme.

"So do you still think we don't know anything about you and what you're doing here, big shot? There's only one part of this story we actually want you to help us better understand, so I'm going to try one more time and ask you a question. How did you weasel your way into your current position? We know you were in an accident and were treated at the Henderson clinic. What we don't know is how you managed to con your way into a position where you could rip off all this money."

Gayle continued her assault, "Have you actually ever stopped to realize how much money you and Amanda bill daily, monthly, or annually? Think about it, smart guy, the four clinics combined are billing services for an average of nine hundred patients a week, and the average charge for each patient visit is seven hundred and forty-five dollars, which by the way, is over four times the mean visit charge for all other Clark County chiropractors.

"You and your fried across the hall are submitting claims for about $670,000 a week, which is nearly thirty-five million dollars a year. Your annual salary is one half of one percent of that amount. Excluding your leader Mirzoyan, total salaries for all the clinics' employees last year was under four million. Have you ever stopped to think where the other thirty-one million goes? You're part of a big scam, but you've been conned, duped, and bamboozled, and now you're left holding the bag."

Lance didn't answer; he simply sat at his desk looking at Gayle, initially refusing to utter a word. Her experience and instincts told her he was ready to talk, to explain, to defend himself by correcting the false assumptions she had outlined. Lance apparently began to realize he somehow needed to shift most of the blame away from himself, but he didn't know exactly how or when to do it.

Gayle suspected he needed time to think, probably to talk to Washburn, his trusted friend and lover, before he said anything. She could tell he had decided to be evasive one more time, and responded to her with indignant confidence. "Your theories about what I do in my job are ridiculous, and I have nothing to say except the FBI wasted a lot of time investigating the background of an innocent man from a small town in southern Illinois."

Gayle sat looking at Lance and realized the interview time was up, then fired a symbolic shot between his eyes, while staring directly at the now nervous young man. "We believe someone else is behind all this, because you and your friend across the hall are getting next to nothing compared to what you're helping them steal. But if you don't help us prove who's pulling your strings, we'll be satisfied with tossing the two of you in jail for the time being.

"Your only chance here is to start talking, and you better decide to do it real soon. By the way, thanks for being so transparent in spite of saying nothing. I'd strongly advise you to stay away from the poker tables in this town because everyone you're playing against will know when you're bluffing, like you were with me for the past hour. You're scared and we both know it, so drop the tough guy routine."

*****

After leaving Lance's office, Gayle found Eli and Hampton already in the conference room quietly talking. Once she'd closed the door, the three quickly debriefed each other about the events and outcomes of their individual assignments. Interestingly, Eli reported Sally made no outside calls, and the incoming calls didn't seem to be from Mirzoyan or anyone else with a leadership or legal role in the business. That was surprising and somewhat unexpected because Hampton had anticipated by now, one of the three employees would have found a way to reach out to Mirzoyan. Nevertheless, it was a safe bet Lance and Amanda were likely placing calls at that very moment, and all those conversations were being monitored.

Because Hampton's interview with Amanda had gone much as they expected, Gayle's report drew the most interest. Clearly their assumptions that Lance might be the key to successful next steps in the investigation were valid, but his unwillingness to cooperate so far was a disappointment. They decided during the case review session over the next hour, their strategy would be to divide any shared interests Amanda and Lance held, making them adversaries rather than allies. All initial questions would be directed to Amanda and Lance would be witnessing her answers.

By shaping every question to Amanda in such a way that the question elicited the same answer over and over again, the finger of blame would soon point directly and consistently at Lance. Emphasizing the strategy, Hampton gave an explanation to be sure Gayle understood. "Every question we ask needs to end in such a way that Amanda will answer in some form or fashion by saying she selects a code for each line on the bill that most accurately describes what was documented in the medical record. So we ask her line by line, why did you pick this code, and if she answers something other than what we want her to say, we ask it again, until she finally understands the answer we want is the code she billed is the code that most accurately described what was documented in the medical record.

"My guess is in less than half an hour, after several restatements of the initial question to get the expected answer, Amanda will robotically start giving us the desired response the first time we ask the question. Once we get to that point, as long as we have thirty to forty consistent answers, we'll excuse her, telling her to take a break for a few minutes until we're ready to review the next case. At that point we'll shift our focus and questions to Lance."

"So you're telling me you expect Lance to realize Amanda's explanations have focused all the blame for the false claims on him because he approves and manages all the medical record documentation?" Gayle asked.

"We're going to drill that prospect into his brain as the likely outcome of the position she chose to take, even with him in the room. What we really want him to begin believing is it's every man for himself when it comes to criminal accusations and avoiding prosecution. We need him to flip and give us Mirzoyan, or more likely Washburn, the way it's beginning to look."

Sally knocked on the conference room door, then opened it and placed an impressive stack of paperwork organized into folders on the table, telling them, "These are the records for the first three patient files you requested. The file for Henry James Lattimer is the top one. I'm still working to assemble the information on the other two patients now. Also, Amanda and Lance are waiting in their offices for me to let them know when you want them for the next meeting."

"Tell them to come right away, Sally. And thank you very much for your help, and especially for gathering these files so quickly. Agent Wilson will return with you to the reception area as soon as Ms. Booth and Mr. Beasley have joined us here," Hampton answered.

The planned questioning began five minutes later. It turned out Hampton was wrong; Amanda figured out how to give the answer they expected within the first five minutes. He allowed Gayle to continue the questioning until over half the bills in Henry Lattimer's file were reviewed, then he decided it was enough; the point was made. Amanda would likely maintain she was innocent because her job was to code what was documented in the medical record.

While Hampton was in the process of telling Amanda she was excused so they could talk with Lance, Eli entered the room and asked him to step out into the hall for a moment. "I just got a call from the agents monitoring this phone line. While we were holding our little strategy session, two calls were made from this office. Amanda called Mirzoyan's cell phone and spoke directly to him, explaining what was happening in the office. He told her to stall as long as she could, say as little as possible, then he promised to get their attorney over here as soon as he could reach him.

"He didn't mention Watson's name or any attorney's name. No subsequent outgoing call from Mirzoyan's cell phone has yet been recorded. The other call from here was placed by Lance, and it went to the Henderson clinic. He asked to talk with Washburn, but was told the doctor was with a patient. He did leave a voice mail, telling Washburn he needed to speak with him immediately, emphasizing there were federal agents at the billing office asking questions about false claims. So far, Washburn hasn't called back, and he's made no other outgoing calls from either his cell or his office phone."

Hampton told Eli he was going to tell Gayle to step out into the hall, and Eli was to share the same information with her. In the meantime he would begin questioning Lance. Hampton had decided things were progressing better than expected, and he wanted his team to finish up and withdraw from the billing office before any confrontations took place with Mirzoyan's attorneys. With the activities at all four of the clinic's offices scheduled for the next morning, he wanted to avoid any legal clashes that might reveal their plans or complicate events already in motion. He also told Eli to ask Gayle to quickly return to Amanda's office and occupy her for the next fifteen minutes in any way she could while he finished-up with Lance.

Alone with Lance, and with their self-imposed deadline approaching, Bryan decided to summarize in an objective and solemn manner what he expected Lance to do if he didn't want to end up in jail. "Mr. Beasley, you can see from what your associate has already told us that she's identified her escape route from this mess you both find yourselves in. She claims she consistently and honestly coded what was documented, and the person responsible for the documentation is you. We know that's bullshit, but it won't look that way to a jury.

"Amanda will obviously do anything possible to stay out of prison, so she can continue to raise her three children. So in spite of what you believe to be your enduring friendship with her, she'll happily throw you under the bus to save herself. You're bright, you're single, and you're in an untenable spot. However, what's of equal importance is you're in a position to help us get to your boss.

"We know Dr. Mirzoyan is responsible, but we need your help to prove it. He's a professional crook and has shielded and insulated himself from direct involvement in the scheme by positioning you, Amanda, and probably almost everyone working for him as the perpetrators. You, on the other hand, are a greedy and naïve novice who wanted something for nothing, and that's why we have all the proof necessary to convict you, and most likely all four of the chiropractors running the clinics. Now we know you have a special interest in one of those men, specifically a romantic interest in Dr. Gerald Washburn."

Bryan saw Lance bristle and attempt to deny the last statement, but warned him not to interrupt. "We don't have time to play games here, so don't mess with me. We know you're gay, as is your friend Washburn, who tries unsuccessfully to hide his sexual preference. But that's not relevant to this case except that your relationship may provide a path for both of you to avoid prison. If the two of you are willing to testify and help provide the evidence we need to prosecute Mirzoyan and any others primarily responsible for organizing this elaborate scheme, we may be able to help you."

Hampton moved from the opposite side of the table and sat in the chair next to Lance, sliding it so close the sides of their seats were touching. "I don't like you, Beasley, nor do I care for anyone else who so easily compromises their integrity by pretending they don't know they're breaking the law every day they go to work. So think our offer over carefully, because if you reject it, then you need to consider the grim reality of your future as a resident of the federal penal system. I'm done with you for today. You have until tomorrow afternoon at four to give us your decision. We'll be here then with a warrant for your arrest, and the only way we won't exercise it is if you tell us what we want to know. And don't try to leave town; we'll be watching you every minute until you decide to do the right thing."

With that said, Hampton left Lance sitting in the conference room looking stunned, visibly shaken, and nearly in tears as he likely considered the harsh reality of his situation. Even to the agents, the office air seemed heavy and thick with the aftermath of what had just taken place.

Within minutes the three agents had left the building and crossed the street to their car, which was now surrounded by a host of Cadillacs, Jaguars, Mercedes, and BMW's parked by the gathering lunch-time crowd. "Who eats steak for lunch?" Gayle asked as she climbed into the back seat.

"If things go the way I hope, it won't be Dr. Mirzoyan for much longer," Hampton answered with a satisfied smile.

Chapter 21

Las Vegas, NV
December 7th
8:45 AM

Dixon accompanied Hampton, Eli, and Abe on their trip to the Henderson clinic on Wednesday morning, and he'd been quiet during most of the nearly half hour drive from the office. As they waited for the nine o'clock hour to arrive, he spoke reflectively and unequivocally to the three men. "You know health care practitioner's offices are intended to be places of therapy, healing, and compassion. They can also be places of sadness and despondency, when patients confront the reality of diseases that change and sometimes end their lives. Caring, competent, and honest health care providers dispense more than therapies and medications. They also administer the hope and reassurance every patient wants and needs.

"When those entrusted with the welfare of their patients abuse the leverage their position of trust provides them by overcharging, over-treating, over-prescribing, or by exaggerating or miss-diagnosing, the end result for the patient can vary from inconsequential to catastrophic. On the other hand, any excessive, unnecessary, or ineffective care is by definition wasteful, and adds tremendously to the overall cost of health care, impacting every citizen, business owner, and taxpayer in this country who pays for medical services and health care insurance. The industry debates about fraud, waste, and abuse as if they were all unique issues. I believe they're simply different manifestations of the same disease and crime. The disease is greed and the crime is fraud.

"In the next fifteen minutes our agents will breach the pseudo-sanctity of all four of Dr. Mirzoyan's clinics. In every case I hope these agents are armed with an attitude of righteous indignation against these crooks that demean their professions, mistreat their patients, and defraud every one of us just because they think they can get away with it. We're going to do all we can to take down every one of these parasites who suffer from this transmissible disease called greed, and we're starting today. I'm glad I'm here with the three of you to see the beginning of this state-wide campaign."

As all four men knew, the show of force this morning was the second manifestation of their strategy of disruption. The unexpected visits were designed to shake Mirzoyan's organization with sufficient force to yield new information in any way they could get it. Some would be gleaned from interviews with the doctors, but the majority of the additional evidence they hoped to gather would come from the expected rash of phone calls triggered by their visits, all of which would be closely monitored. Once the agents left each office, those calls to Mirzoyan and hopefully others yet to be identified would undoubtedly be instigated by the chiropractors in every one of the clinics.

At the Henderson clinic, Hampton's objective was to convert Dr. Gerald Washburn from Ari Mirzoyan's accomplice to a collaborator for the Justice Department. If he could accomplish that goal, it would effectively shut down one of the clinics and at the same time provide investigators with unprecedented access to the inner workings of the fraud operation.

On Tuesday night the FBI had overheard two phone conversations between Washburn and Lance. Oddly, in spite of everything Lance related to his friend, including the ultimatum Hampton had issued, Washburn somehow didn't believe he himself could possibly be a suspect. At the end of the first call he had advised Lance to simply remain calm and not give in to what he termed 'government scare tactics.'

When Lance called back several hours later, he was approaching a state of panic and had again pleaded for Washburn to take him seriously, but curiously his urgings went unheeded. Washburn simply dismissed his friend's concerns and assured him things would look better to him in the morning, then disconnected the call. The intrusion about to take place was designed to be unexpected and to send a clear message to Washburn he was in fact a prime suspect in the investigation, confirming what Lance had already tried to impress on him during the phone call the previous night. Hampton hoped things would look much worse to Washburn after the morning's confrontation, and as a result he would align his interests with Lance's and the two of them would then assist in the investigation against Mirzoyan.

At precisely nine AM, thirteen members of the Department of Justice converged on Mirzoyan's four clinics. A similar procedure was followed by each of the teams. With the exception of Hampton's group, each team was composed of three agents adhering to precisely the same agenda and process. They introduced themselves to the receptionist, explained they were there to interview the doctor in charge, and asked to be immediately escorted to his office.

Two agents met with each doctor in his office for exactly thirty minutes, while the third agent stayed in the reception and billing office observing the activities of the employees in those areas. All office lines were being monitored, so there was no attempt to oversee employees in other areas of the clinics. Each of the chiropractors was asked the same background questions, a formality since most of that information was already known. Next, the doctors were probed about their own specific duties and responsibilities at the clinic. This was immediately followed by a transition into a sequence of queries regarding their legal responsibility to oversee other members of the clinic's staff who provided direct care to the patients.

The issue the agents wanted to better understand was the degree to which each doctor truly understood his legal obligations to oversee staff members treating patients. While ignorance of the law was no excuse for any degree of negligence, establishing a practitioner had blatantly disregarded regulations could have a dramatic impact in a trial.

The licenses of most ancillary health care providers such as radiology technicians and physical therapy assistants required their patient care to be supervised by someone with a more advanced degree and additional training. Failure to properly oversee the activities of those personnel, who in most cases billed their services under the supervising clinicians' license, constituted a violation of the obligations inherent in their professional licenses.

The claims information provided through the MFCB database clearly revealed that the volume of services billed every day in each of the clinics precluded the possibility of adequate oversight by any one person. The unlikelihood one doctor had the capacity to oversee the huge number of services billed each day, coupled with the physical impossibility for a staff of four or even five providers to deliver them, imparted additional credibility to the allegation the clinics were submitting false claims. The MFCB analysts had unwisely concluded the doctors overseeing each clinic's operations likely had no idea about the excessive volume of work billed each day in the clinics they oversaw.

Before the agents left the chiropractors to consider their bleak situations, they all delivered a final message, followed by two questions. Those concluding messages were scripted and were to be delivered almost verbatim by each agent. "Doctor, we have proof you're operating a fraudulent business in this office. We have the data, the witnesses, and all the evidence we need to close your doors and arrest you today. But we're not going to do that, because we want to give you a chance to think about helping yourself, while helping us at the same time. We want you to testify against your boss and whoever else is leading this massive fraud scheme.

"So before we leave, we have two questions to ask you. First, do you understand the consequences of and the penalties for the federal and state laws you're violating? To make this question specific to your situation, what we're really asking is do you realize, if convicted, your fines will exceed your net worth, and you'll go to prison for more years than you can imagine? And our last question is even more straightforward and important. Can we depend on your help?

"You have a very limited period of time to make your decision. All your cohorts are being asked these same questions as we speak. We only need one of you to help, so I wouldn't wait too long if I were you. Here's a card and number. When you make up your mind, please call, and I'd advise you to make the call sooner than later!" All the agents had delivered that exact message as their concluding remark, then left their assigned clinics and returned to the DOJ office in downtown Las Vegas.

Hampton's team followed most of the same processes in the Henderson clinic, with a few variations. When they first saw the young doctor in his office, they were surprised by his appearance. His face was puffy and discolored, one of his eyes was swollen and colored a dark shade of blue transitioning to a yellowish tone, and he seemed to move awkwardly and stiffly. Hampton immediately asked, "What happened to your face, Dr. Washburn?"

Washburn unwisely decided to stick with the story he'd repeated over the last three days to his staff and any patients who had asked him the same question. "Is that why you're here? Did you catch the man who tried to rob me? Did the police send you?"

"No, they didn't, and we're not here because of a mugging, but we are here to discuss a theft. When and where were you attacked and what police agency did you report it to?"

Washburn ignored their question and asked, "If you're not here about my assault, then we don't need to discuss it anymore. I have patients waiting. Why are you here?"

Hampton decided they could verify his story later and sensed Washburn's condition was noteworthy, but they didn't need to pursue it then. He knew they needed to get back to their planned approach and schedule. Dixon was part of Hampton's team, and he was there to conduct a specific part of Washburn's questioning. Abe, in the meantime, tended to the staff in the reception and business area. Hampton and Eli tag-teamed with the standard scripted questions for the allotted thirty minute session, then ended with the, 'We only need one of you to help' line. Then Hampton reintroduced Dixon, this time emphasizing his U.S. Attorney for the District of Nevada title.

Dixon, in a serious but unintimidating tone, began. "Dr. Washburn, I would normally not be here today with these two gentlemen, but I've come along this morning to emphasize the seriousness of your situation and to help you recognize you have a chance to reclaim your career and possibly salvage the next several years of your life. From our perspective, you offer us two advantages not shared by the doctors in charge of the other three clinics. First, you've only been working here a little over a year and you likely didn't understand exactly what you'd gotten yourself into for a number of months. We estimate it took you around eight or nine months to recognize it and admit to yourself something was wrong."

Dixon saw from Washburn's demeanor and body language that their supposition wasn't exactly correct, but he continued anyway. "Second, we know you have a romantic relationship with Lance Beasley, who works in the billing office. We know Beasley looks to you as the wiser, but more idealistic partner, if it's okay to use that term. And because of that, we believe you can influence him to make a decision which will be best for both of you. We know he's running scared. These gentlemen were with him yesterday morning; they've both seen it first-hand.

"His associate Amanda Booth has taken a position that his falsification of the medical records was the reason she fraudulently coded the bills. He's in a terrible position, as are you. You're a young man with a professional degree and you have your whole life and career ahead of you. If you're wise enough to decide to do the right thing, you could dodge a bullet that might otherwise be lethal to you and Lance."

For emphasis Dixon paused and looked directly at Washburn's swollen eye. "What we're asking is for you and Lance to assist us by explaining everything you know about this operation. Who tells you what to do? What other employees are involved and to what extent? We want to know who Dr. Mirzoyan works with. Where all the patients come from? How many services are actually delivered in comparison to what's billed? Where does all the money go? How long have you known about the false claims? What have you done to try and stop it, if anything? What happened to your predecessor? Have you ever spoken with him? I can go on and on, but you must understand by now what we're looking for.

"What I can promise you is we'll provide you and Lance with full immunity if you cooperate with us in every way possible and assist us in identifying and prosecuting all those responsible for the organization and ongoing operation of this conspiracy. You have seven hours to call me with your decision, unless you want to come downtown with us right now and begin the process."

Washburn's mouth was dry; his thoughts were disorganized and muddled. He searched to find a safe answer, but fear seemed to block any prudent response. Dixon, Hampton, and Eli sat across his desk, staring at him and waiting for his response. He wondered why he couldn't face this reality last night when Lance warned him. What was he thinking? What should he do? He'd already been threatened and warned specifically about talking to the authorities. What will happen to him if says one word to them?

He subconsciously touched his still tender eye, and his instinct was to run, to flee Las Vegas and disappear before the brutally vicious man paid him another visit. Suddenly and strangely, he recalled something from all the police shows he'd watched in his lifetime, and one reality jumped out at him. Whenever anyone suspected of a crime started answering questions from the authorities without a lawyer by their side, they ended up getting screwed. NYPD to the rescue, he thought, then he responded to Paul, "I'll consider your offer with the help of my attorney and get back to you within the timeframe you've outlined, provided that's what my attorney recommends."

Hampton started to say something, but Paul preempted him by standing and moving toward the door while he reminded Washburn, "The offer is good until five this afternoon, and we want you to make a wise decision, so make sure your attorney understands the extent of your complicity and the evidence we have condemning you. If by chance your lawyer would like to meet with us, I'll be happy to accommodate him." Dixon then held the door open while signaling Hampton and Eli to exit. There were no handshakes or well wishes as the meeting ended; only grim resolve and determination departing through the door, and fear and uncertainty behind the desk.

Once they were back in their car, Eli offered an observation, "Someone beat the hell out of Washburn within the last week or so. You should have seen him, Abe; black eye, swollen face, and he could hardly move, so he took some blows to his ribs and back, too. I don't think he reported anything to anyone, but I'm planning on following up with all the local police agencies as soon as we get back to the office, Bryan."

"My guess is you're right, Eli. Let us all know what you find out as soon as you're done checking. Once we know if he reported his attack, we can press him more on what happened."

During the ride back to the office, the agents finalized their plans for the remainder of the day. Since both Lance and Washburn were given decision deadlines for later that afternoon, Dixon hoped he would hear from Dr. Washburn or his attorney in the next two hours. They were all hopeful Lance and Washburn would both come to the conclusion it was in their best interests to work with the DOJ, but if the two men decided otherwise, they would need to depend on one of the other chiropractors deciding to help them.

The agents had moved quickly over the last week implementing Hampton's aggressive and risky plans, and for the next few hours they waited to see what the seeds of fear and dissention they had planted would yield. For the rest of the day they were in constant communication with agents monitoring the phones, especially Washburn's and Beasley's cells as well as their business lines. Dixon had already warned the agents listening on Washburn's lines that he was likely to contact his attorney, and if he did, they were only to record the name of his lawyer and the time Washburn placed the call, because those conversations were privileged and not admissible as evidence.

The most vital information, however, was likely to come from conversations between Washburn and Lance, as well as between Mirzoyan and Washburn or one of the other three chiropractors. Hampton had already received a call from the agents monitoring Mirzoyan's lines. They advised him they had recorded calls from two of the chiropractors to Mirzoyan's cell phone voicemail while Hampton was still meeting with Washburn. The messages were simple requests for Mirzoyan to call back immediately. So far, Mirzoyan had not made any return calls.

After hearing that news, Hampton immediately told Eli to contact the agents assigned to follow Mirzoyan and find out where he was. Thirty seconds later, Eli reported to Hampton, "Mirzoyan is at his country club on the fourth hole."

"How do they know he's actually on the fourth hole?" Bryan asked.

"They know because they're on the third hole following him in a golf cart along with their rented clubs. They said it was the only way they could keep track of him. They also mentioned, to avoid being conspicuous, they had to buy shirts, hats, and balls in the pro shop, adding they thought their job should have some fringe benefits."

Paul shook his head. "I'm glad those are FBI guys and they're not on our expense account, Bryan. Two shirts, two hats, two rounds of golf, two sets of rental clubs, two greens fees, and at least a dozen balls will hit somebody's budget at around seven or eight hundred bucks.

"But I guess that's a small price to pay when we need to know where this guy is on a crucial day like today. If Mirzoyan has his phone turned off, and he's only on the fourth hole, then he'll be unreachable for at least another three hours or until around one this afternoon. That may cause his troops to reach out to someone else for advice, and we could get a direct connection to Watson."

"That's too much to hope for, Paul. We'll never be that lucky, but maybe the doctors will believe they're being ignored, then reach out to someone else who's implicated that we're not even aware of yet," Hampton said without much conviction.

"Maybe we'll get real lucky and somebody on Mirzoyan's staff will post a video on YouTube of Mirzoyan and Watson planning how to save their asses," Abe added cynically.

Chapter 22

Las Vegas, NV
December 7th
11:45 AM

Until last night Hampton had barely spoken with Charlie since Monday morning when they both arrived at the office. They did manage to have a long conversation on the phone the previous night, and both agreed to have lunch together the next day. In spite of everything going on with the case, Bryan wasn't about to back out on a lunch date with the woman he was becoming more and more attracted to. They had agreed to leave the office at noon, so Bryan needed to wrap up the meeting with Eli, Abe, and Gayle in the next ten minutes.

For the last hour the group had been discussing messages the FBI had forwarded them from all the clinic phone lines, as well as from Mirzoyan's cell. Dr. Mirzoyan had not retrieved any of his messages, and he hadn't placed a single outgoing call. Fifteen minutes earlier the agents golfing one hole behind the doctor's foursome advised Eli that Mirzoyan and his group grabbed sandwiches from the clubhouse snack shop and had just left the tenth tee after Mirzoyan hit a lousy drive into the left rough.

Hampton's team had reviewed the transcripts of the voice messages left on Mirzoyan's phone, and it was clear the agents' visits to the clinics that morning along with the questions they asked and the messages they conveyed had indeed stirred the pot. Two of the chiropractors were obviously worried, and a third doctor seemed only slightly calmer, but still expressed serious concerns about possible legal actions against him. All three had left several messages each, but the substance of all eight voicemails was fundamentally a request for Mirzoyan to call back as soon as possible.

The prized message of the morning was left by Washburn, and it exceeded all their expectations. After reading the transcript, they requested the digital audio of the actual call and had just completed the second round of listening to it. Each of them had made their own detailed notes on the specific facts Washburn revealed in his telling two-minute dissertation and ultimatum.

Hampton told Abe, "I'd like you and Gayle to aggregate all our individual notes from Washburn's message into a single list of the facts he revealed, especially those that until today we either didn't know about or we'd been unable to confirm. If you can have that done by one-thirty and still get some lunch, we can meet again then and map out a strategy for the rest of the day. We've promised Lance and Amanda we'd be there by four, and we've urged Washburn to contact us before five. Based on what I've heard from his voice message to Mirzoyan, we may need to be more pro-active about our plans for him. Once Mirzoyan listens to Washburn's message, the one thing we do know is Dr. Washburn won't be safe, and we need to make sure he understands the danger he's in."

Bryan decided to take Charlie to Chicago Joe's for lunch. It was an excellent little Italian restaurant not far from the office and a favorite of Las Vegas locals for over thirty-five years. He chose the non-glitzy, reasonably priced and quiet place, so he could enjoy good food and Charlie's great company, and his pick proved to be perfect.

The hour they spent together was satisfying, and both sensed their growing feelings for one another. Despite the disparities in their ages and their stages of life, they continued to discover more and more common ground in their values and outlooks on life. Near the end of the meal Charlie asked Bryan, "What's going on tonight that you thought we better have lunch rather than plan anything for this evening?"

"Well, it's even better than what I suspected last night. We recorded a voicemail Washburn left for Mirzoyan. He called him about an hour after our little discussion with him this morning. It's more than we could have hoped for, because in less than two minutes his message confirmed several things we already suspected. But even more important, we learned a lot of new and damaging information. Unfortunately for Washburn, I think by leaving the voicemail he's placed himself in serious jeopardy.

"Apparently, he got beat up last Friday by some strong arm guy Mirzoyan hired to intimidate him and convince him to wise up and keep his mouth shut. We suspect the message he left today will force Mirzoyan to take some drastic action to contain any damage Washburn might cause. Our next step, as soon as I get back to the office, is to decide exactly how we're going to handle Washburn in the next few hours. I think this is our big chance to bring Washburn and his friend Lance together and get them to realize the precarious and dangerous situation their roles, actions, and relationship have placed them in."

"That's some major drama there, Bryan. Aren't you a little surprised at how fast everything's happening? It seems like you haven't been around long enough for things to be moving this quickly in your favor."

Hampton thought he detected some ambiguity in Charlie's question and comment and felt she intended to convey a double meaning. He decided to handle it with boldness and daring. "You're absolutely right, Charlie. Things are moving along nicely between the two of us, and I hope you feel the same way, even though I'm the new guy in town. If, on the other hand, you're commenting on the case, it too, is progressing nicely. And to be honest, I'm thrilled about the pace both our relationship and the case are progressing and evolving." Hampton quickly leaned over and gently kissed Charlie on the cheek, then signaled the waiter to bring the check.

"You seem awfully sure of yourself, Chicago man. But your confidence is part of what I like about you. However, I was really only making an observation about your case."

"See, you did it again! The term 'your case' is also unclear."

"That's enough. We need to get back to the office so you can figure out how to save Dr. Washburn and Lance from the bad guys."

As the three PM hour approached, the strategy session was well underway, but was still yielding mixed opinions without anything approaching a consensus on what exactly they should do. Hampton decided to invite Dixon into the meeting to update him on the latest information and solicit his advice on what they must and should do next. Fortunately, Dixon was available and eager to join their discussion.

Hampton began by telling him he would first summarize important information gleaned from Washburn's voicemail, then discuss competing options proposed by the team for protecting the doctor and Lance, while at the same time advancing their case and investigation of the fraud scheme. He warned Dixon they needed to reach a decision on how to proceed as soon as possible for two reasons. First, the deadlines set for the agents to meet with both men were minutes away. And second, and definitely more compelling, was the existence of a real threat to Washburn's life that he promised to explain later.

"Let's get on with it, Bryan, I understand the issues and the deadlines, so let's not waste any time."

With that urging from Dixon, Bryan began, "So I'll go through the critical things we learned from the voicemail Washburn left Mirzoyan. Washburn started by telling him he believes the Justice Department knows the clinic files false claims. He confirmed he'd been slow and gullible in recognizing and confronting his boss about the problems he was aware of. He mentioned he approached Mirzoyan about the issues over a month ago and Mirzoyan promised to get back to him, but never did. Instead, he accused Mirzoyan of sending a thug to scare him into keeping his mouth shut and make sure he never bothered the doctor again about these or any other issues. To emphasize that point, he reminded Mirzoyan that the visitor 'beat the crap out' of him, his words not mine. So that explains the condition of his face we all observed today.

"There's more, Paul, but before I go on, any thoughts so far?" Hampton asked.

"None, Bryan, keep going," Dixon urged.

"Washburn then told Mirzoyan he believes he's caught between us and the thug who promised to kill him if he ever complained to Mirzoyan again or went to the authorities about the operations of the clinic. He noted he's not sure what he's going to do, conceding he's caught between two bad choices. He threatened Mirzoyan, saying if he ever sees the hired assailant near him again he'll contact you, Paul, and tell you everything, then ask for protection.

"Then, apparently believing he had an opportunity to piss Mirzoyan off one more time, he informed him he had sent all clinic employees home with pay for the rest of the week, but not before he had them cancel all the scheduled patients for the same period of time. He closed with what I'm sure will further anger his boss, by commenting that irrespective of the fact, there won't be any patients or workers in the clinic for a few days it will obviously not stop Amanda from sending bills to insurance companies, since delivering actual services to real patients wasn't one of Mirzoyan's requirements for generating claims. So that's pretty much what was contained in the voicemail. Any questions, Paul?"

"Do we have a digital recording of Washburn saying all this?"

"We do, indeed, thanks to the wiretaps you requested and we received. Let me go on and talk about options for what to do next. We're worried about Washburn's safety and possibly Lance's as well. Protecting them both is a first priority, and since Mirzoyan is well aware of the deadlines we set for both of them to either cooperate with us or be arrested, we can assume Mirzoyan knows he also needs to act quickly and decisively.

"So our thinking is to somehow accelerate the decision-making process for both Lance and Washburn, then get them into protective custody. We believe we should start questioning them immediately and get their interviews on video, just in case something goes wrong and Mirzoyan's thug somehow gets to one or both of them sometime in the future. Let me stop here and ask if you agree with what we're proposing so far?"

"I can't argue with any of it, but what will we do if they refuse to cooperate?" Dixon asked.

"That's where our group's opinions begin to diverge. We've also considered the possibility one or both may have already retained legal counsel, and when we show up to meet with them, their attorneys might be present and insist their clients not be taken into custody. Another issue is, should we keep them separated and deal with each of them in isolation, or is our original plan to try and cut a package deal with both of them still the best option? We also--."

Dixon interrupted, "Hold on, Bryan. Has Mirzoyan heard Washburn's message, and if so, do we know what time he listened to it?"

Eli answered, "Yes, he's heard it. It was sometime around two, about an hour ago. I can guess what your next questions will be, so let me volunteer more information. He hasn't placed any calls to anyone, but he did listen to messages from all the other doctors working for him while he was driving home from the country club. The agents following him said all of a sudden he made an illegal U turn and headed back toward town. On the way he stopped at the same bar he went into yesterday afternoon, and that's where he is right now."

Bryan jumped from his seat and almost yelled, "He stopped at the same bar he went into yesterday? And right after he picked up Washburn's message? I've read the doctor's background file, and all about his bad habits and drinking in bars in the middle of the day isn't part of his profile. Tell one of the guys watching him to get his ass inside that bar right now and see what Mirzoyan's up to. If he's with someone, and I hope he is, we need to follow that person as well.

"Get another two agents over there immediately, preferably in something like a Prius, so if Mirzoyan or his friend sees the tail, they'll think George Clooney is following them and not us. It's obvious the doctor must know we're watching him, and he's been meeting with someone in that bar while our guys are outside admiring their new golf shirts."

Dixon stood quickly. "Let's take it down a notch, Bryan. Everything you just said is likely right on, but we can't start beating each other up because we're in a tight spot right now. This is what I propose we do, and we need to do it quickly. I'll call Washburn and tell him we have reason to believe he's in danger, and I want him to stop whatever he's doing and drive immediately to the billing office where our agents are meeting with Lance at four o'clock.

"Leave it to me to provide him with sufficient motivation to get his butt over there. In the meantime, Bryan, Gayle, and Abe, you all need to get to the billing office and keep Lance there no matter what it takes. He's already expecting us so hopefully he'll be at work where he's supposed to be. You can call him on the way and tell him you're en route, and that his friend Washburn will be there around the same time you arrive. Tell him we're concerned about their safety and not to make any calls to anyone and definitely not to leave the building. Also, recommend he lock the doors and the only people he's to let in are Washburn and the agents with him whom he should recognize from yesterday."

Bryan interjected further instructions to Eli. "Eli, you manage the teams following Mirzoyan and his friend. If they don't see him with anyone, instruct the new team of agents to grill the bartender and all the employees about Mirzoyan's visit, who he talked to and how often he comes there, and to find out whatever they know about him and the person we're damn sure he met with. Also, get with the LVPD and see what they know about the bar and the owners. I assume you have the name and address of the bar, so if it's nearby, get over there yourself and oversee everything first-hand since you know exactly what we're looking for."

Dixon then resumed his directives. "As soon as I finish talking to Washburn, I'm going to head for the billing office as well. My guess is I'll be about fifteen minutes behind all of you. In the meantime, keep me posted on your progress, and I'll do the same. I'll update you all as soon as I speak with Washburn. What I think we need to do is get Washburn and Beasley in the same room, but not before you get rid of both of the women who work in the office. Send them home and make sure they don't see or hear what we're discussing with Lance and Washburn.

"If one or both of the men have attorneys, we'll need to determine if either of the lawyers is in any way connected to Watson's firm, but obviously without mentioning him by name. If they are, then we need to regroup once I arrive. If they're not, I'll talk to both lawyers alone in a separate room away from our suspects or witnesses, whichever they turn out to be. Once we've resolved any issues with attorneys, then we'll all get in one room and lay out what we know about the threat to Washburn's and possibly Beasley's lives--"

Hampton interrupted Dixon asking, "Paul, do you actually expect their lawyers to take what we're telling them at face value? Will they believe us when we explain the urgency and risks these men are in?"

"Let me worry about getting them to believe us. Unless they're from Watson's firm I'm sure we'll be able to convince them. We won't tell any of them how we obtained the information, but since the facts came from Washburn, he'll accept them as the truth because they're accurate. After we tell them Mirzoyan had a clandestine meeting around three this afternoon with an unidentified individual, Washburn will do all the convincing with Lance we need done.

"When we get to that point we'll suggest we immediately take them both into protective custody. If they accept we'll put them up at the Marriott on Convention Center Drive for the night, and we'll keep a couple of agent teams there to protect them. That'll give us till morning to set up something more permanent. Bryan, how does that sound to you?"

"I like the plan. You have my endorsement. It's now three forty-five, and we all need to get going to have any chance of being there by four. Abe, you drive since this is your city and you hopefully know some back roads to get us there more quickly. And Gayle is dying to ride in your Crown Vic; she thinks my ride is demeaning."

"They're the same uncool government cars, Bryan. The only difference is yours is always full of crap, like food wrappers and gym clothes. Abe's car is neat and clean, and I don't end up with food stains on my butt when I sit on his seats."

Chapter 23

Las Vegas, NV
December 7th
2:00 PM

By two o'clock, Mirzoyan was off the golf course and had retrieved the nine voicemails left by his frightened and clearly agitated staff of chiropractors. Two of the doctors had called three times, first asking, then demanding a reply. The most tenured member of his staff left only two messages, both with the simple request, "Ari, I need to speak with you. Please call me."

Gerald Washburn left only one message, and Washburn listened to it several times as he worked his way through congested traffic in a seemingly never-ending construction project on West Sahara. The message was alarmingly different from the others, and after he heard it for the third time, he realized yesterday's crisis had blossomed into an even more serious problem, and regrettably he needed to once again report trouble to Bennett Watson.

After he spoke with Amanda yesterday, Mirzoyan had almost pressed the single digit on his cell phone to speed dial Watson's number, then hastily lifted his finger off the button after recalling a warning Watson had given him many months before. "Should an emergency ever arise regarding our business dealings, especially one that involves law enforcement, we never want to communicate about the crisis in an email or over the phone.

"If something happens and we need to talk immediately, the person requesting the meeting should text the emergency code 8899, and the person receiving it should respond by texting back the time he can meet, using the military clock format of four digits, but without the colon.

"We should always try and meet within one hour if possible, and until we decide otherwise, we'll set the meeting place at Frankie's Lounge on Las Vegas Boulevard near Oakey. The place is dark, open twenty-four hours every day, and we can have all the privacy we need because I know the owner."

At the time Watson had mandated the elaborate protocol, Mirzoyan believed it was overkill, overly dramatic, and ridiculously complicated. But the day before when he needed to covertly contact the attorney and actually had a need for the process, Watson's idea seemed prophetic and brilliant.

Reluctantly, he dialed the emergency code again, for the second time in just over twenty four hours. He texted 8899 to Watson's cell phone, and in under a minute saw 1435 appear in a return message. Realizing he had less than fifteen minutes to make the two thirty-five meeting with Watson, he made an illegal U-turn and headed back toward the Strip and the same tavern where he'd met Watson early yesterday afternoon.

Sitting at the bar where he could watch for Watson to arrive, Mirzoyan was surprised his business partner was already five minutes late. The man pouring drinks approached him and handed him a folded piece of paper, which he read, and when he looked up, the bartender pointed to a table in the rear of the room where Bennett Watson sat watching him. He quickly walked to the table and asked, "How long have you been here, Bennett? I didn't see you come in."

"Nor will you see me leave, Ari. I wanted to see if anyone followed you in here. Do you realize you're being tailed?"

"What are you talking about? Who's following me?"

"You tell me, but they look like feds of some type based on the car they're driving. They're going to believe you have a drinking problem if we keep meeting here this often. Tell me the latest about what's going on. We need to get this over with as soon as possible. I think we better move to a private room in back, just in case your friends in the car outside get curious and come in here to see what's going on."

Once they'd relocated to the more isolated space, Mirzoyan began by giving Watson an update on the aftermath of the visit from the DOJ agents to the billing office the day before. He informed Watson Amanda had vowed she wouldn't help the feds, and in return Mirzoyan explained he had promised to provide her with a lawyer and cover any legal expenses she might incur. He then explained Lance's plans were still an unknown. "Lance is scared and on edge because the agents who questioned him have convinced him Amanda is putting all the blame for the fraudulent claims on him. I offered to get him a lawyer and pick up all his legal expenses as well, but as of yesterday afternoon he was still extremely nervous and not willing to promise me anything."

Watson frowned at that news and made a mental note to alert Guzman to the situation. Mirzoyan then gave a complete accounting of the day's most recent Justice Department visits and a summary of the messages he received from all four of his doctors. As Watson had anticipated, he was most alarmed by Washburn's threats and even more concerned than Mirzoyan about his state of mind and threatened actions. "Play me Washburn's message so I can hear his exact words and listen to the tone of his voice," Watson ordered.

Mirzoyan located the voicemail and handed the phone to Watson, who then listened to Washburn's message. "Dr. Mirzoyan, this is Gerald Washburn. Two agents from the Department of Justice along with Paul Dixon, the U.S. Attorney himself, just left my office. They said they know our clinics are billing for services that are never provided and filing claims for patients we never see. Apparently, I must be more gullible than I realized because they seemed to know more about our billing practices than I do. They said they have proof we're filing millions of dollars' worth of false claims every month. Based on what they told me, the problem is much worse than the issues I told you needed correcting last month.

"Don't think I haven't noticed you never got back to me as you promised you would in November. Instead, you sent some thug to beat the crap out of me last Friday night. The bastard nearly killed me and promised he'd do just that, if he ever had to come back because I threatened you again or went to the police. So now, I'm up shit creek. The feds are threatening to throw me in jail if I don't cooperate, and your goon has promised to kill me if I do.

"Right now, I'm not sure what to do, but I do know I have a major decision to make by five tonight or they're going to arrest me. I can, however, promise you this right now; if I see that bastard from last Friday anywhere near me again, I'm going to tell Dixon everything I know and ask for protective custody.

"There's one more thing I should tell you. Before I left the office, I sent all the employees home and gave them the rest of the week off with pay. I also told them to cancel all the patients for the next three days. But don't let that stop Amanda from sending bogus bills to the insurance companies, since apparently you don't seem to require patients to actually exist or receive services as a prerequisite to generating claims."

Watson handed the phone back to Mirzoyan, then told him, "He's got to be stopped, and right away, Ari. We can't just hope he keeps quiet, and if your phone is tapped, he's already said way too much. I'm going to have Guzman shut this guy down immediately."

"What do you mean, shut him down? He's already said what he'll do if he sees your guy anywhere near him."

"I mean shut him down permanently," Watson responded. "What the hell do you think I'm talking about? And what about this guy's boyfriend, Lance? What's he going to do? We have no guarantee he's not going to fold, especially after his lover turns up dead. I think we need Guzman to take care of both of them, and soon."

With his chest tightening and his face rapidly reddening, Mirzoyan declared, "Bennett, I'm a healer, not a killer. Having one of my doctors simply disappear last year was bad enough, but now you're talking about killing two more people, and both of them work for me. Isn't that going to look a little obvious, since they're primary suspects in the investigation?"

"First of all, Ari, you are not, nor have you ever been, a healer. You're a charlatan and a scam artist who's been run out of two states already, and it looks like it could be a threepeat, if I don't clean this mess up for you.

"I also don't agree this move is as obvious as you seem to think it is, because three out of your four docs will still be alive and on the job twenty-four hours from now. That's only a twenty-five percent mortality rate. And trust me on this one, those three will get the message real quick that talking to the feds will dramatically shorten their life expectancy.

"Ari, you do whatever's needed to keep the rest of your staff in line, while I arrange to have Guzman take care of Lance and Washburn. Now get out of here before your federal escorts come looking for you."

As soon as Mirzoyan left the room, Watson sent another cryptic text to Guzman, the third in the last five days. This time the message was 'CEJ on DI NOW.' The reply, as always, was almost instantaneous '15 minutes,' and caused Watson to smile at the predictability of his treacherous problem-solving business associate.

The tavern on Desert Inn Road near Eastern was unexpectedly busy when Watson arrived, but he quickly spotted Guzman, who had already claimed a table toward the back of the crowded room. As usual, their meeting was brief with a narrowly focused agenda. Watson spoke first. "Hello, Fausto, I'm sorry to be bothering you again so soon, but we have a crisis that must be dealt with today, and in no event later than sometime tonight. Dr. Washburn, the man you visited last Friday, and his friend Lance, whom you're also familiar with, have become liabilities. They represent a real risk and danger to our ongoing business. They're threatening to expose our operation to the authorities as soon as tomorrow or perhaps even today.

"You need to take care of these two quickly and permanently. I'm thinking, if possible, it would be to our advantage if at least one of them met with some kind of accident, but whatever you need to do, do it quickly! And, Fausto, you should know that Dr. Washburn left Dr. Mirzoyan a message promising him that if he saw you anywhere near him, he'd immediately go to the police and ask for protection."

Watson decided to incite a small bit of rage in Guzman, so he added, "Washburn also referred to you as a thug and a goon in that same message, and since I'm quite sure his phone is tapped, the authorities will be watching for anyone fitting that description. So be extra careful, and act as un-thug like as possible when you're anywhere near him. Since we don't know where he is right now, you'll need to figure that out as soon as you can. We do know he closed the clinic and sent everyone home, so he's likely not there. And Fausto, you'll receive a nice dividend if you get this done tonight, and if you do it right." With that, Watson stood and left the bar using rear door of the building where his car was parked out of sight.

For the next several minutes Guzman nervously tapped a finger on his glass and remained at the table to finish his drink and plan his strategy. He was sadistically motivated by the opportunity to kill two targets before the night was over and particularly pleased the victims were two gay men. He learned long ago in Mexico that bigots make the best killers as long as they're pursuing the right prey, and in this case his bigotry was paired perfectly with the targets. Recalling that he still had listening devices hidden in Washburn's condo, he decided the most logical place to begin his pursuit was there.

By three-thirty, Guzman was situated and listening outside Washburn's condo, and almost immediately he overheard him talking, apparently on the phone since he heard no other voice. He seemed to be making arrangements to meet with someone and agreed to be at their office by four. Guzman at first thought he was talking to Lance, but the office meeting place made no sense.

Perhaps he was meeting with his attorney or possibly with the agents from the DOJ.

The next sounds he heard was a toilet flushing, followed in a few seconds by a door slamming, then silence. As he considered his alternatives, he heard the familiar sound of Washburn's Miata exiting the lower level parking garage. When the sports car immediately turned in his direction, he crouched down in his own car to avoid being seen. Guzman hastily stowed his electronic gear, quickly flipped a U-turn in the middle of the road, and took off in pursuit of Washburn. He exercised greater than normal precautions to avoid being seen by the man he was following.

When the Miata turned off the northbound lanes of I15 and took the eastbound Flamingo exit, it was obvious he wasn't headed downtown to the Justice Department. Several minutes later when Washburn made a left onto Paradise Road, Guzman realized the office he was going to was the billing office where Lance worked. But who was he meeting there, Lance or the FBI?

Guzman needed to know then, before it was too late. When Washburn steered the Miata off Paradise Road and into the billing office's parking lot, Guzman was two cars behind him and couldn't make the turn soon enough to keep the Miata in sight. By the time Guzman entered the lot, he saw Washburn already going through the lobby door and headed toward the elevators.

He was frustrated, but not overly concerned. He now knew where Washburn was going, so he'd leisurely take the elevator to the fifth floor and enter the suite through Mirzoyan's private door. This path would allow him to pass directly from the hall into the doctor's office, and from there he would have unfettered access to the entire suite. After parking his car he opened his trunk and removed an oversized briefcase containing an array of weapons, the tools of his trade. Because he didn't know what or who he'd encounter on the fifth floor, he needed to have a variety of weapons and other options close at hand. And besides, he thought, the briefcase makes me look less like a thug, to quote Watson's phrase.

Just as he started to close his trunk, he glimpsed a black sedan pulling into the opposite side of the lot, thirty feet from where he was parked. He slowly re-opened the trunk lid, acting as if he'd forgotten something, and was searching for it. He saw two men and a woman, all with the serious and humorless look of federal agents, exit the Crown Vic, then heard their three doors slam closed almost simultaneously.

For the first time in many contracted jobs, Guzman was concerned about his ability to take care of the business he'd been asked to accomplish within the time constraints and other specified terms. "How am I going to kill both these guys, make it look like an accident, get it all done by tonight, and do it before they tell everything they know to the feds, especially when they're probably meeting with the three agents I'm looking at in the next five minutes?" he quietly muttered to himself.

His mind was racing with alternatives, but he concluded he couldn't possibly storm the office fortress alone. He was outnumbered and at a huge tactical disadvantage, because he had no idea who else was upstairs in the office, and he also didn't know what the agents planned to do with Washburn and Lance in the next hour or two. So he decided to wait and watch to see what happened next. After all, he thought, it's only four, and I have till midnight to get the job done. There's always a way; I just need to wait until fate shows it to me.

Chapter 24

Las Vegas, NV
December 7th
4:05 PM

Washburn was the first visitor to actually enter the business office a few minutes after four. Sally Blackburn had never met him, and even when he introduced himself as Dr. Washburn, nothing registered immediately until he told her he was there to see his friend Lance. "Oh, you're that Dr. Washburn," she said clumsily. "Let me tell him you're here. I didn't know he was expecting you, too. I guess since you work for Dr. Mirzoyan, it's all right for you to come in the back, but Lance is in the conference room right now meeting with his other guest, so let me check with him first before you go in."

Sally had only been gone for two minutes when a soft chime from down the hall signaled the arrival of someone on the fifth floor. Washburn realized he was trapped if the wrong person got off the elevator, because Sally hadn't unlocked the door into the main part of the office, and the elevator was only a matter of a few feet from entrance to the suite. Before he could even consider what other options he had, he heard the door to the hall open behind him, and quickly turned. His fear was replaced by relief when he saw the two Justice Department agents he'd met in his own office earlier that day. They were accompanied by an attractive woman who, a strange thought popped into his mind, dressed too much like a man.

"I take it by the look on your sore face you're a little happier to see us this time, Dr. Washburn. What a difference a few hours can make, wouldn't you agree?" Hampton chided Washburn, understanding his duty was to be the antagonist once Dixon arrived and assumed the role of a sympathetic, thoughtful, and caring member of the Justice Department team.

"I spoke with Mr. Dixon and he warned me someone might be after me, someone sent by my boss to keep me from talking to you. I didn't know who was coming down the hall, so yes, given a choice between you and someone trying to kill me, I'm glad to see you and Agent Slater and your friend."

Gayle introduced herself, "I'm Gayle Baker from the Medical Fraud Crime Bureau. We're part of the DOJ task force."

Just then, Sally opened the door into the back offices. She looked slightly surprised to see the reception room was now occupied by three more guests, but then quickly recognized them as yesterday's visitors from the Justice Department. Since they had promised to return today at four, she was prepared and asked them to have a seat while she informed Lance and Amanda of their arrival.

Hampton stepped forward and stopped Sally from closing the door and told her, "We have a slight change of plans, Sally. First of all, we're not interested in meeting with Amanda today, and we'd like you and Ms. Booth to take the rest of the day off. We're here to meet with Dr. Washburn and Mr. Beasley and we need some privacy and security. So please let Ms. Booth know the two of you, for your own safety, have five minutes to get your things and clear out for the day. Please give Agent Slater here a key to the office door so we can lock up after we leave, then tell Mr. Beasley we're here to see him. I already called him about ten minutes ago so he should be expecting us."

"Lance is in the conference room with his attorney. He's expecting you, but he wasn't expecting Dr. Washburn, and he told me to have the doctor wait in his office," Sally replied.

"Once again, Sally, change of plans. Tell Amanda the two of you now have less than four minutes to clear out. Agent Slater will go with you to make sure you don't forget to leave us your keys. The rest of us will join Mr. Beasley and his attorney in the conference room."

"I'm not sure Dr. Mirzoyan will approve of me leaving work early or giving you a key to the office. I don't want to lose my job over this," Sally protested.

Gayle approached the perplexed young woman who wasn't in any way prepared for this complicated situation. "Sally, there will be no job for you or anyone else working for Dr. Mirzoyan in a short time. You need to start looking for another job now. Just walk away and don't look back. Consider yourself fortunate to be dodging a bullet here that's about to hit most of the Accident and Injury Health Restoration Clinic's other employees. My advice is to leave now, take everything that's yours with you, and don't plan on coming back."

Before Gayle finished giving Sally advice, Hampton was already past them both knocking on the locked conference room door. After a few seconds Lance opened it and saw Hampton and Washburn standing in the hallway. They were joined almost immediately by Gayle, who a day earlier had scared the hell out of him.

In an unsuccessful attempt to show confidence, he forced a smile and welcomed the agents into the conference room, saying, "My attorney and I were having a confidential meeting and we weren't expecting Dr. Washburn."

"Please introduce us to your attorney, Mr. Beasley," Hampton asked condescendingly.

Seizing on the opportunity to get into the mix, Lance's lawyer stood, handed Bryan his card, then introduced himself as Andrego Mattich, a partner in the criminal law firm of Stipech, Goldstein, and Jurevich. "Mr. Beasley has retained my services to advise him concerning the matter at hand."

Hampton turned to Lance and asked, "Would it be all right with you, Lance, if Mr. Mattich and I use your office for a few minutes of private conversation? Maybe while we're talking you and Dr. Washburn can catch up. Agent Baker will stay here with the two of you to corroborate any details or information you might be hearing for the first time."

Mattich began to object to Bryan's request, but Bryan gave him a stern look, then offered some advice. "Andrego, in about five minutes the U.S. Attorney for the District of Nevada, none other than former Governor Paul Dixon, is going to walk through that door. He's specifically asked me to have a one-on-one with you before he gets here. I don't think either of us wants to disappoint him, so why don't you just come with me for a couple of minutes so we can talk in private?"

Mattich turned to Lance and, before he left, advised him, "Be careful what you say and don't admit or agree to anything while I'm gone. They can't force you to say anything, so be smart and remember you don't know where your friend stands on any of this. You've said so yourself."

Once they closed the door to Lance's office, Bryan continued staring at Mattich's business card. "Fascinating firm you have here, a Croatian, an Israeli, and a Serbian. I'll bet you guys have some interesting and scary holiday parties with that mix of nationalities and faiths. Do you all actually work in the same office, or what?"

"Agent Hampton is it? You're both a rude and highly unorthodox representative of the Federal government, and I'm not interested in your opinions or observations about my law firm. Let's get to what you want to discuss and dispense with the insults and innuendos."

"As you wish, Mr. Mattich. What we first need to know is who's paying for your services? We also want to protect you in the event a conflict of interest exists for you or someone in your firm who could be associated in some way with the fraud scheme we're investigating. What you don't likely realize is there are other potential defendants in this case, individuals who are not associated directly with the clinic's operations, but are in fact part of this multi-million dollar fraud scheme. Additionally, Dr. Washburn's life has been threatened, and by virtue of the intimate relationship these two men share, your client's life is almost surely in danger as well. You are aware of their relationship, are you not?"

"That's an interesting and varied mix of information and questions you just unloaded on me, if it's all true and relevant. I'll answer the easy stuff first, but let me clearly state at the outset of any comments I make, that my client admits to no wrong doing, and anything we discuss now must be taken in that context.

"If you're asking if I knew Dr. Washburn and Mr. Beasley occasionally share the same bed, the answer is yes. That fact is one reason why my client doesn't want to get Washburn in anymore trouble. He claims he's avoided discussing the fraud issue with Washburn because he can't live with the thought that Washburn might be one of the primary benefactors and promoters of the fraud. My client sees a major difference between what his duties are in the billing office and the possibility Washburn might be one of the organizers of the whole operation. He claims he's given him ample opportunity to volunteer information about any deceit and deception taking place, but Washburn never seems willing to venture into even touching on those topics.

"The most relevant thing I can tell you about why I'm representing this young victim is his older sister is a former friend of mine from Northwestern. When I was in law school and she was in medical school, we would hang out occasionally. She called me at home last night and asked me to help her distraught brother. And, although it's none of your business, and inappropriate and improper for you to ask, I'll tell you that I'm being paid by Mr. Beasley. He gave me a small advance on my retainer from his personal checking account and claims he can get additional funds from his parents or his sisters.

"I've spent two hours with him today, and what I can tell you, Agent Hampton, is it's all about the salary for him. He got himself involved because he viewed the job as a chance to make some big dollars and prove to his parents and sisters that he's at least their financial equal.

"My partners and I are honest. We represent dumb-ass criminals and supposedly smart white collar guys who think they can get away with anything, and we see most of them go to jail, not because we're bad lawyers, but because we're representing crooks. We have no interest in joining them in prison, so we play it straight and honorable."

"Okay, Andrego, thanks for making that easy. I'll take you at your word because we don't have a lot of options anyway. I was afraid you were going to be like most of the lawyers we encounter, and we just don't have time now to deal with a lot of legal maneuvering and BS, or someone's going to get killed.

"Frankly now that you've been honest with me, I'm going to be straightforward with you, but I expect you to keep everything we discuss in the strictest confidence. Both of these guys could be dead by morning if we don't manage this all very carefully. Between Dr. Washburn and Mr. Beasley, with their unique roles and perspectives in a varied and complex fraud scheme, we believe we can build a strong case against everyone involved in the entire operation and shut it down permanently.

"We estimate this scheme is defrauding insurers of over thirty-five million dollars a year in health care expenses alone. There's also another cost component to this scam, but as yet we don't have firm cost estimates for those losses, but we expect to have them soon. We think those costs will exceed the amounts we already know about on the medical side. We're sure someone else besides Mirzoyan is involved and likely heads up the entire operation. We don't know for certain who that is, but we have an idea."

When Bryan paused to make sure Mattich was following his explanation and understood the urgency of the situation, the attorney did comment, "I understand what you're saying, but you must admit we're in a highly unusual situation here, and if I'm going to advise my client to admit his involvement and cooperate, then I'll need something in writing first that guarantees his immunity. Since Dr. Washburn has no legal representation, I'd also like to speak with him in private, and if he agrees to retain me as his legal counsel, then I want his guarantee of immunity in writing as well."

After acknowledging Mattich's comments, Bryan continued, "In the next few minutes, Governor Dixon will arrive here and, between the three of us, we need to convince your client and Dr. Washburn it will be in their combined best interests to work with us. We'll guarantee them both total immunity from any prosecution or charges if they cooperate with us immediately and unconditionally, and I'll have that put in writing as soon as they verbally agree to be candid and forthcoming.

"Once we persuade them this plan is their best and only safe option, we then need to place them into immediate protective custody. We'll keep them sequestered at least until, with their help, we identify and arrest all the main players, and especially the killer who's likely pursuing them both as we speak. Can we proceed using that plan and those assumptions, and depend on your help?"

"I'm okay with those plans, but first I need five minutes alone with my client, then a few minutes with Dr. Washburn."

"You have ten minutes then. I'll send Lance in to meet with you while I explain to Washburn what you plan to discuss with him and why he might want to consider retaining your services. Let's get this done quickly so we don't unnecessarily delay Mr. Dixon when he gets here."

Within fifteen minutes Dixon arrived, but not before Mattich had completed his meetings with both his client and Washburn. Once everyone was seated in the conference room, Hampton introduced Andrego Mattich and Lance Beasley to the U.S. Attorney, and Dixon as always was gracious but businesslike in greeting them and in acknowledging Dr. Washburn as well. He then wasted no time in explaining the circumstances which had brought them all together. His presentation was thorough, detailed, and accurate. He summarized the situation while looking directly at Lance and Washburn and their attorney, who only minutes before had announced he was representing both men.

Dixon began, "Dr. Washburn and Mr. Beasley, I apologize in advance for repeating what I and others have already said to you, but we want to make sure there's no confusion about the details of what is a one-time offer for the two of you. You've both aided and abetted a fraud scheme that's resulting in millions of dollars of ongoing thefts. You're both without a doubt guilty of facilitating and executing essential parts of that scheme. But we're primarily after the people who led you down a path which you both foolishly and naively rationalized was acceptable to follow.

"Shame on you both for sacrificing your personal integrity, for disgracing your family names, and for compromising your honor, all because of your indifference or greed. At some point you both must have considered that one of the consequences of your involvement could be a loss of your freedom. But until last Friday when Dr. Washburn was attacked, neither of you probably ever suspected you were risking your lives. But here we are today and both of you are most assuredly at the top of a list that no one ever wants to be on. We're offering you the only good chance you have, not only for staying out of jail, but for staying alive.

"Now, in the simplest terms I can explain, the arrangement is this; you tell us everything you know for as long as we want to ask questions, and eventually you'll testify against everyone we indict. In return we'll grant you both total immunity and will place you in protective custody starting today and keep you there until we're convinced you're both safe. This is an agreement that will be put in writing, but if either of you at any time attempts to hold back information or renege in any other way, we'll prosecute you as well. Are we all clear on everything?"

After Washburn and Lance nodded their understanding Bryan spoke, "Since Mr. Mattich represents both of you, he can be present during your interviews, should either of you make that request. We'd like to take both of you into protective custody immediately. Our plan is to begin interviewing you separately the first thing tomorrow morning."

Washburn interrupted Bryan. "Wait a minute, what does that mean? Taking us into protective custody immediately? And Mr. Dixon said we'll be in that status until someone thinks we're safe. How long is that? It'll be months before you arrest everyone involved and put them on trial. And who believes you can even find the guy who beat me up? Do you even know who he is or what he looks like?"

"No, we don't know either of those things, but you're going to help us answer both of those questions. And you're right; your lives are going to be shit for a long time, but if you'll agree to let us protect you, at least you'll be alive," Hampton explained with passion and some impatience.

"Where will we live? Are you talking about taking us somewhere right now? I ran out of my condo thinking I'd be gone for an hour or two, not for months. I have no clothes, not even a toothbrush or a comb. This is insane," Washburn protested.

Lance then added his concerns and frustrations to the mix. "Gerald is right, I have the same concerns. I need my stuff and someone needs to take care of my cat. How's my rent going to be paid and, if it's not paid, the landlord will sell everything I have or throw it all out. We can't just disappear for months without planning and preparation."

Mattich then offered a suggestion. "Perhaps we could let the gentlemen return to their homes tonight, under your protection, of course, and they could pack a few things and make other necessary preparations to be away for an undefined period of time?"

"I don't like that plan. We don't know yet who we're protecting them from, and the fact Mirzoyan knows they both have deadlines to get back to us this afternoon tells me someone could be sitting outside this building or at their homes waiting for a chance we don't need to give them," Bryan told the group with obvious concern.

"I insist on going home before I'm forced into custody. I need an hour in my apartment to pack what I need, get my medications, and make arrangements for my cat," Lance demanded.

"I need more than an hour to get organized. I'd like to remain in my home overnight or for at least three or four hours, so I can prepare adequately. I've already made videos of myself explaining what I know. They're on my PC, as are several files containing facts, claim numbers, names, and dates of things I know about. I need to copy these files to flash drives, and I need my laptop with me so I can provide the details you'll need.

"I want protection, for sure, but why can't one or two agents guard me in my condo for a few hours? I'll gladly go with you later this evening or in the morning, but I need some time to prepare," Washburn pleaded, now wanting to be cooperative.

"It's too risky. It's a bad plan. Someone else can grab your laptop and PC," Bryan argued.

"My clients have offered reasonable concessions, so it would seem you should accommodate them. This whole situation is both traumatic and unexpected, and I think it makes sense for them to be allowed to take a few hours to get their lives in order when you're asking them to disengage and vanish for months."

Hampton looked at Dixon for advice, but Dixon said nothing, indicating the decision was Hampton's to make. Gayle then offered a suggestion. "Bryan, why don't you have a couple of agents head over to Dr. Washburn's right now, with the expectation they'll need to be on duty there or at the hotel, as Paul suggested earlier, until tomorrow morning when they'll be relieved. You and I can accompany Dr. Washburn to his home, then those agents can take over once he's safely in his condo. I think it's vital he have time to compile the files and other digital information from his home computer. It could save us days of effort and wasted time.

"Abe can go with Mr. Beasley while he gets his things from his apartment, then another pair of agents can be waiting at the hotel to take over his protection in a couple of hours. Then we can all get a fresh start in the morning and Dr. Washburn and Mr. Beasley will be less fragmented when we go through the arduous process of interviewing them."

"I still don't like it. It may sound like a reasonable and fair compromise, but I've got a bad feeling about all this for some reason," Bryan told the group.

Abe then voiced his support for Gayle's proposition. "Bryan, Gayle's offered a sensible plan, and one that should be safe. Would it make you more comfortable if we ask the LVPD to send units to both of their homes giving us additional security while they're packing? I can get that done in two seconds if it helps."

Bryan relented. "Okay, I give up. Those are probably adequate precautions and all the protection they need. I feel a little more confident now, but I'm still not entirely at ease."

Thirty minutes later both Lance and Washburn were safely in their homes. Abe sat on Lance's couch struggling to keep the man's irritating cat away from him, while out of sight in the bedroom and bathroom, vigorous noisy packing was taking place.

Outside Washburn's condo, Hampton and Gayle finished planning the details for the following morning's meetings after leaving Washburn in the care of two somewhat annoyed FBI agents, back inside his home.

Before Gayle and Hampton left, Hampton spoke with the two Las Vegas patrolmen sitting in their car parked outside on the street. "This doctor you're guarding is an important witness in a major fraud case. He was already assaulted just five days ago. Someone has threatened his life if he talks to us, which he'll be doing first thing in the morning. As you know, we have two FBI agents inside with him, and for the next several hours we'd appreciate it if you two make sure no one even gets close to his building. Here's my card. Please call me directly and immediately if you see anyone or anything suspicious."

Hampton and Gayle then walked to their car and prepared to leave. Hampton took another long look around before he started the car. He observed the closed and backlit window shades in Washburn's condo that thankfully prevented anyone from seeing inside where Washburn was packing his clothes and assembling his files. Even in the gathering darkness, the sentinel effect of the police car conspicuously parked less than fifty feet from the building revealed further evidence of their preparation.

Everything appeared to be in order, but Hampton's instincts told him something was wrong. At times when he felt these invisible premonitions of danger they were weak and unpersuasive, but at that moment they were so intense they nearly overwhelmed him.

Something told him the assailant was nearby, but he couldn't see anyone or anything suspicious in the descending dusk. Then the thought occurred to him that, irrespective of Washburn's claim he never saw the man's face, they needed to press him for a better description of his attacker first thing the next morning.

Chapter 25

Las Vegas, Nevada
December 7th
6:00 PM

Guzman kept an anxious eye on the police car, but most of his attention was focused on monitoring the conversations and sounds his listening devices were transmitting from inside Washburn's condo. His growing concern over the likelihood of eliminating even one of his two targets before morning was starting to wear on him. The pressure he felt was also interfering with the rational, but bold planning he believed was his strength as a fixer. Even more worrisome was his fear a failure in this assignment would ruin his perfect record of taking care of everything his current employer had ever asked him to do.

He remembered an effective trick he'd used before to calm himself and relieve stress, so he tried talking quietly to an imaginary comrade. "We got no chance of sneaking in there without first getting rid of the cops sitting out front in their car because they can see the front door and it's the only way in or out. Even if we take out the two cops, from what I'm hearing, there's at least two Feds inside protecting my target. A shoot-out with two FBI men's a big risk, unless they're just desk guys, but how do we know how good they are? No way am I taking that chance.

"This whole mess really pisses me off. We should have taken this guy out last Friday. Wait a minute! The package is still in there. We do have an option, the one Watson told us not to use. But he'll be damn glad we ignored his orders now that this is our only possible solution. I think I left the transmitter in the trunk? I better check and see."

Guzman then carefully exited his darkened car and silently opened the trunk. Seeing the transmitter he resumed his almost inaudible monologue, "There it is, baby, right where it's supposed to be! There's gonna be a hot time in Washburn's bed tonight. It's too bad he didn't bring his friend along with him, so we could nail them both. Now all we need to do is make sure Washburn's in the bedroom, preferably near or in his bed when we deliver our little surprise."

After re-entering his car with the transmitter in hand, Guzman again began listening carefully to the sounds and voices coming from inside Washburn's home. With his ability to turn the devices on or off, he could listen to any of the individual rooms inside the condo. At that moment, he was hearing a conversation taking placed in the dining and kitchen area, and one of the voices was Washburn's.

"I've copied several video files of me explaining what I understand about how the fraud works, at least in the Henderson Clinic, from my PC to my laptop, and also onto this flash drive. On the second flash drive I've listed over a hundred names and ID numbers of patients I know we never treated in our clinic, but I've seen insurance payments recorded under those names on revenue reports I wasn't supposed to be able to look at.

"I'm going back to my PC now to continue copying other files and documents onto my laptop and a couple of other flash drives I have on hand. I came out here to show you these two drives so you'd know I'm making progress. I also wanted to grab a drink and some cookies, and tell you both to help yourselves to any food you can find, since I won't be here to eat anything for a long time."

It sounded to Guzman like one of the agents then followed Washburn into the kitchen. He heard the man thank Washburn for the update on his progress, then he offered to help with anything Washburn needed to facilitate his preparations. While the icemaker was grinding and dispensing ice, the agent asked Washburn a question, but Guzman couldn't hear clearly over the noise of the ice dispenser. But he'd already heard enough!

Originally, he had some concerns about triggering the bomb with the feds inside, believing it would further anger Watson and also enrage the FBI. But now, he decided he must eliminate everybody and everything inside the condo, especially the laptop, the PC, and all the flash drives, DVD's and anything else containing any evidence of the fraud Watson and Mirzoyan were trying to hide.

He considered calling Watson before making a final decision, but decided there were no other options to discuss, and concluded it would be a waste of time. All that was left to do was to activate the transmitter and make sure Washburn was in his bedroom. He already knew from previous visits the doctor's desk and PC were in the room, only a few feet away from the bed.

He listened intensely once again with only the bedroom's microphone active and vaguely heard a toilet flush, then apparently the bathroom door opened and Guzman distinctly heard the sound of the toilet bowl and tank filling. Seconds later he heard keystrokes, then the familiar sound of Windows booting up. Then after several more seconds rapid keystrokes were the only sounds that continued.

Fausto Guzman smiled with the satisfaction only a homicidal zealot could claim. Then he flipped a small switch on the hand-held transmitter, and micro seconds later he first saw, then heard a massive blast that blew out all the windows in Washburn's condo, along with those of his two nearest neighbors. Flying glass and fire quickly filled the inside of the building, while smoke and debris cloaked everything anywhere near it.

Then Guzman felt the concussion of the blast through his car's open windows. He was in awe of what he'd caused and wished he could give himself a standing ovation, but for the time being he had to be satisfied with his unspoken sadistic thoughts. *I should use bombs more often. Everyone in there must be toast. Even I have to admit a blast like that was impressive. On the other hand, it's a lot more noticeable and a lot less personal than taking care of business with a gun or a knife like I usually do. How could anyone ever be fanatical or stupid enough to strap a bomb to their body, then press the button? If I was running the government, my anti-terrorist program would be to get a slow motion picture of some dumb-ass fanatic blowing himself to pieces, then broadcast that twenty-four seven to Pakistan, Iran, and all the other 'Rans' where they train those crazies.*

Through the smoke Guzman could see both of the stunned patrolmen anxiously emerge from the driver's side of their cruiser and into the street. Apparently, the passenger side of the car facing the building was damaged so badly the door wouldn't open. One of the two policemen appeared to be talking to his bicep; obviously the microphone of his two-way radio was attached to his sleeve. The other officer was frantically punching numbers on his cell phone.

No one was coming out of Washburn's condo, and the patrolmen were not yet moving in that direction. Guzman considered trying to get close enough to the building to assure himself all the occupants were dead, but decided it was too risky and unnecessary. He watched the policemen distracted by all the fire and smoke move cautiously toward the broken window of the building, then seized the opportunity their diverted attention offered to pull slowly out of his parking place and drive away.

The sound of Bryan's cell phone disrupted what had been a peaceful and fulfilling five minutes of sharing time with a Whopper Combo Meal, the Whopper doing all the giving, once he had taken his first bite. "Hampton here, who's this?"

"It's Officer Marshall, Agent Hampton. I've got some bad news!"

Bryan and Gayle arrived at what was left of Washburn's condo at nearly the same time. Fire trucks, ambulances, and police cars filled the street in both directions, so they were both forced to jog a block to reach the devastation that only two hours earlier had been one fourth of a neatly maintained rambler-style fourplex. "What happened?" Gayle, who was still breathing hard, asked Bryan.

"Obviously a bomb happened. We need to find someone who knows what's been going on while we were on our way over here. Officer Marshall!" he shouted. "Has anyone seen Officer Marshall?" Bryan continued walking around the periphery of the scene searching for the policeman while shouting his name for the next several minutes, then he heard a frail response.

"I'm over here in the ambulance, Hampton."

Bryan quickly moved toward the rear of the ambulance where he saw Marshall being treated for multiple cuts and burns, primarily to his face and upper body.

"Marshall, I can see you're injured, and I'm sorry, but you'll need to forgive me. I don't have time to be sympathetic. I need to know what happened here and what you saw, if anything. Did anyone inside survive? Did you see anyone come out of the building right before the blast? Did anyone walk or drive by the building before the bomb went off?"

"Agent Hampton, I'm sorry about this, but we didn't screw up here. We were observing anyone or anything that got anywhere near that building. If you're thinking someone drove by and threw a bomb or someone sneaked up anywhere near the place and planted it, there's no chance. The only way we would have missed someone getting anywhere close to that building is if they came across the roof of one of the other units.

"We were keeping a real close eye out, and one of us would even walk all the way around the four units every few minutes to check things out. We never saw or heard anything. To get on the roof you'd need a ladder, and I doubt anyone could have gotten onto the roof without us seeing or hearing something."

"How about the people inside? Did anyone come out after the explosion? Did you or anyone go in to see if someone survived?" Gayle asked.

"My partner and I ran to what was once the front window, when mostly just smoke was pouring out of it, but we could see flames coming from the rear part of the condo, which I guess was the bedroom. We could hear someone faintly calling for help, and no one else was anywhere around, so we climbed inside. The sound was coming from somewhere close to us, off toward the kitchen, not back by the fire.

"We managed to feel our way through the thick smoke, but the heat was starting to get worse. We followed the sound and found a guy in a bathroom by the laundry room where apparently the washer and dryer had partially shielded him from the initial blast. He was semi-conscious, maybe from inhaling the smoke, but more likely from being crushed, then trapped beneath the cabinets and all kinds of other debris that had blown through the walls of the small space.

"We managed to get all the crap off him and drag him back toward the living room window where we came in. Then the flames and smoke got so bad we could hardly breathe. We lifted him out through the window, but it was getting too hot and we couldn't look for anyone else. We were lucky to escape with only minor burns and cuts."

Hampton could see it was highly unlikely anyone else inside had survived the explosion and was anxious to talk to the only survivor Marshall and his partner had been able to rescue. "Where's the person you rescued?"

"The paramedics from the first ambulance that arrived treated him, then hauled him off to the hospital about ten minutes ago. He was wearing a white shirt and a tie, so he was either a Mormon Missionary or one of your guys. Oh, one more very weird thing I should tell you. When we started to free him from the debris, he kept telling us to get his coat, which we managed to find under him on the floor of the bathroom."

"So did you do what he asked? Did you actually recover his coat?" Bryan asked.

"Yes, we did. But it was just his suit coat, nothing special. It looked cheap."

"Where's the coat now?"

"I have no idea, sir. What's the big deal with the coat?"

"I don't know, but if I was being rescued from a burning building and I was worried about my suit coat, there'd need to be a damn good reason. If the agent was that focused on his coat, we need to know where it is and right now.

Thanks, Marshall, for saving a life and for risking your own. I hope they give you some time off to recover."

After he confirmed with firemen and police on the scene that the agent being treated at the hospital was the only survivor of the blast, Bryan also learned the bodies of two other victims had been discovered in what remained of the condo. Hampton asked Gayle to call Eli and request him to come to the site and oversee things for their team while he summoned the Fire Chief and the police captain in charge to a quick huddle.

Hampton was initially frustrated and tormented by an unnecessary and preventable turn of events, and felt his anguish boiling into anger that had approached rage. He was furious with himself for agreeing to the risky scenario in the first place, and he was annoyed with those who lobbied for a dangerous compromise of the agency's strict protocols.

Allowing the suspects to fetch their toothbrushes and feed a cat was an unnecessary risk. Now one of them was dead, and he wanted Gayle to recognize her role in the loss. "I guess your plea to allow our witnesses to collect their belongings from home so they wouldn't be fragmented during our interviews turned out to be a poor choice of words, at least as far as Dr. Washburn was concerned."

"That's a low blow, Hampton, even coming from you. You're a real asshole sometimes."

"This should never have happened, and I let all of you talk me into it. An FBI agent, probably with a wife and kids, lost his life tonight because I made a bad decision. I have to live with that while the rest of you don't give it a second thought. I'm going to make sure this mess gets a thorough investigation and that nothing disappears from the scene before our guys comb through the ashes and find anything they can that might help us. Hopefully, we can salvage a hard drive. Once I'm done here, I'm heading over to the hospital to talk to the FBI guy who survived and see why he was so interested in finding his suit coat. If you want to meet me there, be my guest. Otherwise, I'll see you in the morning. Just make sure Eli gets here before you leave."

By the time Hampton arrived at the hospital he was getting more and more depressed about the evening's losses and tormented by the belief he could have prevented the deaths of two people. Hampton easily found the ER department and asked a nurse if he could see Agent Jeff Young, but was told he'd been transferred from the ER and moved to the another floor. The nurse gave him a room number and pointed him in the right direction, then he began his search.

Because most hospitals had grown from a core building with new wings and floors constantly being added, Hampton found locating a room in any hospital always seemed like a counterintuitive experience. Just when he was getting frustrated, a nurse approached him in the hall, so he asked, "Can you tell me where room B327 South is located?"

"Well, if you were in the south wing of this building you'd only be four doors away. Unfortunately, this is the east wing." The nurse then gave him a series of instructions on how to alter his course to reach the south wing.

Several minutes later he saw his destination ahead and realized he was unsure how severely the agent had been injured. He knocked gently on the door and quickly prayed the man's condition would still allow him to answer a few critical questions. He heard someone tell him to come in, then found himself looking at an open bathroom door, which he had to push closed so he could move into the room. Surprisingly, what he saw next was a battered Agent Young sitting upright in the room's only bed, surrounded by four young children and a relieved wife.

"I'm sorry to intrude, Agent Young. I'm Bryan Hampton from the Justice Department, and I wondered if we could talk just for a few minutes? I promise I'll be brief, Mrs. Young, then I'll get out of your way."

"Take the time you need, Mr. Hampton. I'll run down the hall with the kids and get them something to drink."

"How are you doing, Agent Young? You look better than I expected, based on what Officer Marshall, the guy who hauled you out of the burning building, told me."

"So the guy's name is Marshall. There were two of them, as I remember, but I took a nasty blow on my head, and most of what happened after that is fuzzy. I hope I can remember enough to answer your questions, because I'm also getting groggy from all the meds they gave me to manage the pain."

"Let's go to the critical questions then. Did you have any warning or indication something was wrong? Did you see or hear anything outside or inside the condo that alerted you to any problem immediately before the blast?"

"Nothing; everything was quiet. Washburn was working in the bedroom and Agent Cheu was sitting at the kitchen table reading when I went in to use the head. Thirty seconds later, all hell broke loose. I think I was unconscious for a while, but only for a few seconds. When I came to, there was so much crap on me I couldn't move. I thought I was a goner for sure. All I could do was call for help, and they were pretty feeble calls. I think God was looking out for me, because the two patrolmen managed to hear me. Wow, my head is starting to feel like I'm spinning around."

"Let me ask just one more question then, and we'll finish this tomorrow. Officer Marshall told me that in spite of your injuries, you kept telling them to get your coat, and in fact they did find it in the bathroom on the floor and were able to retrieve it and you as well. Why were you so interested in the coat? And do you know where it is now?"

"That's the most amazing thing of all, I guess. The coat's in the closet over there. I'm sure it's never going to be wearable again, but they managed to save it and me along with it. The weird thing is I had this impression to take it into the bathroom with me. It was on the back of a chair at the kitchen table, and I was halfway out of the room when I had the thought to take it with me. So I actually went back, grabbed the coat, and hauled it into the bathroom. I had just laid it on the vanity since there was no place to hang it, when all of a sudden boom, and I was knocked on my ass."

"The real question, Agent Marshall, is why was the coat so significant?"

"I was getting to that. Could you get the coat out of the closet and bring it to me?"

Growing frustration seized Hampton as he brought the dusty, smoky-smelling suit coat to Marshall. "Why don't you just reach into the inside left pocket yourself, Agent Hampton."

Hampton did as instructed and retrieved two flash drives. "What are these?" he asked Marshall.

"They're the evidence my partner and your witness gave their lives for, and what nearly cost me mine. They're worth more than gold. Dr. Washburn showed them to us a few minutes before the blast. He wanted to let us know he was making progress copying and transferring files. He told us one of them had videos of him explaining the facts of the fraud scheme he knew about, and the other one had a list of patients the clinic got paid for treating, but none of them were actually ever seen in the clinic nor did they receive any services.

"He also told us a list of the procedures the insurance companies paid for were itemized under each of the fake patient's names. It sounded to me like that was some powerful evidence in a medical fraud case so, after he showed them to us, I decided to ask him to let me hang on to them, so he gave them to me. I just put them in my coat pocket so I'd remember where they were, and now you have them.

"Make sure my partner gets credit for whatever evidence is on them if it helps put these bastards away. It's a sobering reality of what our jobs entail, to realize a few hours ago both of us were at home with our families, when we got called to report for what we thought was a babysitting assignment, and now Agent Cheu will never be going home again."

Chapter 26

Las Vegas, NV
December 8th
6:00 AM

Hampton's alarm woke him at the usual time, but he felt exhausted after a fitful night of half-sleep. His first thoughts were about the bombing and Agent Cheu and what developments might have taken place overnight, so he immediately flipped on his TV to the local news, then poked Mr. Coffee into action. When he heard how the headline story was being handled, he fired an angry but resigned comment at the TV, "I'm not a damn bit surprised."

The pictures he saw, and the reporter's narrative, forced him to relive the trauma and angst he'd felt only hours before. Scenes of the burning condo and emergency crews hit him like hard body punches, and when an official FBI photo of Cheu and a picture of a much younger Washburn filled the screen, tagged with the word 'Deceased,' the pain he'd felt last night struck him again like an electric shock. The next static image was an FBI file photo of Agent Young, labeled 'Hospitalized in Serious Condition.'

The concluding segment of the report was an interview of a cavalier fire chief who seemed more interested in prolonging his conversation with the attractive newswoman by telling everything he knew than he was about insuring the integrity and confidentiality of the investigation.

When he responded to the TV reporter's question about possible causes of the blast, Chief Anderson's comments weren't the message Hampton wanted publicized, and he wondered how Anderson was privy to so much information in the first place. "Initially we suspected the explosion might have been caused by a gas leak. But then we were informed that two of the people inside the condominium, which was owned by Dr. Gerald Washburn, were FBI agents. Both Washburn and one of the agents died in the explosion, and the second FBI man was taken to the hospital with serious burns," the chief had answered.

He continued before being asked any additional questions, "When we learned about the presence of the FBI agents, we shifted our thinking about the cause to some kind of incendiary device, a bomb if you will. Our preliminary investigation at this time seems to confirm a powerful explosive device was detonated inside Dr. Washburn's bedroom, which was located in the rear of the home. These single floor condo structures all have shared walls made of foot thick concrete with a two foot air space in between them, so the blast damage was restricted to the one building where the bomb was actually placed. Of course, we have fire and smoke damage to adjacent units but no injuries."

Before the Chief walked away from the camera, the reporter hit him with a final question, as though the topic of her inquiry was common knowledge throughout the city, "Is it true Dr. Washburn was in protective custody as part of a federal medical fraud sting operation?"

Fortunately, that query seemed to have involved new information the captain wasn't aware of, and he simply responded by saying, "You'll need to ask the Justice Department about that. Thank you, I need to get back to my men now."

Hampton thought it might be too early to call Dixon, but he wanted to make sure his boss knew what everyone in the country was hearing on the early morning TV newscasts before he got a call from Washington or Carson City. Hampton checked FOX News and CNN to see if the national outlets had picked up on the blast and murder. He discovered bad news on all fronts.

Every channel was running some version of the bombing. Each network and the AP had slightly different slants on the featured story, but all of them included most of the same elements: Bomb Kills FBI Agent; Witness in Protective Custody Dies; Medical Fraud Sting Operation Goes Bad; Authorities Not Talking. Hampton thought whatever news agency used the Authorities Not Talking line must not have seen Chief Anderson's interview or they doubted he was an authority.

Unexpectedly, Hampton heard his cell phone broadcasting the ring tone he reserved for Dixon. He answered quickly. "I was waiting to call you at a more reasonable hour. I suppose you've already either seen or heard the news coverage about last night's disaster. I wanted to brief you before you got the bad news somewhere else."

Hampton knew Dixon was undoubtedly upset, maybe even madder than hell, but he didn't yet have enough history with him to know how his new boss would react. Nonetheless, he had steeled himself to take whatever Dixon dished out and to accept all the blame, both for the event itself and for the news leak.

Strangely, Dixon was calm and only said, "Bryan, I'm already headed into the office and I'd like you to get there as soon as possible. We have a lot of ground to cover before everyone arrives for the day."

Hampton agreed to leave as soon as he was dressed and the call ended. He was astonished at how calm and composed Dixon seemed, and he thought, this guy is either on tranquilizers or he's got ice water in his veins. How can he possibly be so controlled? I'm worried as hell, and I'm not the one who's going to be getting any calls from big shots in Washington or placing any bereavement calls to loved ones.

By seven-fifteen, Hampton was sitting at the conference table in Dixon's office waiting for him to finish a quick email to his immediate superior at the Justice Department. As soon as he'd sent his message, Dixon began the conversation without any preamble, and before he'd spoken a dozen words, Bryan's mind was reeling.

"Bryan, have you ever heard of *Deliberate Misdirection, DM* for short?"

"I can't say that I have, Paul. What's this about?"

"*DM* is a term and idea one of my professors taught me long ago and I want to explain the concept. *DM* has a first phase, a reasoning process used to develop a hypothesis about the problem you're attempting to understand or solve. This process is where the uniqueness and art of *DM* begins; I call it Imagine the Unimaginable. *DM* is another of those concepts, like the *Success Failure Matrix*, that have stuck with me since I first learned about them. To me, they seemed to have universal applicability across many fields of discipline.

"I came to the conclusion it's imperative for us to use this approach in this case while I was watching the press coverage of the bombing last night and heard the confidential information being revealed by the reporters. That's when I first started to actually consider the unimaginable.

"I decided then we needed do some unorthodox thinking and take some radical action or the death of two men and all the work we've done on this case was going to be for nothing."

Hampton struggled to see where the conversation was leading and *DM* sounded like something from a spy movie. Paul read Hampton's confused expression and offered, "Maybe I can best explain the theory by relating last night's circumstances. You called me three times to keep me updated on the events of the evening. Your initial call came after you first heard about the blast and you were on your way to the scene. I immediately turned on the TV, and there was nothing on any of the stations about the incident at that point.

"Your next call to me was made during your drive to the hospital to check on Agent Young. You told me Washburn and the other agent, whose name you didn't know, had been killed in the blast, and you were heading over to see how Young was doing and find out why he was so concerned about having his rescuers retrieve his coat from the condo. I went back to my TV right after we ended our call, and by then three of the local outlets were already on the scene televising pictures of the burning building.

"Some of the reporters had started to interview police and firemen. Before you called back about half an hour later to fill me in on what you had learned from Agent Young, the TV news people were already reporting the destroyed condo belonged to Dr. Gerald Washburn. They claimed police on the scene told them two FBI agents were in the building at the time of the blast, but only one of them had been rescued, and he'd been taken by ambulance to the hospital and his condition was unknown.

"Five minutes later, I got a call from the Special Agent in Charge of the FBI's Field Office here in Las Vegas. His name is Harry Graves, and he wasn't a happy man. He had no idea until he saw the same TV coverage I was watching that he had agents deployed last night working on our case. As it turned out, he knew little about our investigation, irrespective of the fact that eight of his people had been working on the case on and off for the last several days.

"Before he contacted me, his staff told him Agents Cheu and Young were hastily assigned to protect a witness in a DOJ fraud case, after a last minute request came from my office, but that was all they knew. The unpleasant task of informing him Young was in serious condition and Cheu was the agent killed by the bomb fell to me.

"After a long pause, Graves solemnly told me Agent Cheu was a former Marine and a veteran FBI Agent with three teenage children and one in college. Then he let me know what he thought about our risk awareness and asked why we recklessly and negligently placed his men in such a perilous environment without adequate planning."

Bryan felt his remorse deepen with the new burden of Cheu's four fatherless children, and Paul's run-in with Special Agent Graves added to his already full plate of guilt. "Paul, I'm sorry, it was my call, and under the circumstances I should never have agreed to let Washburn or Lance go home, much less calling the FBI into an environment we hadn't adequately assessed. It's my fault, and you shouldn't be taking any blame for my mistake. Please let me call Graves and explain it to him."

Dixon finally noticed Hampton was grieving and realized he had inadvertently shifted more blame on him when he had no intention of doing so. Bryan, we're not in here this morning to pass the blame buck around. I'm sure there will be plenty of that later on. This is all of our faults. Things moved too damn fast and we were sloppy. We totally underestimated the ruthlessness of whoever is running this entire operation.

"I never dreamed they would be crazy enough to go after Washburn when we had police and federal agents in and around his home. And how did they get a bomb inside his condo anyway? This killing must have been pre-planned and the device was already in the bedroom somewhere. Why didn't Cheu and Young search the place? That's standard practice, isn't it? These are the questions we should and will be asking, but we don't have time for that now. Let me go back to last night and what my thinking was after Graves called and what I've decided we need to do."

Dixon waited a few seconds to make sure Hampton had no questions or comments, then continued. "I started asking myself several questions about the events that took place all day yesterday and last night. I thought about people who were involved on our side of the case, and I also thought about the suspects. I considered the timing of everything we know took place yesterday. I explored both events and non-events.

"One of the strangest non-events was the absence of outgoing phone calls from either Mirzoyan or Watson all day long, like they may have known we had wiretaps on their phones. When you consider the events side of the equation, we had several atypical ones over the last two days. First Mirzoyan goes into the same bar in the middle of the day, two days in a row, something profoundly unusual for him.

"Even stranger is that on the day after we set the bait by raiding his billing office, Mirzoyan decided to spend most of the day playing golf, neglecting to answer his phone and ignoring his messages. And then, a bomb goes off in

Washburn's condo, and within fifteen minutes the newscasters know that FBI agents were there protecting a doctor who's involved in a fraud case."

Bryan listened, then apparently realized where Dixon was headed with his commentary. "Mirzoyan and his thug probably knew our plans!"

"Now you're thinking the unthinkable, Bryan. You just completed phase one of *DM* and you reached the same hypothesis I arrived at. Now using mathematical terms, if that's the proposition or theorem, then what's the corollary? Or in other words, what can we likely deduce from your hypothesis?"

"That the information must be coming from someone inside on our investigative team and the person must be communicating with Mirzoyan by some means other than his phone, perhaps even meeting him in the bar? Or maybe the informant is communicating with Watson, and Watson is relaying the information to Mirzoyan. Watson could be meeting Mirzoyan in the bar, or Mirzoyan could be meeting the thug-bomber in the bar telling him what to do."

"There are countless possibilities, aren't there, Bryan? After processing all this information for most of last night, I've decided we should narrow our first corollary to your initial statement, but with a condition. So let's conclude we have a leak, a mole, an informant somewhere on our team, and that individual is somehow sharing our plans with someone in Mirzoyan's organization. But right now we don't know who or how.

"One of our challenges in finding the informer is our team involves the FBI agents, our Justice Department staff, and Gayle's group at the MFCB. It's risky, but for now I want to rule out the FBI since they have only a limited understanding of our case, and we've only asked them to do specific tasks like background checks and monitoring the wiretaps. My chief discomfort in excluding them is they do know Watson, and the attorneys working for him are suspects in the scheme. But in weighing that knowledge against the possibility that if the informant is an FBI employee, he or she would need to be a ruthless SOB to have condemned two of their own to a death sentence last night.

"That leaves us with the DOJ team and whoever has access to our plans at the MFCB. Once again, I'm going to take a leap of faith here and show my partiality by saying, for now, I think we should exclude our team, unless there's someone here you think might be a suspect."

Bryan squirmed, then answered carefully, "If you're true to your model of thinking the unthinkable, then that's a huge leap, maybe an unsupportable one. I think I know our agents, but with the exception of Abe, Eli, and Charlie, I'm not willing to bet anyone's life on the rest of them yet."

After he gave careful consideration to Hampton's painfully accurate observation, Paul recognized he had no rational or defensible reason to dispute Hampton's logic, so he simply told Hampton, "I'll own this error in judgment if it's the wrong decision. I just don't believe we have time to use resources looking internally. I trust the people in this office, and I don't want to send that kind of message to them."

Dixon continued confidently, "I feel strongly we need to assume it's someone on the MFCB staff, perhaps someone we've never met and Da Silva and Gayle don't know about either. We need to adopt a plan moving forward that excludes their group from critical information. Then at the right time we'll send some misinformation their way and see where it goes."

Bryan understood the pitfalls and mistrust that would result from withholding information about the investigation from Gayle and Da Silva, and he knew where all their anger would be directed, once they realized what was happening. "Does that include Da Silva and Gayle? Are you telling me I'm not going to be able to include Gayle in our planning meetings and our interviews, like the one taking place with Lance at nine this morning? You do realize she was his only interrogator on Tuesday, don't you? How do you expect me to navigate this minefield?"

"For starters, you're going to tell her the session with Lance has been postponed for now, because that's precisely what's going to happen. You're also going to tell her we're moving him to a new location and we're not telling anyone outside our internal team where he's being held. You'll stress that we're only using our own agents on twelve hour shifts to protect him until we get this mess under control.

"What you're not going to tell her for now is that all planning and any information related to what we're proposing to do next, and when anything is scheduled to take place, will be limited to five people, even here with our own staff. Anyone we need beyond the inner group of five will be brought in at the last minute. You've probably guessed who the five are, but in case you haven't, they're you, me, Abe, Eli, and Charlie. You choose the four agents guarding Lance and get Abe to help you, because he knows all these men and women better than either of us do.

"Now that we've reasoned our way through all the tricky stuff--"

"In an exceptionally scientific manner, if I may add," Bryan said jokingly.

"Yeah, well, we're a couple of lawyers, not scientists or mathematicians, so what we've come up with will need to be good enough for now. As I was saying, our next step is to plan our misdirection strategies and determine where that misdirection will be targeted. Here's another assumption we didn't discuss yet. My gut tells me Mirzoyan wouldn't have authorized his thug, as Washburn called him, to kill two FBI agents, and I believe the bomber did know there were federal agents in the condo with Washburn."

"I agree with both those theories, Paul. So let me add my reasoning to this pot of stew. If the bomber knew the agents were in Washburn's condo, and we assume Mirzoyan would never have authorized killing the FBI guys, then either the bomber didn't tell Mirzoyan what he was going to do, or someone else besides Mirzoyan was handling the killer. I'll add one more bold assumption; Watson was and is the one managing the assassin."

Dixon emphasized his agreement with Hampton saying, "Bingo! Let's take it one step further. We've always suspected Watson was the real leader of this pack of thieves, and if that's true, Mirzoyan takes orders from him, and he would never be allowed to authorize the murder of federal agents without permission from Watson. So we have a doctor who'll be panicked because he knows we'll suspect he's the one who ordered the killing of an employee who was going to expose him, and the two FBI agents who were protecting him."

"And Paul, this particular doctor has been a scammer for a lot of years. He's been run out of two states already, but until last year when one of his chiropractors dropped off the face of the earth, there was absolutely no evidence of any violence associated with any of his crimes."

"One more last important fact, Bryan. We hope Mirzoyan has no idea we suspect his fraudulent medical practices link him to Watson or anyone else, or to the staged auto accident scams we know are part of the overall scheme. So first, we have Mirzoyan, a slippery character who knows we're on to him, and we have his employee to help us prove it; and second, he believes we think he's responsible for killing two people, but he knows he didn't; and third, he now realizes he's all alone out there in an ocean of serious trouble, on a sinking raft. So how do we blow him out of the water and force him to swim for his life?"

"I'm sure this is where the *Deliberate Misdirection* comes into play, so let me take a shot at it, Paul. Since deliberate means intentional, I assume that means were planning a strategy intended to confuse the two individuals we're after, Mirzoyan and Watson. And we're trying to misdirect those two people, who on the issue of guilt have opposing interests, and we want them moving in the wrong direction, which would be directly at each other destined for a head-on collision."

"Bingo again! Did you learn to reason like that at the University Of Utah College Of Law or at the DEA?"

"They must only teach *DM* at Stanford because I've never heard of it in either place, and I think you're making this all up anyway, but I like it, so let's keep at it because now I think I know where this is going to end up."

"You're right, Bryan, we're going to turn these two crooks against each other, and we're going to do it by forcing Mirzoyan to confront Watson about the ill-advised attempt to kill two FBI agents."

Hampton still felt skeptical about the strategy working and asked Dixon, "The question is, how exactly are we going to force the confrontation?"

"Through a two-pronged attack, one of which you'll lead, and the other one will be my responsibility. First, you'll find Mirzoyan, at home, at work, or on the golf course. When you go, take Abe with you, he's intimidating as hell just seeing all six foot six and three hundred pounds of him staring down at you. Your job will be to panic Mirzoyan into taking action. The two of you must be unsympathetic, serious, and uncompromising when you're confronting him.

"Ask all the questions you want. It's important for you to pepper him with so many accurate facts we already know about the fraud going on in his clinics that he won't doubt all the BS about everything else you're going to misdirect him with.

"It's crucial you convince him we're going to prove he ordered the bombing that killed Washburn and an FBI agent. Tell him we have a witness who saw the bomber at the scene outside Washburn's condo, but we don't need to wait to catch the killer before we come back for him. Emphasize we already have other evidence to prove who was giving the killer orders, so it's just a matter of time. You'll need to get all this done today because it's critical it be coordinated with my part of the strategy. Do you have any questions on any of that, Bryan?"

"I got all of it, and I'm looking forward to my conversation with Mirzoyan. I'll be on him as soon as we're done here."

"And we're close to done now, Bryan. I want you to brief me fully on how Mirzoyan reacts and what he tells you, if anything, as soon as you're done meeting with him.

"Now I'll explain my part. I have a close relationship with several reporters locally, and I'm going to make sure there will be a major news story on every channel on the evening newscasts tonight. It'll go something like this: 'An unnamed source at the U.S. Attorney's office--Blah, Blah, Blah.' The gist will be we're closing in on the people responsible for the murder of a local chiropractor and an FBI agent.

"The story will stress that witnesses have provided a description of the suspected bomber who fled the scene after the blast. We'll imply Federal law enforcement authorities are close to proving a prominent local professional man ordered the double homicide. The reporters will be asked to stress that the owner of the clinic where Dr. Washburn was employed was questioned by federal authorities today about the murders.

"They'll also mention several other employees at three other clinics owned by that doctor were interviewed earlier in the week concerning possible fraudulent billing practices, and one of those employees remains in federal protective custody. The same information will appear in the morning papers tomorrow, and I suspect the national news outlets and networks will be all over the story tomorrow as well. Bryan, maybe you and Abe can scare Mirzoyan enough to get him to make a run for it on the freeway. Coverage of his escape attempt on live national TV would be helpful."

"Are you asking me and Abe to force him into a car chase, Paul?" Hampton asked sarcastically.

"Just find him somewhere and scare the hell out of him. There's one more important thing. Have Eli tell the two FBI agents following Mirzoyan to get conspicuous. We want him to know we're tailing him everywhere. If he goes into a restaurant or bar, one of them needs to be two feet in back of him. If he goes into a public restroom, they follow him in. The only privacy he gets is when he's in the stall.

"Also, have Eli get the FBI guys to immediately put a tail on Watson, as soon as they can assign someone. But we don't want them spotted until an hour after you have your little session with Mirzoyan. But once we give them the word, they follow Watson closely everywhere he goes, just like we're doing with Mirzoyan."

"Paul, I'm worried about how treacherous Watson might be if Mirzoyan ends up biting on this bait and threatens to expose him. Isn't it possible Watson might have his enforcer eliminate Mirzoyan?"

"It's possible, but we should be able to mitigate the risk, if the agents are doing their jobs. This plan is obviously also designed to flush out the killer. That's why we're saying someone saw him leave the condo after the blast, and that misdirection should make him more cautious, less effective, and less inclined to take chances, especially once he sees Mirzoyan is being tailed.

"The FBI guys should be able to keep him safe by preventing anyone who looks threatening or suspicious from getting close enough to him to do any harm. And if they do their job, and the guy does go after Mirzoyan, we'll catch the murderer in the same net. I'm going to call Special Agent Graves and request their help and tell him there's a chance we might flush-out the guy who killed Cheu. We'll remind him the agents following Mirzoyan need to be on their toes at all times."

"This is risky, Paul. A lot could go wrong."

"A lot already went wrong last night. I'm old school Bryan. I'd like to convict all these guys in a court of law. But if they want to impose justice on each other and help us out, and it saves another law enforcement officer's life, then let them do whatever they will. Now, make that call to Gayle and let's get to work."

Chapter 27

Las Vegas, NV
December 8th
11:00 AM

Ari Mirzoyan left his home at eleven AM heading north toward town, but ten minutes later exited I15 and headed east on Flamingo Road for about four miles. Just before reaching Eastern Avenue, he zipped the Mercedes into the Kinkade Outpatient Surgical Center's staff parking lot, then rushed off to the main entrance. As previously planned, one of the FBI agents immediately followed Mirzoyan into the facility, but was soon forced to end his pursuit after Mirzoyan disappeared through a door marked *No Admittance Authorized Personnel Only.*

Agent Blascoe promptly went to the patient registration window, and after showing his credentials, inquired if Dr. Mirzoyan was scheduled for surgery that morning. The attendant reviewed the day's schedule and explained Dr. Mirzoyan was assisting another surgeon on a case that was booked to begin in five minutes and was projected to last approximately two hours.

Jake Blascoe realized the doctor wasn't going anywhere for a while, so he returned to the car to update his partner on the situation. "It looks like we're in for a little wait Bill. I saw Mirzoyan enter the OR suite and was advised he's tied up for the next couple of hours. He can't leave unless he uses the door he went through a few minutes ago, so I'm heading back inside to plant my butt in the waiting room. I'll watch the traffic going in and out and make sure he doesn't leave earlier than expected." As it turned out, it was after one-thirty before Mirzoyan reappeared at the door Agent Blascoe was observing.

Alerted earlier by Agents Simmons and Blascoe that Mirzoyan was expected to leave the hospital between one-fifteen and one forty-five, Hampton and Abe parked the Crown Vic in the staff lot and waited near Mirzoyan's Mercedes. The doctor spotted the two men when he was still twenty yards away, but didn't slow his approach, nor did he seem surprised. "Can I help you two gentlemen with something?"

The agents presented their credentials, then Hampton spoke, "Dr. Mirzoyan, my name is Agent Bryan Hampton and this is Agent Abe Slater. We're here to ask you a few questions and deliver a message from U.S. Attorney Paul Dixon. Is there somewhere inside where we could talk, or would you prefer to come downtown to our offices?"

"My schedule is tight today, so why don't we just talk right here. Presumably this is about Dr. Washburn's horrible accident, or are you just planning to harass me like you've been badgering my employees the last two days? As I said, I don't have much time to give you now, so you'll need to make this quick."

"Doctor, you'll give us the time we need or we can arrest you here and now, then we'll all have plenty of time to chat. Where were you last night between six and eleven PM?"

"I was at home with my wife, reading, then watching TV."

"When did you last see Dr. Washburn?"

"I haven't seen him face to face for several days. He did leave me a voicemail after your agents raided our offices yesterday. He wanted to assure me that nothing was wrong with the billing practices in the Henderson clinic where, as you know, he's in charge. He also wanted to meet with me to discuss details of the false accusations you were making against him."

Abe and Hampton remained in the parking lot and continued questioning Mirzoyan for over thirty minutes. The doctor consistently responded to the questioning by spinning some version of the truth mingled with outright lies. Both agents assumed Mirzoyan's belligerent attitude was driven by a conviction there was no way he could be linked to the bombing. So they decided it was time to rattle his cage and shake some of his self-confidence.

Hampton abruptly moved closer to the doctor in what any casual observer might describe as a confrontational stance. "Dr. Mirzoyan, we know you're directly responsible for the death of Dr. Washburn and FBI Agent Cheu. U.S. Attorney Dixon wants you to know in no uncertain terms that we intend to prosecute you for at least two murders, and the attempted murder of a second federal agent. We know you ordered the assassination of Dr. Washburn to prevent him from identifying you as the criminal mastermind of your long-standing fraud scheme.

"We have an eyewitness who can identify the man you sent to kill Washburn, and all law enforcement agencies are aggressively looking for him at this very moment. We have information linking you to the killer, and as soon as we find him, we'll have more than enough evidence to convict you. We'll coordinate with local prosecutors and determine what jurisdiction will give us the best opportunity to guarantee your eligibility for the death penalty. Evidence is mounting that connects you to both these homicides as well as one that occurred over a year ago. You're the worst kind of murderer, Dr. Mirzoyan, because you kill not out of anger or passion, but simply because of your unbridled greed."

Hampton and Abe could see Mirzoyan's smug attitude evaporating, and Abe couldn't resist the opportunity to add his own version of an intimidating message. "Mirzoyan, you're as done as a Thanksgiving turkey that's been in the oven too long. The entire Department of Justice is at the table waiting to feast on your bones, and we won't rest until our main course is consumed. Paul Dixon said to make sure we tell you to enjoy what little freedom you have left."

Then Hampton moved in even closer. "We're done with you for now, Dr. Mirzoyan." Then he pointed to a black sedan parked near the exit of the staff lot. "Those are two FBI agents waiting just for you. They're going to constantly be in your rearview mirror or three paces behind you from now on. They'll make sure we know where you are at all times, so when it comes time to arrest you they'll have you in custody before the ink's dry on the warrant. Have a nice day, and hopefully you're not operating on anyone else today because you're looking a little shaky right now."

Mirzoyan sat in his car and watched the DOJ agents drive away. The black Ford remained near the lot's exit, its occupants staring at him, obviously expecting him to make a move, any move. The Mercedes' powerful engine was running, but the car sat motionless waiting for instructions from its driver. But Mirzoyan's thoughts were scattered and muddled, and he was unsure of what he should do. He reached into his pocket and retrieved the note Bennett Watson had somehow managed to have slipped into his locker in the surgeon's lounge. The note instructed Mirzoyan to meet Watson at two-thirty that afternoon at yet another bar, and again cautioned him against any use of his cell phone.

Mirzoyan's sweaty hands grabbed the steering wheel when he realized he had only thirty minutes to get to the meeting place. He guessed based on the address it would take at least twenty of those minutes to make the trip if traffic was normal. His eyes darted to the dark sedan parked at the exit, and he had serious doubts if he should actually go to the meeting with the FBI following him. After a few more indecisive minutes, he remembered Watson had established an extreme emergency code intended to alert him to any unforeseen problems. He decided to ignore the no cell phone instruction and text the three numbers **666** to Watson and see what message came back, if any.

Mirzoyan waited only seconds before receiving a one-word response, "NOW." Baffled by what seemed like a reckless decision by his usually cautious and restrained business associate, Mirzoyan resigned himself to follow the instructions, reasoning Watson knew the risks and must have some contingency plan.

The bar was located on Industrial Road, one of ten questionable businesses in a run-down strip mall. True to his expectations, another quick glance in his side mirror confirmed the dark sedan still followed closely. After he arrived in the parking lot, Mirzoyan thought, a strip club in a strip mall. This is an all-time low for me. But it was the right place, and now was now, so he hastily got out of the car and entered the dark smelly bar. Almost immediately someone grabbed his arm and asked, "Are you Mirzoyan?"

"Yes, who's asking?"

"It's not important who I am. You need to come with me right now and don't screw around."

The man immediately rushed Mirzoyan through a doorway at the back of the bar. It led to a storage area that also served as a dressing room for the 'exotic' dancers. On the wall opposite one stacked with cases of liquor and beer sat three too old, mostly naked, 'showgirls' working in vain with a variety of cosmetics to cover the damage that age, too much sun, and hard living had done to their bodies. Mirzoyan realized then why the owners kept the lounge as dark as possible. While he was observing the women, his escort had unlocked another door and was urging him to hustle through it, then wait. As soon as he was on the other side, he heard the man replacing the padlock he'd removed only moments before.

Almost immediately a door opened on the far side of the well-lit room, and Bennett Watson casually strolled into the space. Taking charge, he invited Mirzoyan to sit in one of two cushioned chairs that appeared to be part of a movie set that also included a heart-shaped bed. Then he noticed the video and sound equipment, and several spotlights on large stands, and in an adjacent smaller glass-enclosed room a bank of servers and monitors glowed.

"Online, interactive sex is what we deliver here, Ari. It's another of my profitable enterprises. The world is full of perverts and suckers with credit cards, and we give them a variety of opportunities to use them."

"Well, my world is full of FBI and DOJ agents, Bennett. They're out there right now following me everywhere I go. They think I had Washburn killed, and they claim to have the proof. They also said they have an eyewitness who can identify the killer, and they're looking for him right now. I'm not taking the rap for killing anyone. You should never have let that crazy bastard Guzman off his leash. I've never even talked to him; he's your damn assassin, not mine."

"Ari, calm down and shut up! The FBI can't prove anything. No one even noticed Guzman at the condo or he would have let me know, and there's no way they can link Guzman to either of us anyway. You're panicking, and that's exactly what the FBI wants you to do. I already know they're following you, and as a matter of fact they started following me today, and that's why we're here meeting where they can't possibly find us in the few minutes we require for our little talk.

"I ditched the guys following me half an hour ago, so no one knows I'm here. The agents watching you will be looking for you in the bar, expecting you to be meeting someone. When they don't see you, they'll start nosing around the bathrooms and the dressing room, but they won't find you. When we're done here, my men will sneak you back into the bar, and when you're ready, you can simply walk out the front door. We even have witnesses who'll confirm you were at a table having a beer alone the whole time."

"Listen, Bennett, I'm telling you right now, if they arrest me, I'm not going to keep quiet and take the fall for any killings. Hell, fraud is one thing, but murder is something I never signed up for. I told you that last year after you and Guzman arranged to have one of my doctors disappear."

"Ari, please calm down. They have no proof of anything. You had nothing to do with the bombing and neither did I. Guzman is a professional, and they'll never find him because they don't even know who they're looking for.

"Also, don't ever threaten me like that again. If you tell anyone anything about the business arrangement you and I have, I'll send Fausto after you. Do you understand what I'm telling you? If they haul you in for questioning, you don't say a damn word about me or claim to have anything to do with me. And for sure you don't admit to any fraud in your clinics. If you do, you won't need to worry about a trial because you won't live long enough to have one. Guzman has friends just like him everywhere. There's nowhere you'll be safe if you betray me, Ari. Do you understand?"

"Bennett, I'm scared. This is way out of my league. I don't know what to do. I can't deal with the feds following me everywhere and harassing me and my employees. How can I run my business? How can I have a life?"

"Everything will be fine, Ari. Now listen, you need to get back to your car and get out of here before they decide to look around more closely and start asking questions about the padlocked door we used to get you in here. One more thing, like I told you a few days ago, all of our phones are tapped, so don't call me and don't even text anything anymore. Be careful what you say to anyone on any phone you use.

"Here's a burn phone you can call me on in an extreme emergency. It's untraceable and should only be used once. If you need to call, use the only number programmed into the phone. It goes to a similar phone I have in case I need to reach you. Now go, my friend, say nothing to anyone, and don't worry. I have everything under control."

Chapter 28

Las Vegas, NV
December 8th
2:30 PM

When Bryan and Abe arrived back at the DOJ building, Lance Beasley was already waiting in the interview room with his attorney Andrego Mattich. Abe realized Lance was worried when he'd left him in the care of the two FBI agents at the hotel the previous night, but now he looked terrified, pacing erratically around the room trying to deal with the complex emotions of loss, and fear for his own life. Lance had gone to bed shortly after he was left alone in his hotel room, long before news of the deaths of Washburn and the FBI agent reached TV audiences.

After he learned about the bombing, Hampton had sent Eli and another agent to the hotel to team up with the FBI agents, hopefully preventing anymore disasters. When morning came, Eli was there to give Lance the grim news of the previous evening, and as expected, the young man was devastated. They continued guarding him at the hotel until one that afternoon, then the four agents vigilantly transported Lance to the interview room where he now waited.

The first words Hampton spoke were sincere and apologetic. "Lance, we're truly sorry for your loss and for our failure to anticipate the unprecedented level of brutality Dr. Mirzoyan and his associates demonstrated last night. I hope you now realize who we're dealing with and the danger these people you're trying to protect represent to anyone who might cross them. We need your help and we need it now. Every minute we leave these people on the street means someone else is at risk. It's now obvious they'll stop at nothing to protect themselves from anyone who knows enough about the operation and its organizers to threaten them.

"We're guaranteeing you complete immunity and we'll keep you in protective custody for as long as any threat exists. If we discover there's any connection to organized crime or it appears there's a long-term danger to you, we'll place you in the witness protection program."

Lance looked directly at Hampton. "Weren't you supposedly protecting Gerald last night? That didn't work out too well for him, so why would I trust you to protect me?"

"Letting both of you return to your homes was a breach of protocol and a mistake. Had we followed policy, Dr. Washburn would still be alive along with our fellow agent. That was an error of judgment on my part, and I can promise you no such mistakes will occur in the future."

"I need to know what will happen to other employees like me who were just doing their jobs if I tell you what I know. Are they going to jail? Is it going to look like I ratted-out everyone just to save myself? What about people like Amanda? She's got kids and a no-good husband. What's going to happen to her? Besides, I'm not even sure I know enough to do you any good. Yesterday you said it was what Gerald and I knew together that would give you the information you needed. He had to know way more than I do about who's involved and how it all works. All I know about is my job, and what I do is a small piece of what you need to know."

Hampton knew Lance had made an excellent point, but Lance didn't know about the videos explaining the fraud scheme or the list of counterfeit patients and claims his friend Washburn had compiled and given to Agent Young. He also had no knowledge of the providential sequence of events that had preserved that digital evidence. Hampton also didn't want Lance to have any second thoughts about being fully cooperative. So he reassured him, saying, "You'll be surprised to see how much more you actually do know compared to what you think you do, Lance.

"If you just answer every question we ask you, you'll discover one fact leads to another fact that sometime leads to a crucial piece of information. The process is like finally understanding what the next piece needs to look like when you're putting a puzzle together. People don't generally recognize how unique the information only they possess can be, because they use it so often. To them, it seems like general knowledge. We'll ask the right questions, and all you need to do is give truthful and complete answers."

"I'd like to try and get Amanda to talk with you guys. Can you offer her the same deal you're giving me? She's been part of whatever's going on longer than I have, and I'm sure she could tell you stuff I don't know anything about."

Hampton paused before answering, because he realized Lance was probably right. "Lance, let's keep that possibility open and we'll work just with you for a few sessions, then sometime tomorrow we'll revisit the possibility of talking to Amanda again. Right now I'm convinced she's loyal to Dr. Mirzoyan, and I don't want her to know you're helping us for fear she may report anything we tell her to Mirzoyan."

"That sounds reasonable. I know she thinks Mirzoyan is just looking out for the patients, but if she sees the news and believes he's responsible for what happened to Gerald, she'll change her mind, won't she?"

"You never know, Lance. We can't be certain she will, but we can hope. Let's get started and cover as much ground as possible this afternoon. Eli's going to leave now because he's been up all night, so Abe and I will be asking the questions today. We'll be video recording this session, and we note your attorney Mr. Mattich is present."

Lance raised his hand to ask a question. "Before we start, may I ask why Agent Baker isn't here? She already asked me a lot of questions and maybe it would help if she was part of this process."

"Agent Baker is with the Medical Fraud Crime Bureau not with the DOJ, and she isn't available today, so we might be asking you to repeat some information you already gave her, but from what I understand, you told her very little. Let's get started and see how it goes."

The questioning continued for over four hours, and the group only paused for coffee, food, and bathroom breaks. When Dixon entered the room just before seven and saw how exhausted everyone looked, he called a halt to the marathon session. "Bryan, I think Mr. Beasley has had enough for the day, and I'm sure the rest of you all feel the same. The FBI agents are here to escort our guest to his new accommodations for the next several days where he'll be diligently guarded and kept safe."

Dixon then turned to Beasley. "Lance, I've observed some of the interview proceedings today, and I want to thank you for what seems to me like a sincere effort on your part to tell us everything you know about operations in the billing office. The information you've provided will help us put an end to this fraudulent criminal operation. You've told us enough today to allow us to request warrants for several arrests. We'll secure those warrants first thing in the morning and execute them before end of day tomorrow."

Dixon had then offered Lance a handshake. "Your work is not yet done, so we'll see you back here tomorrow morning at ten. We can't let you communicate with anyone tonight. I've instructed the agents to confiscate your phone, iPad, and laptop if you have one. If I thought you could send smoke signals to anyone I'd have your lighter seized as well. I hope you understand we need to keep you incommunicado for a few days while we round up some dangerous people, so no one else gets hurt."

After the agents escorted Lance away, Mattich thanked Dixon and Hampton for their thoughtful treatment of his client, then left. Almost immediately afterwards Abe packed up his papers and promised Bryan he'd return before eight the next morning and hurried out the door.

Dixon and Hampton decided to reconvene in the comparative comfort of Dixon's office. "I didn't see the entire interview Bryan, but what I did observe was helpful. At least it's enough to go after Mirzoyan and the three chiropractors who are still breathing. I'll request the warrants in the morning and, as soon as they're signed, I'll have Charlie let you know. Let's pick all four of the doctors up immediately, before anyone leaks the news of their pending arrests."

Bryan nodded cautious agreement, but then expressed concerns about the timing. "Paul, I know we don't want these guys slipping out of town, and what we have so far makes a good case against Mirzoyan and his principal co-conspirators who run each of the clinics. But we have nothing implicating Watson, only statistics from the MFCB. We also haven't learned anything about the killer or who's actually giving him orders. Doesn't that concern you?"

"Those are the very reasons I suggest we immediately start questioning the four men we plan to arrest. I think this is a well-compartmentalized operation, and we won't get any closer to Watson until one or more of the doctors panics and begins telling us what we need to know. Ideally, we get Mirzoyan to give up Watson in exchange for some reduction in charges we plan to file against him.

"If we can't make that happen, we should be able to piece together enough information from whatever we obtain from the other three to get something solid on Watson. We need to zero in on one of them. Focus on the doctor with the most to lose, family wise and financially. Get them profiled as soon as possible and identify the weakest link, then grill the hell out of him and Mirzoyan as soon as we arrest them."

"Sounds like a plan, Paul. Tomorrow should be a big day for us."

"If all goes as planned, I hope it will be, Bryan, but for now it's time to call it a day."

Bryan finished picking up his notes in the interview room, then spent a few more minutes trying to organize the piles of paper that had accumulated on his desk during the day. As he prepared to leave his office and head somewhere for dinner, he was shocked to see Charlie waiting for him in one of the cubicles just outside his door.

"Hungry, Agent Hampton?"

Determined to be atypically charismatic, Bryan paused before responding, "Charlie, what an awesome surprise. You're an answer to an unspoken prayer. I was just wondering how I could motivate myself to get dinner, then drag myself home to bed. My exhaustion just vanished. Seeing you, by the way you look amazing, just cleared away the fifty problems churning around in my head. Spending some time together without talking about this case will feel like a mini-vacation, a brief escape from reality. How did you know how drained I was feeling?"

"When I was leaving late this afternoon, I could see it was going to be a long day for you, and I thought tonight you might need a hot meal and some good company. So I had my parents pick up the boys and keep them till later on tonight. We still have a couple of hours to have a relaxing meal and get your mind off things. By the way, that was a fairly charming response for someone who looks too tired to think. Where would you like to go for dinner?"

Chapter 29

Las Vegas, NV
December 8th
7:30 PM

An already unnerving day had suddenly worsened for Bennett Watson after he heard the local newscast on the drive home. The reporter alleged the information had come from an unnamed source in the U.S. Attorney's Office.

"Federal authorities are said to be closing in on those responsible for last night's bombing that killed Dr. Gerald Washburn, a local chiropractor, and FBI Agent Roland Cheu. An eyewitness provided a description of the suspected bomber, and local law enforcement officials are now actively searching for the man. Our source informed us agents today interviewed Dr. Washburn's employer, a local professional man with alleged links to the suspected bomber. The source also hinted that other arrests are anticipated in what appears to be a fraud scheme gone bad."

Until that moment, Watson had managed to control the anger and escalating anxiety he felt since meeting with Mirzoyan. But the day had brought him a succession of increasingly disturbing news, and his inclination to resist making any rash decisions was rapidly weakening. He was still struggling to rationalize conflicting information coming at him from multiple sources. He somehow needed to know which facts were true and which were false, and which impressions and instincts he should follow.

He decided he might reach a clearer vision of what to do if he reexamined the day's events in chronological order. First he,d heard the perplexing news of the bombing that killed Washburn and the FBI agent. Had Guzman gone crazy? He recalled he had immediately picked up the phone to send the meeting code to Guzman, but then decided against it. Not now, he thought. I'm too upset, he's apparently irrational, and the police might be watching him.

Next he received an unexpected mid-morning call on the untraceable phone used to talk with his covert source at the MFCB. In that conversation, he was told the bombing had apparently caused a temporary shift in DOJ policy concerning information sharing with the MFCB or anyone outside of the DOJ. He was reassured this was likely only a temporary problem but the informant wanted him to be aware of the change.

The source was expensive, but the information was always well-timed, accurate, and vital. The unidentified person had first contacted him several weeks earlier on his home phone offering information that could "keep you out of prison, because the Feds are looking into your business dealings with a local chiropractor." The caller had then immediately disconnected the call. Watson had slept little that night.

The next day a FedEx package marked 'personal' arrived at his office. It contained a disposable cell phone, a phone number, and a note that simply said, "Call if you want to know more facts about the topic of our conversation last night." He resisted calling the number for two weeks. During that time, the mystery phone was silent. He finally made the call after deciding he could no longer risk waiting to know exactly what the source actually knew.

The voice that answered was mechanical, the gender undeterminable, but the emotion unmistakable, "Don't ever play chess with me again, Watson! Your future depends on information I have that will keep you out of jail. This is how you and I are going to do business. I'll call offering you information to keep you one step ahead of the Feds, whom you should know are already investigating one of your major fraud schemes.

"Each time I call, I'll tell you what the information I'm offering will cost you. If you're interested, and you better be, you'll agree to wire the specified fee to an account number I'll provide you. Then I'll call back and give you the information as soon as my bank emails confirmation of the specified deposit. We'll always communicate using the untraceable phone I sent you."

"What makes you think I need to pay you for information about my business dealings?"

"You called me back! You realized you couldn't risk not knowing whatever information I might have for you. We both know you're a crook, Watson, so let's cut the crap and get down to business. What I'm offering today is to tell you exactly what information the Justice Department will soon know about your relationship with Dr. Mirzoyan and his bogus clinics. I was willing to sell this information to you for fifty thousand two weeks ago, but you made me wait, so now it's seventy-five thousand."

He had resentfully agreed to pay that day, and since then had dished out another three hundred thousand dollars in exchange for advanced warnings about wire taps, the FBI surveillance on both him and Mirzoyan, the planned raids on Mirzoyan's billing office and clinics, and the DOJ's current theory that Mirzoyan wasn't the real organizer of the complex scheme, which was also seemingly associated with a series of staged auto accidents.

For Watson, the most alarming aspect of the news the DOJ had even temporarily stopped sharing information with the MFCB, was that it likely signaled a loss of confidence or trust in the organization. Lost trust probably meant someone at the Justice Department suspected information was being leaked, which meant he would no longer be getting advance warnings of any pending DOJ actions. He could only hope his MFCB source wasn't already under investigation and had been shrewd in obtaining the leaked information and meticulous in purging evidence that might point directly to its source. But if by chance that wasn't the case, he had already demolished the phone and disposed of its remnants.

That call had prompted him to arrange the meeting with Mirzoyan. And after speaking with him for ten minutes he'd concluded there was nothing complicated about that decision; it was only a question of timing. He had no doubts Mirzoyan would tell everything he knew as soon as he was taken into custody. The only viable solution was to eliminate him, and to do it quickly. Before he left the room with the heart-shaped bed and cameras, he called Guzman's cell and left him a message to meet him in the Deuce Lounge at the Aria at ten that night.

Now, he thought about the latest bad news. Do they really have an eyewitness who saw Guzman, or do I trust he would have warned me if someone saw him? In the past he's always been ghost-like when he works. No one ever sees him, just the bedlam he leaves behind. Does the DOJ really have any information linking Guzman to me or to Mirzoyan? How could they possibly know anything about Guzman's association with Mirzoyan, because there isn't one? The only possible connection they could uncover linking me to

Guzman is if Fausto or Mirzoyan divulged it. There's no way they've talked to Guzman or the headlines would be, 'Bombing Suspect Arrested,' so that leaves only Mirzoyan, who could tie me to Guzman. Mirzoyan is a dead man.

The Aria was one of three hotels in the vast City Center complex. With over four thousand sleeping rooms and numerous bars and show rooms that featured live entertainment, Watson recognized it would be nearly impossible to follow him through the place at ten at night when the crowds were at their peak. He was also well enough acquainted with the hotel that he believed he could safely disappear and elude anyone who followed him by walking through the casino and slipping into the Deuce Lounge.

As soon as he pulled into the valet parking lane, a young man opened his door and handed him a claim ticket. "Keep it close, I'll be out in less than twenty minutes, and you'll get the other half then," he told the attendant while handing him half of a one hundred dollar bill.

He moved quickly then, because he knew the dark undercover sedan with the two agents was only three vehicles back in the line of cars already forming in the drop-off lane. When his peripheral vision revealed one agent already opening the passenger side door, he felt an uncommon sense of urgency, perhaps even fear, prodding him to move even more quickly to the entrance, through the lobby, and finally into the casino where he paused and looked back.

Already having disposed of the ridiculous baseball cap he placed conspicuously on his head before leaving his car, he then ducked behind a bank of slot machines to switch his reversible jacket from red to dark blue. He saw the FBI man standing near the entrance frantically looking for him in every possible direction, so he relaxed and continued through the casino, now moving more slowly with the crowds toward his destination.

Seconds later Watson spotted the menacing hulk of Fausto Guzman in a secluded corner of the Deuce Lounge. He paused for several minutes at one of the Blackjack tables near the entrance to make sure Guzman was alone and not under surveillance. Watson also wanted to be certain his FBI friend hadn't followed him. Then, when everything appeared safe, he moved casually toward the killer.

He was growing more fearful of Guzman as time passed, and he now knew Guzman had disregarded his earlier explicit instructions to remove the bomb under Washburn's bed. Guzman's decision to trigger the bomb with two FBI agents inside the condo and the police outside was confirmation of a reckless arrogance that both troubled and frightened him.

"So what do you think of my problem-solving last night counselor? You almost got three for the price of one."

Arrogant and unbelievably stupid, Watson thought. Trying to project strength and courage he didn't feel, Watson asked, "I told you to remove the bomb the night you put it there. How is it that you ignored my instructions, then set it off with two FBI agents inside? Did you know they were in there? Do you know what kind of trouble that decision could bring down on us?"

"What do you think, lawyer-man? Of course I knew who was in there. I listened to every word they were saying and everything your doctor friend was about to tell them, and that's when I decided they all needed to be eliminated."

"Well, for the record, it was an unauthorized and dangerous decision, and now we have a colossal mess on our hands. The FBI claims they have a witness who saw you at the scene and has given them a description."

"That's bullshit! Nobody saw me, no one paid any attention to me and, if that was true, why haven't they posted the police sketch of me all over the place? What's this mess you think we got?"

"Are you serious? You killed an FBI agent. You think that's not a problem? The Feds are already tailing me and Mirzoyan. They questioned him this morning, and he's scared shitless. He's threatening to tell them everything he knows if they arrest him and try to charge him with the bombing. They've already told him they're going to haul him in as soon as they catch you."

"Well, I got a quick and permanent solution for that problem. And I'll be more than happy to take care of him before morning; just give me the word."

"I'm afraid we have no other choice. He knows too much and he can't be trusted. The longer we wait, the more dangerous it is for us. He knows your name and he knows you work for me, and that's enough to get us both executed. With the FBI tailing him, it's not going to be easy for you to get to him. I don't want anymore bombs, and I don't want anymore unnecessary killings."

"Define unnecessary, counselor. You send me into impossible situations with no notice and expect me to still get the job done. Then you second guess me when someone else is in the wrong place at the wrong time. What if Mrs. Mirzoyan is in the way tonight when I visit her husband? Should I leave her alive as an eyewitness who can identify me and tell the police about the doctor's relationship with you? The reality is she probably knows too much already, and we need to get rid of both of them. So what do you want me to do?"

"I'm asking you to fix the problem. This scam is over now, and you've made an excellent point. We can't afford to leave any witnesses who can tie Mirzoyan to me or to you. A scared rabbit like him has most definitely told his wife enough about me and you, and that definitely makes her a threat. You're right, take care of them both, and do it tonight. You understand?"

"Of course I do, Mr. Watson. I must tell you I'm looking forward to getting rid of the doctor. He's an embarrassment to criminals everywhere. He has no cajones."

"Fausto, there's one last, important thing you must do. You need to leave town for a few months. Go back to Chicago or somewhere else." Watson then handed Guzman a bulging legal-sized envelope. "Here's a nice bonus for you, and I'll keep paying you our agreed upon monthly retainer for as long as it takes the Feds to give up on this investigation. But you must disappear. Stay out of sight for the next several months in case someone did see you at the bombing and the Feds have your description. When everything has settled down and it's safe, I'll text 'All Clear' to the phone I've put in the envelope with your cash. It's critical we have no further contact until you get that message."

"You're a fair man, amigo. Everything will be taken care of by morning, and I'll vanish and become a ghost again. You'll not see or hear of me until you either stop paying me or summon me to return."

Watson looked around to make sure no one was paying any attention to them, then slowly stood, watching nervously for any sign of the FBI agent. "Give me a five-minute head start before you leave, and don't go out the front."

When the automatic doors opened, Watson stepped out under the canopy where a steady stream of cars arrived and departed. He immediately saw the promised hundred dollar tip had secured him a spot on prestige row where attendants deliberately parked high-end cars, sending the message the rich and famous were patrons at the hotel.

His timing was perfect because it had been exactly twenty minutes and the attendant with the torn half of the hundred dollar bill was watching for him. Now that his jacket was red side out again he was easy to spot even without the hat. "Your car is right here, sir," the valet said, handing him the keys, while Watson smoothly slipped him the other half of the hundred dollar bill.

After starting the engine, he looked for the dark sedan. At first he couldn't see it, but then as he pulled forward he spotted the car farther down the driveway, both agents sitting inside impatiently waiting for him to return to his car so they could resume their regrettably interrupted surveillance.

Fausto had watched Watson disappear, then quickly began planning the evening's executions. First he searched the contacts on his phone for Mirzoyan's exact address. Afterward he pasted the copied address into Google Maps and selected the hybrid view so he could plan his approach to the doctor's house. It took less than fifteen minutes to map and plan his strategy. Then, ignoring Watson's instructions, he left the hotel through the main entrance. But it made no difference because Watson and his FBI chaperons were now long gone.

Chapter 30

Las Vegas, NV
December 8th
11:00 PM

Guzman was thrilled when he discovered Mirzoyan's home was located in an exclusive golf community in Henderson. People who live behind gates and walls always think they're safe, he thought, so the impact of my work will terrify the neighbors long after I'm gone.

The rear of the house overlooked the fourteenth green, the back lawn ending along the cart path. The entire development was gated, with an impressive-looking guard house situated less than a hundred yards from the doctor's home. Despite the location of the guard house, unobtrusive access to the residence looked fairly simple, at least when viewed on Google Maps. But Guzman wanted to see the site first-hand before the actual incursion when he would carry out his grisly assignment.

He took the Bruce Woodbury Beltway to Green Valley, briefly headed east on Locust Ridge Parkway, parked in a small strip mall, and walked across the street. Incredibly, he saw a sidewalk leading from Locust Ridge Parkway directly into the grounds. No gate obstructed foot traffic, and it appeared anyone could walk directly down the path and into the surrounding neighborhood, especially in the dark, late at night when the guards were catnapping. He thought about testing his theory, but decided against it. If someone noticed him now, another sighting later that night would be more noteworthy and likely problematic.

As always, Guzman identified an alternate way he could use to get into or out of the complex, depending on whatever situation he might encounter at the time. The secondary path was only a short distance from the preferred one, but it required him to scale a five foot stone wall. He eventually decided it might be wise to exit the grounds using the wall route rather than chancing the sidewalk that took him past the guards.

Guzman knew he had other tasks to complete in the next three hours, so after taking one last look around, he headed for his car. Knowing he planned to drive out of Vegas that night, he returned to his small apartment, packed what few things he actually kept there, then carefully wiped down every surface in the entire place. He removed all the bedding and towels and later disposed of everything in two different dumpsters, both miles away from the apartment. During an extended late meal at an all-night restaurant, he carefully finalized details of his murderous plans.

Usually Guzman wanted his victims to experience pain when he executed them. Rape, too, was always an option, depending on his mood and how much the target appealed to him. But he decided without the luxury of more advanced planning, and a more thorough survey of the doctor's home and grounds, he would need to forego some pleasures for the sake of efficiency and stealth.

His plan was simple; access the grounds, go down the cart path to the rear of the home, cut the phone lines, disarm the alarm system, then break into the house. He hoped he could first locate Mrs. Mirzoyan and quietly strangle her. For Guzman, bare-handed assaults were always the most rewarding. Next he would find the weasel chiropractor and spend a little more time dealing with him. If he came across the doctor first, he'd duct tape his hands and feet, gag him, and force him to watch the execution of his wife. His plan was to be safely back in his car at the strip mall in no more than twenty-five minutes after he parked it.

Dr. Mirzoyan and his wife had both gone to bed slightly after midnight. They shared a bedroom, slept together in a king-sized bed, but seldom retired at the same hour. Tonight had been an exception, but long after his wife was quietly sleeping, Mirzoyan was still wide awake, replaying in his mind the conversation from his meeting with Watson. The more he reflected on the attorney's harsh warnings, the more troubled and uneasy he became. Sleep was impossible, and shortly after one-thirty he got up and took two twenty milligram tablets of

Ambien, twice his normal dose. He left the bedroom and went downstairs to his office, washed down the Ambien with a double shot of Johnnie Walker Blue Label, and settled into a favorite chair to read while he waited for the drug and alcohol to take effect.

Something startled him, causing him to bolt forward in his chair. He noticed the book he was reading on the hardwood floor beside the partially reclined lounger where he now sat. Disoriented, he struggled to think clearly and tried to shake the confusion from his overmedicated brain.

I heard a thud, he thought. Was it just the book falling off my lap? He glanced at the clock on his desk, 2:10 in the morning; he'd slept only a few minutes. He flinched, then clearly heard another noise, a creaking sound this time, and then he heard it again! Before he could lift his body from the chair he sensed someone standing in the doorway, a large man. There was an object in his right hand; it looked like a hammer, but the stranger was moving so quickly toward him his eyes wouldn't focus. He was defenseless. A horrific, agonizing blow to the middle of his forehead drove him into blackness.

Icy water and horrible pain were his next conscious sensations, and he thought he tasted blood. Yes, it was blood, a lot of it. Then more ice water, followed by a hard slap, then many more; he lost count. He realized he was sitting on the floor, leaning against something hard, a chair? He struggled to raise his throbbing head and focus his eyes on the face of the man working the hand pounding his face.

"Dr. Mirzoyan, wake up. I need you to see this, because this is what happens to cowards who can't keep their mouths shut. I better help you keep your head up so you don't miss the show," Guzman said sarcastically, while wrapping a long piece of duct tape around Ari's forehead and the chair in back of him, forcing him to stare straight ahead. What he saw only further terrified and devastated him. His wife sat on the floor directly across from him, gagged and tied to the footboard of their bed.

The man spoke to him, "Do you know who I am, Ari? I can see you're having a hard time concentrating, and I'm running short on time, so I'm just gonna tell you a few things, then I'll finish up and leave. You know me as Guzman. I solve problems for Mr. Watson. I'm here to take care of you and your wife tonight, because the boss says you're both problems, and he hates problems."

Despite the incapacities the drug, alcohol, and a fractured skull had imposed on his brain, comprehension of his horrible circumstances had eventually registered in Mirzoyan's cerebral cortex. He tried to shout, but Guzman shoved a washcloth into his mouth. Guzman slapped him to attention again, then crossed the room and began choking his wife. Mirzoyan saw her struggling to breathe, but Guzman released his grip. Mirzoyan thought for a moment maybe the man was just trying to scare him and he would let her live. But then Guzman grabbed her head with his two massive hands and while smiling at Mirzoyan, savagely twisted it until her vertebrae shattered and her spinal cord stretched, then tore.

Before he could close his eyes to the horrific sight, the killer was kneeling in front of him, sneering and laughing, seemingly relishing the horror and pain he was suffering. Then more ice water assaulted his face, probably intended to sharpen his awareness and increase his pain and terror. He saw the hammer coming at him again, but this time the blows struck his chest and crotch, blow after blow until he could hardly breathe. He nearly blacked out, but more ice water and harder slapping brought him back to an unbearable awareness and the intolerable pain.

Mirzoyan knew his life was ending when Guzman's huge, rough hands grasped his neck. He felt his airway collapse, stopping any air flow into or out of his lungs. The sudden lack of oxygen intensified his panic for what seemed like forever, but in reality it was only a moment. The last thing his brain registered was a cracking sound; it was his hyoid bone fracturing, then blackness, permanent blackness.

Guzman was forced to stop torturing Mirzoyan sooner than he planned. Somewhere in the distance he heard sirens. They're probably coming here, he thought, but why? Was there another alarm system he missed? Had he tripped an infrared sensor? Did Mirzoyan have a cell phone backup that activated after he cut the land line? None of that mattered now, he decided. It was time to leave.

As he exited the sliding glass doors through the back of the house, he could see flashing red lights reflecting off the guard house. He decided to leave the grounds using the path that took him over the wall, rather than chancing the sidewalk past the gate and guards again. He was at the wall in less than two minutes. Peering over it, he saw no cars coming from either direction, and he also saw the red lights moving away from the guard house canopy, making their way to the street in front of Mirzoyan's house. Quickly he crossed Locust Ridge Parkway and trotted the short distance to the strip mall parking lot where his car waited, well-hidden from the street by the surrounding buildings.

Guzman started the engine and exited the lot onto North Encinitas Drive. He drove north for a couple of blocks before switching on the headlights, slowly making his way back to the beltway. He joined northbound I15 and continued driving through the night. He had breakfast in Beaver, UT at six that morning, then headed north again until he reached I70. Seven hours later he pulled into a Holiday Inn Express in Wheaton, CO.

He stayed in the Denver area for the next five nights, moving once to another hotel. His plan was to be back in Chicago the following Friday. Leisure driving, he had decided, from Denver to Chicago, only about 320 miles a day would get him there in three days.

The FBI agents had been parked a few houses away for over six hours, keeping an eye on Mirzoyan's home. Every thirty minutes one of them circled the doctor's house on foot. Apparently, by blind luck, the killer had entered the house right after the last patrol. The FBI man was just stepping out of the car to make the next circuit when he saw the red lights on the Henderson Police car come speeding onto the street.

Chapter 31

Las Vegas, NV
December 9th
6:20 AM

Ten minutes before he usually began his day, Hampton's phone startled him out of a restless sleep. Any call before seven wasn't good, and when he saw the display on his caller ID read 'PAUL,' he braced himself for bad news. He just never imagined how bad it would be. "Bryan, it's Paul. Mirzoyan and his wife were murdered early this morning."

The news was so devastating Bryan struggled for a moment to say anything, desperately trying to form a clear thought. But then he heard Dixon continue the sobering story, "Special Agent Graves called me ten minutes ago, and details are sketchy, but it happened at their home, between two and two-thirty, while the FBI agents sat outside in their car.

"After evaluating the scene for three hours, the police and FBI have come up with a working theory. Someone apparently slipped past the guards at the gate house, approached the back of the home from the golf course, attempted to disable the alarm, but failed to do so, then jimmied a sliding glass door and went in. The killer must have found the doctor in his office on the ground floor based on the mess they found there. He then went to all the effort of dragging the victim upstairs to the couple's bedroom, where he tied the wife to their bed and apparently forced Mirzoyan to watch as he strangled her to death.

"At some point, the killer viciously beat Mirzoyan, breaking his ribs, fracturing his skull, and smashing his genitals, all apparently done with a large hammer left at the scene. The assassin apparently finished him off by choking him to death and was out of the house in less than twenty minutes.

"We know the exact times because the alarm was triggered at 2:10, the police arrived at the security gate at 2:24, but didn't enter the house until 2:28. The FBI agents did a walk-around of the exterior of the house every half hour. The last patrol began at 2:00 and ended five minutes later."

After pausing a moment, Dixon continued, "The delay of fourteen minutes before the police arrived was the result of inexcusably bad judgment on the part of the attendant at the alarm call center. She first tried calling the Mirzoyans, then attempted to reach two others on their call list before she finally got around to notifying the Henderson Police. Her explanation was customers get angry when the police charge them for responding to false alarms."

"Is the media aware of the killings yet?" Hampton asked Dixon.

"Of course. I haven't seen any of the broadcasts yet, but apparently several of the six o'clock newscasts even had overhead pictures of the scene taken from helicopters. Graves told me the videos show a variety of emergency vehicles surrounding the house, and he also told me the gist of all the headlines are basically identical, *Local Doctor and Wife Murdered in Home*. Turn on your TV and see for yourself. The 6:30 news cycle will start in another minute."

"What about evidence? You mentioned a hammer was left at the scene. Has it been checked for prints?"

"Graves told me the FBI and Henderson Police forensic teams are combing the place for evidence as we speak. Confidentially, they found a couple of usable prints on the hammer. They don't know if the hammer belonged to the Mirzoyans or if it was brought there by the killer. They're comparing the prints with the victims to rule them out. If they don't match, we might catch a break."

"Not to change the subject, Paul, but do we still wait for warrants to arrest the three chiropractors?"

"I'm thinking yes. Why do you ask?"

"I believe we need to get all three of them into protective custody immediately, before this crazed butcher goes after them, too. I don't think we have time to wait for warrants. I suggest we assign three teams of agents to locate them and bring them in immediately. That way, they'll at least be off the street. We can hold them for questioning while the warrants are being processed. I'm afraid when they see the morning news they'll panic and attempt to disappear. That is, if they're still alive."

"More than likely, you're right, Bryan. Go ahead and make the calls and assign teams to pick all three of them up before they have a chance to go anywhere."

"Abe, Eli and I will team up with other agents to form the three teams. That way we'll know we're not tipping off anyone else to our plans. I'll keep you advised of our progress throughout the morning, Paul. I think we should bring them to the office, so you can meet with them as a group and explain in no uncertain terms the dangers they face."

"Bryan, I don't think we'll need to preach about the dangers they face. There's no doubt the news of the bombing coupled with these grisly murders last night will have already made that point. Our problem is going to be convincing them if they do tell us what they know, we can protect them and their families from a similar fate. You and I need to assure them the evidence they provide us will make it possible to arrest and detain whoever is the mastermind behind this along with his hired executioner. Be sure and keep me informed as your teams work to get them all into custody."

Bryan called Abe, brought him up to date on the events of the previous night, and told him to contact Eli and explain everything. He asked them to arrange for the additional three agents and require everyone to meet at the office no later than 7:30, which was less than an hour away. "No one but you and Eli are to know this morning's assignment until we're all in the same room. At that point I'll inform everyone what the mission is and the identity of the doctor each team is assigned to take into custody. We'll keep the agents we're partnered with from communicating with anyone until we have all three suspects back here at the office. I'm worried about leaks and losing another witness in this case. It's getting too damn messy and out of control."

Bryan was showered, dressed, and in his car headed to the office before seven. As he drove, he tuned to 720 AM, the local FOX station, to hear the morning newscast. The murders, of course, were the lead story, and although the newscaster didn't name the Mirzoyans as the victims, he did disclose the house where the victims were found was indeed owned by the couple. He also emphasized Dr. Mirzoyan had been questioned by authorities earlier in the week about the murders of his employee Dr. Gerald Washburn and FBI Agent Cheu, both victims of a bombing less than thirty-six hours before.

After hearing the report, Bryan decided they had no time to waste and flipped on his car's red and blue emergency lights, maneuvered into the HOV lane, and sped as fast as possible toward downtown. He walked into the DOJ offices at

7:20, slightly surprised the front doors were already unlocked and all the lights on. He was even more surprised when Charlie intercepted him just as he was about to enter his own office. He smiled and quietly said, "It seems like I just said goodnight to you. Why are you here so early?"

"Paul called and asked me to get to the office ASAP. He's expecting a busy and messy day, and wanted me here to help both of you with anything you might need, and something difficult has already come up. I needed to warn you about it before you go into the conference room. Abe and Eli are already in there waiting with the three other agents and, this is the problem; Gayle Baker."

"What's she doing here?"

"She showed up ten minutes ago and asked for you or Abe. The receptionist told her you weren't in, then I arrived and she latched onto me. She was aggressive, no 'Hello, Charlie' or anything. She just demanded to know if you met with Lance yesterday, and if you did, why she was told the interview had been postponed. I explained she needed to talk to you about anything pertaining to the case because I wasn't at liberty to discuss it with her.

"She backed off a little and said she definitely would talk to you about it and wanted to know when you'd be in. I told her I had no idea what your plans were for the morning because there had been developments overnight, and it might be better if I just asked you to call her as soon as you arrived.

"Then she said, 'Developments? You call two murders developments?' By then, I had about had enough of her attitude, and if Eli hadn't shown up in the nick of time, Ms. Baker was about to get some major actitud Hispanica from me.

"The next thing I knew, she was asking Eli the same questions she grilled me with. He listened to her, then politely told her she needed to speak with you, and he expected you in the office before 7:30. Abe was already in the conference room, but came out to see what was going on. He actually invited her to go and wait with them in the conference room, deciding it was the best way to discretely deal with all the commotion she was causing."

"Hells bells! Why did he do that?"

"He sent her ahead with Eli and told me why. He said you needed to deal with her, because you're in charge and she'll only back off if you put her in her place. Then he told me to do exactly what I'm now doing, tell you what happened before you walked into the conference room and got blind-sided."

Bryan was aggravated by this complication, but had known yesterday that sooner or later this conversation with Baker needed to happen. He steeled himself for the conflict he knew was coming while he waited for Charlie to bring Baker to his office.

In spite of all the stress and problems he was dealing with that morning, when Charlie escorted Gayle into the room, he couldn't escape what Malcolm Gladwell calls a 'BLINK' moment, a fleeting impression that raced through his mind. Those are two of the best looking women I've ever known, but as he briefly made eye contact with Gayle, he sensed something was not right. Then the impression was gone, and he was back in real time. "Come in, Gayle. Thanks, Charlie. Please tell Abe no one is to leave the conference room and I'll be there in a minute or two."

"What's going on, Agent Hampton? You told me Lance's questioning was postponed and he was being moved to a secret location, and some operational changes were being made. Were you lying about Lance? Why wasn't I involved in his interview yesterday?" Gayle demanded with no preamble.

"Gayle, I'm sorry, but I'm doing what Paul told me to do. We suspect a leak somewhere, either at the FBI or the MFCB, and he's instructed me to stop sharing any advance operational plans or other critical information beyond five core members of the DOJ staff. Too many strange coincidences have occurred during the investigation of this case, with the bad guys seemingly always one step ahead of us. As of yesterday, even the FBI is on a need to know basis, when and if we do ask for their assistance. Until further notice, I'm not to share any confidential information about our plans or what we learn from suspect interviews with you or Da Silva or anyone at the MFCB."

Gayle didn't react the way Hampton expected. She was quiet for a few seconds, the wrath and indignation he expected evidently toppled by uncertainty. "So have you told your brothers at the FBI you think there's a leak?"

"No, there's no need to, because they only provide help when we make specific requests. They do background checks and help with surveillance and witness protection."

"Yeah, and they've done a damn fine job with both those things, haven't they? It seems to me like they're a far more likely source of a leak than the MFCB."

"I don't have time to work through this with you right now, Gayle, but I want you to think about something. Will you do that for me?"

"What do you want me to do?"

"I want you to make a list of anyone in your organization who has access to information about the plans and progress of this investigation. Who might have known about our wire taps or our plans to raid the billing office or the clinics? The list I would think should be short. Get Da Silva to help compile it. Today's going to be busy for me, but let's plan on getting together tomorrow, and we'll go over the names and see if we can figure out if anyone jumps out as a possible source of the leak."

"Do you actually know there's been a leak? It seems you're only guessing and have no real proof. Aren't you just trying to find an excuse for letting four people get killed?"

Another 'BLINK' moment for Hampton, this one so fleeting he wasn't sure it even happened. And once again he was uneasy. "Gayle, we're suspecting and assuming, and doing so based upon cause and effect logic. It's unfair to call it guessing, because you know as well as I do that good investigators usually have a sixth sense guiding them, if they're tuned in and wise enough to listen to it. Now I have to go. I have five agents waiting for me and a lot of work to do."

A second later, Charlie opened the door and asked Gayle to follow her. How did she know I was ready for her to come and get Gayle at exactly that moment? Hampton wondered. Maybe Charlie's got a sixth sense too, he thought then headed off to his meeting.

Before 9:30 all three teams of agents had returned to the DOJ offices with the chiropractors. Hampton briefly introduced himself to the doctors, explaining they weren't under arrest, but were being held in protective custody. Then he turned the meeting over to Dixon, who began by describing the DOJ's earlier meeting with Dr. Washburn, Lance Beasley, and their attorney, emphasizing it had preceded the fatal bombing by only a few hours. His objective was to gradually nudge them toward an understanding that becoming cooperative witnesses was their only real option. His approach was to stress the brutality and recklessness of the killer and to embellish the specificity of the information Washburn and Beasley shared about the fraud occurring in the clinics.

Dixon next shared his augmented version of the parking lot meeting Bryan and Abe held with Mirzoyan. Hampton guessed the U.S. Attorney hoped his account would cause the three doctors to conclude Dr. Mirzoyan had been prepared to disclose the details of the fraud scheme. Dixon strongly implied Mirzoyan planned to name the killer as well as the individual who masterminded and directed the entire fraud operation and ordered the murders. "We had hoped to meet with Dr. Mirzoyan and his attorney today, but as you all must have also concluded by now, someone, we suspect it was his business associate, ordered the brutal execution of the doctor and his wife last night."

Pausing for effect, Dixon continued, "Of course we already know all three of you are central figures in the overall fraud scheme. Dr. Mirzoyan and Mr. Beasley have been clear about that. You're here because whoever you're all mixed up with seems ready and willing to do anything to keep from being exposed. Four killings in two nights could become seven or more, unless the three of you tell us everything you know. Our expectation is that your information will provide what we need to find and arrest the head of this ring and stop the slaughter."

Dixon went on with additional details of the previous night's killings, then followed up with further warnings about the dangers the men and their families faced, if they remained unwilling to help get the killer and the person directing him off the street. When Dixon finished, none of the three said anything, and surprisingly during the fifty minutes he spoke to them, they had asked no questions.

Hampton looked at Dixon, shrugged, then told his agents to escort each of the doctors to separate interview rooms and begin questioning them. After an hour of constant demands to talk to their attorneys and refusing to answer any questions, it was clear all three had decided they would take their chances with being prosecuted for medical fraud rather than risk being next on the extermination list.

The start of Lance Beasley's second interrogation session had been delayed for nearly two hours. The FBI agents guarding him already reported Lance had seen the morning newscasts and was extremely agitated after learning of the slayings. Hampton's concern was Lance might now fear the risks were too great and also refuse to cooperate. But when Abe and Hampton entered the room where Lance was waiting, he stunned them with his demeanor and with his recommendation. "We should call Amanda now and get her down here. I know she'll help us after what happened to Dr. Mirzoyan last night."

Bryan adjusted to Lance's unexpected attitude quickly. "Why do you think that Lance?"

"I don't think it, I know it, because she worshiped the guy. She'd do anything for him, and there's no doubt in my mind she knew what she was doing with the insurance claims was fraudulent. But you've got to promise her immunity because, if you don't, she won't tell you anything. Her goal now will be to stay out of jail for her kids' sake. So she's not going to cooperate if she thinks there's a chance she'll be prosecuted."

Hampton had already spoken with Dixon about granting immunity to Amanda if she was fully cooperative and provided conclusive information about the inner workings of the fraud scheme, as well as who directed her billing activities. So after a thoughtful pause, he responded, "Lance, Amanda would need to give us clear evidence proving she was following orders from Mirzoyan and the other doctors. We would need conclusive proof, such as emails or notes from meetings, or some other clear-cut evidence showing Mirzoyan and the others instigated and supported fraudulently billing insurers."

"That should be no problem, because I've seen notes she made when Dr. Mirzoyan gave her instructions on what services to bill for every diagnosed problem. The whole process for both of us was cookbook. If someone was a legitimate patient, the doctors in each office would document the injuries with a written medical diagnosis.

"The ancillary staff in the clinics had a list of every procedure or supply that should be billed for a patient with every diagnosis, and Amanda had the same list. If the clinic didn't bill all the services, or if I missed documenting something, Amanda added the missing procedures and made me update the documentation before the claim was sent to the insurance company. And it made no difference whether the patient actually received the service or not; it got billed by the clinic or by Amanda."

"So, you believe Amanda knew she was committing fraud by filing false claims when she did what you just described?" Abe asked.

"You're asking a legal question about exactly what law she was violating, and I can't answer whether or not she knew she was violating the False Claims Act. But anyone knows if you charge for something you don't do, it's wrong. She knows that much for sure, and she's also shrewd enough to know she got bonuses for every procedure she added to a claim that someone in one of the clinics failed to bill."

Lance then looked at Hampton and Abe as though they still were missing the big picture. "You guys, the patients and claims we're talking about right now are the nickel and dime stuff. These patients actually had something wrong with them, and that scheme is about loading on as many extra charges and visits as possible. There's another whole category you need to be looking at."

"What's that category, Lance?" Hampton asked, eager and curious to find out how much Lance knew about the fake accident victims.

"They're the patients with a 'GS' indicator on their files."

"What does 'GS' mean on a file?" Abe asked.

"Officially, they told me it means 'Gold Star,' and I was instructed it meant these patients deserved premium treatment, and I was to make sure their medical records were documented flawlessly. But I figured out the patient records with 'GS' on them belong to real people, but there was nothing wrong with them. Their reported injuries were fake.

"I can give you fifty reasons why I know this, but there are two main ones. First, these patients always have identical combinations of diagnosis codes. And they never have a problem with only one arm or leg, it's always three or four appendages, and they always have multiple sprains and ligament tears on every one of them. If it's a back problem, they always have injuries in at least three regions of the spine. Also, the injuries are always the most severe possible, not just a simple back strain, but a herniated disk or multiple herniated disks. And the treatments are always the most intensive and most prolonged of any patients we ever see in the clinics.

"But here's the clincher. I started seeing records with 'GS' and a number. Like 'GS2' or 'GS3,' so I got curious and discovered the appended digit is a record number for the unique medical file we retain for the patient. And it also indicates the number of times we've sent the same diagnoses and series of treatments or bills to an insurer, but obviously never to the same one.

"I figured out the number was there to make sure we pulled up the right medical record if it was ever requested, so we didn't bill a patient with exactly the same injuries to the same insurer more than once. Supposedly it also prevents overuse of any single patient. The highest 'GS' number I've seen is five, meaning we've billed five different insurance companies for the same set of injuries, and we have five unique records for the same patient."

"Lance, do you know who actually creates the medical records for the 'GS' patients? Are they generated in the clinics or do you do it?"

"Agent Hampton, I don't know. It's not me, but I know there are standardized lists of services and doctor's notes related to every medical problem. A doctor or someone in each of the offices can select a problem, and the medical record system can generate lists of services, doctor's notes, and even an insurance claim as part of a new or existing patient's medical record.

"The new systems have modules allowing users to create standardized descriptions of exams, clinical findings and procedures provided to patients. This functionality allows doctors or other staff members to cut and paste, and when necessary, modify any section of the information for an individual patient. They hardly ever create new information, so the documentation on the 'GS' cases is usually flawless. I'm sure it's because it's copied from existing versions already in the system."

Hampton stopped Lance by raising his hand, then asked, "Let's be sure we state this correctly for the recording we're making. You're saying that 'GS' patients have nothing wrong with them, their bills are completely fabricated, their medical records are false and replicated over and over, and sometimes a single billing scenario for one patient can be submitted to as many as five different insurers? Are you also saying Amanda knows this, and the doctors in the clinics know it, as well as the billing people in the clinics?"

"I'm positive the chiropractors all know it, but I'm not sure about the people in the clinics who normally generate the bills. And I don't know how Amanda could not know it. I figured it out just from the medical documentation. She would definitely see how often a patient had the same set of injuries billed to multiple insurers. And so she would have asked Mirzoyan about it long ago, as soon as she picked up on the duplicate records and billings, probably suspecting someone in the clinics was up to no good. Who knows what he told her, but it doesn't make any difference because she'd do whatever he asked her to do, no matter what BS explanation he gave."

Eli and another agent brought Amanda into the office shortly after two that afternoon. She was badly shaken by the news of Mirzoyan's execution and devastated by the loss of the man who apparently had become her mentor. After Hampton explained her two options, cooperation or indictment, she requested a private conversation with Lance. Following their talk, she decided to cooperate in return for guaranteed immunity.

She knew almost everything about the operation of the fraud scheme. She confirmed the complicity of all the chiropractors, except Dr. Washburn, whom she described as naïve and innocent, explaining that once he figured out what was going on a few months earlier, he had likely pushed Mirzoyan too hard to stop the fraud. "Dr. Washburn and Dr. Mirzoyan were both killed when it was obvious they were going to tell what they knew, so what's going to prevent that from happening to Lance and me?"

"You're going to tell us who's directing this whole operation and we're going to arrest him. That's what will keep you and Lance alive," Hampton explained.

"Then we're both dead, because I can't give you any names. All I know about is what happens in the billing office and what I would sometimes hear when Dr. Mirzoyan was on the phone."

"You probably know more than you think, Amanda. Let's walk through everything you can tell us," Hampton said reassuringly. But five hours later, he resigned himself to the reality Amanda didn't have the information that could directly associate Bennett Watson with the fraud occurring in Mirzoyan's clinics.

****

Paul and Bryan sat reviewing the day's events long after everyone else had headed home for the night. They were looking at a white board with four lists: *What We Know; What We Can Prove; What We Suspect; and What We Need to Prove.* They knew a great deal about the inner workings of the fraud operation, and after today's interviews they could prove nearly all the details necessary to assure convictions. The columns they were now focused on were the last two.

Amanda, without being prompted, had said she believed Mirzoyan's silent partner was part of the legal profession or perhaps in law enforcement. Her suspicions were based on her employer's response when she questioned some of their unconventional billing techniques. She told them Dr. Mirzoyan had reassured her the clinic's legal expert guaranteed there was nothing to worry about.

Amanda had also mentioned overhearing a recent phone conversation between Mirzoyan and possibly the partner in question. She described Mirzoyan as being highly agitated during the call, saying at one point he had shouted, "How can you be sure of that?" Then soon afterward he seemed to calm down and said, "Well, that's different, if you have someone on the inside."

When their meeting ended, Bryan and Paul understood where all future efforts needed to be focused. Staring at the white board made it clear. They suspected and needed to prove just two things; Bennett Watson was the organizer and mastermind of the fraud, and Watson was directing an unknown killer to eliminate anyone who could link him to the clinic's fraud schemes.

Chapter 32

Las Vegas, NV
December 15th
3:00 PM

After a weekend of rest followed by four more days of intensive questioning, the agents learned little if any new evidence from Lance and Amanda. Attempts to get at least one of the chiropractors to cooperate had also been unproductive. No new information had emerged to help prove their suspicions about Watson. But the killings stopped and, earlier that afternoon, Dixon had received some encouraging news from the FBI's forensic team. A print found on the hammer used to batter and kill Mirzoyan was matched with one alleged to belong to the killer of Illinois Congressman Horowitz.

Dixon recalled the Horowitz homicide and Hampton's suspicions about the motive for the killing. The problem with the fingerprint was neither the FBI nor Illinois authorities had been able to match the print to any known individual after comparing it to millions of records in multiple databases. Now there were three murders linked to the same unknown person, and Dixon was anxious to share news about what could be a real break in the case with Hampton.

Hampton had seen the text from Paul asking him to come to his office as soon as he returned, and as he stepped through the door, he knocked lightly and asked, "What's up, Paul?"

"We may have caught a break today. The FBI guys matched the print on the hammer that killed Mirzoyan to one they believe belongs to the suspected murderer of Congressman Horowitz. Since I know you have definite opinions about that killing and who arranged it, this could be a significant development."

Hampton was stunned by one part of what he'd just heard. "Wait a minute, Paul, there was never any news the police found fingerprints in that case."

"All I know is what I've been told. You'll be able to ask all your questions fairly soon. I've arranged for a conference call in twenty-five minutes to speak with the lead detective from the Morton Grove Police and one of Las Vegas agents Graves had call me with the news. For now, we're not involving anyone from the U.S. Attorney's Office or the FBI in Chicago, because we don't want to tip Tacovic or anyone else off to this development. So far, no one outside of one or two people at the Las Vegas FBI office knows we've made a match."

"Does this mean we have a contract killer involved in two different murders? Could they both somehow be linked to two separate cases of health care fraud, or is this possibly just a coincidence?"

"Be careful about connecting any dots just yet, Bryan. What we know is one murderer likely executed five victims in two different cities in the last three months. His methods have included explosives, strangulations, beatings, and staged car accidents. That means he's likely a hired killer and is indiscriminate when it comes to technique. He could be working for two entirely different individuals or organizations. The fact you happen to have connections to both cases is interesting, but is it a coincidence, is it by design, or is it even relevant?"

When the conference call began, Detective Barnes from the Morton Grove police seemed guarded about disclosing any details of his ongoing high profile investigation. The FBI agent from Las Vegas had spoken with Barnes earlier and explained the source of the print that matched one from the case Barnes was handling. After brief introductions, Dixon and Hampton both stressed the importance of this link to their case and the urgency of solving the related murders in Las Vegas. Then Hampton asked Barnes why the fingerprint discovered in his investigation hadn't been made public.

That caused Barnes to pause and set some ground rules for the discussion and possible investigation. "I want some guarantees you won't leak any information we discuss on this call, especially to anyone in the news media. I also need you to agree you'll limit knowledge about the existence of our print just to people working directly on your investigation. We've managed to keep this quiet for three months, hoping for just this kind of break, and if you'll cooperate in keeping this confidential, I've got other evidence to share with you."

Dixon responded quickly, "Detective Barnes, we're as concerned about leaking the existence of the print in our case as you are in yours. The last thing we want known at this early stage of our investigation is that we even have a print. The news it matches one in your case could force the people who hired this killer to make sure he disappears forever. And if that happens, we might never solve either case.

"As far as I'm concerned, going forward we need to work closely together on these cases and share any information we develop about the identity of the killer. No one should know these fingerprints exist until we jointly decide it would benefit both investigations to disclose it."

"Then let me tell you about something else the public isn't aware of. We have two eyewitnesses who saw the killer at the site where the Congressman was killed. It was dark and the witnesses are a couple of teenagers, but they got close enough to describe him fairly well. Do you have any witnesses who may have seen your killer?"

"Unfortunately not, but if you have a description and a sketch we could show it to the officers who were at the scene of each crime. They might not realize they saw him, but his face in a sketch could jolt their memories. What's his general description according to the kids?"

"Huge guy, apparently not tall, around five ten, but the kids said he was big and looked powerful. Both agreed he's Hispanic, and they were both sure his hair was black. They described him as just plain ugly, if that helps, which you'll clearly see from the artist's sketch. They couldn't find him in any mug shots, and they couldn't agree on several of his facial features, but both felt the final drawing was close to what they remembered. To me, the guy looks like the Hulk, just not green. We're still keeping the witnesses' existence and their identifications completely hush-hush."

Hampton had an idea. "Send us the picture as soon as possible. It just occurred to me the killer must have inspected the layout of the home and the grounds where he murdered the doctor and his wife sometime before he went in. There's a guard house with cameras at the entrance of the complex, and I also saw cameras on the lights at a nearby intersection. We can pull the tapes and see if anyone who looks anything like the guy in the sketch shows up in the twenty-four hours before the murders."

"Wow, Hampton, your idea about checking the traffic cameras shocked one of my apparently non-functional brain cells back into action. I just remembered something that happened around three years ago down in Chicago. It involved some kind of drug deal. Three guys from one gang were shot to death by a single gunman. A bystander was also killed, and the shooter also wounded several others during the shoot-out.

"The whole thing was caught on a traffic camera, and for days we had a fuzzy face-shot of the shooter in all the papers and on TV. As far as I know, they never caught him, but he looked Hispanic, and he was definitely ugly. I'll run down that picture and send it and the sketch ASAP. But to be clear, as of now, you guys don't have anyone you know of who ever saw this guy, is that right?"

"No one who's still alive. He gave an up-close beating to one of the men he killed a few days later, but we never got a description because the victim never really saw him. He only heard his voice and smelled his breath."

As soon as the call ended, Bryan could tell by Dixon's resolute expression he had come to a decision. "Bryan, we're now knee-deep in a murder case that involves the execution of our suspects and witnesses. I don't want to get bogged down waiting to find this killer and delay prosecution of a fraud case we know we can prove."

Dixon hesitated briefly and seemed to consider something, then continued, "Let's put the Watson connection on the backburner for now. With our current evidence, unless we find the killer, we can't link Watson to the executions or to the operation of the fraud scheme. For now, Mirzoyan's death eliminated the only obvious connection between Watson and the clinics. I'm sure there's a money trail somewhere, and we can pursue that moving forward. But for now I want to file charges against the three chiropractors and anyone else in the clinic offices we can clearly show had knowledge of the phantom patients.

"With the video evidence Washburn left us along with his listing of phony patients and their insurance claims, and the details he provided citing the falsely billed services they never received, we have all the evidence we need to expose the fraud and identify the participants."

"Aren't we giving up too easily on proving Watson was directing the whole operation by putting this on the back burner?" Hampton asked with growing frustration.

"Bryan, we both know the arrogance of people like Watson is eventually their downfall. We'll continue to watch him, and we know he's not going to entirely give up on the huge amounts of money the staged car accidents and bogus medical claims generate. We can even begin with an entirely new angle on those cases by investigating every claimant represented by his firm.

"We'll follow the money and get him eventually. There's no doubt in my mind he has other medical insurance scams he's working right now. We just need to look harder for them. For now, let's close down the clinics and prosecute every person working there who knew about and profited from the fraud. We'll tie up all Mirzoyan's assets and follow the money."

"If that's what you want us to do, then I have my marching orders, Paul. We'll get our financial investigators to tear apart the clinic's finances as well as Mirzoyan's personal finances, and maybe we'll find a connection to Watson in the process. How far down the food chain with clinic employees do you want us to go?"

"In addition to the chiropractors themselves, for starters let's focus on any licensed medical people working in the clinics, along with anyone handling patient scheduling and billing. We may decide to go deeper or eliminate some of those in the initial groups, but my philosophy is licensed medical personnel should be bound by ethics, as should anyone handling financial affairs. Turning a blind eye to fraud just to keep your job isn't an acceptable excuse."

"Should we be trying to expose links to Watson as we question the employees? Or would we be tipping our hand if he still has someone there feeding him information?"

"Your team should be judicious with those types of questions. Maybe you only ask leading questions like 'Are you aware of any one law firm that represented most of your patients?' or 'Did anyone or any organization routinely refer accident victims to the clinic?' I don't think we should ever ask a question using Watson's name as a routine approach. However, there is one question I would ask every employee at some point in their interview, Bryan."

"I think I can guess the question, Paul. What does 'GS' mean on a medical record?"

"That's it. And if the person being questioned starts to turn red, begins to sweat or gets fidgety, grill them until they tell whatever they know. My opinion right now is if they were aware of what the letters meant and how those patient records were used, then they're complicit and we should charge them."

"There's one more issue we need to discuss, Paul. The leak we suspected is unresolved, and I need to deal with Gayle and determine our policy regarding continued work with the MFCB. It's awkward right now, and if we're moving ahead with the prosecution, we're going to need the statistics and data from the MFCB database to support and prove our case."

"What's your gut on this, Bryan?"

"On the surface Gayle seems genuinely offended we would suspect their staff as the source of the leak. I've asked her to compile a list of their people who had access to information on the wire taps and planned office raids, and she's never gotten back to me. I don't know what that means."

"I've received two calls from Da Silva this week, Bryan. Have you spoken with him?"

"No, I've been avoiding it, I guess," Bryan admitted.

"Maybe Da Silva told Gayle to let him handle it. I'll call him tomorrow and get a read. You call Gayle and ask her why she's never gotten you the list, then let's talk. We need their data and expertise, and we don't have any proof they were the source of what we suspect was a leak. We should try to work with them particularly since their data is the best proof we have there's a connection between Watson and the clinics."

"Okay, Paul, but there's one more thing I need to tell you, something you might think is crazy. Last week when I met with Gayle to discuss the leak, I twice had what I can only describe as inklings or impressions something wasn't right about her. I keep trying to rationalize away those feelings, but when I've had them before I've always regretted ignoring them."

"Bryan, I'm a big believer in what you're describing. I call them impressions, and others label them intuition. Whatever they are, when I get one, I try never to ignore it. So let's proceed cautiously in our work with the MFCB until we identify the leak or vindicate the whole organization."

Hampton shared an idea with Dixon. "There's no doubt in my mind our plans were somehow being disclosed to Watson. What if we just let some time pass, and be careful about anything we share with Gayle in the meantime? When we do have new evidence pointing to Watson, and we're ready to pursue it, we could leak false information through her to the MFCB. Then we'll see if Watson acts on the phony facts, which could only have come from a mole somewhere in their organization."

"I like that approach, Bryan, but be sure you alert anyone working on your investigative team to be careful about discussing anything that could be helpful to Watson while Gayle or anyone from the MFCB is present. Also, don't under any circumstances discuss the connection with the Chicago murder or the fingerprints or the pictures we'll be receiving with anyone but Abe and Eli, and explicitly tell no one from the MFCB!"

"I've got a good feeling about our phone call today, Paul. I think we're on this guy's trail, and he has no idea he's made two mistakes."

"I hope you're right, Bryan. Time will tell."

****

Twenty-one hours later, Dixon received an encrypted email from Detective Barnes with five attachments. Three were photos, two from the traffic cameras, and one that looked like a software-enhanced version of an artist's sketch. The sketch could have been labeled 'Generic Mexican,' one traffic camera close-up was blurry, and the other one was too far away to be definitive, but all three might be the same person.

The fourth attachment was a report from their facial recognition software. The bottom line, according to the software report, was the close up and the sketch had a forty-eight percent probability of being the same face. The fifth document was a transcription of both statements made by the teenagers. Each included their separate descriptions of the suspect, and interestingly, they both described the killer for the most part in almost identical terms.

Hampton and Dixon decided to give the close-up and the sketch to Abe and assign him to privately examine the video from the guard house and the traffic camera outside the entrance to Mirzoyan's subdivision. Hampton told him to look at every face on the videos over the twelve hours preceding the murders and determine if any came close to matching the images he was given.

He emphasized, "Talk to no one about this and don't tell the police or guards or anyone else what you're looking for. Your story is you're just checking for anything suspicious. If you discover possible matches, do screen prints and we'll all look at whatever you find. You may need to do twelve more hours as well, if the first twelve don't give us a hit."

At nearly the same time Bryan sent Abe to look at week-old surveillance videos for a big, ugly Hispanic man snooping around Mirzoyan's residence, Fausto Guzman was traveling east on the Stevenson Expressway, nearing the Chicago city limits, the end of his journey. Perfect timing, he decided; two hours before the Friday night rush hour. He'd made the trip exactly as planned, and now he was back home.

It was colder than Vegas, he thought, only in the mid-thirties now, but the radio was promising snow overnight and for most of the next day. But he didn't care; his plan was to check into a nice hotel on North Michigan Avenue and enjoy the Christmas decorations and the season in general. He thought after the holidays he'd look up some of his old friends and see if he could get some part-time work. The next few months were a chance for him to double-up; while the checks rolled in from Watson, he could pick up a job or two and bank some extra cash.

Guzman always loved Michigan Avenue. Strangely, perhaps, but somewhere even in his warped mind the sights his sadistic eyes recorded registered as beauty and gave him a sense of peace, especially during the Christmas Season. But he also understood the Miracle Mile was one of the most intensively scrutinized places in the entire country. The public knows there are thousands of surveillance cameras in Manhattan, but Times Square has nothing on Michigan Avenue. Guzman realized the image of every pedestrian and driver of any vehicle traveling along this famous street was recorded twenty-four hours a day. The cameras were the reason he always wore a cap and kept his head down at intersections, where he knew the observer's remote eyes were always watching.

Most of the expensive stores and high end hotels along Michigan Avenue had their own security monitoring systems as well. The Ritz Carlton was no exception, and the street level entrance lobby was particularly well scrutinized to insure wealthy guests were kept safe. During his stay at the Ritz, Guzman was careful to avoid directly facing the hi-tech, state-of-the-art monitoring cameras. But he had missed noticing two of them.

Chapter 33

Las Vegas, NV
February 8th
1:00 PM

Dixon recognized the holidays had slowed progress on their case during the last half of December, but over the first five weeks of the New Year the DOJ agents had dramatically ramped-up their investigation. After charging the three chiropractors with multiple counts of health care fraud, he hadn't opposed releasing them from custody a few days before Christmas. The judge set bail at a million dollars each, which Dixon felt was reasonable.

Late in January all three were indicted by a grand jury on thirty-six counts of health care fraud each. Dixon was disappointed on one level, because as is usually the case with most professionals' licensing panels, the Chiropractic Physicians' Licensing Board didn't revoke nor suspend their licenses. So while they were awaiting trial, two of the doctors continued to practice. Since Mirzoyan's clinics had all been closed and his assets seized by the government, the doctors were forced to find work in other clinics and offices.

Dixon doubted the efficacy of any vetting process that allowed accused fraudsters to be assimilated into a clinical staff actively caring for patients. He'd accepted the position as U.S. attorney because, for him, it was an opportunity to crusade against fraud and waste in a health care system that could no longer afford it. He understood the real costs fraudulent providers were inflicting on U.S. citizens by driving up everyone's health care expenses.

With all the fears about the additional taxes and added costs for expanding health care coverage to all Americans, wasting hundreds of billions of dollars annually rewarding fraudulent providers could no longer be ignored nor accepted. Dixon hoped prosecuting, penalizing, and imprisoning more of these criminals would get the public to wake up and assist in stopping the waste by becoming wiser consumers of medical services.

The questioning continued for a few members of Dr. Mirzoyan's former staff, but after four weeks of interrogation the investigative teams informed Dixon they were recommending that in addition to the three chiropractors, only twelve other individuals be charged with felonies. In addition to the chiropractors, each office had two non-medical personnel who proved to be deeply involved in the fraud schemes. These staff members were in charge of patient appointments and billing. All eight were deemed accountable, and Dixon agreed they should be charged. Additionally, the senior radiology technician and three physical therapists had all routinely falsified medical records and were charged under the false claims act.

When the interrogations of Mirzoyan's employees first began, Hampton had told Dixon about his previous experiences with the staffs of doctors accused of fraud. "Paul we know from former cases that most staff members don't participate in the schemes, but they're usually aware of the irregularities and choose to ignore them. They often simply follow the example of their peers and go along with practices they know are inappropriate, and it's not just limited to insurance billing.

"Employees can turn a blind eye to violations of OSHA regulations, sterilization protocols, and a host of other important procedures and guidelines. Doctors have an obligation to their patients to manage every aspect of their demanding and complex practices and to hire principled employees who'll respect and oversee the set of high standards doctors are expected to set for them."

As a result of Hampton's warning, Dixon wasn't surprised, but was still disappointed when the agents' interviews revealed at least eighteen other clinic employees had actually suspected or observed fraudulent activities taking place. Some had seen bills for services not provided, others were aware of claims generated for phantom patients never treated in the clinics, and several others had seen patients over-treated.

The interviews revealed that several employees had reported ludicrous examples of trumped-up care, such as one patient who complained only of an ankle problem, but was also diagnosed and billed for non-existent back and neck ailments. It became clear to Dixon the standard practice at the clinics was to falsely document additional needs for treatment unrelated to a patient's real complaint. This strategy made it simple to charge for added tests as well as unnecessary care.

One medical assistant in the Henderson clinic told of reporting irregularities to Dr. Washburn, in particular about extra services being routinely added to insurance claims. She explained his reaction and subsequent events to the agents. "He thanked me and asked me to report any future occurrences of bill padding, so he could deal with it. I informed him of twelve other incidents over a two-week period in late October. A few days later, Dr. Washburn told me to stop the reports, because it could be dangerous for me if anyone discovered what I was doing."

As he carefully planned and choreographed before their regular weekly meeting, Dixon began summarizing the current status of the investigation to the small inner circle of the DOJ team and Gayle Baker. "Out of the forty-two employees in the four clinics and billing office, it looks like we'll ultimately charge fifteen of them. But four others could have been indicted had they not been murdered or given immunity. That means forty-five percent of Mirzoyan's employees were felons in embryo, and he simply nurtured their greed.

"Sadly, eighteen others suspected or knew something was wrong but ignored it. That's another forty-three percent of the staff. As we know, prospective employees were given a special test the doctor had designed to measure their corruptibility before they were hired. The test seems to have been accurate eighty-eight percent of the time since only five people in the whole operation seemed unaware of the reality they were working in a fraud mill."

"Maybe those five were hired before there was a test. I'll bet employees who suspected something was wrong but didn't report it wish they'd known about the Whistleblower rewards. Someone could have earned themselves a nice retirement fund just by reporting what they were seeing to someone who cared, like the Justice Department," Gayle caustically observed.

"I know you're being sarcastic, Gayle, but the Whistleblower Laws and the related rewards are something we should be stressing to people who find themselves in situations where they see fraud and lack the motivation to report it," Hampton noted.

"I don't think the public understands how large these settlements can be," Dixon added, then continued. "Medicare and Medicaid fraud whistleblowers can be awarded between fifteen and twenty-five percent of what the government recovers. Stop and think about some of the recent settlements. Just weeks ago one person was awarded over forty million dollars for reporting fraud at a drug company, and a couple of years ago in another drug award a woman received ninety-six million."

"Maybe some of them thought about it, but two things probably made them think twice about the idea. First, in this economy, some may have believed any job is better than no job. And second, the mysterious disappearance of Dr. X some months ago was probably an object lesson," Eli observed.

Dixon then initiated their prearranged deception by asking Hampton to summarize progress on other aspects of the investigation. "It looks like we're nearly done with interviewing the staff, and although we haven't been able to get any of them to tell us Watson was involved, our forensic accountants have identified a money trail from one of Mirzoyan's personal accounts to an account allegedly set up to pay his personal bills and fund three investment accounts. What we've discovered so far is few, if any, bills were every paid from the master account, and nearly all the funds were transferred to the investment accounts."

"Were all the accounts in Mirzoyan's name?" Gayle asked.

"The master account and two of the investment ones are owned by entities that he or his wife controlled. The third investment account is the one we're focused on because over seventy percent of all the money flowing through the master account went to that one account. We're talking about millions of dollars here. We don't believe Mirzoyan controlled it, and the entity that does is a shell comprised of a series of LLC's and corporations, so we're digging to discover who the individuals are who control those entities."

"That account must be the link to Watson. It's got to be how the insurance payments to the clinic are funneled back to him," Dixon unequivocally observed, making sure Gayle, one of only five people in the room, grasped his point.

"It definitely could be the case, Paul. And as you know, there's another odd thing about that account. Money flows into it multiple times a month, usually five or six deposits. But there's only one withdrawal each month. It's always on the last business day, and it drains off an amount close to ninety-eight percent of whatever's in it. It doesn't appear to be an automated transaction, and the total withdrawal goes to an offshore bank, and we don't yet know who owns that account."

"Since the clinics have been closed down for nearly two months, I would assume these accounts are no longer being funded, so have the withdrawals stopped?" Gayle asked.

"Actually, since remittances from many insurance companies are made electronically, payments for some claims filed before we shut the clinics and billing office down in December continue to hit Mirzoyan's accounts even as we speak. We've allowed deposits and transfers to accounts we've seized to continue without interruption. But we just recently discovered the existence of the investment accounts, unfortunately too late to stop the January withdrawal from the largest one. With end of year payments hitting in January, it was a big month, and they pulled over six million out of that account before we could stop it, over twice the usual transfer amount."

Bryan was uncomfortable with what he and Paul were up to, but the discovery of these accounts offered a perfect chance to set-up an opportunity to track the leak. If Gayle or someone else at the MFCB was the source, and the false transfer information they were discussing caused Watson to react the way they expected it would, the leak could only be from Gayle or someone at the MFCB. Everyone else in the room was aware of the ploy and knew some of the details in the information they discussed were false.

Most of what Bryan had explained about the large investment account was true, except for two crucial facts. The investigators had already identified three of the individuals who were the primary owners of the four entities that controlled the withdrawals from the account. Watson wasn't one of them; he was too smart for that, and had wisely created another layer of protection for himself. Each of the accounts' four owners participated in a monthly rotation withdrawing funds from the account. So in a twelve-month period any one individual was only responsible for three transactions on the account.

The FBI was able to determine once the owners withdrew the funds, they quickly deposited them into another account, which they alone controlled. Ninety percent of the amount withdrawn and deposited into the owner's individual account was immediately wired to another offshore bank. The remaining ten percent stayed in the individual's personal account, apparently the commission for laundering the funds. The wire transfers sent by all four individuals went to the same offshore account, and that account was probably controlled by Watson. But the money never stayed there long; it was immediately dispersed within minutes of arriving.

Dixon had decided this situation presented the ideal opportunity to identify the source of the leak if it was coming from Gayle or someone else at the

MFCB. They would set the trap by telling Gayle the January withdrawal had been over six million dollars, when in fact it had only been half that amount.

Hampton had convinced Dixon to set the transaction at six million dollars, telling him, "The average monthly withdrawal has always been around three million, but last January four million had been withdrawn. Owners and executives of health care businesses know provider receipts in January are typically higher than average due to insurance reimbursement cycles, so Watson should be expecting more than three million to be wired into his account at the end of January.

"Watson will be surprised the amount wasn't higher than the $3.1 million actually transferred, but he's likely already anticipated the closure of the clinics would reduce revenues below the previous January's amount. When he hears the DOJ is aware of the accounts and just missed preventing a six million dollar withdrawal at the end of January, he'll be incensed; maybe so furious he might even directly contact the individual responsible for the last transaction," Bryan explained.

"If he calls, emails or pays a personal visit to this guy, we've got him," Dixon had told Bryan. "The FBI has combed through all the LLC and corporate ownership documents for the four entities controlling the investment fund, and we have the names of the people who actually control the shells. With the exception of one of them, the owner of a web-based security company, WeSolveProblems.com, we currently have them all under surveillance.

"The person who made the January withdrawal is the key to the whole trap, Bryan. If Watson goes after him or sends his enforcer after him, we might catch both of them in the same net," Dixon said optimistically.

"On the other hand, if Gayle isn't associated with the leak, we've created another trust issue for any future work with the MFCB," Hampton pointed out.

"I'll take that chance, Bryan. And don't forget we now have the names of the people who are laundering funds coming from this fraud scheme. If nothing comes from the false information we planted, we should still be able to put some pressure on those four individuals and maybe get one of them to give up Watson."

"Paul, two of these men are big shot attorneys, and Anton Littski, the ex-felon who made the January withdrawal, owns half the car lots in Chicago. These people aren't going to just roll over for us and answer all our questions. These guys are all serious criminals. And as for the WeSolveProblems.com guy, you and I both know there's no way his name is Rondo Ganado. We're probably never going to find him. I think we're hoping for too much here."

Dixon realized Hampton was probably right, but a week ago they'd both agreed to go forward with the plan, and the trap was set. New wire taps had been authorized for Watson and Littski the day before. And now the FBI agents watching Littski in Glencoe, IL and Watson in Las Vegas had been alerted to keep a close eye on both suspects over the next several days.

As soon as Gayle left the DOJ offices, she morphed into the corrupt entrepreneur she had become. She knew she should capitalize on the opportunity to get this lucrative information to Watson as soon as possible. She planned to tell him the six million he pulled out of the account in January needed to be his last withdrawal, because the Justice Department investigators were monitoring the accounts and investigating the owners.

Gayle hadn't contacted the attorney since December, because she'd been excluded from the DOJ's investigation until the second week of January, and since then she had gathered little information she believed Watson would pay for. Gayle had formed her own warped ethical boundaries limiting the information she would sell Watson. She convinced herself that helping Watson continue his financial crimes was acceptable as long as he paid well for the help. But she had decided she'd never offer information facilitating a murder or thwarting the arrest of his brutal enforcer, at least not up to that point in time.

But this staggering news should be worth at least a hundred grand or more to him, she thought. She believed the wiretaps on Watson's phones had expired, but didn't want to chance a direct call in any event. She decided on an overnight letter for next morning delivery and went straight to a nearby FedEx store, typed out a cryptic message, *Have Important Information on January $6M Account Transfer, Text Interest and Availability for Call to 702-897-2613, Untraceable Number, An Old Friend.* After completing the mailing label with fictitious sender information, she used cash to pay the fees and dropped the envelope in the outbound box.

Bennett Watson opened the sealed envelope marked *Personal* that his secretary had removed from the FedEx mailer and placed on the seat of his chair where he couldn't miss it. He'd known immediately who it was from, but the message baffled him. *January $6M Account Transfer*; what the hell does that mean? he wondered. He grabbed the burn phone he always carried and texted the number of the phone he was using followed by *ASAP*.

His phone buzzed four minutes later and an electronically modified voice said, "Mr. Watson, you apparently got my letter."

"I got your letter, but don't know what you're talking about. "

"What part of my message confuses you?"

"All of it."

"I'm hanging up now if you're going to deny facts I know are true. If you want the information, the price is two hundred thousand dollars. If I were you, I wouldn't wait long."

"Wait, two hundred thousand is a bit excessive. What makes you think anything you know is worth that much?"

"Have you ever overpaid for anything I've given you before? What I know is worth more than what I'm asking for it, and you'll realize that as soon as you hear it."

"Tell me how confident you are of the six million dollar figure you mentioned."

"As confident as you would be looking at your bank statement."

Watson paused a few seconds, then conceded, "I'll wire the funds before noon."

"As soon as I confirm the fee is in place, I'll call you back." Gayle then promptly disconnected the call.

As soon as he hung up, Watson found Anton Littski's number on his directory and used the burn phone to call him. Four rings later, Anton's booming voice came through loud and clear. "Who the hell is this?"

"Mr. Littski, this is your brokerage firm calling about January's balance. Could you please verify the amount of the last transaction you made, and please text it to the number you see we're calling you from?"

Littski was initially caught off balance, but quickly caught on. "You're asking about the one on January thirty-first, correct?"

"Yes, that's the one."

"You'll have the exact amount in the next five minutes."

"Thank you, Mr. Littski, we appreciate your cooperation."

Four minutes later Watson's phone vibrated and, when Watson looked, he saw, *$3,127,689* clearly displayed on the screen. Watson couldn't process all the possibilities running through his mind. The first thing that occurred to him was Littski was skimming the account and the three million dollar transfer should have been six million. Was that possible? That would definitely make the source believe the information was worth two hundred thousand. Actually three hundred would have been the right price, ten percent of the three million that was skimmed.

He contacted his offshore bank and gave the wiring instructions for the two hundred thousand dollars. Two hours later his phone buzzed. "I see you're anxious to hear what I have to tell you."

"Cut the crap. I didn't pay to hear you gloat. Tell me what you know, and don't skip any details."

The conversation lasted nearly ten minutes and, once Gayle was finished, Watson again asked the one crucial question, "Are you positive that six million dollars was transferred out of the account on January thirty-first?"

"That's what the Justice Department believes, but I would think you'd be more focused on covering the trail of money, especially before it leads to you."

"Goodbye for now. If you have anymore information like this, contact me again."

Gayle was surprised by Watson's focus on the six million dollar amount rather than learning investigators had found the accounts and were now attempting to trace the funds directly to him.

Thirty minutes later it hit her. Somehow, someone must have skimmed the account, and Watson didn't get the full six million. I undercharged him. I probably could have gotten twice what I asked for if I'd known that, she thought.

But something still troubled her. She just couldn't figure out what it was. Uncharacteristically, she allowed her greedy focus on the two hundred thousand dollars she'd earned in one day to divert her attention away from the real but illusive problem that was troubling her.

Chapter 34

Las Vegas, NV
February 9th
11:30 AM

Special Agent Graves called Hampton just after eleven-thirty. "Our agents on the Littski wiretap just reported a call made to his office phone from an untraceable cell number. It was cryptic but not very subtle. But clearly the information you guys planted has already been leaked, and it almost surely went to the guy you're after. But we got nothing conclusive from his end. All he asked Littski to do was verify the exact amount of the last transaction to his brokerage account in January and told him to text it to the number he was calling from, which we assume Littski did."

"Thanks, Graves. Tell your guys they better stick to Littski like glue for the next few days because our suspect has a pattern of quickly disposing of people who mess with him. If he thinks Littski stiffed him for over three million dollars last month, you know he'll assume it's happened before. As soon as Paul gets back from lunch, we'll call you. I think we better talk about letting your guys in the field know what the suspect might look like and how dangerous he is."

As soon as he hung up, Hampton saw Charlie standing in his office doorway. "Looks like you're going to cancel our lunch date. What's up?"

He thought for a few seconds, then said, "No, I'm not. As a matter of fact, some good food and sound advice from you is exactly what I need right now."

Hampton was finally realizing Charlie had become an important and vital part of his life, and he was determined to make sure she knew it.

They had been seeing a lot more of each other since the holidays. The extra time off between Christmas and New Year's Day had given them unplanned opportunities to do everyday simple things together, like Sunday afternoon drives, dining out, and taking the boys to movies, trampoline centers, and skate parks. Most people were more caring and patient during the holiday season, and those feelings were infectious, so both of them had grown more relaxed and comfortable with each other.

Hampton had spent Christmas Eve with Charlie's family and her boys, and after Aaron and Becham finally went to bed, they worked for over an hour assembling toys and arranging the gifts from Santa around the tree. When they were done, they rested and shared tales of their childhood Christmases over cups of hot cider. Charlie's stories were unquestionably more inspirational and traditional than any account Bryan was able to share.

More than the usual kissing and touching seemed to have naturally accompanied the cider and stories. Charlie expected the boys would likely be up before the sun rose to see what Santa brought them. She invited Bryan to spend the night on the living room couch so he wouldn't miss the early morning festivities. He'd declined the invitation, unsure of what it implied, then kissed her goodnight and promised to return before six-thirty in the morning.

From Christmas Day through New Year's Day they'd spent more time together than apart. Charlie even watched three of the six college bowl games with Bryan on the day after New Year's. Over the past six weeks after work and school schedules resumed, they managed to find more and more time for one another. Today's lunch date was the second of the week, meeting a goal they had mutually set. They went to a dine-in Mexican restaurant close to the office and, after placing their orders, Charlie asked him, "What's going on, Bryan?"

"Just before we left, I got a call from Graves, the FBI guy. Littski, you know Watson's suspected accomplice in Chicago who made the January transaction, got a call half an hour ago from an unlisted number. I'm betting it was Watson, but we can't prove it. He asked Littski to validate the exact amount of the January withdrawal from his brokerage account."

"Wow, that didn't take long. So now you know the leak is coming from the MFCB, but is it Gayle or someone else?"

"How can it be anyone else but Gayle? She's been told to guard against sharing anything we tell her with anyone but Da Silva. And there's no way he's sharing secrets with crooks."

"You're positive about that?"

"I'd bet a year's salary it's not him."

"What if someone in their IT department is reading emails or recording phone calls between Gayle and Da Silva? Is that possible?"

"It's possible, but as much as I hate to admit it, I have a feeling Gayle is the leak, and she's probably selling the information to Watson for big bucks. We need to start investigating her, looking at her finances and checking everything she does. This is discouraging; she's a former FBI agent with an excellent record, she's extremely knowledgeable about health care fraud, and she had a great job and future ahead of her. What the hell is she thinking? She's going to end up in prison."

"Bryan, all I can tell you is you can't let people's bad decisions sour your own attitude, not with the job you have. You've told me at least twice there was something about her that was slightly off. Maybe you were sensing her true character and looking beyond what she tries to project and wants people to believe. I know she's never had a family and she takes care of an ailing mother. It's possible she's convinced herself money is her only path to some level of happiness and satisfaction. It's sad to see someone so accomplished destroy her own life by making wrong choices."

"I remember someone telling me that life is all about our choices and living with the consequences of the ones we make. I guess there's more truth than poetry in that idea," Hampton told Charlie.

After finishing what evolved into a gloomy lunch together, they headed back to work. As soon as they arrived, Bryan went directly to Paul's office and related the news Graves had shared about the call Littski received.

"Sorry, Bryan, I know you were hoping it wasn't Gayle, but it must be her passing the information and not just someone else at the MFCB. It's highly improbable she was careless enough to have accidently disclosed such precise details to anyone there."

After discussing what to do next, they decided to get Special Agent Graves and Detective Barnes from Morton Grove on a conference call and talk about this development. They also wanted to ask the detective if he had any new leads about the identity of the man who owned the fingerprints and if he was continuing to search for other possible images of the suspect. Paul asked Charlie to coordinate the call with the other two men as soon as she could arrange it.

While they waited, Paul proposed the next steps in dealing with Gayle. "I believe our suspicions about Gayle shouldn't be shared outside of the five people here who already know. We can add Special Agent Graves to the short list and caution him to be equally prudent with the knowledge. I don't think we should confront Gayle at this time. It may turn out we need her later to feed Watson more fabricated information, so he'll take some action to further implicate himself in these crimes. We won't say anything to Da Silva about our suspicions either."

"Paul, this is really tough for me. Da Silva put us together by getting me this job, and betraying him this way just seems wrong."

"You're not betraying him; you're protecting him from himself. And by the way, it's true he did help you get this job, but he also hired Gayle Baker, so those two personnel decisions offset each other in my book."

"I hope he'll still consider me his friend when all of this is over."

"He'll be fine. Let's get back to Gayle. We'll keep her peripherally involved in this investigation, making sure we never discuss anything important with her that she could leak to Watson. If we can't find someone else to tie him to the fraud, we'll either use her again to force him to tip his hand, or we'll confront her and offer a deal of some sort in exchange for her testimony against Watson."

"Why don't we just try your second option today?"

"Because she's smart enough to know right now we can't prove what we suspect. The evidence we do have is circumstantial, and she could just deny everything and walk away with her money, and there's nothing we could do to stop her."

Charlie was able to get both Graves and Barnes on a conference call half an hour later. Bryan explained the latest developments to Detective Barnes, then asked him to update them on any progress in identifying the owner of the fingerprints.

"I was going to call you this afternoon, Bryan, and tell you we may have caught a break, a total fluke actually. Just after Christmas, I asked a friend, a Chicago Police detective, to see if he could get his guys to run facial recognition scans, comparing our suspect's image to people on the streets in downtown Chicago. I suggested they start with the busy shopping season, maybe a couple of weeks before Christmas when everyone loves to visit the city and shop on Michigan Avenue."

"What happened? Did you get a match or an ID?" Bryan asked anxiously.

"Man, this is an incredible story, so let me tell it at my own pace. To answer your question, he came up with over fifty possible hits during the week before Christmas. Most were multiples of the same eight people. But my investigators ultimately focused on one guy as our likely suspect. We had six different views of him, but none were much better than the traffic camera images we sent you in December. The highest probability we had a match was fifty-two percent, so we didn't burden you with anymore inconclusive pictures."

"Okay, Barnes, when do we hear the good news?" Special Agent Graves asked.

"Yeah, I'm getting to that. This is the fluke and the actual break. One of my detectives moonlights as a guard at the Ritz Carlton Hotel off North Michigan Avenue. Last night he shows up for work, and the head of security hands him a picture of a suspected pick pocket who may have been working in and around the hotel's street level lobby the week before Christmas.

"One of the hotel's guests had his wallet and five thousand dollars cash lifted somewhere in the Ritz on the twentieth of December. The picture he gave my guy was a mug shot the victim identified at the police station. He asked my officer to review three days of lobby video, the nineteenth through the twenty-first, and see if he could spot the guy."

"Are you going to tell us the picture of the pickpocket is our suspect?" Bryan asked.

"No way, but get this; my detective did find the pickpocket milling around two of the three days. However, the big discovery, which all of my staff has now agreed on, is our detective spotted our murder suspect coming and going through the lobby all three days. We have four crystal clear shots of his face, two-head on front views and two profiles, one from each side. We even got the back of his head and one of him walking through the elevator door all alone. That one's allowed us to estimate his height at five-nine and his weight north of two-thirty. Facial recognition software rates the probability of a match between the Ritz images and the traffic images from three years ago at seventy-eight percent."

"It looks like he might have been a guest at the hotel during that timeframe then. Is that what you're assuming?" Graves asked.

"Yes, we're searching more video to see when he first showed up and when we no longer see him coming and going. Once we have that, we'll compare that period of time to the registration data, and we'll get a name. In the meantime, we're also interviewing the desk staff and room service personnel to see if any of them recognize him and can give us a name."

"I doubt he'd be dumb enough to register with his own name. Wasn't he identified three years ago as Ernesto Morales and then he disappeared?" Hampton asked.

"That's right, Bryan, and we've already checked and no one with the name of Morales was registered at the hotel during the week of December in question. So he's using another name."

"Don't assume he's even the one who's registered. He could be staying with another guest, male or female. So you've got to look at those possibilities as well," Graves urged.

"So far we've never seen him with anyone when he's passing through the lobby or in the elevator, but we're not done looking."

Dixon sincerely and gratefully wrapped up the call by saying, "Good work, Barnes. This could be the break we've both been waiting for. Please send us the pictures as soon as you can so we can start working with possible witnesses on our end."

Without Graves asking, Detective Barnes offered him some help. "Do you need me to get these pictures to someone here in Illinois so your agents watching Littski know exactly who they're looking for?"

Graves answered, "I appreciate the offer, Detective, but just email them to me and we'll get them to our agents in the field immediately. I've asked the Chicago special agent in charge to assign an old friend of mine, Agent Phil Reese, to head up the surveillance teams, and he'll coordinate directly with our Las Vegas office. Thanks again for all your help. We're going to get this guy, I can feel it."

Chapter 35

Chicago, IL
February 9th
6:00 PM

Guzman had been struggling with the fourth knot he'd attempted to tie in the last ten minutes. He decided the problem was unsolvable. Once the blue and white length of polyester made the trip through his eighteen and a half inch collar, it was too short to look decent no matter what kind of knot he tied. He looked in the mirror and saw six inches of white shirt beyond the end of the now mangled necktie. He thought about the problem. Ties get more expensive and shorter every time I buy one. And then he arrived at his usual solution to every problem. I'll kill the bastard who made this one when I find him.

Tonight he had a crucial role in an important political campaign event. With the Illinois Primary Elections just over a month away, emotions were heating up, and the crowds were growing larger and more unruly. His former friends had lined him up as part of a security detail for one of the congressional candidates. His job was to protect the man from threats of any kind, keep the crowds at least three feet away at all times, and watch for anyone making any aggressive moves toward the candidate. He was to watch for suspected weapons of any type in the crowd and was to never be more than a few feet from the candidate, especially when he was speaking at a podium.

Today marked the beginning of the fourth week he'd been guarding Al Tacovic, the current U.S. Attorney for the Northern Illinois District, and the favored candidate in the Democratic Primary for the 9th Congressional District. But until that day, Guzman had never been assigned to be out front with the crowds and the candidate. He'd always been given backup roles, guarding the limo, watching for intruders backstage, observing the catering staff, and any other support roles the security people were usually responsible for.

He was excited and needed to be on his way to Evanston. Guzman was always on time for everything, and usually he liked to be early. He pocketed his wallet and keys and put both his cell phones into his suit coat pockets. As always, his final step before leaving his apartment was to check his gun, making sure the clip was fully loaded, a round chambered, and the safety on. Then he holstered the weapon in the small of his back.

Just as he was about to open the door and leave his apartment, one of the phones vibrated. He double checked to make sure who the call was from, because unless he had accidently switched them and put them in the wrong pockets, it was Watson's special phone that was summoning him. He saw his perception was correct; it was Watson's phone. He answered it immediately. "This is Fausto."

"Where are you right now?" Watson asked.

"I'm just leaving my apartment."

"What city and state are you in was really what I wanted to know," Watson asked with little patience.

"I'm in Chicago."

"Perfect, that's where I hoped you'd be. I want you to take care of something tonight, or tomorrow at the latest, but it's going to require extra time, because I need you to extract some information from the target before you finish your business."

Watson identified Anton Littski as the target, providing Guzman with both his home and office addresses. Then he specified the exact information Guzman must get from the man before he killed him. "I need the bank names, account numbers, and the name on every account where he's been stashing money he's stealing from me. And you also need to find out how long he's been skimming the funds from my account. And finally, I want you to make an example of him, so others will never attempt to steal from me again."

"Do you have a picture of Littski?"

"Google him. There's pictures of him anywhere they sell cars. Haven't you heard of him? He's the king of cars in Chicago."

"Okay. Now I know who he is. I'll take care of it, but it's going to take some time to plan. I don't know how long it'll take to get the information you want. This isn't just an In-N-Out Burger kind of deal."

"I'm not interested in your procedural problems. I pay you to do what I ask. If you get the account numbers and the money's there, I'll give you an extra hundred grand this month."

"I'll get the numbers, don't worry. I'll call you on the phone you're using when I have what you need." Then he pressed 'END' and headed out the door to protect Tacovic from the electorate.

It was a little after ten, and Fausto was just leaving the parking lot at Evanston Township High School where Tacovic's jam-packed rally had ended over an hour ago. He enjoyed his assigned duty that night; being by Tacovic's side throughout the evening was new and exciting. TV cameras, newspaper reporters, and photographers had covered the event as well as the news conference afterward, and Guzman had never left Tacovic's side for three hours. He'd even been part of the security detail escorting the SUV transporting the politician's entourage from his home to the high school and back.

After he declined their invitation to have a few beers with them, the three other members of the security team dropped him off at the school lot where his car was parked. They jokingly told him to stay out of trouble, reminding him to be sure and be on time for the press conference early the next morning.

Because Guzman was already in Evanston for the rally, it was an easy fifteen minute trip north to Glencoe to check out Littski's house. He'd already seen the general layout of the grounds and surrounding streets from the Google satellite pictures. Littski lived on Walnut Court, a relatively short street that coursed in a general U shape from Sheridan Road to Beach Street. Most of the homes on the street were actually mansions with the waters of Lake Michigan splashing onto beaches in their scenic and exclusive back yards. Dense trees surrounded every home, but in February they offered less cover, and most houses were visible from the street.

The satellite view also showed a narrow sandy beach stretched across the rear of Littski's home and three others next to it before widening into a longer section accessible to the public. A manageable wall, he thought, separated the private beachfronts from the wider stretch where dozens of boats were now stored waiting to be launched in a warmer season.

He decided to do a slow drive-by entering Walnut Court from the north end, using the southbound lane of Sheridan. It was nearly ten-thirty, and traffic on

Walnut Court was non-existent, so his journey might look suspicious to anyone watching. Rounding the first turn to take him past the target's home, he immediately spotted an unmarked police car parked two houses north and across the street from the end of Littski's driveway. With no possible way to turn back, he instinctively slightly increased his pace, making the next turn at what he thought would appear like a resident's normal speed. Then he turned onto Beach, quickly putting as much distance as possible between him and the undercover car and its passengers.

During the thirty-five-minute drive back to his apartment, Guzman devised two different plans for gaining access to Littski's home. Both required additional surveillance during daylight hours, and he already had a bias for one of them. He also knew he needed to get a closer look at the guys in the car doing the surveillance. He wanted to know what branch of law enforcement they belonged to, so he could predict how dangerous they might be. Maybe they had nothing to do with Littski. They might be watching someone else's house on the street, but he knew that was highly unlikely and risky, wishful thinking.

Tacovic's large donors' breakfast event was held the next morning for anyone willing to pay two thousand dollars to attend. Over two hundred and fifty citizens from the 9th District showed up only to be packed into a hotel conference room where they ate a mass-produced hotel breakfast and listened to their candidate deliver his standard stump speech. Anyone willing to chip in another five hundred could have their photo taken with Tacovic and be rewarded on their way out of the event with an autographed souvenir.

Guzman counted the guests, did the math, and thought about the money, over five hundred grand, even if nobody went for the photo deal, which at least fifty or more of the crowd did. TV cameras were all over the room and the reporters were filming and interviewing anyone who would talk to them. Guzman fantasized about someday becoming a politician.

The fund-raiser was over before ten, and within thirty minutes Guzman was parked in a church lot in Glencoe. He was several blocks from Littski's home, but it was impossible to park anywhere near the house without being noticed. He dressed like a jogger, with a big baggy hooded sweat shirt to hide his face. He found the boat place and jogged on the beach as far as the wall and saw he could scale it easily.

Circling back through the frozen sand, he worked his way to Beach Street, then decided to chance a slow jog on Walnut Court past Littski's house. The undercover car was in a slightly new location that morning, one house farther south, but still on the opposite side of the street. The two men in the car watched as he approached. He needed to discreetly get a good look at them, so as he passed their car, he pretended to be checking his pulse while looking at his watch. Federal cops of some sort, not locals; must be FBI, he decided. Satisfied he had passed without them suspecting anything, he turned on Sheridan and circled back to the church parking lot, smiling at his good fortune.

It was clear there was no way to drive anywhere close to Littski's house without being seen by the surveillance team, at least on a normal night. But what he'd spotted in the driveway of the house next to Littski's revealed this wasn't going to be a typical Friday night. He saw four men unloading a large truck carrying chairs, tables, linens, and more boxes than he could count. Colorful balloons, hats, and noisemakers were painted on the sides and rear of the truck along with the company name, Carl's Party Rentals. This was going to be easy, he decided. Lots of people will be going into the party next door, and I can tag along with a group of them, then detour to Littski's house. What a stroke of luck, he thought.

Guzman had gone back to his apartment after stopping at an Ace Hardware store to buy a pair of heavy duty wire cutters, a hedge trimmer, a plastic tarp, and duct tape. By six he was back in Glencoe waiting for guests to show up for the party. He saw the FBI car was still exactly where it had been that morning, at the end of the neighbor's driveway where the party was being held, but on the opposite side of the street. They couldn't see Littski's house from where they were parked, but the end of his driveway was clearly visible to them, so no one could drive or walk in or out without them noticing.

It was cold, below freezing, and it turned out he had arrived nearly an hour earlier than necessary. People began showing up at ten minutes before seven, but the heavy traffic didn't begin until around seven-fifteen, which was when Guzman came out of the bushes, his tools and tarp hidden under his large overcoat, and his head and part of his face obscured by a loose fitting wool ski cap.

He tagged along at the rear of a group of guests heading to the party and passed right by the agent's car, but on the opposite side of the street. He continued trailing the group of eight legitimate guests up the driveway toward the party. At his first opportunity after the driveway curved and he could no longer be seen from the street, he slipped away from the group and disappeared quietly into the wall of evergreen trees and leafless bushes separating the neighbor's lot from the Littski's property.

His initial plan was to simply knock on the front door and force his way in when someone answered it. But just as he started to step from the trees onto the lawn and then the sidewalk leading to the front of the house, the huge oak entry door opened and an elegantly dressed woman walked out. He ducked back into the bushes and watched as she adjusted her fur coat against the cold wind. Before she closed the massive door, he heard her call back to someone inside, "Don't be long, Anton, we're already late."

Guzman watched the woman start to leave the sidewalk and move toward his hiding place in the trees, but then she seemed to change her mind and remained on the path that led her to the well-plowed driveway. Fortunately for Guzman, she had decided to take the longer and safer route to the party next door rather than chancing the snow and slippery frozen ground.

After she disappeared onto the street, Guzman quickly headed to the front door and tried it, but it was locked. He thought about ringing the bell or knocking, but decided it was safer to wait for Littski to open the door as he left for the party.

Five minutes later, Guzman heard the clicking of approaching footsteps inside on the hard foyer floor, then a louder clunk as Littski unlocked the door and opened it. Before the man even saw him, Guzman burst through the partially opened doorway and crashed hard into Littski, knocking him onto the unforgiving marble floor. After quickly closing the door, he punched the startled, smaller man viciously in the face, kneed him twice in the groin to take his breath, then bound and gagged him with the duct tape.

After locking the entry door, Guzman asked Littski if anyone else was in the house. Anton shook his head no. "Where's your wife?" he asked, trying to assess his victim's candor. Littski tilted his head twice toward the party next door. "Good answer, Anton, but I already knew that. If you can continue to be truthful, we'll be done here quickly."

Then for good measure, Fausto shouted, "Is anyone home?" three or four times to be certain the house was empty. Silence reigned, bolstering his confidence. He quickly walked around to locate an interior room without windows, and preferably with a good thick door, where he could move Littski for questioning. He settled on small space with a desk, computer, and two chairs, probably an assistant's workplace, he decided. It was adjacent to Anton's spacious corner office which looked out onto the pool and front yard.

After forcing Littski into the room, Guzman duct taped him tightly to one of the chairs, then removed the tape and gag from his mouth. "Mr. Watson asked me to come by tonight and get some information from you. You know who Mr. Watson is, don't you?"

"Of course I know who he is. What's this about? Who are you and what are you up to?"

"Here's the first rule, Anton. I ask the questions, not you. Your job is to give me answers. Are we clear on that?"

"Yes, I'm clear, but you and Watson are going to regret pulling this stunt."

Guzman punched him twice in the stomach, then continued, "To make this real simple, I'll explain the rules one more time. I'm going to ask you questions and you're going to answer them. If I don't get the answers I need, I'm going to hurt you until you tell me what I want to know." Guzman had been unfolding the tarp while he talked to Littski, who could now see the wire cutters, hedge trimmer, and Fausto's large knife. For emphasis, Guzman removed his gun from his holster and placed it on the blue tarp alongside the other tools.

"First, here's a little background so we're both on the same page. Watson knows you've been skimming his account, but he doesn't know how much you've taken or how long you've been doing it. He wants the money back, and I'm just here to get information; account numbers and bank names where you've parked Mr. Watson's money, the date you started stealing, and the exact amount you've stolen. Anton, did you really think you could skim off three million in one month? I guess you've been screwing customers at your car lots for so long, you think you can get away with anything."

"I don't know what you're talking about. I've never taken a dime more than our agreement allowed. Why does Watson think I stole three million from him? He called me the other day and I told him exactly what amount was transferred out of his account. I make more profit moving his funds three times a year than five of my dealerships produce in the same twelve months. Why would I jeopardize that?"

"Wrong answer, Anton." Guzman punched him several more times. One of the blows fractured Littski's jaw, and unfortunately for Guzman, knocked him unconscious. Realizing he just ended their Q and A session and needed to revive Littski, Guzman headed off to the kitchen hoping to find a bucket or a large bowl to hold ice and some water. Maybe if I can find a beer in the refrigerator I'll grab one while at it, he thought.

Earlier in the day when the party truck started unloading, Phil Reese, one of the FBI agents sitting in the parked car on Walnut Court, went to the neighbor's door and asked what was going on. The owners weren't home at the time, but the maid filled Reese in on the details of the anniversary party being held that evening. She told him they were expecting over 150 guests, and Reese quickly realized it would be difficult for one team of agents to effectively protect Littski with that number of extra bodies roaming around the neighborhood next to the house they were watching. He returned to the car and immediately requested an additional team be assigned to watch Littski's house that night.

He was advised no extra teams were available, but was told the two-man team scheduled to relieve them would arrive at five. Reese suggested he and his partner stay on duty at least until the party was over, and the agent in charge approved the extra time.

Reese later spoke with the neighbor giving the party and explained there would two FBI cars on the street that night and they would be watching for anything suspicious as their guests arrived. At the suggestion of the neighbor, the two agents who joined the surveillance at five left their car two blocks away and were now sitting in his Mercedes, parked in his driveway.

"This way," the neighbor explained to Agent Reese, "they won't alarm the guests as much as the two of you, who are obviously law enforcement officers trying to be undercover. You guys do realize no one but police drive Crown Victoria's, don't you?"

Agent Reese had noticed something strange shortly after seven. He saw what looked like four nicely dressed couples approaching the driveway on their way to the party. A stalky man walked behind the eight people, seemingly with them, but two things caught Reese's attention. First, the man had on a loose fitting stocking cap, and under his bulky overcoat Reese thought he saw a sweater. Everyone else going to the party was dressed formally, some even wearing tuxedos. The other unusual thing was no one talked to the straggler, and he made no attempt to speak to anyone in the group. He appeared to be alone.

Rather than embarrassing the man on such flimsy suspicions, Reese called the agents watching from the Mercedes and told them to keep an eye out for the group and the guy trailing them in the stocking cap. He advised them to get a better read on his clothes and to stop and question him if necessary. The group disappeared down the driveway toward the house, and Reese shifted his attention to the other people streaming into the party, including the woman who emerged alone from the end of Littski's driveway.

"Is that our guy's wife headed for the party? Where's Littski, I wonder?" he asked his partner Ben Scott.

They watched her come up the street, then take the neighbor's driveway to the party. Reese then returned his attention to the end of Littski's driveway, wondering how long it would be until the man followed his wife's path to the party. Five minutes passed and no Littski, then he suddenly realized the other agents hadn't radioed back yet to report what they found out about 'stocking cap.'

"What do you mean, you never saw him?" Why didn't you call me back and report that?" Reese shouted, "Did you see the four couples come by?"

When the agent said they had seen all eight of them go into the house a few minutes ago, Reese ordered Agent Preston and his partner to get out of the Mercedes and find the man with the stocking cap. If they couldn't locate him in five minutes or less, they were to call him back immediately. Reese also told Preston to find Littski's wife and ask where her husband was.

Preston and his partner entered the packed and bustling house and quickly searched for someone stalky and possibly wearing a sweater, with or without a stocking cap. Preston decided to ask the two men at the front door who were checking coats if someone had come in wearing a knit ski cap. "Absolutely not!" he was told. Just as Preston was about to head back outside, he saw Mrs. Littski talking to another guest at the party. He walked over to her and quietly asked, "Where's your husband, Mrs. Littski?"

"He's running late. He's still next door, but he'll be here soon. Who are you, and how do you know my name?"

"My name is Agent Michael Preston. I'm with the FBI. I need you to come with me immediately." Preston allowed the woman to examine his credentials, then discretely escorted her to a guest bedroom where coats were being hung on mobile racks and also piled on the bed.

Preston's partner had seen them moving toward the bedroom and followed. "Mrs. Littski, this is Agent Field. He's going to stay here with you while I locate your husband. You're not to leave this room until I come back." Preston dashed from the room and out of the house. He ran the full length of the driveway almost to the street, talking all the way to his wrist, letting Reese know they couldn't find the man with the stocking cap, but they did find Littski's wife, alone at the party, and she was now safe. He saw an opening in the trees that would allow a short cut to Littski's house and took it.

Reese and his partner ran toward Littski's driveway and got there about the same time Preston emerged from the snow and trees. Reese felt his cell phone vibrate, looked at the screen, then held up a hand, a sign all of them should wait while he answered it.

"How long ago? Do you have anyone on the way? Tell them no sirens, no red lights, no noise. We're at the house right now and, if necessary, we're going in. We've learned Mr. Littski is in the house and our suspect could be in there with him."

Reese quickly explained the call to his companions. "That was the dispatcher at the Glencoe PD. Littski's silent alarm went off fifteen minutes ago. The alarm service notified the police nine minutes ago. She has a unit still four or five minutes out, but she was bright enough to remember her captain telling her the FBI had a surveillance operation going on at the same address. It took her some time to get her captain on the phone; she needed to get my number from him."

"Do you think stocking cap is in there with Littski?" Preston asked.

"If stocking cap is the crazy bastard the guys in Vegas warned us about, Littski could already be dead or maybe still alive, with a few parts missing, which could be worse for him. You two make a quick and silent trip around the house and check if any of the windows give us a view of what's going on inside. I'm staying here to make sure nobody comes out."

Moments later, Preston called Reese, almost whispering, "Our suspect is in the kitchen rummaging around in the refrigerator. It looks like he's opened half the cabinets searching for something. No sign of Littski. What should I do?"

"Do you see a door from outside leading into the kitchen?"

"Yes, across the room from the window I'm looking through."

"How sturdy does it look?"

"Glass on top, wood below, with a dog entrance. There's no bolt. The door looks relatively flimsy."

"Get your butt over to that door as fast as you can without him hearing or seeing you. Is my partner Ben there with you?"

"Yes, what do you want him to do?"

"Tell him the two of you are going to crash through that outside door and to get ready. As soon as you're both in position, let me know. I'm going to break the side window panel by the front door, then try and reach through and unbolt the door to get in. The minute he hears the noise, he's probably going to dash out of the kitchen to find out what's going on. But before he can turn and run, the two of you are going to bust through the door and confuse the hell out of him. You got that so far?"

"We understand."

"Now listen to me. This guy's a killer, and he's not going to surrender or give up easily. He's crazy enough to come running at you with his bare hands, a knife, or a gun. One of you needs to have a gun pointed at him every second; two guns would even be better. If he makes any kind of aggressive move, shoot fast, shoot straight, and shoot to kill. If he gets near you, you're a dead man. Now if you're both ready, I'm breaking this window on the count of three. One--two--three."

Guzman was holding a beer in one hand and the bowl of ice water in the other when he heard glass break somewhere back by the front door. He dropped both items, reached behind him for his gun, then realized where he'd left it. His hand was still touching the empty holster in the small of his back when the kitchen doorframe seemed to explode and two men in suits holding guns came rushing through it. "FBI, FBI, don't move!" they were yelling at him.

Out of the corner of his eye, on the counter, he saw a knife rack near his right hand. He realized without his gun his only chance was to surprise the two men. Maybe they would freeze for an instant. He hesitated and pretended to raise his hands, but instead he grabbed the largest knife and charged the two agents. He heard three loud shots, looked down, and saw blood spurting out of three gaping holes in his chest. He thought he recognized the sound of a fourth shot, then felt a sudden, horrific blow that snapped his head back, then nothing.

Reese managed to get the bolt unlocked and the front door open at about the same time he heard the four shots coming from the kitchen. He moved behind a wall in the entryway and called, "Agent Preston, what's your status?"

"Suspect down. We're both okay, except I'm about to throw up," Preston called back with a shaky voice.

"I'm going to search for Littski. One of you needs to help me, and the other stays there with the suspect. What's his status?"

"Three to the chest and one to the forehead. I think he'll be fine here without either of us," Reese's partner Ben Scott answered sarcastically.

They found Anton Littski with all his body parts intact two minutes later, but his face was already badly swollen. His left orbit was fractured so badly they could barely see his left eye, and there was bone protruding from the right side of his lower jaw. He was unconscious, and at first they thought he might be dead, but Reese checked his carotid pulse and confirmed at least his heart was still beating.

Reese pressed his callback button, got the Glencoe dispatcher on the phone, and told her to get an ambulance there as fast as possible. He also said she should let the responding units use their sirens and red lights if they were needed.

He then went to the kitchen to check on Agent Preston, who was sitting on a chair looking down at Guzman. The killer had collapsed and fallen to the floor with his back against the cabinets, his lifeless face staring blankly across the room.

Reese stood there for a few seconds looking at the dead man's face. He told Preston to check on Scott and see if he needed any help. Then Agent Reese did something which was undoubtedly against numerous FBI regulations. He took a picture of Fausto Guzman's face with his phone's camera and emailed it to Detective Barnes, Special Agent Graves, and Bryan Hampton. His message was brief; 'Run this through the Facial Recognition Software. I'm betting it's a ninety percent match. It could have been a hundred percent, but part of his head seems to be gone.'

Chapter 36

Chicago, IL
February 11th
9:00 AM

At first, news of the Friday night killing and home invasion in the exclusive suburb of Glencoe, IL spread slowly, even in and around Chicago. Avid readers of the Saturday morning papers learned more about the Bulls victory over the Hornets Friday night than anything they might have discovered about the killing. By mid-day both the local TV and the national networks had marginally improved reporting on the story.

Most showed pictures of a depraved looking man initially identified as Fausto Guzman, who was shot and killed by the FBI in the Glencoe mansion, which was also pictured in most accounts. Additional facts and critical details began emerging on Sunday after reporters had more time to piece together all the elements of the shooting and conduct interviews with authorities and witnesses.

On Monday, Morton Grove police announced the man killed by FBI agents the previous Friday was unquestionably the same person who assassinated Congressman Reuben Horowitz on the morning of October 15, 2011. Detective Barnes was interviewed on national television and explained how a previously undisclosed fingerprint had been the key piece of evidence leading to the identity of the assailant. He went on to defend the strategy of keeping the existence of the fingerprint confidential, explaining the killer likely would never have returned to Illinois had he known about the evidence he had carelessly left behind.

On Monday afternoon a sophisticated and provocative video was posted on YouTube. The tweeting started soon afterward and quickly gained momentum. The online discussions and observations centered on the validity of the visual evidence viewers had witnessed. The intent of the video was clear, to establish an undeniable resemblance between pictures of a deceased murderer and photos of Al Tacovic's chief of security.

The YouTube production was skillfully produced and successfully achieved the goal of convincing most viewers the Glenview murderer and the U.S. attorney's security man were without a doubt the same person. Viewers first saw an image of Tacovic and Guzman standing side by side. The picture zoomed in on Guzman's face, which was then moved to one side of a split screen. On the opposite side, one-by-one in succession, three different images were shown.

As each image was posted, a caption appeared revealing its source: Artist's sketch the Horowitz murderer; Traffic image from a drug shootout; and finally, the image from the Ritz lobby, from which witnesses of the Congressman's killer had made a definitive identification. After each of the three images was shown, it was merged with the campaign event photo of Guzman with Tacovic, which could still be seen on the opposite side of the split screen. The implication was clear; all four images were the same man. Tacovic's chief of security was a murderer.

Several of the early evening newscasts showed the video and also mentioned the tweets, and by eight o'clock Eastern Time the story had gone viral. Nearly every news network dedicated at least five or more minutes to the story every hour and continued to do so for the next twenty-four hours.

When the ten o'clock newscasts hit the air Monday night, most stations showed the video again, along with carefully chosen side by side photos of the killer and Tacovic's security man. The consensus was they were clearly the same person, unless Tacovic could produce the dead man's twin. When the candidate's campaign manager was asked about the story, he downplayed the question as being a political smear tactic and a preposterous allegation.

On Tuesday morning FOX National News broke what turned out to be the real story. After running the YouTube video, the network exhibited four different photos of Tacovic and Guzman together. Guzman, dressed in a suit and tie, was always close to Tacovic and looked like an overweight Secret Service Agent. In one picture a smiling Guzman and Tacovic were face to face, and the politician appeared to be laughing at something Guzman had said.

The newscaster's narrative was decisive, judgmental, and condemning.
"Fausto Guzman, also known as Ernesto Morales, a long-time strong man and
known executioner for one of Chicago's illegal drug rings, was shot to death by
FBI agents last Friday night after he invaded the home of Anton Littski, a
prominent Illinois businessman. What you are seeing now are photos of the dead
man and U.S. Attorney Al Tacovic taken at two separate campaign events last
Thursday and Friday. Tacovic is a candidate in the Democratic Primary for
Congress in the Illinois 9th Congressional District, and Guzman was one of the
most trusted members of his security team."

The image then shifted to a video showing a tow truck, surrounded by police
and fire engines. The tow truck was pulling a car out of a river several yards
below a bridge. The newscaster continued, "Many will recall these pictures
taken last October, when Morton Grove Police found Republican Congressman
Reuben Horowitz dead in this car, in what was initially believed to be a single
car accident. Evidence later established the Congressman's car had been forced
off the road and was badly damaged after crashing into a barrier on the bridge
seen in this video. While he was still pinned in the wrecked car, severely injured
and likely unconscious, an unknown assailant ended his life.

"Police withheld, until yesterday, information provided by two teenagers who
witnessed the killer's SUV ramming the already damaged Volvo over the
guardrail and into the river. Before he raced off, the witnesses had clearly seen
the driver as he examined his SUV for damages. The killer later abandoned his
stolen car several blocks away. Saturday morning when Skokie Police found the
SUV, they discovered a flashlight with the killer's fingerprints carelessly left
under the front seat of the stolen vehicle.

"Republican Congressman Horowitz was heavily favored to win re-election
in the 9th District against likely challenger Al Tacovic, who most believed would
easily defeat Leah Kerrigan in next month's Democratic Primary. Before his
death, veteran observers of Illinois politics dreamed a Republican victory in the
probable race between Horowitz, the popular staunch Tea Party conservative,
and Al Tacovic, the son of Ed Tacovic, a long-time Chicago machine politician,
would usher in a new era of ethical and honest politics in Illinois."

The reporter then continued with the most damaging allegation. "The
conclusive fingerprint evidence, along with the witness' identification, proves
Congressman Horowitz was murdered by one of Al Tacovic's trusted security
men, a known killer responsible for at least five murders in the Chicago area.
Many Illinois citizens, including Leah Kerrigan, who opposes Tacovic in the
upcoming primary, are demanding an immediate investigation to determine

Tacovic's complicity in these despicable crimes. But Chicago observers tell us any serious investigation is unlikely, because Al Tacovic currently serves as the U.S. Attorney for the Illinois District, and his office would be responsible for undertaking the investigation."

The picture then shifted to video of Tacovic's Democratic Primary rival, Leah Kerrigan, delivering a prepared statement. "This latest revelation is yet another case in a long list of questionable instances where my opponent claims the allegations against him are unsubstantiated or simply guilt by association. It's doubtful any direct evidence will ever be found proving U.S. Attorney Al Tacovic ordered Fausto Guzman, also known as Ernesto Morales, to kill Congressman Horowitz, but we've all seen photos of this heinous criminal and my opponent publicly smiling and laughing together at a campaign event just a few days ago."

Referring to a large blow-up of Guzman and Tacovic laughing and smiling, which most viewers had already seen several times, she continued, "Do we, the voters of the Illinois 9th Congressional District, want to elect a man who would allow a killer to be part of his inner circle? Do we want to send someone to Washington who jokes with a man who only hours later was killed by authorities as he attempted to torture and murder yet another victim? Do we really want another machine politician controlling our destiny? Shouldn't we be asking Mr. Tacovic why he sent Fausto Guzman to Mr. Littski's home last Friday night? Could the reason be Anton Littski is a major contributor to my campaign?"

Then Kerrigan concluded with her political pitch. "I think it's time the citizens of Illinois get answers to these questions. I know it's time for voters to send a clear signal to the nation that we will no longer elect underhanded, corrupt, and deceitful machine politicians to Illinois public offices. You can begin sending that message by voting for me, Leah Kerrigan, in next month's primary election. Thank you and God bless the USA and the FBI for their excellent work last Friday."

Missing from all the news stories was any reference to the brutal crimes the dead man was responsible for in Las Vegas. Detective Barnes and his investigators were silent on that aspect of their case. Barnes had agreed with Dixon to withhold any information linking Guzman's crimes in Illinois to his grisly murders and the callous bombing in Nevada. Dixon understood this temporarily left four murder cases and one missing person case in the unsolved category, but Special Agent Graves had agreed to the arrangement hoping it would eventually allow them to link Watson to Guzman. "It'll be much easier to find the connection if he has no idea we're looking for one," Graves had told Dixon.

Chapter 37

Las Vegas, NV
February 14th
2:00 PM

After the Fox News story aired with Leah Kerrigan accusing Tacovic of ordering Guzman to torture and murder Littski, Dixon called a series of emergency sessions for that afternoon to discuss how they would manage all the new and curious developments coming out of Chicago. The first meeting involved only Hampton, and Dixon asked the first question, "Has Littski changed his mind?"

"No, he's sticking with his story, maintaining he's in the dark about who Guzman was, why he was there, or who sent him. We've tried everything we know to get him to admit he's part of the money laundering operation, but he claims he has no idea what we're talking about. Frankly, we don't have much to work with because he only makes three deposits a year to an account in the Caymans. And all we know about the account is the money instantly moves twenty different directions out of it as soon as it gets there." Hampton answered.

"But we haven't mentioned anything to him or anyone else in Chicago about suspecting Watson, have we?" Dixon asked.

"Not even your friend Phil Reese knows anything about the Bennett Watson connection. Special Agent Graves has promised me that information has gone nowhere outside of a small group of agents here in Las Vegas, and they're completely on board to help us get Watson for what they suspect his part was in the bombing of Washburn's condo."

Then Dixon asked for Hampton's opinion. "Are we sure Leah Kerrigan won't back off her accusation that Tacovic sent Guzman after Littski because he supported her campaign financially?"

"She'll milk it as long as the reporters and public are asking her about it. According to the papers, she's got a good shot at beating Tacovic after all the attention she's getting. Does it really matter whether she sticks with it or not at this point? Once the idea is out there, it's almost impossible to take it back," Hampton reasoned.

"Bryan, we should talk about future plans for any further investigation of Watson. It's clear we lack sufficient evidence to prosecute him now, and I'm convinced our best hope is to let him believe we hit a dead end in Chicago and can't link anything to him. In the meantime, we'll keep pressing the three chiropractors to see if any of them might decide to cooperate, and we'll also keep our experts digging into Mirzoyan's finances. We'll track the accounts in the Caymans and wherever else the money leads us, but we'll do it as covertly as possible."

Dixon paused expecting a reaction from Hampton, but none came so he continued, "No more wiretaps or surveillance on Watson for a while, but we'll come at him from other directions. We'll look at other schemes we know he's involved in and see where those leads take us. We know he's implicated in a prescription drug diversion scheme, and we have the name of a pharmacy we know is somehow associated with him and the scheme. We'll shift our focus to drugs, persist in our investigation of the staged auto accidents, and see what we come up with."

"I don't like taking the pressure off him, Paul, but I guess you're right. Maybe he'll get sloppy believing we bought into the Chicago connection between Littski and Tacovic, but we know Gayle told him we were onto the clinic money being laundered through the offshore accounts. The money trail might lead to something productive and we need to keep monitoring the accounts we've identified for future activity while continuing to aggressively investigate the entities owning the accounts, but I doubt he'll every use them again."

"But don't forget, Bryan, we still have a long list of bogus claimants from the phony accidents to investigate. Since most of them were represented by attorneys from Watson's firm, I'm confident we'll prove those who actually used their real names on the false claims were complicit in the schemes. All we need is one of them to testify they were recruited by Watson, and that's how they got involved in his fraud scheme."

"Paul, you're probably being overly optimistic again, and I guess that's one of your best qualities. But we've already interrogated eight of them, and apparently they were all recruited by Guzman, and without him alive to tell us Watson was behind everything he did, it's a dead end.

"Just this morning we got a look at Guzman's one and only business account for his sham organization, WeSolveProblems.com. It shows weekly wire deposits of ninety-five hundred dollars for the past two and a half years. We're sure the deposits were payments coming from Watson and we'll investigate the accounts the money was wired from, but it's doubtful they'll easily link back to him. This guy's tricky and ruthless, but we're going to get him, I can promise you that," Hampton said with passion.

"Bryan, I know this will be difficult for you, but before you bring it up again I need to be clear. We don't want to pull the plug on Gayle just yet. As we discussed before, I think we can use her to get to Watson when the right time comes. She already knows we suspected Mirzoyan wasn't directing Guzman's activities, but apparently she's never told Watson we suspect him or he never would have sent Guzman after Littski. Let's string her along until we can trap them both, then we'll make her an offer she can't refuse," Dixon explained.

"You're right, Paul, I hate the idea, because I find it impossible to passionately work with the type of person she's turned out to be. Ignoring the fact she's a traitor giving information to a person like Watson while we allow her to work with us like nothing's wrong is BS as far as I'm concerned. What if she does tell Watson we suspect he was directing Guzman? I'll do what I'm told, but she may start reading the vibes I'm giving off because I despise her," Hampton said emphatically.

"I appreciate any effort you can make to hide your true feelings Bryan. You'll find it was worth the struggle when we catch Watson," Dixon promised with intended sarcasm.

It was Valentine's Day, not that Bryan had given it much thought. On her way out of the office, Charlie reminded him their dinner reservation was at seven. His mind froze for a second, then he realized the date; it was February fourteenth. Too late, his blank expression had said it all, and Charlie knew he'd forgotten. But she just smiled and said, "See you at six forty-five," then waved and left.

It seemed hopeless trying to find a gift in the time he had to shop, and he'd almost given up as he passed the jewelry case on his way out of Dillard's. A large red heart on the counter drew him to a display case filled with expensive jewelry, all designed to ease the conscience of forgetful, guilt-ridden male shoppers. He found a watch he liked, but wasn't positive she would. He paid more than he'd planned, but chalked it up to the cost of his negligence. Searching for a decent valentine in the picked-over greeting card section of Walgreens near his apartment was an even more frustrating process. He had to settle for one that was sappier than he liked, but a little less cheesy than others left to choose from.

Charlie had planned ahead and had several surprises for Bryan on that special Valentine's Day night. She knew he would love driving his Corvette, so she had removed its custom cover, dusted off the seats, and driven the car out of the garage so he would see it was ready to go as soon as he arrived. When she answered the doorbell, his handsome smile proved her surprise number one was indeed a success.

The restaurant was packed, but their table was ready and unexpectedly secluded for a busy holiday primetime meal. During dinner they spoke of everything but work, and over dessert, exchanged gifts and cards. Charlie's second surprise for Bryan was his gift. She had bought him four season tickets to the University of Utah football games the following fall. Her message in his card hinted the tickets could be used to take her and the boys to at least half of the six games played in Salt Lake City.

Bryan seemed speechless, finally saying, "Charlie, what an incredible gift. You shouldn't have spent this much money, and the idea of all of us going to the games is awesome."

"Not to all of the games, Bryan. You have friends who would love to go to some of them, and three trips to Utah each fall will be plenty for me. I'm glad I could get you something you liked and something that'll take your mind off work for a few weekends."

Charlie gave Bryan what she believed was her best surprise of the night just after they finished replacing the custom cover on the Corvette. She put her arms around him and gave him her most passionate Latino kiss, then leaned back, looked at him tenderly, and said, "Bryan Hampton, I know I love you, and I want to marry you. It seems to me like you're never going to make a move, so I want you to know I'm ready whenever you are, and neither of us is getting any younger, so I hope you feel the same about me."

She could tell he was shocked, and feared she might have gone too far, but had no regrets for speaking her heart. This man was more than just good. To her and her boys, he was heaven sent. She needed to be loved and respected, and her sons needed a role model who would love them and help them become the type of men their father and this incredible man both were. She had come to love him deeply and looked forward to every minute they spent together. What's he thinking and what's he going to say to me now, were the compelling questions spinning through her mind.

"Charlie, I love you, too," he said without much hesitation, but she worried because his response had been a little slow.

"There's a 'but' in there, Bryan, isn't there? I know you too well now, and you hesitated. I'm sorry if I made you uncomfortable, but we're not kids, and we've spent a lot of time together in the last four months. You should know by now if I'm someone you're interested in or not."

"Charlie, I hesitated because I'm a lot older than you are. I think about that a lot, and it makes me uncomfortable at times. Have you ever thought how I'll look to you, and how we'll look together, in ten or fifteen years? People will probably think I'm your father, and the truth is, people probably think that now."

"I don't care about what anyone thinks, Bryan, so why do you? Do you love me, and do you love my boys is all that matters?"

"Of course I do, Charlie. It scares me sometimes thinking you might get tired of me, and it must be obvious to you I don't do well with losing people I love."

"You're not going to lose me, Bryan, not unless you betray my trust. I believe a husband and wife should be completely dedicated and honest with each other. As long as we can promise that type of devotion and commitment to each other, neither of us should ever fear losing the other."

While he drove home later that night, Bryan couldn't help smiling. It had been over ten years since his divorce, so the joy of being loved and feeling capable of loving someone so deeply in return was overwhelming. As he waited at a red light, his smile faded, forced away by a troubling thought; why the hell didn't I buy her an engagement ring for Valentine's Day? I probably disappointed her and she still thinks I'm a putz stumbling my way through our relationship.

Then the light changed to green and his smile started to return as he thought of a solution. First thing in the morning I'll tell her we need to go shopping together Friday night, with one and only one objective; to find her a ring. He liked his idea and expected a good outcome, but he was still nervous.

Epilogue

Las Vegas, NV
June 27th

Only one of the former employees working for Dr. Mirzoyan's now defunct Accident and Injury Health Restoration Clinics claimed he was innocent and chose to stand trial. Everyone else indicted pled guilty to various charges, and they all had been sentenced by mid-June. Penalties were less severe for those with minor roles; most of them received sentences of a year or two of probation along with substantial hours of community service.

All participants in the schemes with a professional license of any kind, as well as six others who had clearly facilitated the fraud, were dealt with more severely. Their sentences ranged from two years imprisonment to over fifteen years for the two doctors who pled guilty. Both chiropractors were also ordered to pay over one million dollars each in penalties and restitution.

Dr. Sabatta, Mirzoyan's longest tenured chiropractor, chose to plead innocent and went to trial. The trial lasted five days but the jury spent less than thirty minutes deliberating. The foreman announced the verdict just after noon on Wednesday, June 27th. Because he pleaded innocent, prosecutors decided to send a message and maximized the charges against him. Sabatta was tried and convicted on fifty-seven counts of medical fraud and various other crimes. He wouldn't be sentenced until late August and would no doubt appeal.

His upside was the judge allowed his bail to continue while he awaited sentencing. The down side was pending a successful appeal, if the judge imposed the full penalties, he faced a total of fifty-five years in prison. If the jury's recommendations were honored by the court, his fines, penalties, and payback of fraudulent payments would strip him of every tangible asset he owned and still leave him over three million dollars short.

At two Eastern Time the same day, Stan Birch in a Fox Breaking News segment, reported a major announcement just released by the U.S. Department of Justice. "DOJ officials revealed today that Al Tacovic, the U.S. Attorney for the Illinois Chicago District, has resigned his position. Tacovic's resignation follows his three-month battle with Washington officials to retain his post after allegations he was involved in the murder of Congressman Reuben Horowitz. In March, Tacovic unsuccessfully ran in the Democratic Primary for the late Congressman's 9th District Congressional seat."

Birch went on to detail allegations against Tacovic. "Most experts believe his surprising defeat by newcomer Leah Kerrigan in last month's election was the result of his still unclear association with his security chief, Fausto Guzman. Guzman was the undocumented illegal alien who murdered Tacovic's one-time likely rival in this fall's upcoming general election, incumbent Congressman Horowitz. Further doubts were raised about Tacovic's fitness for office as a result of serious allegations Kerrigan made against him after FBI agents shot and killed Guzman as he battered, tortured, and nearly murdered Kerrigan's principal financial supporter."

Birch, the Fox reporter, next lost any pretense of objectivity and concluded his coverage with his own commentary. "After all the incriminations against him, it's doubtful even in Chicago Mr. Tacovic will ever again regain his political standing in this state. It's beyond any reasonable stretch of a rational person's imagination to believe it was mere coincidence Tacovic's chief of security killed his Republican rival and four months later attempted to torture and murder the primary financial supporter of his Democratic rival.

"Clearly, Mr. Tacovic is accountable and deeply involved in this dark tragedy. We as citizens of this state can no longer tolerate politicians who ignore the rules and laws we elected them to uphold and enforce."

The piece concluded with Birch lamenting the loss of Congressman Horowitz and emphatically demanding Tacovic be brought to justice for such overt acts of brutality.

Two months later, as Hampton was about to leave the office for the day, he heard his PC chime the arrival of a new email. Something told him not to wait for morning, but to check the message right away before he left for home. When the screen came to life, he smiled. It was a note from Ted Kucharski, his friend from the Sidereal HealthCare SIU. Before he even opened the message he noticed there were two sizeable attachments. Curiosity got the better of him, even though he was anxious to be on his way home.

He first read the message, "Hampton, I'm passing on an attachment containing a news article that will appear in the *Chicago Tribune* tomorrow. They'll likely edit it, but a summary of the message goes something like the following: *Agents from the US Department of Justice* (now minus Tacovic's crooked leadership) *late yesterday arrested Evanston dermatologist Dr. Hugh Patterson and charged him with 122 counts of filing false medical claims. The DOJ was assisted in the months-long investigation by agents from Sidereal HealthCare in what is being celebrated as part of the new joint effort between the public and private sectors to clamp down on health care fraud.*

"The second attachment is a memento of our work together. It's your own personal copy of a little video my skilled IT friend and I put together and posted on YouTube last Valentine's Day. It's been a raging success and stars your good friend, Mr. Al Tacovic, and his personal security man, Mr. Fausto Guzman, AKA Ernesto Morales. I think the way we took the images of Guzman smiling and laughing with Tacovic and merged them with the three other images was brilliant. We were concerned some might not see the resemblance was perfect, so through the magic of digital imaging we helped those with limited imaginations clearly see all pictures were the same man. I just checked it again today, and so far it's had over twenty-three million viewers.

"Just in case you've forgotten, Bryan, I promised you we'd get Tacovic and Patterson. This Guzman guy was a bonus, but I not sure exactly where he fits in."

"Be well, my friend. Come and visit me this fall and we'll go see the Packers and Bears beat the crap out of each other."

END

ACKNOWLEDGEMENTS

After practicing dentistry for twenty years, I was privileged to have a second, career in two related fields, first as an employee of a midsized health care database, software and publishing company, and then as an entrepreneur of a start-up medical fraud prevention company. Both of the companies I worked in were eventually acquired by large public corporations, but the principles and foundations of what I, along with many others, helped build and operate, are still vital tools and services used every day in the commerce of health care. I have retired from active work with both of my former companies and this book is an outgrowth of the passion I feel about the need to end the ongoing waste caused by health care fraud and abuse.

After fifteen years of leading a staff of clinicians and software developers who created sophisticated systems and processes to detect fraudulent and abusive claims and identify the providers who billed them, I consider myself an expert in the field of health care fraud detection and prevention. The success and widespread use of the tools and services we created by numerous health care payors and property and casualty carriers covering tens of millions of lives and policies is testimony that something can and is being done to effectively stop the waste. The hundreds of millions of dollars these services have saved by detecting and preventing the payment of fraudulent claims is evidence that billions more can be saved every year in both these industries that are currently struggling to provide affordable coverage to policy holders.

I have spoken on numerous panels, written many articles, co-authored part of a book on health care fraud, and been interviewed by dozens of authors for various newspapers and magazines. I have appeared on national TV as well as local radio stations and several webcasts. In spite of all those opportunities to communicate the seriousness of this continued waste of health care resources, I believe most of our industry's efforts to inform the public about a three hundred plus billion dollar a year problem have been largely unsuccessful.

So, I thought, perhaps the seriousness of health care fraud and the need to do something to prevent it could best be communicated through a novel. I'm an avid and constant reader of mystery, suspense, and sci-fi fiction, so I've written a story rooted in truth, but not about actual characters or explicit events. Readers may not believe it, but the fraud schemes presented in this book are variants of actual fraud that occurs every day, somewhere in the U.S. health care system.

I hope this book will be the first of a series, so you the reader, will be introduced to several characters I hope you find interesting, engaging, humorous, and either likeable or detestable, depending upon their character and your preferences and tastes.

There are many people to thank, and I have already dedicated this work to Joyce, my wife, friend and cherished companion since 1965. I also want to express my appreciation to Michael Garrett, who edited the manuscript and taught me a great deal about writing throughout the process. If grammatical or punctuation errors remain, they are my fault and not his. He's an outstanding coach and a talented writer, and most of all an exacting teacher, the only kind I ever want to have. Michael also recommended a book, *Characters & Viewpoint*, by Orson Scott Card, and that too was a source of critical and valuable information for me and any writer, if in fact I can call myself a writer just yet.

I also want to thank one of my sons, Mica Johnson, an amazingly talented man in numerous genres. He writes music, sings and makes his living as an artist and graphic designer. He created the cover, but only after reading the manuscript to make sure it was representative of the story.

It would be negligent on my part to not also recognize our four other children, Shawn, Ardie, Darin and Jodi, who are all grown with kids and lives of their own, but each of them has consistently taken the time to provide me with ongoing encouragement over the nine months it has taken to create this work. I want to mention an incident that occurred early in the process with our second son, Ardie, who works in the movie industry for a major studio. He was one of the first to read an early draft of my first two chapters. He offered some thoughtful criticism and several valuable suggestions that were sorely needed, and I thank him for that specific advice.

Finally I want make it clear that I have incredible respect for the FBI and other Department of Justice agents as well as state, local and private industry fraud investigators, who tirelessly work to detect and prevent fraud and expose those who commit it. The vast majority of health care professionals are hard-working and honest, but we are plagued with a growing number of individuals who feel it is permissible to push the envelope of honesty beyond acceptable boundaries. It's my hope readers of this work will be better informed about some of the ways they, themselves might be victimized by unscrupulous and opportunistic interlopers and what all of us can and must do to help prevent health care abuse and fraud.

Our health care reimbursement system was based on an assumption of trust, but it has become infested by organized crime rings and rogue opportunists who cannot be trusted, and they continue to steal a billion dollars a day from all the rest of us. We must stop it!

Agent Bryan Hampton and U.S. Attorney
Paul Dixon continue their covert pursuit
of fraud mastermind Bennett Watson.

Please turn this page for an excerpt from

DELIBERATE MISDIRECTION

Chapter 1

North Las Vegas, NV
July 1, 2011
3:45 PM

Eddie Collins sat in Dr. Schiffman's reception room waiting for his chance to see the dentist. Eddie was a new patient. He'd called late in the day, less than an hour earlier, for his emergency appointment. Eddie had pleaded with the doctor's assistant for medication to relieve his excruciating toothache. The sympathetic receptionist had consented to 'squeeze him in at the end of the day,' before the beginning of the long holiday weekend. Dr. Schiffman was nearly eighty and he was tired, not only from an extended day of caring for patients, but he was worn-out in general, from a too-long career in a demanding profession. Eddie was eventually seated in the treatment room and heard the elderly dentist enter the operatory, then ask, "John, what can we do for you today, son? I hear you're in pain." At that point Eddie knew he would get what he came for.

An hour later, Eddie was filling out another 'New Patient' form in Dr. Kerrigan's reception room. It was after five, even later in the day on the eve of the July 4th weekend. Bradley Kerrigan, a newly-graduated dentist, had only recently opened his office and any prospective patient, in the fiercely competitive environment of Clark County, was a prize worth staying late for, even though it meant delaying the beginning of an extended weekend outing his family had planned.

Eddie expertly completed all the forms he was given, but not a single item of the information he provided was true. He knew an anxious to get home dental assistant would soon summon him, and he and smiled to himself when he heard, "Danny, we're ready for you."

Half an hour later, Eddie Collins partially paid a nominal emergency exam fee with cash, then left Dr. Kerrigan's office with two prescriptions and an appointment card for the following Tuesday morning. He discarded the appointment card in the parking garage trash can and pocketed the prescriptions. Not bad, he thought, eight legitimate scripts for oxycodone in one day, a total of 160 tablets and at least 50 of them are forty milligrams.

Eddie was not an addict, but he was a pill-shopper, a reseller, and a prescription drug dealer. On that particular Friday, Eddie had visited ten different doctor's offices and clinics and managed to score eight prescriptions for the popular drug. None of them bore his real name, and he would need to use eight different pharmacies to fill them all, every time with the cheapest generic available.

As with every drug distributor, he understood his market. The general rule of thumb was a dollar a milligram, meaning the street value of was ten to forty dollars per tablet, but the thirty and forty milligram tablets brought a premium. He figured after paying for the generics he should clear at least three thousand dollars for his day's work.

But that Friday was a not a normal workday for Eddie; he was free-lancing, as he usually did on the day before a holiday. He knew many doctors adjusted their normal work schedules, by adding one or two extra vacation days around the legal holidays, especially if they fell on a Friday or a Monday. Prior experience had taught him the combination of the staff's eagerness to start their vacations, and a credible and explicit story about his symptoms, would likely earn him pain medications and antibiotics to sustain him, until the office opened-up again after the long weekend.

Eddie had sound and well-practiced tales to deliver to each type of health care specialty doctor, who routinely treated patients in acute pain. Dental problems were easy; he had routines for an early abscessed tooth, for an old root canal treatment flaring up, for pain from a wisdom tooth, and the impossible to diagnose easily, TMJ problem. His favorite medical ailments were back and neck pain, with lower back pain being the condition he alleged most often.

Recently, he'd been successfully trying a new story, centered around the complaint of severe pain from an ailment he learned about on the internet. He'd actually Googled, 'how to get oxycodone,' and discovered a scam that sounded bizarre, but he had worked it successfully four times so far. It involved the complaint of severe testicular pain, specific to the left testicle. When asked, he would describe the symptoms very simply and eloquently as, "Severe pain and extreme tenderness in my left nut."

The pain was easy to fake and difficult for the doctor to disprove as long as he convincingly jumped and shrieked of acute pain, with even the most gentle manipulation of the organ. Unlike most dental pain, which normally yielded only a ten or twenty milligram dose, testicular pain, got him thirty or forty milligrams every time.

But Eddie's real job, the one he worked at three and sometimes four days a week, was illicit trafficking in high cost HIV and oral cancer medications. This form of medical fraud was one of the most deplorable, because there were multiple victims. The drugs were obtained by exploiting seriously ill Medicaid patients, who depended on those very medications for their survival. Eddie bought the drugs from these hapless Medicaid recipients for less than a third of their actual value. Going without their drugs was an alternative some chose, because the proceeds were often needed for other living expenses. But in some cases, the life giving drugs were sacrificed to support dangerous lifestyle preferences. Irrespective of motive, the consequences were always the same for the sellers; they suffered increased pain and shortened lives.

Eddie's profits were predictable and consistent. He would sell the drugs to his unethical pharmacist partner, who would dilute the normal dosages of the drugs or even substitute a lookalike placebo. The pharmacy then dispensed the ineffective prescriptions to other unsuspecting patients, who depended on those drugs to treat the same serious diseases. In this deplorable type of fraud scheme, two patients are seriously harmed, while Medicaid and taxpayers are defrauded.

****

Eddie's pharmacist accomplice, Ravi Bodner RPh, originally migrated to the United States from Germany in the early nineties. He eventually secured his RPh in Nevada in 1995, then worked for several large national pharmacy chains over the next eleven years. It was during his tenure at the chain stores that he recognized multiple opportunities to take advantage of what he regarded, as weak spots in the system. But the large chains had so many checks and balances, he never risked anything major, but remained content with ongoing petty theft. In 2007 he accepted a position with a small, reputable, independent pharmacy, owned and operated for many years, by an ethical and honest man.

But in Ravi's perverted way of thinking, he got lucky nineteen months after he took the position, when the owner of the pharmacy died of a massive coronary. Ravi had saved some money and managed to purchase the store from the man's widow, and at last, he had the chance to pursue the corrupt opportunities he'd only dreamed about for the past fourteen years. His master plan however, required an accomplice, a middle man or broker. When Eddie showed up one day with a script for a supply of Fentanyl transdermal patches, Ravi realized he'd filled narcotic prescriptions for Eddie twice before, but each time they were from a different doctor, and Eddie's name was never the same.

So unless Eddie was a clone, Ravi figured he might have found a partner. Ravi dispensed the Fentanyl but before he handed Eddie the bag he asked him, "You're not fooling me, you know that, right? How would you like to make some real money?"

It was a match made by the Devil himself; so profitable that Ravi had acquired a second store a year later, in another area of town where over half the residents in the neighborhood were on Medicaid or Medicare. The two crooks trafficked in any and all expensive medications. The pharmacies provided a never-ending source of new patients for Eddie to approach. The first time a Medicaid or elderly Medicare patient showed up at the pharmacy to have a prescription filled for a high cost drug, Eddie would get a referral, complete with address, phone number, the name of the drug, and the suggested price to pay for it, if the patient was willing to sell.

Eddie had a seventy percent success rate convincing Medicaid patients to sell him at least every other dose of their medications. He would pay them, then deliver the drugs back to the pharmacy, and Ravi would dispense a diluted dose of the drug to the next patient. It was possible for the same patient to receive the identical pills they had previously been charged for, then subsequently sold to Eddie. But then Ravi never kept track of where Eddie got the drugs or to whom they were re-dispensed.

When Ravi purchased the second pharmacy, it came with Baadal Joshi, a PharmD, RPh who had been educated in India, at the University of Delhi. Baadal had been recruited and brought to the U.S. by one of the large national chains that subsequently lost the strategic battle for neighborhood store locations. Baadal had been unemployed for several weeks when he landed the job as the nighttime manager and pharmacist at the Washington One Stop, a convenience-style store that doubled as a corner grocery and full service pharmacy. A short four months later, he had a new employer, Ravi Bodner.

Ravi had not included Baadal in the circle of corruption during his first few weeks. Baadal had a family of four to support in Las Vegas, and relatives back in India, who also depended on his salary. He could not afford to lose his position at the Washington One Stop, and as soon as Ravi realized that vulnerability, he explained the parameters of continued employment to the susceptible and unlucky young pharmacist.

Ravi had also been in the process of vetting another business association over the past few weeks. He wasn't quite sure yet if, in the long run, that partnership was going to be a good one. Several weeks before, Ravi had received a mysterious phone call from an investigator at one of the large national auto insurance companies, requesting verification about numerous prescriptions his pharmacy had filled for five different claimants. After specific questions about each of the customers had been handled, the investigator asked Ravi if his pharmacy was associated with any of the law firms in Las Vegas. Ravi had immediately denied any connection to any other individual or organization, noting he was the sole proprietor of his two pharmacies.

Ravi had then asked the investigator, "Why are you asking these questions? What's the law firm, you're inquiring about?"

The investigator didn't answer the questions but commented instead, "Perhaps this firm's in your neighborhood and that's why several of your customers are represented by their attorneys."

"What's the address and name of the firm, if I may ask?"

The investigator gave him the address, then said, "I really can't disclose the firm's name, but I'm curious because twenty of their claimants fill their prescriptions at your pharmacy."

Ravi knew the address was in downtown Las Vegas, nowhere near either of his stores, so he informed the investigator about the lack of proximity of the two businesses. "Look, that address is miles from here. Can't you tell me the attorney's name, so I can check into it?"

"Well, I really shouldn't, and if I do, you didn't hear it from me. There are three different attorneys on these cases but they're all from the same firm, which we discovered is owned by Bennett Watson."

Ravi responded, "I've never met him, but his face is all over town on billboards, bus stop benches, TV, you know the routine. It's probably just a coincidence that people in these neighborhoods have sought him out, to represent them in an accident, because his name has such high visibility."

"Maybe so. Well thanks for all your help," the agent said and they both hung up.

Ravi had no idea how many of his customers were actually represented by Watson, but he planned to see which doctors prescribed for the five patients the investigator asked about. The research proved interesting. All five patients shared one physician, a doctor Ravi had never met. Equally unusual was the fact that every script was for exactly the same drug, dosage and quantity.

The next thing Ravi checked was how many of his other pharmacy customers had narcotic prescriptions from the same physician. The query listed fifty-six different patients in the last twelve months, and they all received potent narcotics. So, he reasoned, twenty patients from this one insurance company, and another thirty-six, probably from other auto carriers, because the pharmacy benefit management companies reimbursing me for these drugs generally work for property and casualty companies, not health care companies. I wonder if all thirty-six of these other patients are Watson's clients as well. How can I find that out? He'd decided he would do two things. First he would randomly call a few of the thirty-six patients and ask two questions; who their insurance company was and if they were represented by an attorney. If a patient asked why he wanted to know, he would claim he was being audited by the insurer's PBM, the company handling payments for the drugs. The second thing he would do is to locate the prescribing doctor's office and send Eddie there in search of pain medications.

He decided if he discovered over half of his randomly chosen customers were using the attorneys in Watson's firm as their lawyers, he would ultimately call all thirty-six of the patients and ask the same two questions. If most of them were linked to Watson, and if Eddie managed to easily get drugs from the same physician writing all the other scripts, then he would decide how to turn that knowledge into hard cash, probably by offering his services as another useful and accommodating resource to the organizer of this intriguing fraud scheme.

Ten days later, Ravi had decided on a course of action, after he and Eddie had done all the leg work and placed all the phone calls. They were meeting to discuss what they should do next with the information they had accumulated from their snooping. Eddie told Ravi what he believed they should do. "Boss, there's never any doctor in that office. I've been there five times and it's always locked up. I call the number and the phone always rolls to an answering machine. I leave my number, but no one ever calls back. The doc is either dead or he's sitting at home writing the prescriptions and someone comes and gets them from him."

Ravi answered, "I checked into his profile. He was a legitimate general practitioner and practiced for years in the office you say he's never in. My guess is he's getting paid to write for pain meds for all these patients, who probably have nothing wrong with them. I asked a few of them I called, if the doctor who wrote the script ever treated them. Every one of them told me their doctor was a chiropractor at the Accident and Injury Health Restoration Clinic over on Owens, and claimed they were handed the prescriptions by the office receptionist, when they left the clinic."

"Maybe he's working out of the clinic's back room, since the chiropractors can't write for narcotics," Eddie answered.

"Maybe there's a whole pile of scripts already written and the chiropractors just hand them out, after filling in a name. In any event, we've found ourselves a fraud scheme and I want in on it." Ravi said unequivocally.

"Who do you think is running the scam, Ravi?" Eddie asked.

"It's gotta be the owner of the clinics or the lawyer, one of them for sure." Ravi answered then explained, "I did a little checking and found out there are actually four Accident and Injury Health Restoration clinics spread out all over the valley, and they're all staffed by chiropractors. But apparently, a chiropractor by the name of Mirzoyan owns all of them. So it's either him or Watson, the attorney, or maybe they're both running the scam as partners.

"It's one of them, I'm positive, and we're going to make a run at them and find out which one. I'll probably start with Mirzoyan. I have a logical connection to his patients since fifty-six of them use our pharmacies." Ravi explained.

"I got a better idea, Ravi. Why don't I head over to the clinic on Owens and claim I was injured in a car accident, and tell them I hurt my back and I need an attorney. If they refer me to Watson's firm, we know for sure they're in cahoots," Eddie suggested.

"You may have hit on a more effective way of making the connection we need to expose, Eddie. Get that appointment as soon as you can. Do you have a phony auto insurance card you can use somewhere in your bag of tricks?"

"What do you think?" Eddie answered, and they both laughed.